PRISONER
OF THE
ELEMENTS

ZIAN SCHAFER

Prisoner of the Elements by Zian Schafer
Published by Zian Schafer
Visit the author's website at www.zianschafer.com

Cover by Hazel Lockwood.
Map by Zian Schafer.
Interior designs by Hazel Lockwood.
Editing by Christopher Beattie
Typesetting by Nathan Grice

ISBN: 978-0-473-61942-8
Printed in U.S.A
First Edition

TRIGGERS AND WARNING

Note: *This book is not suitable for persons under the age of 18.*

WARNING: This book contains sexually explicit scenes, adult languages, and violence. It may be considered offensive or disturbing to some readers. It is intended for sale to adults only, as defined by the laws of the country in which you made your purchase. Please store your files wisely, where they cannot be accessed by underage readers.

Triggers:

Violence, adult language, gore, abuse, derogatory language, sex, blood, mental illness, self-harm (hitting objects and scratching/ picking skin), reference to sexual assault and rape, thoughts of suicide.

This is for me.

Esca
Novalis
Land of th
EMPIRE OF EARTH | FERAXIS
Basi
Barra
OCEAN OF THE
Ziema
K
AEC
EMPIRE OF WAT
Sloga
Zeph

Mount Polis
Ignis
Dunes of Harena
EMPIRE OF FIRE | AUDOR
Exsolutus
Kaen
Penare
EVIATHAN
Brathu
R | VESI
Misko
Amare
yire

CHAPTER 1

Lasciare ogne speranza, voi ch'intrate.
"All hope abandon, ye who enter here."
The Inscription on the Gates of Hell
— *The Divine Comedy, by Dante Alighieri*

The sacrificial bell's toll reverberates down my spine.

A child this time.

Tucked between a mass of bodies and against the temple wall, I can see the boy standing as clear as day on the platform. He can't be more than ten years of age.

He's what the Empire would consider a 'forgettable.'

I've heard him crying, mourning his long-departed parents, during my midnight escapes from home. During the day, I've seen him begging alone on the streets of the market square, in a ripped tunic two sizes too small for him. Peeking between the rips of the unwashed fabric was his stained, prematurely-leathered skin. Poverty gifted him a layer of grime to paint that skin: the poorest protection from the cold. I know it well. I've worn the same varnish for twenty-three years. At least that's what my parents think.

He's the perfect candidate for a sacrifice; no one will remember him. No one will cry for him once his flailing heart falls still, once the strands of his life are prematurely ripped apart. No one will mourn him. He will be forgotten, like the rest of them. Except by me. I'll remember his thin hair and watering eyes. Just like I'll remember every one of the hundreds whom I've seen on the altar before him.

My gift *lurches* through me as I spot the scrape on his arm. I dig in my heels, steadying my hand stealthily against the wall, trying to ignore the animalistic *need* to run up to him and to help him. It's like dangling meat in front of a starved dog.

But I can't help him.

I can't allow myself to help him.

I can only watch him suffer, too scared and alone up there to even cry for his life. I must watch his suffering as I have watched the suffering of every tired, forgotten body dragged by every reluctant pair of feet that reaches that altar.

I must keep my gift hidden or I will put Ma and Pa in more risk than they're already facing.

Stay covered and stay hidden, Althea. Mother's order rings in my head.

I tug my brittle sleeve down to make sure my marks stay hidden under the safety of the fabric. A sudden panic grips my heart, and my eyes dart about to make sure that no-one has seen my weakness or noticed me pulling at my clothing. It would only take one person to panic, to point and shout, to scream their deluded assumption that I might be harboring a new type of plague.

No eyes are cast my way.

They are all fixed upon him. The boy on the platform.

The beast deep within my core threatens to suffocate me. It wants to unleash itself upon Audor, a desire that grows more with each passing day. A beast that doesn't feel like it belongs to me. Yet another secret under lock and key from any eyes that may pry.

I am pushed aside with surprising abruptness and a woman drenched in jewels arrogantly takes my spot by the wall, forcing me to drop back into the press. I can't see her arm from here, but I know it will be branded with a 'C'. No mortal would be able to afford what she is wearing, nor would a mortal dare to shove others aside with such confidence. She must be a Cintis.

The woman wears a deep scowl. We all do. None of us want to be here, but we could be the next one slaughtered if we don't attend. Those with the misfortune to arrive first are marched into the temple until it fills to the brim. Everyone else stands outside to bear the weather. They'd rather have hail batter their skin than watch the carnage that will unfold inside.

The young boy stands in front of the obsidian altar, which is raised above the marble floor. The story of the Sun is carved in a dance of gold and rubies on the sides. His cleaned toes curl with dread on the golden platform; his azure eyes pinning themselves to the floor.

The Priest prefers sacrificing the young, saying it's because they are at their most pure and untouched: a clay that the Anzeth could mold as they please.

The bell chimes again, the same noise heard throughout the Empire every month for the past seventy-five years.

The Priest of Audor walks through the oak doors leading from the prayer room. A loose, crimson robe drapes his slender frame, and a cloth of gold hangs across his shoulders and chest, trailing along the floor behind him. A gold circle is painted onto his wrinkled forehead, making his red eyes appear to sink further into his hooded sockets. But they are not sunken nearly deep enough to hide his animosity over the failed attempts to appease the gods.

Terror suffuses the boy's features.

A loud crack rips through the air from outside. None of us flinch at the sound anymore. We all know the noise is from the Cintis using their fire to whip mortals into submission.

The boy moves his right arm from behind the cover of the cloth, and I can see the red band which every citizen of Audor bears. Above the red line, the letter 'M' is seared into the boy's skin. *Mortal*, a lesser being compared to the fire-wielding Cintis. The branding makes it easier for the Cintis to know who they can abuse without consequence.

My fingers brush over my branding, tracing the scars of the letter 'N.' I lost control of my gift and removed a line. Now I have to hide my wrist for the rest of my life. All the gift can do is heal and save people, but despite that, I'll be hunted and killed for it.

Because people hate what they don't understand.

The Priest raises his chin at the sight of the boy, causing his hairless head to reflect the glistening light of the altar. The same pattern of the Sun that borders the walls and floors of the temple is tattooed from the top of his head, down his skull and goes on under his robe.

A parade of acolytes shuffles behind him, all of them sporting the same robe, but theirs are in full black. Some wear crimson cloth across themselves instead: a show of their rank within the temple.

During the ceremonies, the acolytes wear black veils that cover their eyes, splitting down across the bridge of their nose to look like claws. Under the headpiece, they all share the same baldness of head, and the same sun tattoos in the center of their head, with flames radiating outwards.

In the late hours of the night, Evander and I would snigger at the thought of the Priest and acolytes without their veils.

"The skinhead and his ducklings," he would laugh. Evander always said that Audor has two suns, the one in the sky and the reflection from the Priest's head. His father, the King's Royal General, would never approve of such a statement; it would be blasphemous on their family's name.

The Priest walks up to stand next to the boy, while the acolytes circle the altar at the bottom of the platform. They look to the sky and raise their arms into the air, entranced by the red Sun through the open ceiling directly above — making the altar gleam with misguided innocence. Some days the Sun gives a golden glow, while others the Sun burns red or purple. It's always red on the days of the sacrifice.

Shadows cross their faces from the hoops that float above the altar toward the sky, an array of gold rings in different sizes with the language of the gods inscribed into them. As a child, I always thought that it looked like a halo, but now I know there is nothing holy about this place.

Footsteps echo down the hallways as soldiers wearing pitch-black armor emerge, their blood-red capes dangling between their legs. Engraved on each soldiers' chest piece is a half sun pierced by a flaming sword, the symbol of Audor, which represents the King's power to control the Sun across the sky from dawn to dusk.

Behind the soldiers, Queen Mellonia walks in, her heels clicking along the marble, and a crown of flames atop her red hair. Haughty, with her sharp cheekbones and upturned nose, she refuses to give her people a second glance as she saunters over to her throne behind the altar. A black silk gown hugs her slender frame, exposing her protruding shoulder through the lace trim. An onyx belt in the shape of a spine wraps around her waist as beads of black gems bleed to the floor. Her soft black opal earrings and rose blush forms a stark contrast against her ghoulish features and smoldering eyes.

As she moves to sit, she waves a dismissive hand in the air and says, "The King wishes he could pay tribute in person, and he gives his assurance to you that he's present through the eyes of the Sun."

She doesn't even turn to look at us as she speaks, adjusting her dress against the chair.

Seated next to the Queen, Prince Auberon's halo of fire dances above his hair. The resemblance to his mother begins and ends at the precise shade of his curling locks, which frame his contrastingly soft features. His black eyes search the crowd, looking anywhere but at the boy. They meet mine for the briefest second before moving on. My gift pulsates, wanting to get near him. How do his eyes always find me during these dark moments? Like the blazing red Sun high above, his eyes sear against my skin and make my power burn. Is it an omen, or the effect of his onyx stare?

He wears his signature sword, with its ruby hilt and blade made of obsidian, which was forged in the fires of Mount Polis. He once brought it to the blacksmith's forge that Pa and I work at. We handled the sword like a newborn baby as Pa taught me how to sharpen such a blade.

The Priest turns to the Queen and Prince, bowing before launching into the same speech he makes every month: "This is a necessary sacrifice from the people living in the Empire of the Rising Sun; the Empire that controls the flames that rage beneath the earth. Today is a day to remember the First Treaty that ended the War of the Elements. May their sacrifices appease the Anzeth, the council of nine gods, and make the realm whole once more."

The boy winces at his words, tears streaming silently down his sallow cheeks. His death will be meaningless because the gods aren't listening. Thousands have been murdered in their name already, but earthquakes, plagues, and famine still pollute the realm.

The Anzeth don't want the life of a mere mortal.

They want to annihilate Zephryine.

In the distance, the sound of thunder shakes the walls of the temple, and the taste of unease clings to the back of my throat. The boy sways on his feet, shifting his weight from side to side, and avoiding the Priest's gaze.

The only thing he can hope for is a quick death.

The boy's hair is braided into three long rows that trail down his back, to symbolize the three Empires of Zephryine. That's what the acolytes told us during our religious lessons as children. A thick, white cloth wraps around the boy, revealing boney arms tattered with cuts and bruises, as he sways on his feet. The image of purity and debatable perfection washes away as the boy's throat wrinkles under the thick, brown collar buckled there. A gold chain hooked at the back of the collar connects to spikes in the floor. Rumor has it that the collar is made from a scale shed from the dragon of Audor, Niran, who sleeps under the Palace.

My stomach churns and bile rises up in my throat as the Priest pulls out the sacrificial dagger.

I made that dagger.

I stayed up late into the night designing a weapon which I thought would be used for mere decoration.

I sharpened the weapon that will now take an innocent's life.

The guilt is suffocating.

It's also one of Pa's finest works. I made the dagger, and he embellished it. The heads of two gold dragons that look like Niran rest at the top of the hilt, with their tails wrapping around the handle. At the middle of the crossguard sits a golden sun with the emblem of the Empire engraved into it. Flames have been chiseled into the onyx blade, with dried blood stuck in its grooves.

I long to lean on Ma or Pa, to feel their comforting embrace as we watch the life drain from the sacrifice's body. This is the only time that I'm grateful for Ma and Pa's back-breaking jobs. They're no longer required to attend the sacrifices.

At the Priest's movement, the acolytes that were circling the raised altar disperse into the crowds.

Let the sacrifice begin.

A shiver licks my spine as the Priest stalks towards the boy, going up to stand behind him. I hate when the sacrifices are standing as the Priest takes their last breath. You can see everything when they are standing. The Priest only seems to do it when he's feeling especially desperate. He thinks making us watch every single twitch of terror that crosses their face as they die will make the Anzeth happier, joyous in the knowledge that the people of Audor would do anything to be in their good graces.

Behind them the Queen looks bored. She picks at her long, talon-like nails. Ma said the King has made her watch every single sacrifice, and that she kept count of every single soul lost in the War. I guess years of counting death has made her inured to the cries of mourning and the spilling of blood.

The way her finger taps on the chair has my heartbeat hammering against my chest. I stare at the dip in one of the steps, trying to erase the Queen's boredom from my mind. I can't show emotion. Showing emotions means that I will be noticed. My family has already lost far too much to afford such a slip.

Prince Auberon, at least, has a shred more dignity. He stares at the back of the Priest's head as he always does, as though watching the perpetrator is easier than watching the victim. There are rumors that he visits the families of those who lost someone to a sacrifice, and that he even gives them coin.

It is an empty gesture, in my eyes. He may have been born just before the first crack appeared in the earth, but he is as complicit as his parents are for doing nothing to stop the aftermath.

People shift their weight anxiously through the deafening silence in the temple.

The Cintis fae, many of whom fought in the War of the Elements, stand with grim faces and slouched shoulders. Their actions helped to cause this, forcing us to gather to witness another murder in the name of calming the raging gods. Despite their willingness, their lack of hesitation, to throw mortal children into the heart of the war two centuries prior, their eyes now glisten with self-pity for witnessing yet another bloody slaughter.

I turn my head and my eyes lock with those of Evander. He stands tall next to General Fornous, whose hand is on the hilt of his blade, as if daring anyone to speak up against the horrors. Evander's eyes show no sign of warmth or comfort, only disdain towards the Priest for his histrionics.

"The almighty Anzeth. Take this offering, and every soul before, to make Audor whole again. We are your loyal servants; ask and you shall receive. On behalf of the entirety of Zephryine, we ask for your forgiveness for the war," The Priest's voice thunders through the temple the same way I imagine our gods' voices would. I wonder if all nine of them would laugh, seeing our deplorable sacrifices and knowing nothing will come of it.

Lifting the dagger to the sky, the Priest holds it for a few of our labored breaths, planting a kiss on the dagger before he lowers it.

His face is almost devoid of any emotion, save the hunger that flickers in his eyes. Taking slow, predatory steps towards the boy, his knuckles turn white from gripping the dagger so tightly. He stops before the boy and a muscle in his jaw ticks, as he considers how the boy should die.

With unnatural speed, he slides the blade across the boy's throat just below the collar, causing an echo of gasps to come from the crowd.

It is all I can do not to flinch. The blade *I* made killed yet another child.

The gift in me rebels against my inner restraints, begging to be released onto the boy.

I squeeze my eyes shut.

I can't look.

He died because of my creation.

The crowd inhales sharply when the boy drops to his knees. In the distance, I hear someone hurling at the sight. The smell of bile fills the air, mixing with the metallic scent of his blood that clings to the back of my throat.

The sound of the boy choking on his own blood resonates in my ear; another sound I will remember until the day I die. Despite how many times we have seen someone fall to that blade, these sacrifices never get easier.

A thud makes me snap my eyes open. I can't see the boy, limp on the floor beyond the hunched shoulders of the men and women in front of me. We all stand in silence until we can no longer hear the boy's sputters and coughs.

Ecstasy paints across the Priest's face as the blood drips from the dagger. "For the Anzeth!" he roars, throwing his head back as he raises the bloody dagger to the Sun.

"For the Anzeth," we all strain in unison. But not Prince Auberon. I've never seen his lips move to say those words.

The halos floating in the air seem to vibrate, sending an energy through the realm that feels as though rope is being tied around my throat. The beast groans in pain, whimpering as the vibration echoes. My hands find the wall again to steady myself as the blood rushes from my face.

No one else seems to be affected by the halos. No one else ever reacts. I've never understood why, and I'd likely be dead if I ever dared to ask.

Two acolytes come forward from the crowd when there is nothing but a corpse before us. They throw a white sheet over him that instantly blooms crimson. The acolytes grab one of his arms each, and the crowd parts before them as they drag him to the morgue.

His blood trails along the floor behind them. Blood that will be gone by morning.

Tomorrow this temple will stand tall like death doesn't wither within it. There will be no sign of the boy or any person before him. Tomorrow, we will all go about our day like this never happened.

Queen Mellonia and Prince Auberon jump to their feet even before the doors to the mortuary shut. Onyx eyes meet mine again, and the breath hitches in my throat as my gift buzzes. Prince Auberon looks away as if it was nothing more than a passing gaze.

But it's not.

This has happened too many times to be a coincidence.

Neither of them looks back at the carnage as they hurry out of the temple and to the lawns where their gilded carriage awaits.

CHAPTER 2

An inaudible exhale leaves my lips as people quickly file out of the temple.

Next to me, the Cintis woman that shoved me hugs the swell of her belly, speaking in hushed whispers to the man next to her. His thumb wipes away the tears streaming down her face, and I spy the letter 'C' under the edge of his shirt.

"We need to get out of Audor," she says frantically, with tears welling in her eyes, looking around to make sure there are no acolytes or guards nearby.

His eyes widen at her comment as he slams his hand over her mouth. "Don't say such things," he whispers, "This is not the place for it."

A whimper escapes her lips. His saddened eyes turn into a burning glare as he notices me eavesdropping. "Did you hear any of that?" he hisses.

I shake my head vigorously. I was stupid for not doing something to try and stop their conversation. I should have bumped into her or coughed.

"Good, because if you did hear anything, I will cut off your ears and feed them to you." I snap my mouth shut. It's a promise which the

Empire has given him, a fae, the right to make good on. He turns on his heels and drags his wife with him from the temple.

I turn my attention back to the altar. I hate looking at the aftermath of a sacrifice, but I force myself to take in every single detail. We owe it to those sacrificed to never forget them. They're more than an object to be killed on a whim, despite what the acolytes believe.

Especially when I have the power to save them.

Swallowing the lump in my throat, I turn back to the altar to take in the pools of blood splattered over the gold floor. Everything about the image makes me sick. The chain from the collar glistens against the red as it drips down the steps. The acolytes' footprints create morbid patterns in the boy's blood. Bile makes its way up my throat and the world seems to spin, but I keep it down. I must, or else someone might notice me.

I keep staring until the image is burned into my mind. I can never forget Audor's cruelty.

Looking up from the altar, my eyes lock with Evander's; standing next to his father on the other side of the temple. Pity laces through his features. He looks at me like this after every sacrifice. I never know if it's pity for the life just lost, or pity over my internal struggle each time I must lock down what instinct tells me to let free.

With a sigh, I pull my hood over my head and tug my sleeve down, turning away from Evander to slip through the dispersing crowd.

Below my feet, the rocks and bark threaten to rip my dress with every crunch of my boot. It's the same walk I take after every sacrifice. It's the longer route back into Ignis, but it's the quietest. I can't stand watching people go back to their regular lives as though they didn't just watch a child get slaughtered. Maybe they have the luxury of forgetting, but I couldn't forget even if I tried. Every single one of their faces will haunt me forever. The carnage after each sacrifice will be engraved in my mind until my last breath.

Pa once spoke of a Feraxian belief: that one reaches immortality in death for as long as the living do not forget them. Though their names are not paved into the street like the Cintis are, remembering them is the only thing I can do to give their deaths any meaning. Immortality in death is a better state to be in than that of reality.

The charred trees tangle and dance in the wind, rustling against each other in a fight to see who will break and fall to the snow-covered ground first. Even though the branches look like the Queen's bony fingers, the burnt trees against the russet sky give me a sense of home.

The forest lets me find a moment's peace before returning to the bustling of Ignis, Audor's capital. Before the First Treaty, birds used to sing within these forests, jumping from branch to branch, unaware of the war that lay to the South. Now the forest is blanketed in an eerie silence, broken only by the steady beat of my steps and the buzzing of the city in the distance.

A shiver creeps up my spine as the snow's moisture steadily soaks the hem of my dress. I hope tomorrow will be summer. The gods' rage changed the seasons as well as causing earthquakes and plagues, pushing autumn, winter, spring, and summer all into a single week.

My stomach grumbles as I walk past the dried-up crop fields, past the reams of polluted soil that race up the cracked hills. I've never seen anything grow on those lands. The Anzeth's rage over the war changed the air within the soil so that even the Terra, the Earth Fae in Feraxis, can't bring life to plants. Now, the realm starves.

I wonder if the King is lounging on his throne, feasting on a sumptuous buffet of food, oblivious to the suffering of his people. People who are suffering all because he used his power to keep the Sun to himself.

I squeeze my eyes shut, reopening them to focus on the field. It's hard to imagine what the once fruitful lands of Feraxis, the Empire of Earth, might have looked like before King Cyrus plunged the other empires into darkness. Perhaps this is the gods' punishment to Audor for freezing Vesi's water and killing Feraxis' crops under the cold moon. Or for the queens of Feraxis' greed and refusal to share their bounty with other realms. Now, they have nothing to be shared.

My thoughts are at odds with each other. Part of me wants to hate the nine gods of the Empire of Wind for sitting in their Palace, laughing at their own cruelty. Another part of me feels some strange familiarity and a kind of devout love towards them that I can't explain.

As the dirt beneath my boots changes into the pavements of the Ignisian streets, I look up at the clothes that hang from the balconies of the quarters. A mixture of dark colors paints the familiar walls in gloom. Triple-story buildings border the streets. Sputtered coughs echo among them, and my muscles tense. My body screams to find the cougher and help them. Whether it's because they have the plague that's tearing through Zephryine, or if it's because they're choking from the ash in the air.

The city of Ignis was designed to resemble the Sun.

At the very heart of the city is the Fire Palace, with its curved towers reaching towards the sky. Streets radiate outwards from the Palace, with the nobles and the more successful merchants living closer to the center. As the streets reach into the forest, the houses begin to break down, and the stench of shit and plague chokes the air. I call the outskirts of Ignis, 'the Remains.' Those mortals fortunate enough to have a roof over their heads live there.

To get home from the temple, I have to pass the Palace. But after every sacrifice, I can't bring myself to lay my eyes on the Palace or any other Audorian. I want to throw up on the culprits' doorstep, but the act itself will probably result in my death. Instead, I spend an extra hour skirting the Palace just to get home.

The streets are deserted, save for the occasional rat darting across the street and jumping over the drunk men sleeping face-first on the concrete. I've noticed that drunken men don't seem to fear being sacrificed, because they know they would never be deemed worthy enough to be given up to the Anzeth. They're too tainted. They aren't even worthy enough to get a job cleaning the shit off the noble's shoe.

As I walk, a woman's eyes meet mine, and they widen as though she realizes who I am. She turns to the man beside her and whispers in his ear. His eyes widen before he looks at me with a sneer. I pull my hood lower onto my face and goosebumps prickle my skin. Being noticed goes against everything I've been taught; I'm meant to blend into the crowd and remain unseen. Unfortunately, when I wear hoods and dresses that cover every inch of my skin when it's a summer's day, I tend to stand out. But that's likely not why he's uncomfortable at the sight of me.

Maybe they've heard the rumors about a female blacksmith. The 'Cloaked Ironsmith,' as people say. Perhaps they were whispering that I was a 'spoiled maiden', because no man would ever want a woman who does a man's job.

The sky begins to glow purple as the Sun makes its slow descent when I finally reach our quarters. The steps up to my home dip in the middle from years of wear. White paint chips decorate the door. A rope hangs inside a hole where a door handle should be. I pull on the rope to open the door and climb up the two flights of stairs.

With Evander's help, I've tried to find another place for us to move so Pa can get home without using his crutches to hoist himself up to the top. But we don't have the coin to move anywhere else. And Evander can't give me anymore without bringing attention to my entire family, because a mortal in the Remains who can afford to move is unheard of.

I hurry up past the second floor as the sound of coughing echoes through the concrete hall. If it's the Plague, they might not make it through the night. No healer could help them then. The Plague is the Anzeth's essence eating away at their being, only the gods can help them. Or maybe me. There might be a vacant apartment below us soon. Another gift bestowed to us from the Anzeth.

My skin prickles with the urge to turn around to help them. To actually save a life and make a difference. Fighting the pull in my blood to break down the door and do just that, I push myself up the final steps instead.

The latch to our quarters is open, with the padlock hanging around a hook. Taking my cloak off, I dust off all the ash that has fallen on it. The air outside is polluted with char, but we try to keep the inside of our apartment as clean as possible for Pa's sake. I slide open the door and restrain myself from wrinkling my nose at the smell of Ma's cooking, mingled with the mustiness of our quarters. The place is small, but it holds everything we own.

Pa's leg sticks out from under the sink as he grunts, working on something down there and muttering curses under his breath. His sandy hair drags along the grime below the sink, coating it in a layer of soot. The skin of his knee pokes through the hole in his breeches. Ma steps over his leg, moving to the stove.

"Damn sink done shit itself again," he says as a way of greeting.

Ma stands by the stove mixing some sort of concoction in the pot. I'm not sure what it is. 'Edible' tends to be the only standard we can hope for in her cooking. Her salt-and-pepper hair is tied back into a loose bun. She is still wearing her maids' uniform from work, filling the maroon smock that falls down to her ankles. The material turns into a deep pink closer to the seams, discolored from Ma's growing thickness stretching the dress almost to its breaking point. A black apron ties around her neck and waist, covering her chest and down to her knees. Ma's curves, accentuated by her short build, declare her mysterious personal victory over the paucity of food that is given to the mortals of Audor, a rare feat amongst those in this neighborhood

When looking at my lankiness, many wonder how it is possible that she is even my mother. Yet, Pa says that she looked just like me when she was my age, even down to my full lips and button nose. The thought that I could have her softness envelop my sharp features bewilders me.

Not that appearance matters in the Remains. Beauty, even the beauty found in the lines of a healthy-looking figure, is important only to those who stand above the needs of survival. What is beauty to one scrabbling for their life, save one more source of potential harassment?

Ma claims that before the gray seeped through, her hair used to be as brown as mine. Her tired emerald eyes still hold a light in them, whereas Pa gave me his hazel eyes and perpetual frown. A frown that matches our sunken cheeks from years of eating scraps. Ma always complains that both of our eyebrows are like furry beasts that need to be tamed. The only thing I hope is that I don't end up with his hunch from bending over at the blacksmiths all day.

As Ma goes about moving a pot from one place to another, she winces. I watch her gingerly flex her arm. I grimace at the thought of what the sentinels did to Ma after I was born, all because she wouldn't reveal my skin to them. Perhaps they suspected what my parents had carefully hidden. Pa said they put her arm on a stone and used their boots to crush her bones.

She screamed so much, writhed so much in pain and terror, that they forgot about me. They took so much enjoyment from hurting her, they forgot what the purpose for the punishment had been.

I managed to make it seem like a healthy elbow to the naked eye, but in my mind's sight, my gift shows me there's still work to be done to it. There's very little I can do to cure it completely because of her grueling tasks at work. Easing her pain is the only thing I can do for her after all her sacrifices.

As I step inside, Ma spins on her heels and her eyes go wide with a panic that rarely appears. She storms towards me, her face drained of color.

"What do I keep telling you, Althea?" she barks.

She only ever calls me 'Althea' when I'm in trouble.

She grips my wrist as her eyebrows knit in worry. "Stay covered and stay hidden. What if one of those acolytes saw this? What if they noticed? What of you then?"

She points to my exposed wrist.

I blink a few times. I hadn't even noticed.

How could I not have noticed? What if someone saw?

The Anzeth played another cruel joke on me when I was born. They covered my body in marks and patches, and bold purple lines that spread like thunderbolts throughout my body.

"Leave the girl alone, Phaedra. After that what was happenin' today, I'm doubting anyone was lookin' at the girl's marks," Pa huffs as he shuffles out from under the sink. With a grunt, he sits up and looks me up and down, like I'm a weapon he's made for a nobleman.

Ma rolls my sleeve up, tracing the 'N' with her thumb.

"No one can ever see this. They will take you away from us if they know. You know that, right?" She looks up at me as her eyes start to water. Her fingertips are feather light as she touches the dark lines that begin at my forearm, trailing up to my shoulder like a meandering river.

I clamp my hand over hers as she raises her other hand to cup my cheeks. She always tries to see the bright side, ignoring reality in the process. She thinks the Empire would leave her alone if they discovered my secret, but there's no way they'd let her live for hiding my abilities. They'd kill her before she could breathe out the truth.

She inhales a deep breath and exhales a staggering sigh, "I love you, my Thea. I can't lose you."

"I'm not going anywhere, Ma," I say through a practiced smile. It feels forced, but I mean it. There's nowhere I will go without them. I reach over to embrace her, letting her tears soak my shoulder.

The beat of her heart is a comforting song against my stomach. Eventually we pull away, still holding onto each other's arms.

"Well, do ya have it on you, girl?" Pa raises an eyebrow. It almost feels like a threat. I reach into the pocket of my dress, pulling out the silver dagger he gave me on my twelfth birthday.

He made it out of the scrap metal I collected from the ground before I became his apprentice. I watched him make it from start to finish, completely entranced the whole time. My initials are engraved into the handle in cursive writing, inlaid in red. He thought it would be funny to add an extra letter to the handle, making it say 'A.G.V.'

"It's because you're Althea Girl Viteri," he'd snickered to himself.

AGV didn't exactly have a nice ring to it, and it was the type of humor only Pa would find funny. So, I decided to name the dagger Cornibus, after the great warriors that used to protect the women and children of Audor before the war.

"You know it never leaves my side, Pa," I say while rolling my eyes. He nods in approval at my answer. He just doesn't know I've been learning how to use it on a Cintis.

"She doesn't even know how to use the damn thing!" Ma protests.

"Aye, she knows what counts. Aim for the heart. If not, sink that blade into whatever flesh you can."

She blanches at his retort but huffs and returns to the pot.

"About time ya got back. I thought I'd have to eat the table waitin' on you," Pa grumbles as he tries to get up. We rush over to him, each placing a hand under his arm to hoist him up. He used to get angry every time we rushed to help him, but he eventually learned his complaints were falling on deaf ears. We guide him over to the stool at the small table, where he continues to grumble that the sink won't fix itself and that plumbing is harder work than making the Empire's weapons.

I help set the table, remembering to nod every once in a while so that he thinks I'm still listening. I bring over the olive mug with three stick figures that I painted along the side as a child and place it on the table before collecting the rest. Ma's mug has pink and yellow flowers covering the handle and on the inside of the bottom of the mug. The bottom half of the handle broke off last year when Pa's crutch knocked it off the table. Ma was so furious that she refused to speak to him for days. When the gods take almost everything from you, that which you have left holds a place in your heart. My mug is the plainest, a red mug with a white cloud in the middle of it, the lip chipped from years of me running around the house with it, using it as a toy.

I sit down on the stool once the table is set.

"I made your favorite!" Ma exclaims as she takes her apron off and sets down a pot of corn soup. Pa groans at the sight, and Ma smacks him with the apron.

"Thank you," I say, smiling up at her. She makes corn soup after every sacrifice. It's her attempt at cheering me up from the horrors of the day. I don't have the heart to tell her that I haven't enjoyed it since I was a child.

I pretend not to notice that Ma has poured the largest helping out of the three into my bowl. She always gives Pa the second biggest serving. I know that she worries I'm not eating enough, but she doesn't know what happens when she goes to sleep. They need the food more than I do.

When she turns away, Pa and I slip some of our own servings into her bowl, like we do almost every meal.

Throughout dinner, Ma gossips about the other housemaids and the things they overhear in the manor. Pa only grumbles in acknowledgement, even though I'm certain it's going in one ear and out the other.

"That baker's boy came over before, asking to see you," she sings, making Pa jerk his head up. He starts to open his mouth to say something, but Ma continues before he can say a word, "Ms. Cleo's boy is gentle with a kind heart, he's so madly in love with you that he would never say a word about your skin. Imagine how full all of our bellies would be thanks to him."

Her eyes light up even more at the idea, making heat rise to my cheeks.

Pa shakes his head, deepening his perpetual frown, "Exactly. Said it yourself, just a boy. The girl needs a man," He scrunches his nose in disgust, causing Ma to give him an exaggerated eye roll while I try to sink lower in my seat.

"A boy *becoming* a man, then. It's about time we start making use of *that* again," she says, pointing towards the crib next to the couch. Pa made it before I was born as a gift to Ma. She refuses to give it away or break it down, cleaning it every week 'just in case.' She says that it is a reminder of the greatest thing that ever happened to her. Pa always objects, saying *he* should be the greatest thing that happened to her. A warm smile crosses her face, making her rosy cheeks pop.

"Plus, he's an innocent boy for our innocent girl," she says.

"Oh please. No boy is innocent," he says.

A wave of nausea makes its way through me from the overwhelming guilt that consumes me. I want to tell them about what happens as they sleep. I want to tell them all about where I run to and the dangers that I put myself in when they lay safely in their bed.

"Please, Ma. He's a nice boy, but I still have my whole life ahead of me," I plead through heated cheeks.

"It'll go faster than you think," She winks as she waves her spoon, "You won't see me frowning about having a little one run around this place again."

I stifle a groan and Pa massages his temple. She leans over to me, raising a hand to her mouth while side-eyeing Pa, "Don't forget, Ms. Cleo's line has been known for making extra handsome men."

"Phaedra!" Pa all but yells in disbelief while I choke on a corn kernel. She simply giggles and shoots another wink my way and wiggles her eyebrows. The heat isn't contained to just my cheeks, it's over my whole body. I wouldn't be surprised if Pa could see just how embarrassed I feel.

Pa buckles over and grabs the table for support as his cough shakes the entire home. I jump off the chair and rush to him without a single thought. My power seeps from my skin into his, healing him until his breathing steadies. In my mind I can see his blood pump through his body as my power soothes his aching lung. Somewhere over the years, one of his lungs stopped working, and my gift of healing is only just enough to remove the layer of ash lining the remaining lung.

I don't know how much longer Pa can continue breathing in the smoke from the coals. His breathing is getting worse every week, and it's not like his lungs ever get a break with all the ash in the air outside of the Forge.

I need to help him out at the blacksmith shop more often, so that he doesn't need to bend down and pick up things he's dropped or clean up after himself, especially when he only has one leg. I need to ask Wayland to convince General Fornous that it's time for Pa to retire. I know Pa's attention to detail makes him a favorite of the King's men, but he can't keep working.

I encourage him to finish his supper, but he heads into the bedroom instead, muttering his goodnights under his breath. He slumps a little more than usual, and he doesn't lift his eyes to meet mine, but I swear I can see his eyes water.

"Don't worry about him; another one of his blacksmiths died from the plague last night," Ma chimes in hesitantly as she busies herself with cleaning the kitchen. Just last week, one of his friends lost his arm to an earthquake. We used to lose someone we knew once a month, but now it seems to be someone every week.

"You shouldn't worry either, Ma. He's going to be fine. At least you know that without his leg, he can't run off with Ms. Cleo," I say, trying to lighten the mood. We both laugh at the thought of the baker trying to steal Pa from us with the leftover bread she brings to him at work in the morning.

"I'm so glad the Anzeth gave you to us," She smiles. She tells me this every day. They prayed and prayed for the Anzeth to give them a child, until finally, long after Ma's womb went dry, she was gifted with me.

She gives my arm a comforting squeeze before retiring to the bedroom as well, leaving me alone with the ash that always seems to creep through the window and coat the quarters as soon as we clean it.

I make my way over to the couch and pull the blanket I fold every morning that sits tidily to the side of the couch. Without a mattress to sleep on, the ripped brown couch has been my bed ever since I started to wriggle around too much to sleep with Ma and Pa.

I stare at the single candle in the center of the dining table. Its glow is small compared to the oil lanterns Pa has strategically placed around the quarters. But still, I watch the flame dance over the walls and paint the room in an ocean of red and gold, hoping and praying to the Anzeth that if I stare hard enough, it'll make me forget the events of the day.

Grabbing the pillow, I hit it in a useless attempt to fluff it up. Laying back down, closing my eyes, I can still see the trail of blood across the temple floor. I can still see the grotesque patterns made as the acolytes dragged the boy away.

I take a deep breath and throw the pillow onto the foot of the couch and settle under the blanket.

Sleep never seems to find me after a day of sacrifice.

I toss and turn for what feels like hours while my mind wanders back to all the deaths that I've seen.

The sound of stone hitting my window draws me from my thoughts and sharpens my anxieties. Then another rattles the pane.

A low whistle echoes into the street, followed by a third incessant pebble.

Please, not today. I beg to the Anzeth, *I don't feel like seeing him today.*

It's the same plea I've said again and again this past year, muttering it to myself every time I hear that whistle. The whistle that comes after a sacrifice.

Of course, the gods don't seem to listen. I've already told him that I don't want to be summoned after a sacrifice; summoned like a fell spirit called from the pit. I just want to wallow in my thoughts, but he always says that I need the distraction.

I lay still in my bed. Still, as if my own darkness will somehow go away if I hide under the blanket.

Another stone rattles against the window, forcing me to react before my parents wake from the noise. Pushing the blankets off of me, I sit up, peering over the ledge.

My breath hitches in my throat.

Scrambling my hands under the pillow, I wrap my fingers around cool metal. I pull my hand out and clutch Cornibus to my chest, readying to take it with me into the darkness that awaits.

Please gods, any day this week but today, I beg again.

Just like my last plea, the gods do not listen. Neither does he. Why does this have to be the one thing he refuses to listen to?

In the middle of the street, a cloaked figure awaits me.

CHAPTER 3

"Fas est ab hoste doceri.
One should learn even from one's enemies."
— Ovid, *Metamorphoses*

The cloaked figure bends over to pick up another stone from the street, but stops once he sees me looking at him through the window.

Groaning, I shove my head in my hands, taking deep breaths to steady myself for an even longer night.

Slowly, I lift myself up from the couch, dragging my feet to where my gray cloak hangs next to the door. The bottom of the cloak is already ripped from the countless nights of jumping over fences and sneaking through back alleyways.

Stopping before touching the latch, I turn around, hoping to see one of my parents stirring from their sleep, catching me sneaking out and giving me a good reason to not go with him tonight. But like every other night, they never leave their room until the crack of dawn.

I quietly slide the door open, praying the hinges don't squeak and wake the entire floor. I wouldn't be able to explain where I'm going. My years of hiding from sentinels and the prying eyes of acolytes have made me quick and silent in my steps. I run down the stairs, never making a single noise. With a deep breath, I pull my hood over my head before stepping forward to pull the rope. Swinging the door open, I study the street for any sound or movement.

A mischief of rats huddles around a piece of moldy bread in the middle of the street. Coughs and sneezes escape through the window of the second floor. Out of the corner of my eye, I see the hooded figure push himself off the wall and walk down the street.

I quickly pull the rope again, closing the door behind me, jumping over the three steps leading to the door, and darting from pavement to pavement to steer clear of the rats.

The moonlight illuminates the rundown quarters with a sheen of silver, making the streets look peaceful and ethereal. I follow the figure as he turns down the familiar alleyways, always keeping a sizable distance from me.

Being caught with a mere mortal would be a shame worse than death to him and his family.

A lone woman dressed in the Empire's colors hovers to the side, brushing dirt and rubbish into a pile. My chest aches at the sight. The King places more importance on trash than on mortals. We're rejected like the very garbage this woman's been tasked to clean. The only difference is the filth has a place to go once it's been cleaned up, unlike the mortals who will lay on the same stone they cleaned just hours before. At least Ma has a roof to go back to after cleaning the General's Manor.

He avoids the busier streets, where mortals and fae go to drink away the horrors of the day. Nights after sacrifices are the one time the Cintis don't seem to want to abuse mortals — I think, because in some sick twisted way, the horrors we endure bring us together to face a common enemy.

The deeper we travel into the city, the more families there are laying on the streets, bodies huddled together to fight the chill of the night. People of all ages jump up as we walk past, holding out cans or hats and begging for coin.

As we pass the main square, he turns towards the City Garden. It's one of the few places where the plants haven't been burnt or withered away from the drought. Every time we run through here, I feel nauseated thinking about the King's treatment of his wives. The

Garden was a gift from the King to his third wife, who was said to like the smell of the roses from Feraxis, the Empire of Earth. She mysteriously died hundreds of years before the war. Ma said that the third queen coincidentally died when the first wrinkle appeared on the Queen's skin.

I shake my head to clear away my thoughts of the King as we hurry through the Garden, until we reach an area thick with trees. We duck under the branches and hop over tree roots that have escaped onto the surface. Hundreds of thorns and twigs catch my cloak by the time the canopy clears away, bringing the moon into full view.

He stands in front of a tall concrete wall, his regal leather clothing peeking through the same servant's cloak he wears every time that he summons me in the night.

As I walk closer, he pulls the hood from his head to reveal his inky black hair. His full lips glisten under the moonlight as if he had just run his tongue along them. Shadows hug his sharp jaw and curve under his chiseled cheekbones. Even in the darkness, I can see the thick row of lashes resting above his sharp steel eyes.

He grabs my waist, flattening me against the fence with his body. He presses an achingly warm hand to my cheek, making my heartbeat accelerate and my knees threaten to fail me. His thumb traces my brow, traveling over the curve of my cheek, stopping on my lips.

It's always like this. I always feel like I don't want to see him, but once I'm in his company, there's no place I'd rather be.

He bends down, pressing his cheek to mine as his hot breath tingles my ear. "I've been wanting you all day, Althea," Evander purrs in my ear as he brushes his thumb along my bottom lip, pushing me harder against the wall with his body. The warmth emitting from him is a welcoming feeling compared to the coldness of the concrete that seeps through my cloak. He's always been the most beautiful man in all of Ignis, and I'm his for the taking.

He withdraws, dropping down onto one knee, he watches me expectantly—ready to give me a boost over the fence.

Placing my foot on his thigh, I feel him push me up as I swing my other leg over the wall, trying to land on the ground with as much grace as possible. I stumble over my feet but catch myself before I fall. Behind me, in one swift motion, Evander swings himself over the wall, landing lightly on both feet with the stealth of a spy.

The Fornous Manor is enormous compared to the quarters in the Remains, but tiny in comparison to the Fire Palace. All of the King's generals live around the City Garden. As the right-hand general of the King, General Fornous and his son Evander have a grander manor than most of the other generals.

Oil lanterns surround the building, illuminating the crimson-red bricks that climb up the two stories. One obsidian phoenix sits above the back entrance. Two towers are perched at either side of the Manor.

A statue of a Niran wraps around the sharp points of the roof, just like the Priest's dagger. I can't help wondering if the Anzeth look anything like their children, with scales and wings, or with fins like Leviathan.

I can't imagine living in a realm where those beasts aren't slumbering. All I know is that I'll never stop thanking the gods that they incited the Dragon War to force their nine children to kill off their offspring and each other because of the havoc they caused.

My heart pumps against my ribs as we quickly dart through the charred trees, going around the building to where the servants' entrance awaits us. Only one guard watches the back of the manor at this time of the night. He knows about Evander's and my arrangement, or *relationship* as he likes to call it, and has kept quiet about it for the past five years.

Despite my countless visits to his manor, the fear of being caught has never eased.

Evander goes in first to make sure none of the servants roam the hallways. Several heartbeats later, he comes back out and nods towards me. I run forward, welcoming the warm embrace of the manor. He waits until I am inside before coming in to lock the door behind him. We scurry through the halls, occasionally pushing ourselves up against nearby walls or behind a convenient pillar every time we hear footsteps.

It's the same dance we have been doing since the day he first saw me use my gift.

The big mahogany door leading to his room comes into view. He opens it with another key before we both slither inside. Once in the safety of his room, I let the smell of sandalwood fill my lungs.

His room is bigger than my entire quarters, decorated with mahogany furniture and the furs of extinct animals. Sheer red curtains drape from the top of the bed. Leather bound books line the shelves and an array of weapons decorate the walls.

As the door handle clicks, his slow footsteps tap against the floor as he stalks towards me. He reaches around my body to unclasp my cloak, letting it drop to the floor. His hot breath caresses my neck, and he nestles his nose into my hair, taking a long deep inhale.

He grabs my wrist, spinning me around to face him. The space between our bodies is enough to let me breathe, but the look in his eyes takes my breath away. He walks closer toward me, moving me backwards with him until my back hits the wooden pillar of the bed. My eyes dart to an oil lantern sitting atop his desk, bringing my attention to a single leather rope that hangs from the chair and making the muscles in my stomach tighten at the sight.

He lifts both my hands above my head and lowers his head, his steel eyes bore into me while he brushes his lips against mine, "You were a very bad girl today, Althea," he whispers.

I tense, all the blood rushes from my face, and my skin goes cold. A heavy weight feels like it's crushing my chest. Has he finally made my fears come true? Is he finally just going to betray me after all our years together? Was it all a lie when he said that he cares about me?

I think, in my heart, I know he will never betray me. But still, a small voice in my head, the voice of years of paranoia, screams at me to never trust a Cintis.

As a Cintis, he has the right to hand me over to the sentinels for whatever made-up crime he sees fit, because they would never trust the word of a mortal over the word of a fire wielder. A part of me has always felt it was only a matter of time before he was done with keeping my secrets.

Noticing my reaction to his words, he eases the pressure on my wrists and his eyes soften.

"I saw you close your eyes at the temple," he says.

Blood rushes through my ears and my heart begins pounding so loud that I'm sure he can hear it. Shutting your eyes or looking away from the sacrifice is punishable by death. The image of the boy replaces Evander's face before my eyes as I start thinking about how broken Ma and Pa would be if I died just because I couldn't do what the Empire expects from me.

Bile makes its way up my throat and my breathing starts to stagger. If Evander saw me close my eyes, then someone else could have spotted it as well. Panic steals all my senses, and a storm of fear takes hold of my mind. If I'm gone, there would be one less mouth for my parents to feed, but my death would break them. There's also the very real possibility that the Empire kills them as well.

Evander lets go of my hands, placing them gently at my side.

He wraps one arm around my waist as his free hand cups my face.

"We both know what would have happened if it was anyone else that saw you close your eyes. There is only so much I can do to protect you, Thea. If I wanted to put you in the hands of the Empire, I would have done so five years ago during the accident."

His words are soft, but my fear turns into a burning sadness that thrums through my veins. Nausea rips through me as I remember the bargain we struck to save my family from death at the hands of the King.

I shake my head. Evander and I would have never started talking if he hadn't seen me at the stables. He and I would never and could never be.

Grasping my shoulders, he steers me to sit on the leather trunk.

He towers over me, lifting my chin up towards him.

"Don't worry, Althea," he smirks, "Your secret is safe with me."

My fingers tingle, remembering my power's warmth spreading from my hands into Pa's leg. It's one of my greatest secrets. There was nothing more I could have done to save his leg—it was practically severed. I could only just stop the bleeding from where the beam sliced through his skin and bone. I long to feel that sensation once again, the way my soul felt lighter and the tension from my heart eased as I poured my gift into him. The astonishing correctness in my being as the skin began to grow over the wound, stopping the blood that sprayed over the earth. It was the first time my power had been unleashed without remorse and had achieved its true purpose.

I want to wish I hadn't seen Evander lingering in the shadows as he watched me save Pa's life that day, but I would be lying if I said that I don't lean into his touch whenever he's around. Part of me looks forward to the days that I see him.

I thought it was an empty promise that he threw my way to make me feel comfortable. When he first confronted me after the incident with Pa's leg, he found me and cornered me when I was walking home after a sacrifice. He told me that we can arrange for something mutually beneficial; he keeps my secret, and I keep his, just by sneaking around to talk.

First, he would take me to the ash forest, and he would pry into my family life and any hobbies I had. In turn, he'd tell me everything about his life. He'd bring me leftover food, sometimes enough to feed my parents and me. He bought me a new pair of boots once because, as he said, "the greatest weapon a person can have is their silence."

Eventually, he started training me on how to use Cornibus, then how to use a sword.

Two years later, after a sacrifice, when the smell of mortal blood on the altar was still fresh in our minds, he snuck me into his home under the cover of a snowstorm that ripped through Ignis. Ma's housemaster had died the week prior to the snowstorm, and she was out of a job. That day he offered to give Ma a position at the Manor and promised to keep my family safe.

Our time together in his room was innocent at first. He'd sneak me into his bedchamber in the middle of the night and train me in combat, or we would play cards while tossing back Feraxian wine. He was mischievous from the beginning, flirting and joking until the lines blurred. But I held firm against temptation, convinced that a Cintis in a place of power would never lower himself to bed a mortal, and that his flirting was just a way to mock me.

One day, when the General was out of Ignis, we both had a little too much liquor and danced around to the sound of the rain when, abruptly, my lips found his. At first, he didn't kiss me back. My heart plummeted to the ground, heavy with regret and humiliation. As I pulled away, his hands suddenly locked in my hair, and he kissed me like I was the last person alive, and he had waited his whole life to finally touch me.

Heat exploded in my core at the need of his kiss. His hands had roamed my body feeling everything he could, planting kisses on my marks, trailing his lips along the line that goes down between my breasts, until they went lower. The night became a flurry of deviance and pleasure. Just when I thought he was done, his hand found my center and he brought me over the edge all over again.

Back in the present, I shake my head and take a deep breath. I wish it didn't have to be like this. I wish I could enjoy his company without remembering the secret he holds over me.

He's promised to take my secret to his grave, but he's a Cintis. Pa says you can never trust a Cintis. All Evander wanted was for someone to listen and talk to, but somewhere along the way, I decided that I wanted more. It's hard to forget what he's given to my family. I owe him the world. If it wasn't for Ma's job, we would be living on the street. Ma is completely innocent in all this. She has no idea that the reason she received the letter in the mail was because of what I do with him in the night.

Only once have I thanked him for getting a job for my mother, and never again will such words pass my lips in front of him. When I said thank you, he laughed then winked at me, saying, "It's so I can keep a closer eye on you, *princess*."

It was the same day he started calling me that wretched nickname. He said that it's because only a princess would be feisty enough to pull a knife out on a General's son.

My entire life has been a concoction of secrets and lies, all to save me from reaching death sooner rather than later.

Saving Pa is a phenomenon Evander said that King Cyrus and the Priest would kill for. I don't doubt for a moment that my gift would force their hands to slaughter my parents and I to stop word from spreading across the Empire about a new curse from the gods.

His hand moves from my chin to the back of my neck as he bends forward, touching his forehead to mine.

"You know I care about you, right?" he says.

Lie, the voice in my head whispers uncertainly, *he doesn't care about you. He cares about the way he can speak freely to you without any reprimand.*

I don't think the voice is right, because of everything he's done for me. But nothing he's done has made sense to me.

How can a Cintis care for a mortal?

"I cared about you from the moment you tried to wave that silly little knife at me when we first met," he whispers as my face betrays me.

I fight the urge to quiet the voice in my head as he tells me the same thing he says almost every time we meet, "Tell me, if I didn't care for you, why would I teach you how to use that knife on me, my rough-handed maiden?"

There's a hint of playfulness in his tone.

He's never given me a reason not to trust him, but each glance from him sends my heart into a confused sputter. It wants to throw itself at him, while years of conditioning and racial division holds me back.

There is one thing I haven't quite figured out. Why did he teach me how to use Cornibus? He said it's so I can defend myself properly and learn how to use the weapons I make. Although, there is no way I stand a chance against him in hand-to-hand combat, he still knows Cornibus rests at my side while he sleeps.

I search his heated gaze, looking for answers. Does he actually care about me? I think back to what Ma said about the baker boy and the life we could have together, warm and simple and free of sneaking around and keeping each other's secrets while lying to everyone around us.

No, my throat burns at the thought. Evander doesn't care about me in that way. This is just a mutually beneficial relationship to fill both of our lonely hearts. He probably just wants to keep me alive long enough so that he can eventually kill me once he gets bored. That's what a Cintis would do.

He sighs, shaking his head softly, knowing I won't respond to his comment.

"I told you not to call for me after a sacrifice," I whisper. Being in his arms is the comfort I need to get me through the events of the day, but sometimes it feels like I didn't get to process what really happened if I'm too busy spending time with Evander.

"We've tried that before, Thea. You spent the whole week feeling down about not being able to save them. You know I've stopped forcing you to sneak around with me a long time ago," he says as a jest, yet a hint of sadness plays behind his glistening eyes.

But he's not summoning me just for my own good, he's doing this for himself as well. I try to find malice in his eyes, and as usual, I fall short.

"Come now. I had a servant draw a bath for me before I got you. It's been a long day for both of us," standing, he offers me his hand. I take it freely, and he leads us to the corner of the room where the door to the bathing chamber waits.

A granite tub sits in the center of the room, engulfed by stone. A large, circular stained-glass window takes center stage in the room, showing a red sun setting into the golden flames of Audor. Evander said that at the opposite end of the manor, there is a window of the rising sun.

He leads me to the tub and slowly turns me around to face him, bending down to take my boots off, and he moves back up to touch my face. My breathing shortens as he slides his hand from my cheek down to the tie of my dress, his eyes never leaving mine. He gently tugs at the knot as the outer layer of the dress opens wide to reveal my cream tunic. Turning me away from him, he presses his body against mine and wraps his arm around my waist. He buries his nose into my hair inhaling deeply, and I lean into his touch. His heartbeat pounds against my shoulders as he moves his hand from my waist up to my collar bones, pulling the dress off. He catches the dress before it reaches the floor and throws it to the side. Lifting my arms up, he pulls the tunic over my head and piles it in a heap with the dress.

"Turn around," he whispers. His eyes run over me like molten lava as I face him, he takes in every curve and mark of my body. His gaze follows his hand as it idly traces the deep purple line starting at the nape of my neck, running his fingers along my collar bone, following the line as he deliberately slows down his movements where the line travels between my breasts. His hand brushes against my nipple, sending a raging fire to my core as my heart slams against my chest and pleasure curls in me. He follows the line down to my navel and stops, looking up to meet my eyes again. With his other hand, he tangles his fingers into my hair and pulls me to him, kissing me with deep hunger. He stops as quickly as he starts.

A glimmer of shame dances across his features as he looks down at his feet, trying to control his breathing. It's the same expression he wears every time we're about to do something intimate. I once asked him why he looks like that, and he said it's because he feels guilty about having forced me to spend time with him when I first confronted him. There was nothing but truth in his eyes.

He turns away and quickly undresses himself. I watch every muscle that flexes in his back, and a timid smile reaches my lips. He has the body of a born and bred soldier, with decades of training to form each and every single muscle. As he turns, the light from the oil lantern casts a shadow over his abdomen, making his body appear sculpted by the Anzeth themselves.

The water ripples and splashes as he steps into the tub.

"Come, princess. Let me bathe you."

I sigh and step in with him.

CHAPTER 4

"Ira furor brevis est: animum rege: qui nisi paret imperat.
Anger is a brief madness: govern your mind temper,
for unless it obeys it commands."
— Horace, *The Odes of Horace*

Between the splashes of water, I stroke Evander's ego as he brings up Prince Auberon, like he does every time I come over. Born three months after the Prince, Evander lives his life in the shadow of a royal. Brothers-in-arms and best friends to the eyes of the public, but a constant battle brewing beneath the surface.

"I've always thrown a better punch than him," he growls.

I roll my eyes, mentally preparing to hear the same story again.

"You know that I gave the Prince a black eye when we were younger? Queen Mellonia forced my mother to punish me for harming a 'member of the royal family,'" he says in a mocking tone, "I swear that King Cyrus was actually proud of me, because it was Auberon's fault for not blocking it."

"Yes, you've said this many times," I snigger, splashing water his way.

It makes sense. From the day the Prince was born, he was taught the art of charm and manipulation, learning how to sway a court or win wars with strategy and diplomacy alone. While Evander has always been a warrior trained to win fights with his fists rather than his words—he was never meant to lead anything more than a group of soldiers into war.

He seeks comfort from me, because no one will ever see him as more than the great General's son, or the Prince's shadow. I refuse to give pity to any person whose greatest weakness is their egotistical rivalry against the son of a king. Still, I play his game, nodding my head in understanding or laughing at his jokes.

Once, in the dead of the night, when the sheets were tangled between our legs and his fingers traced love letters down my spine, he whispered that I'm the one thing the Prince can't take from him.

Maybe he does genuinely want me, not for the venom that spews from my lips which I unleash on him whenever I get the chance to, but for the mere fact that I am his to keep. I am the only thing that isn't part of a childish competition.

I'd be lying if I said I don't enjoy my nights with him. Beyond the marks on my body or the power coursing through me, we just want the same thing — to forget. To forget that the world is crumbling. To forget that our people slaughter children every month.

The crackling of the hearth and the plumpness of the pillows makes me forget about Pa's ragged breaths, or the pain lingering beneath Ma's eyes. These forbidden nights are a temporary escape from the emptiness in both of our hearts.

"I've been meaning to ask, how have you been coping?" he asks, and tension climbs up my back.

I sigh, running my fingers through the water, considering what to say.

"I had another episode yesterday," I strain. It's hard to keep my mask up around him.

"What happened?" he whispers, placing a soft kiss on my shoulder.

I close my eyes and take a deep breath.

"There was a Cintis in the market," I pause, not wanting to continue. I know I can tell him. He's been my shoulder to cry on for years now. I just want to keep lying to everyone that nothing bothers me, even when it destroys me inside. It's easier to pretend. But he deserves to know.

"He groped me on my way home. Ma was working that night, and Pa was staying late completing an order, so when I got home, I let all my emotions spill out of me."

His hands run over my skin in soft, comforting motions. He says nothing for several moments, before holding me tighter.

"I'm so sorry, Althea. I wish I could have been there for you."

"I know you do. I keep telling myself that I should be used to being treated awfully by a Cintis."

His body tenses, but he knows by now that nothing he says to me will change what it is like being a mortal in a world ruled by fae.

"I keep my brave face on when everyone is watching and break as soon as I'm alone." My voice stays solid as I speak, as if I weren't talking about my own experiences. In the past he says that it's my mind's way of detaching itself from my own reality to keep itself 'safe'.

"You shouldn't need to. This realm shouldn't have taught you to keep your feelings pent up to the point that you self-destruct," he says.

Another kiss lands on my shoulder. I know he's right.

"If you keep lying to yourself that you're alright, at some point you might end up believing it," I say with a light tone, not wanting to acknowledge my emotions.

He sighs, leaning his head against the tub.

"You don't need to keep that mask on just for your parents."

I don't respond. There's nothing I can say that will make him accept that being this way —wearing a mask— is the only way to stay alive and pretend to be more confident than I feel. But he's wormed his way into my heart and made me feel comfortable enough to bring my mask down in front of him. He's the only person who's seen me cry.

"I tried to practice my breathing like you said; breathe in for seven seconds, and out for eleven," I say when the silence stretches for too long.

"And did it work?" he asks with a hint of hope in his voice.

"I ripped one of my dresses when I was breaking down," I whisper, worrying that I'll disappoint him.

"At least your knuckles didn't receive the brunt of it," he says softly, giving my arm a squeeze, "It'll work next time. I promise."

"Don't make promises you can't keep, boy," I say, mimicking Pa's voice in an attempt to distract from the topic. He always sees through it, but he still chuckles, planting a kiss in my hair.

"Let's get out of here before we wrinkle," I say.

He nods and wraps a fluffy towel around me when we get out, kissing my brow. He gently lifts me into his arms and carries me to the bed.

Water drips from my hair, trailing down my bare back, leaving a damp spot on the bed. He walks towards the mirror, tightens the towel wrapped just his hips, just below the deep V. Admiring himself in the mirror, he ruffles his wet hair, dragging his hand through it to style it.

It's the little things like this that reminds me how different mortals and fae are. They worry about their appearance, making sure that they keep up with the latest fashion and that there isn't a single hair out of place. Meanwhile us mortals can't afford to focus on anything other than staying alive: food, shelter, and survival. Rare few humans foolishly try to care about their appearance, but we all know nothing will hide the stench of poverty.

He saunters back to the bed, with a mischievous smirk etched across his features as he plops down beside me and sits up on his elbows.

"You really are quite beautiful, for a mortal."

I can hear the playfulness in his voice as he reaches over and lightly flicks my nose.

Scoffing loudly at the backhanded compliment, I say, "So, the noble Evander sees mortals and fae as equal? Except we petty mortals can't possibly be attractive unless we have something that sets us apart? Have you forgotten it's *your kind* that forced us into this type of life?"

The playful sparkle leaves his eyes, as a gleam of shame filters through, mingling with a tight anger.

"You know that's not what I meant. You know what I want to —"

I cut him off before he can continue, "No, Evander. I don't know what you want. Because what you *do* and what you *want* are two very different things. Tell me this, what exactly are *you* doing about these things you apparently want?"

Challenging him on something like this is a very dangerous game, but it has been a long day, and the desire to make it all stop fuels my fire.

A swirl of anger and helplessness flashes across his features. "It's not my place to change the realm," he says.

"You're saying that like someone who is nothing more than General Fornous' son."

The words slip out before I can stop myself and my blood runs cold. There are many things I can get away with; this is not one of them. My breath hitches as a drop of guilt laces through me at the sight of the pain that rocks through him. I tense, readying myself for a blow or to smell burning skin—though he's never harmed me. Nothing but his burning eyes sear into mine. I hurt him, and I can only pray he doesn't decide to destroy my life as vengeance for my snide remark.

"I'm sorry."

With shaky fingers I reach out to him, wanting to *forget* like we always do, and forget what I just said.

"I think it's time for you to go home."

He inches away from my touch without looking at me. I scramble out of the bed, all but running to the bathroom to shove the dirty clothes back on. The soot on them stains me just as thoroughly as my guilt. I should have kept my mouth shut.

His eyes still do not meet mine as I walk back across the room. I stop halfway to the door, swinging my body to face him.

"Please," I beg, standing there, hoping to get some kind of reaction out of him.

His face is unreadable as he stares at the hearth. He doesn't even flinch.

Knowing he won't say anything, I slip from the room, brushing the brass door handle before I slink into the darkness of Audor.

Sleeping families line the streets, and drunken laughter fills the air as the rest of the world continues on as though nothing happened. I duck from shadow to shadow, trying not to be seen or heard. I want to take my family and get out of Ignis to a small village so my parents can stop killing themselves at work just to provide for us.

It's nothing but a whirlwind of foolish dreams that we may be free from tyranny, to be happy with full bellies at the end of every day. But Pa can't run because of his leg, and Ma's optimism means she always says our life in Ignis is good.

Rounding another corner, a group of men stand by the entrance of a tavern, each man looks angrier than the last. I try to steer clear, picking up my pace as I stick to the shadows on the opposite side of the street.

"I'm telling you, it's those fuckin' Vesians that started the war," one of the men's voices carries down the street, and I slow my steps. I've heard of the theory, but never gave it any weight.

"Them Acolytes ain't sayin' in anymore so we don't try fightin' those blue shits," another huffs, taking a swig of his drink.

"I say, screw the treaty, we gut the next Lympa we see!" says another man.

They all erupt into agreement, yelling out all the ways they'll kill a Vesian. I pick up my pace, breaking into a run to get some distance from them. Ma said never to listen to anyone that points fingers about which empire caused it.

Dashing up the steps to our small home, I am finally greeted by the familiar metal latch. As I step in, the sound of Pa's snore breaks the deafening silence.

Good, they're still asleep. Like they always are.

The clock ticks nearby. It's only a few more hours until dawn when the quarters will start to buzz as mortals run off to perform their back-breaking duties.

I creep back onto my couch with a heavy heart. My eyes close, but my mind wanders. What if my slip-up seals our fate? Will they be kind and kill us quickly, or break our spirits until we wish for our deaths?

So, the question remains; do we wait here like sitting ducks, or do we run to our certain death?

CHAPTER 5

"Omnia mutantur, nihil interit.
Everything changes, nothing perishes."
— *Publius Ovidius Naso, Metamorphoses*

On nights like tonight when I toss and turn, the thought of death burrows into my mind. Death by Cintis or death by the Anzeth.

Death is a contagion no Cintis or mortal can run from.

Somewhere between the angst and fear, I drift off to sleep only to be jolted awake by Pa's coughs that shake the walls of the quarters. The door to their bedroom swings open as Ma hobbles out.

"He doesn't look good today. He shouldn't go to work. Water won't do nothin'," she mutters to herself.

I sit up on the couch, and she turns to me as she pours water into Pa's mug.

"Oh Thea, lie back down. You've got a few more minutes before we need to get up."

I stand, making my way toward her to plant a kiss on her cheek. Taking the mug from her, I say, "Rest, Ma, you have a big day ahead of you. I'll take care of Pa. I'll go to work with him today."

I try to reassure her with a forced smile.

She sighs, shaking her head slightly, "One day your Pa's gonna die for those damn Cintis."

Her shoulder slumps forward as her head hangs low, looking down at her hands.

As our eyes meet, an understanding settles between us. This moment is not about us. It is about what we can do right now for Pa. She gives me a strained smile and places a heavy hand on my shoulder, saying "I love you, Thea. Thank you for taking care of our family."

I squeeze her hand, saying "You never need to thank me. Go, rest, let me do what I do best."

I try to sound as comforting and confident as possible, even though we both know my power isn't enough to cure him completely. I won't be able to do that unless he manages to retire, giving him time to rest and heal. She must have seen through my mask because worry laces her brows.

"Just be careful at work. Stay covered, stay hidden, and don't you ever use that little gift of yours outside of these walls, you hear me?" She waves her finger at me with a warning tone.

I chuckle as I walk away with the mug in my hand, hoping to lighten the mood.

"I know. When am I not careful, Ma?"

I walk into their musty bedchamber, as the sheer curtains dance against the draft seeping through the cracks in the window. Pa's wheeze doesn't sound as dangerous as it did when it startled me from sleep. Behind me, I hear Ma scuffling through the kitchen, her pots and pans clanging against each other. I plop myself down next to Pa on the bed, making him mutter in annoyance.

Handing him the mug of water, I say in a joking tone, "Can you please try being a little quieter? There's no need to wake the whole neighborhood with your coughs."

Ma's face would go white if she heard the way we spoke to each other.

He tries to laugh, but a choked cough comes out instead. He takes a long sip as I place my hand on his arm to let my healing powers trickle into him and warmth spreads to my skin.

His lung flashes through my mind as his breathing starts to steady under the thrum of my fingertips, and his eyes flutter close as he rests his head back on the pillow, taking deep breaths.

I wish I could do more, by the time I had control over my powers and harnessed it properly it was too late. There's nothing I can do to regrow Pa's lung.

"Old man, you should quit your job while you're ahead. We both know I can craft a better sword than you anyways," I provoke, reminiscing that the one weapon I made when I was younger that could barely cut a slice of bread. I know challenging his craftsmanship gets him riled up.

He scoffs.

"Girl, ya couldn't even lift a hammer with that tiny arm."

I laugh, knowing just how untrue it is.

"Even with a missin' leg, I'm still better than you," he continues, "Everyone in Audor knows my craft, I'm one of the best -"

"Yes, yes, I get it." I interject, "The only thing you've still got is your wit and your eyesight. And even that's pretty debatable."

I smile from ear to ear, knowing there's no counter he can make to my argument. He deflects instead, grumbling, "Anyways, rest up. We need to go to work soon."

I start to leave, but he halts me with a word.

"Girl," Pa coughs, and I stop in my tracks, turning back to him. There's an uneasy look on his face. He clears his throat and continues, "The Priest is coming today for the dagger."

My stomach lurches at the mention of him. I hate when he comes to the Forge.

"I know..." I reply slowly, "Is something wrong?"

He looks around the room slowly like something is watching him, and my body tenses.

"Nothin' wrong. Just don't like when he comes. He could see your marks."

I shift my weight on my feet, unconvinced that's the whole reason. But it makes sense: we all hate when the Priest comes.

"Are you sure?" I push.

"Yes," he nods uncertainly. I stare at him for a moment longer before making my way back to the kitchen.

~

The Royal Forge hasn't been fixed or improved since the war. It's a few blocks away from the Fire Palace. Ma said when I first came here as a child, I called it a gray hole.

It's still a fitting description.

Four rounded walls entomb the forge. In the center of it sits a pile of charcoal, mingling with a mountain of burnt, broken and unwanted pieces within the ash. Anvils, bellows, swages, nails, and other tools scattering over the dirt in the Hole. The outskirts of the Gray Hole are sheltered under brick. The walls have been layered with centuries worth of char, turning the brick into a miserable patchwork of gloomy shades of black. The smoke from the furnaces travels along the walls, coating even the ceiling in mottled grays.

Whenever I work, I wear Ma's old uniform from before I was born. The dress is far too small to fit her, and it was already decorated in rips and stains. The once-red dress is now a dirty brown, the hem has a thick black coat of muck.

Wayland, the foreman, doesn't want to give me breeches because they're 'reserved for men.' He doesn't seem to hesitate to buy a whole new set of forge appropriate clothing every time one of his many sons takes a brief interest in becoming a blacksmith.

I wear the same gloves as the blacksmiths, except they are three sizes too big and fall off whenever I drop my hands to my side. When I asked a seamstress to make me a pair that fits, she laughed in my face saying she didn't offer her service to a *Spoiled Maiden* because it would 'do her struggling business no good'.

Sweat breaks across my forehead as I pull out steel from the forge and embers fly out, threatening to burn me. I set the steel, still bright red from the heat, flat onto the anvil bringing the hammer down. Eventually it will be ready for Pa to decorate the hilt and inscribe the blade.

I want to be the one to do the etching and carving. It's like painting with someone else's coin. But in order to keep Pa as far away from the forge as possible, alas, I have to be content with designing a weapon every once in a while, and otherwise spending my days breathing in the smoke.

The blacksmith I've always hated looks at me with disgust as the sound of clanging rings in the air. I've seen the envious glances he throws my way because he doesn't have the strength or speed he had in his younger years. He doesn't like that a woman can produce more weapons than him in a week.

After years of working here, my muscles don't struggle to keep up anymore. Not to mention because of my gift, I've never had any injury which impacts my work.

"I've been meaning to ask you, what's with the whole 'Cloaked Farris' thing?"

My hammer stops, hovering before I strike again, and I look up to meet a pair of golden-brown eyes. Cal has been trying to catch my attention ever since he started his apprenticeship.

I sigh.

"I played a little too close to the forge when I was young."

Another lie. Everyone has fallen for the lie, except Wayland, because he knows he would have heard if such an accident had happened. Saying I was burnt by ordinary fire isn't enough when most mortals have scars given to them by a Cintis. If Cal saw my marks, he'd run away screaming that I've come to bring another plague.

"Get lost, boy," Pa grumbles, waving his crutch around like he's about to use it on him as a weapon. He waves that thing around every time he catches Cal's wandering gaze. Yet the young man never learns his lesson. I smile.

The apprentice's eyes widen, and he quickly goes back to cleaning up the Hole like nothing happened.

Pa looks around with an edge of fear spread across his features.

"Althea," he breathes, and my heart stops. He never calls me Althea. There's a terror in his eyes I've never seen before which shakes me to the core.

"Yes?" I whisper.

His throat bobs as he swallows the lump in his chest.

"The dagger —" he stops mid-sentence, darting his eyes around the Hole to make sure no one can hear him speak, and his hand starts to shake.

"What is it?"

"I didn't tell you. I lost a ruby," he whispers, and the blood rushes from my face.

"What?" I hiss, stepping closer as my heart hammers against my chest.

"The rubies fell out of my pouch. I found all but one."

Shame coats his voice, and he can't even look me in the eyes. Panic runs up my spine as the realization sinks in.

"Why didn't you tell me? When did this happen?" My voice comes out frantic. The Priest is coming to collect it today, there's no time to fix it, and it's not like there's a ruby lying around we can just take. He says nothing, turning away to face the fire in contemplation. "Pa, what happened?" I press.

"Weeks ago. I didn't want to worry you," he says guiltily.

"Don't worry yourself, we've got to work," he says before turning to walk back to his table. My jaw drops as goosebumps spread all over my skin. A blacksmith was whipped for being tardy to one of the Priest's visits. If such a severe punishment is given to lateness, the repercussions for losing Audor's property would be catastrophic.

Worse yet, what if they think he stole it?

"Pa, stop!" I yell, staring at his receding figure. I sprint up to him, putting an arm on his shoulder before he can sit. They could kill him. These could be my last moments with him.

"Be quiet," he hisses, "Don't tell anyone."

His lip quivers slightly.

"We can fix this. We have to fix it," I try to whisper, but it comes out more like a sob. Tears burn my eyes, and I wipe them away before they can fall.

"Drop it, girl. It's done. There's nothing we can do," he grumbles as he turns to sit, pulling out the dagger he's been working on.

"There has to be something," I choke out. How can he pretend it's fine? Nothing about this is fine. If he had just told me, I might have been able to ask for Evander's help. I could have fixed it.

An unexpected slap thumps me on the back and I lurch forward. I twist around and meet Wayland's face.

"Get to work. We have a big order coming up and we don't want to be behind," he says, turning away to go outside.

I swallow the lump in my throat and make my way over to the barrels to check there's enough water and coal. I can barely focus on my work, thinking about the dagger. When I saw the design, there were at least twenty rubies on there. Maybe, he won't notice one missing.

I shake my head and take a deep breath, forcing the anxiety from my thoughts. I don't want to add to the trouble if we're late for an order. I need to focus and do what I do best.

From the corner of my eye, I can see Cal make his way back over to me. I sigh as he opens his mouth to speak, "Hey, about what I was saying before, I was wondering —"

"Quit chatting! Hurry up and clean faster. The Priest is coming," Wayland yells to Cal from across the Hole, and he snaps his mouth shut. He turns away to trudge through the filth with another bucket, picking up scrap metal discarded on the ground. Wayland continues, "They're going to bless your father's dagger to gift to the Anzeth. I want this place tidy."

My stomach turns at the mention of the dagger. The real reason they're coming to the forge is to bless the new sacrificial instrument that will 'appease the gods.'

Every so often, Pa's coughs overpower the heavy breathing of all the other blacksmiths. My power begs me to run over to him to heal him, but it's too suspicious if every time I go near him his coughs suddenly disappear.

"Everyone stop and line up outside!" Wayland orders, running inside from the front doors.

Sentinels and other royal patrons come into the Hole, but not for long. Like the Priest, most don't even come inside. It's ironic: a fae that can yield fire can't stand a crater filled with smoke to make the very weapons they use. Yet they expect mortals to spend their days choking on it. Sometimes the fae stands at the entrance and beckons one of the blacksmiths to come to them.

Cowards.

Pa hobbles out of the Hole and into line next to the other men, while I drag my feet in frustration over to the corner of the Hole out of sight. I plant my feet in just the right place so I can see any commotion unfold. The blacksmiths never let me stand with them in the line-up, because they say it's a discussion between men and I'd be better off cleaning up the Hole—even though I'm as good a smith as any one of them. Better even.

The shine of the Priest's bald head catches my attention. He pairs the blinding reflection of his head with an arrogant smirk which sickens me to my stomach. Though the Priest's hands have been washed from the boy's blood from yesterday, I can still smell the metallic scent radiating off him, and the image of *my dagger* being plunged into the boy replays.

Next to him, the Prince opts for a crown of gold flames instead of using real fire like he usually does. Standing among the sentinels, he looks like one of them with his broad chest and grave expression—though his embroidered jacket and ruby-encrusted sword distinguish him.

Terror makes its way into my throat as my eyes finally land on General Fornous, who stands on the other side of the Priest. He has the same black hair and steel eyes as Evander, only his eyes aren't filled with any playfulness. But something is wrong. Getting a holy weapon is the Priest's task. The general has no place here.

What if he's here because Evander told them about me, and he's already dealt with Ma and is now here to take Pa?

Wayland walks hurriedly towards the Priest, bowing before kneeling on the ground with both knees planted in the dirt as he raises his hands toward the Priest to offer him a folded black cloth. The Priest snatches it out of his hand, making Wayland jolt to his feet and scurry away to stand in line with the other men.

With bony fingers, the cloth is unfolded to reveal the dagger. Nausea crawls through me hoping he doesn't notice the missing ruby. It has rubies embellishing the curved guard, and an obsidian snake wraps around the hilt, with its mouth wide open at the center, making its way to the steel blade. He lifts it up closer to his eyes, then holds it up to the sun to inspect it, his face unreadable. A barely audible huff leaves his mouth, and he trails his fingers along the rubies plastered across the guard, counting under his breath. The entire line of mortal men tense, helpless to the Priest's every whim.

The Priest steps forward, clicking his tongue as a predatory smile paired with innocent eyes dresses his wrinkly face.

"Who was in charge of making this?" His words drip with malice. The line stills even more, as each head turns to Pa. At the same time, I stop breathing.

Pa uses his crutches to swing himself a foot closer to the Priest, bowing his head at his shoulders. I start scratching the outside of my palm at the sight of the devil himself referencing Pa.

"Ay, Holiness, I drew it up and made it."

I was surprised his voice oozed with confidence, not a single word cracked or wheezed.

"You are in the presence of Royalty and the Spirit of Audor. What do you call that despicable bow? Show us respect, or we will teach you it, mortal," he sneers, taking a step closer towards the line.

Pa hesitates, unsure what to do. He throws a crutch to the side, and drops onto his knee, using the other crutch to keep him upright as he lowers his head level to the ground.

"Please forgive my rudeness, Holiness," This time his voice cracks as his breathing breaks into a wheeze.

The Priest's face morphs into a scowl before replacing it with his predatory smile.

"So, you were in charge of the rubies and tried to steal them?"

My shaking hands touch my lips to silence the urge to yell to the Priest that Pa would never be foolish enough to try and steal from the Empire.

Pa's knuckles turned white as his grip on the crutch tightens.

"Ay, I was in charge of the rubies, but I ain't never tried stealing them, your Holiness."

"So, are you calling me a liar?" The Priest spits. I am sure the entire line has stopped breathing completely. I have never seen Pa look so helpless.

"Of course not, Holiness. It fell out of its pouch at me workstation. I couldn't find it through the mess," he says with a slight plea to his tone.

The Priest looks at the top of Pa's head for a moment considering his options before he walks to General Fornous to hand him the dagger.

Turning back around to face Pa and the rest of the men, the Priest says, "I should punish all of you for lying and trying to steal from the Empire."

His eyes darken as they lower like a beast about to kill its prey, "But I am a forgiving man, and the Empire of Audor has a kind heart. Look at me mortal. You will thank me for my generosity."

The tension in my shoulders releases.

"Thank the gods," I whisper to myself, taking a deep breath as my body leans against the wall.

He gets to live another day. We all get to live another day. Maybe after today's threat, I can finally convince Ma that it's time to leave Ignis.

The Priest gives a slight nod toward the General, and says, "Because of that, not *all* of you will be punished."

My thoughts take flight at his words.

My eyes barely register the flurry of movement.

The General walks towards Pa with the dagger in his hand. With a single swipe, the blade tears through Pa's throat, spraying the blood across the yard.

The crutch falls to the side, and his body goes limp as he drops into a pool of his own blood.

CHAPTER 6

"Death may be the greatest of all human blessings."
— Socrates

Red.

Everything is red.

A scream rips through the air. My scream.

Something in my core snaps, releasing a darkness into my veins which overpowers the gift that usually thrums loudly through me.

With each beat of my heart, more darkness floods into my lungs from my core, and before I can get control, it seems to surge toward the line of men, sentinels, acolytes, and the General. I watch as time slows, and the men go flying through the air before landing on the ground. It feels like I hold the power of the gods at my fingertips, ready to kill those who stand before me. But it does not feel like those powers are my own. I have no control over it. It's as if I've become a vessel for the darkness.

I should tremble with fear about what I just witnessed. Fear of consequences, fear of my secret finally being revealed. But I am beyond feeling. I've become the beast.

The darkness hones in on General Fornous; his face splattered with my father's blood; his steel eyes wide in shock. My sight blurs, turning him into nothing more than a speck of white in my vision, as rage courses through me, buzzing through my fingers like a fire storm.

Out of pure instinct, my hands flick. And, like dust, the General's body rips through the air again to land on the ground.

I don't know when I started moving, or when my tears started to drip onto the dirt covering Pa's face. I also don't know when my shrieks weren't the only noise piercing the air. The clanging of metal and groans are nothing but white noise, as Pa's eyes scream for help. I can barely hear my own heartbeat.

A pale-blue hue engulfs his skin, and his lips turn the crimson red of Audor. Bubbles of blood spray out of the slit across his neck.

Words refuse to leave my lips as my hands speak for me. They find their way to his chest and forehead. The red in my vision disappears and spirals into a swirl of gold, silver, blue, and green as the firestorm on the tips of my fingers turns into an ocean of familiar warmth. It flows from me into the body beneath my hands.

It's like ecstasy compared to the wails and tears that pours from me in a torrent.

Blinding light flashes through the laceration in his throat, as if King Cyrus moved the sun from the sky and into Pa's core. Slowly, the slit draws itself closed, covering the blinding light, leaving behind a healed thin red line where a fountain of blood once flowed. Shades of pink return to his skin, and the call of death in his eyes is replaced with shrill fear.

As the last bit of light disappears beneath the scar, a rough hand curls around my shoulder and tears me through the air, and I land on the ground with a heavy thud. Pa props up onto his elbow as footsteps narrow in on me, until I'm engulfed in a sea of acolytes and sentinels.

Fury emanates from the General. The Priest's eyes widen, as he stalks closer to me he whispers, "My gods." Next to him, Prince Auberon's mouth gapes open in disbelief and our eyes lock, and a surge of familiarity floods into me.

Like a tsunami, the realization of what I just did in front of an audience knocks the breath out of me. Their gazes burn holes through me as my promise to Ma lies shattered in the dirt. My one duty to our family was never to reveal myself.

All for nothing.

They saw me use my gift.

It turns out my greatest enemy was me, all along.

The General pulls himself from the ground, ignoring the hay coating his jacket as his once-black hair turns into a blazing fire. "You're an abomination," General Fornous growls.

All around, hay bales turn into an inferno as the Cintis summon the flame to light their drawn weapons on fire.

The General's steel eyes never once leave mine. He does not move. He does not breathe. He's ready to attack.

The Priest steps forward to kneel next to me, his nose still held high as he looks down at me.

"What are you, girl?" he sneers.

Girl. Pain shoots through my chest from using my father's term of endearment for me just after he ordered for his death.

What have I done? I've ruined everything. I need to get through the sentinels to Pa, and we need to run. Even if it means we live in the forest. We need to escape.

Through the mass of legs, Pa reaches for his crutch to prop himself up.

"Leave her alone! Run, Althea! Run!" he screams.

I would never leave him here. A sentinel walks over to him and sweeps his foot under Pa's crutch, and he crashes to the ground.

"No! Leave him alone! It's me you want. Take me!" I beg, saying a silent prayer to Anzeth that they might listen for once. I stare at Pa as he is hauled upright by a sentinel.

"You didn't answer my question. I'm sure your father can help me convince you to cooperate," the Priest snarls. The threat in his tone burns me. I try to meet Pa's eyes, but the Priest moves to block him from my sight.

"Please, leave my father alone and I'll tell you everything." This time, my tear-streaming eyes lock with the Priest's cold sapphire ones.

He looks me up and down, studying every inch of me, from my hunched form to my splayed shaking fingers.

Powerless. I'm powerless.

The same realization dawns on him that I'm powerless. I'm left helpless at his will. A triumphant smile stains his cold demeanor.

"You're in no position to be making any demands, are you? Where are your powers now, girl?"

His sinister laugh joins the chorus of cackling flames around us as he stands up and walks away from us without looking back.

"Take them to the King," he barks.

"No!" I scream.

I don't need the powers to help Pa. Out of the corner of my eye, something silver glistens against the hay. I lunge towards it, wrapping my hand around the ruby hilted dagger. "Stay back!" I hiss, sweeping the blade around me in an attempt to keep the sentinels at bay. Like muscle memory, my arms move into the fighting stance Evander taught me. I need to get to Pa. I need to get us out of here. My feet slowly shuffle toward Pa.

I can feel the darkness stirring in my core. The caged beast thrashes around and it becomes harder to breathe as the men turn into a blur of movement.

Fire rends the air. Then suddenly, everything goes black.

A throbbing pain clings to the back of my skull, leaving a high-pitched ring that makes its way behind my eyes. Through the ringing, hushed conversations and yelling rumbles through the walls, and the smell of charred soil and damp decay assaults my nose.

A burning ache consumes my wrists, making me gasp for air from the combined pain. Waves of exhaustion hit me as I try to lift myself up to see the carnage around my wrists.

My muscles feel raw beneath my skin, like I scaled the top of Mount Polis ten times over. Yet somehow, my gift and the beast still swirl hungrily.

I pry my eyes open, fighting the pulsing rhythm behind my eye sockets, and stifling a whimper as I push myself upright. I study the ribs and crook of the stone wall, and in the corners, I see jagged purple stones peeking through. The Infra stone climbs down each corner, spilling onto the floor into a pool of sharp points. The acolytes at the library said all prisons are lined with Infra stone to dampen a fae's power and make them what they hate most: mortal.

They said its name derives from the language of the Anzeth—*Infra; to be less than, below and beneath.* They left out the final part of that sentence; *to be beneath fae by becoming mortal.*

Small cracks lace through the ribs of the stone walls, letting a cascade of golden light cast jagged shadows through my prison. It almost looks ethereal.

A sickly wet feeling runs down the back of my neck to my collar bones. My brown hair sticks to the red seep of blood. Just beneath the red line around my wrist, jagged thorns of black metal and vines wrap around my wrist. The sharp points dig into my skin, threatening to draw blood with the slightest movement. Dirt webs across my hand, covering my sleeve and dress.

The clanging of chains dragged along the ground echoes through the room, pulling against the thorn shackles. Scorching pain penetrates my wrist when I move to touch the ache at the back of my head. Blood pebbles my mud-washed skin like rubies in a forge. Like the beads of Pa's blood across General Fornous' skin scorches my mind.

Pa.

All at once, I remember Pa's blue skin, the white dust flying out of sight, the firestorm that broke free, then suddenly—nothing.

I can still hear the gurgling sound of Pa choking on his own blood. A stifled whimper leaves me. I'm not sure if the tears that come are from the memories or the gnawing sensation in my body. I try not to retch as I search the shadows for Pa, begging to hear his raspy breathing.

I saved him. Pa has to be fine. There's no way he could be dead. They need him. If not for his skill, then to control me.

What if they have Ma? They won't need him anymore if they have her. They may still want to use him to teach mortals a lesson for losing the Empire's property.

As the thoughts race through my mind, the throbbing at the back of my head peaks. Panic thunders through me and my breathing quickens. I'm trapped.

I need to calm down.

I need to keep it together. I have to be strong for Pa. I have to get out of here.

I close my eyes, letting images of General Fornous and the Priest being slaughtered like an animal on the altar consume my thoughts, and a steady stream of calm rolls through me, extinguishing my fire and releasing the throb from my head.

Stay covered and stay hidden.

I promised Ma that I would keep to the shadows—to hide my powers from everyone and keep away from fae, as if they carried the plague.

I do a once-over of myself, searching for any exposed skin. I may not have been able to keep one promise, but I can still try to keep the other. Slowly moving my arms against my body in small motions, my sleeve falls lower down my arm, hiding the purple line.

As the moonlight starts to trickle into the cell, exhaustion sinks its teeth into me. Screams from a cell nearby pry open my eyes and my blood runs cold.

I try to summon the darkness that I felt at the Hole to find Pa and get out of here. If only I knew how to summon it. I'll kill everyone in my path if I need to. I close my eyes and dig deep into my core. I can see the beast swirling hungrily just out of my reach. As I focus on that well of primal power, I can feel its anger radiating out of it, like it wants to destroy this Palace and everyone in it. When I offer my hand to let it do just that, it pulls further away from me and the swirls slow. It's asking me to be patient.

I try grasping onto that darkness for hours. Trying to wrap my fingers around it. Trying to make it mine. Each time I try, the beast recedes away like it's intentionally avoiding my touch. A frustrated scream leaves my lips, and I hiss as the thorns drag along my skin from my movement.

I hope they treat Pa with more kindness than this. I don't think his lung will endure living in this filth.

As the silver light changes into a golden yellow, signaling a new day, my fingers ache with the slightest movement, my stomach groans, and my mouth turns to dry ash.

As night begins to crawl in, violet fades to indigo, and three sets of footsteps echo down the corridor, stopping right in front of my cell door.

They've come for me.

CHAPTER 7

"Damnant quod non intellegunt
They condemn what they do not understand"

— Cicero

The once hushed whimpers of other prisoners turn into a chorus of wails and banging. They all beg for freedom, screaming bloody murder at whoever waits on the other side. Behind the black metal slab, keys rattle as the door shakes with the sound. My breath hitches in my throat, reigniting my tears of dread. I roll my fingers into fists and a soft cry leaves my lips as the thorns cut deeper into my skin. I try to reach for the darkness from before, but the well is empty.

With more force than is necessary and a predatory smirk that rivals the Priest's, a dark-skinned sentinel walks in with a bounce in his step that has my stomach sinking. He looks at me like a cat, amused to toy with its prey. Two other sentinels step into the room, visibly tenser with the effects of infra in play, and tighten their grip around their holstered swords as their most powerful weapons are smothered by the rocks.

I pull my shoulders back, hardening my exterior to seem more confident than I feel. The lump in my throat grows bigger, and I try to ignore it.

The sentinels wear the armor of the Empire of Fire, with the emblem of Audor engraved into the breast plate. The light coming through the cracks illuminates the dips in their muscles, reflecting off the chainmail dangling at their sides.

My fingers tick, wanting to jump up and take the swords from their hands and feel the comfort of the heavy weight in my grip. If these shackles come off, I can try to take them down and find Pa.

That's optimistic, the voice scoffs.

No, I have to be optimistic. He'd be in here somewhere. There's no way they'd let him walk free after what I did. If he's even still alive.

Wrapping his hands around my collar, the sentinel pulls me to my feet, slamming me against the wall. I hiss through my gritted teeth when the stone pierces into my skin, bringing ruby beads to the surface for my gift to heal.

I say a silent prayer to the Anzeth pleading for help, for rescue, anything but this incessant pain and humiliation.

Behind the man, the corners of one of the sentinel's lips curls into cruel satisfaction. The other stands rigid and grim. I swear I can see terror and guilt in his eyes, but I push it aside, labeling it as imagination. The armor hangs loosely over his frail figure, and he's half the size of the two other sentinels. There's a slight hunch in his back. I've seen his face before. Probably harassing mortals on the street.

A pearlescent, maniacal grin spreads across the dark-skinned sentinel's face. He pulls out a blade, the cool metal presses into my neck as he lowers his lips to my ear.

I need to ask about Pa, but there's a voice in my head screaming that if there's a time to shut up, it's definitely now.

"You've been summoned," he spits, throwing me down, landing on the chain's spike sticking out of the ground.

My body hits the ground with a crack, and my eyes burn with unshed tears as I hit the chain's spike.

I reach deep into my core to find the darkness. It's there, I just need to get to it. The well swirls away from my reach. *Come here,* I beg to it as it bares its teeth at the Cintis, disregarding my plea for help.

I can feel its rage clawing at my insides, readying itself for something. But I don't know what. Only the spark of my gift rumbles through me in full force, scrambling to my ribs to repair the broken bone like the infra has done nothing to slow it down.

Please! Desperation chokes me as my face scrapes against the ground, stopping me in my attempts to get up. The thorns dig into my skin, and I scream in agony. My gift thunders through me to heal it, trying to push the intruder out and failing. *Help.*

The beast does nothing but watch.

I eye the dagger at his side. It looks pathetic: the hilt is too big for the actual blade. I won't hesitate to plunge it into his heart, and every other person who gets in my way. If the beast wants to slumber, then I will take matters into my own hands.

Breathing in the grit and dirt from the floor, a choked cough strains out of me as a hand grabs my hair, yanking my face up to look at the other sentinels.

"Now let's see what an abomination you are," he spits into my ear, "Let's show everyone that you're a vile curse that needs to be destroyed."

"You're right, Belve. She's an abomination," one of the other men laughs.

Abomination.

The word stings, but I clench my jaw. *I'm not the abomination*, I long to retort. The monsters that he worships are. His own kind is the real abomination in this place.

I can't swallow my scream when his dagger pierces my shoulder. White dances in front of my eyes, the darkness thrashes at the impact, and as if noticing where the non-fatal wound was delivered, it slithers back into its well, watching and waiting to see whether death will unfold. I feel helpless without it.

A rush of air whips into me as the sound of cloth tearing fills the air and my skin goes cold.

No.

He's going to see my skin. He's going to see the one thing I thought I could keep hidden from them.

"Help me!" I roar, not for the prisoners to hear, but for the darkness. My world feels like it's going to shatter. I can barely move. I can barely breathe. I try to get up, try to fight, but he's too heavy. All my attempts do is move the thorned shackles, ripping the skin in its wake.

"Get the fuck off me!"

I can barely hear Belve's yells of hatred toward me beyond the ringing in my ears as my breath grows ragged and quick.

He moves to my other arm, this time slicing my skin open. I can already feel the wound in my other arm start to heal as the pain slowly subsides. He pivots his body as his foot lands on the ground near my head and his hands pin my legs to the floor to stop me from kicking. My skirt pulls and tears under his blade.

His dagger cuts into the neckline of my dress, catching my skin in the process as he moves his blade up to the very top of the dress. I thrash around under him, and my heart thunders painfully under his knee as I see pure greed and excitement spread across Belve's face, which only makes my heartbeat reverberate through my bones.

Sheathing his dagger, he pulls the torn dress aside to expose my collar bone and neck.

Grabbing my hair, he pulls me up. The room spins as I stand. I can't remember where the sentinels keep their weapons. Right side? Left side? Who was it that didn't carry a weapon? I force my eyes to blink quickly, trying to get my bearings.

Just as the room stops spinning, he finally lets go, pulling out a chunk of my hair. I sprawl onto the floor, skin exposed, dirty, shamed, as he joins the other sentinels.

Belve puts his arm around the smiling one and pats the other on the shoulder, laughing.

"What do you say, boys? Reckon they'll take one look at her and decide she needs to be put down like a dog?" Belve lets out the type of laugh I hear coming from the taverns at night.

The fog in my mind clears as I get my bearings. Resolve mingles with my anger. I'm going to kill him. I'm going to kill him even if it's the last thing I do. As soon as he takes these shackles off, I'm going to shove that dagger into his neck.

"Look how fucking disgusting she is. Look at her skin. Maybe she's the walking plague!" the smiling one retorts playfully.

I look down at my bare arms, to my naked legs and to the pile of ripped fabric on the floor. Shame engulfs me in its cold fire as the sentinels feast their eyes upon me. He stripped me so everyone can see that I look exactly like what I am: an abomination.

Tears of humiliation and despair threaten to spill down my cheeks, but I can't stop the tear that runs down my face.

They made me break my promise to Ma. I'm not covered.

Reaching for a set of keys in his pockets, Belve walks back to me and wraps another shackle around my wrist. My eyes burn into his, waiting for the moment he unlocks the thorns. My heart skips a beat as the thorns fall away, I try to reach for the power while angling myself for his dagger, but Belve moves quicker. Pulling my neck to him until his face comes mere inches from my own as a grin stains his face. Through a smile that's all teeth, he says, "You're going to die today."

A scream fights its way through gritted teeth as he yanks me to my feet. My hand moves to the weapon at his side, and he throws me against the wall.

"Don't even think about it."

Belve turns on his heels, as he pulls me out with him. Unable to hold it at bay any longer, my bottom lip quivers as my tears fall.

You're weak, the voice inside my head hisses.

As we exit the cell, Belve and the smiling sentinel release an audible sigh of relief. They're back to feeling *more than* mortal without the infra.

My feet barely keep up and I struggle to remain upright as we move quickly through the hallways. Exhaustion nips at my heels as we walk down the long corridors and the winding stairs. I blink back tears, trying to steady my thundering heart. I can't help anyone if I'm too consumed by emotion.

Belve's grip around my arm holds firm as we walk down rows upon rows of black doors. Torches line the walls, muffled groans and cries filter through the corridor making my skin prickle. Banging noises come from behind the doors as they hear us walking past. At every turn, another sentinel stands guard.

My bare feet shuffle along the floor, picking up dust and dirt and whatever manure they haven't cleaned since the war.

A sudden chill cleaves the air and seeps into my torn dress—a natural indicator that night has completely fallen, and the King has laid the sun to rest. A shiver slithers up my spine as a perpetual nausea settles in, making me tremble as each step becomes heavier than the last.

My eyelids threaten to close whenever light from the oil lanterns shines in my eyes. Each time I have to force them wide open, all while attempting to keep track of where each sentinel is and listening for changing patterns in the way their scabbards clang against their legs as they walk. And looking for an opening to escape their grips and navigate the endless corridors and stairs of the dungeon.

It's a fool's hope to think they might lead me to Pa, but I will go from door to door until I find him once I free myself. I'm not going anywhere without him. I can't fail him.

I swallow the lump in my throat and try to straighten my back. Belve yanks my arm in an attempt to make me stumble, and I spit on him.

Rounding a corner, a sharp object pierces my foot, making me stagger. My shackled hands fly out to catch myself. The pain isn't that bad, but the hole in my foot compounded with the overwhelming fear of what the future brings is enough to send me toppling.

Belve lets go of my arm and watches me fall to the filthy ground and impatience paints his features. He steps forward, kicking his boot into my ribs with a loud crack. The beast within me perks up, ready to protect its own. *Finally.* The darkness fills my heart and my fingers curl to welcome the storm.

"Get up." His voice is laced with venom as he spits on me.

No! I plead as the darkness recedes, leaving me defenseless all over again.

Hands grip my hair, yanking me to my feet. "I said get up!" Belve growls, sadism oozing from every word. He starts pulling me along the corridor by my hair.

The smell of dirt and must dwindles as he pulls me up a spiraling flight of stairs. As we ascend the stairs, the sound of groans and screams get louder. My eyes dart from door to door, desperately trying to sense Pa. He could be in any one of these.

Once we reach the top, the same torches and black doors line the hallway. It looks exactly like the corridor we just walked through. We walk a few more feet before Belve pulls me to an abrupt stop to open another door.

The ground under my feet shifts to clean concrete, then polished marble that glistens under sconces shaped to look like a dragon breathing fire. A sigh leaves my lips as my feet feel reprieve from the abuse of the dungeon floors. My feet slide along the marble floor, leaving a trail of mud and filth. A distant part of me relishes in the mess I'm leaving on their pristine flooring.

I try to memorize everything I see as Belve drags me under arch after golden arch that are held up by obsidian pillars that reach into the painted ceiling. Every few pillars, a carved dragon curls around the column, then the flooring changes.

More paintings of war and the King's power over the sun cover the ceiling. The plush black carpet under my feet feels like ecstasy after the shit I've been walking on. As we make our way along the halls, carved golden statues of the King in different poses tuck into more gold arches in the walls. If an archway doesn't hold a statue of the King, then paintings of all the queens that died after being unable to bear a son decorate the walls. I am surprised they haven't taken the paintings down when they're a stain on the Empire's history. Some of the queens are painted doing mundane things such as gardening or reading. One painting depicts Queen Mellonia laughing, along with who I assume is a baby Auberon on her lap. The painting almost makes me laugh at the thought of her being capable of feeling joy.

Rage boils within me at the sight of such opulent decorations. So, this is why we starve? Because the Royal Palace is too busy commissioning artists to paint or sculpt golden statues just to stroke the King's ego? Meanwhile the people in the Remains are living amongst rats on the streets, scavenging through rubbish bins in the hopes that they'll find crumbs to feed their children.

We pass servants and other sentinels who move aside as we parade by, gawking at me. The layer of blood and soot aren't enough to keep my marks hidden. I feel naked. Exposed. Vulnerable. I swallow the lump in my throat, cowering into my own skin.

I look like the plague. I look like I'm here to take their families in the night. After all that mortals have gone through, the thought that I've given them something else to fear makes guilt pulse through me, making my figure crumpling further inward.

Eventually the carpet gives way to cold obsidian floors, and the ceiling rises even higher. Turning around a bend, we come to large oak doors as tall as the apartments lining the streets.

Two sentinels guard the colossal doors. Their armor is completely plated in gold, down to the tasset. The insignia of Audor is engraved directly in the center of their chest plate molded to their abdomen, curving around each muscle as scales run up the sides of their ribs. They wear a helmet made to look like something crossed between a phoenix and a dragon. Gold fangs protrude down the side of a sharp beak, tusks shoot out from the side of their head between a web of golden scales.

They look vicious. They look the very image Audor wishes to portray; an Empire of power and wealth.

As we come to a stop in front of the doors, Belve nods at the sentinels. The taller one marches to the side and pulls on a rope. I expect an earth-shattering creak to come from the door as it opens, but it barely whispers. I have to stop myself from flinching when the throne room from hell is revealed in all its frightening glory. My flight-or-fight instincts are begging me to run, or fight tooth-and-nail just to get out of going into that room.

A dragon head is carved out of steel and obsidian above a single throne, looking down on the subjects of Audor. Two symmetrical curved staircases with giant claws coming out of them protrude from the side of its head, down to the raised dais. A stream of lava spills down the steps from the throne that has been carved from the tusks of some great beast, and knives radiate out from the throne like lighting.

Tears of hellfire run down the dragon's eyes, pouring directly above the King's throne and enshrouding him in fire. The fire continues pouring down onto the dais, circling King Cyrus, dripping down the steps and engulfing the edges of the room. Red banners fall from the beast's horns, as if it were the blood of war dripping from it.

This is a throne room fit for a King of monsters. A place where demons are birthed from the bowels of hell.

In the center of it all stands a horrifying sight.

Eyes of piercing blue stare into mine, a depraved grin crawling along his ghost-like face. The darkness in my core seethes at the sight of him. A crown of fire as tall as my arm sits on his head, reaching toward the ceiling. Unscarred knuckles grip the arm of the throne. The King's long red hair cascades down his back, leaking over the side of the throne. His strong fingers release and grip the armrest in a battle rhythm.

The sound of my feet sliding along the floor and clinking chains is drowned out by the raging fire.

General Fornous and the Priest stand on the right side of the seated King, with Prince Auberon on the other. Queen Mellonia stands at the foot of the stairs, lips tight as she stares at the man sitting on the throne. She's wearing another garment inspired by a skeleton; a golden spine sticks out from the back of the tight-fitting black dress. Her raging eyes snap from having to be in the presence of another mortal, looking down her nose at me when Belve forces me to a kneel. The Prince's eyes twitch, while the Priest raises a pleased brow.

I clasp my trembling hands together. Sweat cascades down my back from the heat emanating from the room, but somehow my skin feels cold with fear.

The King raises a dismissive hand and the steel grip around my arms disappears as the sentinel's footsteps move to the edge of the room.

I drag my eyes over the room, noting the towering columns, and scarce escape routes besides the stairs by the throne and the doors we came through. Notably absent is Evander. Part of me was hoping that he'd be here. Even when we are at odds, my soul feels lighter when he's around.

I look around, hoping to see Pa to make sure he's alive. I'm not sure whether to feel relieved or frightened that he's nowhere in sight. He could be sitting in a dungeon, or he could be dead.

The glint in General Fornous' eyes and the way he scrunches his scarred nose makes me certain that if he knew Ma was working under his roof, she would not survive to see the sun rise. With that thought, the strain in my heart returns. I try to tell myself that they have more reason to keep my parents alive than have them killed. But the more I say it, the more doubt bores into my heart.

King Cyrus relaxes and leans back in his chair, bringing his hand up to stroke his stubbled chin. The Priest notices the gesture and steps forward.

"You've caused a lot of trouble, *girl.*"

Pa's nickname for me. That one word causes the darkness in my core to roar as my rage flutters to life. It shouldn't bother me as much as it does.

With slow strides, the Priest descends from the dais. The flickering light from the flames cast dancing shadows over the tattoo on his naked head.

I lift my chin in an attempt to retain as much dignity as I can when the Priest circles me. His eyes study every line snaking over my limbs, and he peers closer to look at the different colored patches of skin. Then he touches me. His bony fingers feel like ice against my skin, burning my stomach with nausea.

I spin on my knees, yanking my body away from him.

"Don't fucking touch me!" I scream.

Searing pain burns my skin when his hand collides with my cheek. The slap echoes through the room and not even the crackling flames drown it. His nails grip my chin before I can react to the assault.

"You speak when spoken to," the Priest says through gritted teeth.

From up close, the aging of his papery skin is more apparent, making him look as old as time itself. His frozen fingers do nothing to calm the rage bubbling inside of me. I dig my nails into the palm of my hand to stop from spitting on him. He lets go of my chin, shoving me back in the process, giving me a pointed look, commanding me to stay put.

The Priest shrugs his shoulders, uncaring of my pathetic display.

"Tell me, Althea," he starts, and the way he says my name makes my skin crawl. "What's on your skin?"

"Birthmarks," I manage to say without my voice breaking.

I reach into my core, trying to grasp at the darkness, but the beast sits there watching and waiting until my life is at risk. She refuses to rise to my command.

The Priest yanks at the torn sleeve ripping it completely off my dress. I jump back as panic cripples my system. "You'll have to do better than that, or I'll have to find some more creative ways to present you as an appealing offer to the Anzeth." A smile slithers across his face like a giant serpent waiting to strike.

"Enough," a voice booms from the dais, and the darkness hisses.

King Cyrus rises from the throne and makes his way toward me. A crimson cape flows behind, rippling against phantom wind. As the cape moves, threads of gold shimmer under the flames' light. The Priest bows and shuffles back. The King stops a foot away from me, looking me up and down with curious eyes. At once, the darkness in my core dissolves, leaving me empty.

"Do you know who I am?" he says.

His question shocks me. I expected venom to drip from his words, or that his mere presence would make me tremble in fear. Yet he asks a simple question that he knows the answer to. Unless he thinks so little of mortals that he doesn't believe we would have the mind to know our own ruler.

I nod my head shakily.

"That is your King. Show your respect," the Priest snaps.

"Yes, Your Majesty. I know who you are," I say with raw disdain

A deep laugh rumbles through the room before the Priest can ignite his fire. The King smiles down at me like I'm a child. In a heartbeat the smile disappears, replaced by the stern expression of a general of war.

"What are you?" he questions without a trace of emotion.

"Human," I say without hesitation. It isn't a lie. Both my parents are human.

"What can you do?"

There it is, the question that truly King Cyrus concerns him: am I a threat?

"Heal," I state.

I can't bear to say more than a single word under the weight of his powerful gaze. I know if I say more than one word, my voice will come out breathless and I'll lose what little appearance of strength I have.

The King crosses his arm over his chest, nodding in encouragement for me to continue. No, not encouraging. He's threatening me to continue, because kindness from a Cintis is an illusion.

"I can heal others. Aches and pains, the common cold. That's all," I say.

"How do you explain what happened to your father? I was told that it was a fatal wound," King Cyrus presses.

"I've never healed anything like that before. That's the first time I've ever done it," I pause briefly. If the King is asking this, then no one has figured out Pa's leg—yet. And if I admit that I am capable of healing mortal wounds, will he just send me into battle as a combat healer? I run through the risks in my head again, and swallow the lump in my throat, and breathe out, "Successfully."

The Priest and the King stand up straighter at the last word. Behind, Prince Auberon takes half a step forward, tensing like his body moved against his command.

"What do you mean, 'successfully'?" King Cyrus asks, uncrossing his arms over his chest, clasping them behind his back.

"That was the first time I've healed such a wound successfully, *Your Majesty*," I say. I know that won't be enough to please them, so

I continue, "A man at the forge accidentally sliced open his arm. I couldn't help him, and he died of infection a few days later."

Not a single word out of my mouth is a lie. I couldn't help him. Only because Pa held me back to stop me from trying.

Seemingly satisfied with my response, he begins to pace.

"What about what you did to my men?" He cocks his head.

"Shock. I've never done that before," I say quickly.

He eyes me suspiciously for a brief moment.

"Very well," he says, turning on his heels and ascending back up the dais.

A breath of relief leaves me. Had I just passed some twisted test? His cape flares as he spins dramatically to sit on the throne. The sentinels that brought me from my cell walk back towards me, stopping several footsteps behind.

King Cyrus turns to the general and nods. General Fornous then looks at the sentinels and gives them a barely noticeable nod.

Behind me, the sound of a blade being unsheathed rips through the sound of fire. I pivot towards the noise, raising my hands in defense. I look in time to see Belve plunge a sword into the stomach of the skinny sentinel from back in my cell.

I drop my shackled hands in a gasp, stepping backwards as Belve removes his sword and the sentinel drops to the ground.

The sentinel's eyes meet mine, and he reaches his hand towards me.

"Please," he whispers, "save me, Althea."

CHAPTER 8

"I came to see a king, not a row of corpses."
— *Augustus Caesar*

"Heal him," King Cyrus orders.

Blood seeps through the sentinel's armor, and white foam starts to drip out of the corners of his mouth. Bile burns my throat as my mind replays his words. He's a monster.

This shouldn't surprise you, the voice says in annoyance.

I turn to the King who would kill his own sentinel for an experiment. "He's Cintis. He will heal," I urge, looking between the dais and the sentinel as he launches into a fit of coughs, spluttering blood across the floor.

Showing off my gift *again* is not part of my plan.

"The blade was tipped with poison. He will not survive unless you intervene," the gravel voice of General Fornous grates my ears.

He couldn't care less that his man is dying in front of him.

A pool of blood starts to spread from the sentinel's stomach. Every fiber of my being screams to run to him to help him. To answer the yearning in my bones—to heal. The gift begs for just the slightest release; to place my hand upon his chest and let my gift seep into him, to feel as the skin fuses back together and expels the poison.

I turn back to the King, with his chin resting in the palm of his hands, watching to see what my next move is. He wants to know if I am a weapon, an asset, or a liability. I have seconds to think which one I want to be to the Empire.

If I'm a weapon, he'll send me to the trenches to play with his soldiers and tend to their wounds on the battlefield, just for those men to kill others. If I am an asset, my future is unknown. What's the point of a healer for the fae if they heal on their own?

Running my mind through a marathon, I try to think of something important to the King outside of his ego. Maybe if I could speed up the process of a fae's healing, I'll prove useful; not so quickly that I become a weapon, but quickly enough that an injury isn't an inconvenience.

The only thing certain is that as a liability I will find myself dead by sunrise. He's already risking fear amongst the populace that an abomination has been roaming the streets with powers unknown to history.

I give into the ache in my bones and run to the sentinel. A green hue coats his skin, and the foam still oozes through his lips. I can't help the uneasy feeling that I've seen his face before, but I can't remember where.

I'm not surprised that I've seen him. As one of the Royal sentinels, he would have attended his fair share of sacrifices. He was probably one of the fae who rounded up children and marched them to the slaughterhouse. Nausea coats my stomach at the thought. All sentinels are Cintis. This man dying before me deserves whatever death that he finds. I can only hope the afterlife is as cruel to him as his kind is to us.

As our eyes lock, there's a hope in his pleading eyes which dissipates, and I think I'm too late. Somehow, I don't think that's how I know him. There's a familiar kindness in his eyes that wouldn't have come from a Cintis. Then the only thing I can see on his face is the look of betrayal.

Betrayal that the Empire he'd give his life for took his for a sick test.

I place my hands on his frail sternum, letting my senses open and my gift seeps through my skin into him. In my mind's eye, I see the weak beating of his heart and a green toxin flowing through his veins. I always expected I would feel fire when I looked into a Cintis, but I only feel the familiar warmth of him like I do with Ma and Pa, and all the other mortals I've healed without them knowing.

He's a Cintis, not a mortal. Just focus, the voices grate.

Usually, I wouldn't try to see inside the persons' body: I'd let my gift run wild to find and heal on its own accord. This time I need to control it.

I close my eyes and find every stream of poison that has flowed through his system. The green has made its way down his legs and pumped its way through his heart chambers. I curve around the wound, not letting any of my gift find its way to it. I inhale deeply, grasping every sliver of poison in his system with a white thread brighter than the sun. As I exhale, the toxin disappears.

The show of colors that came out of Pa when I healed him doesn't appear on the sentinel.

I open my eyes and watch as the sickly green hue disappears from his skin while the hole in his stomach continues to bleed onto the floor.

I did it.

I bite my lip to hold back the smile that threatens to curve across my lips. The greater the problem, the more my gift wants to reach out to cure. Part of me had hoped I would fail and completely heal him. But this path will at least give my family and I a fighting chance.

Schooling my face into a practiced emotionless mask, I stand and turn around to face the King. "I can't save someone from such a mortal wound. I don't know how I saved Pa. The poison in his system is gone, but there is nothing I can do to heal the wound itself. His fae powers will heal him," I say, straightening my back.

King Cyrus raises his chin towards the sentinels, and I watch as they kneel down next to their fallen comrade to sniff his wounds.

"The poison is gone, Your Majesty," the smiling sentinel says once they stand, then both bow their heads in unison.

The King turns his attention back to me. "Are you sure you can't heal him?"

I hesitate, because I know I could heal his wound and the sentinel would be in his own bed before the moon peaks. I don't know much about a fae's healing speed, but I can't imagine it will be more than a week before he's back on duty.

"No, my gift won't be able to fully heal him like I did to Pa," I say with as much confidence I can muster.

"Very well," King Cyrus says consideringly, he looks at the two sentinels and nods, "Finish him."

My heart jumps in my throat as realization kicks in. I've sentenced this man to his death. Just like every other person before him where I had the opportunity to save a life, but instead I watch their soul rip away from their body.

Belve takes out his sword and plunges it into the sentinel's heart. His body jerks as the blade enters him, then the rise and fall of his chest stops. His eyelids flutter before they widen, staring at the ceiling lifelessly. A gasp leaves my lips and I stumble back, struggling to believe they just killed their own kind.

"I do hope you don't mind watching mortals die," the Priest says, lurking in the shadows of a towering column. He must read the confusion in my face, because he steps forward with a sigh. "Such a pity you couldn't save him really. I would have rather he died on the altar."

My cold hands wrap around my torn dress as I try to make sense of his words. They've never had a sentinel offered to the Anzeth. The trained Cintis are far too valuable to the Empire, they'd much rather have them killed in battle.

The Priest walks towards the corpse and grabs the sentinel's arm, pulling down the sleeve to reveal the man's bony wrist.

I take a step back and fall, lifting my hands to my mouth to stifle a sob. Around his wrist is the red line of Audor, and just above it is the letter 'M.' Then, he pulls off the gold helmet to reveal a scar running across his scalp.

He's mortal. And I know him.

Elex.

He's one of Wayland's sons. He helped out his father at the Hole a few times when I was much younger, but I haven't seen him in years.

Rolling onto my hands and knees, I let out what little contents there is in my stomach. I may not have plunged the blade into him, but I did nothing to save him when I had the chance. Still, he would have been sacrificed at the altar. But then it wouldn't have been directly by my own hand. I'm just as bad as them. I killed the son of Pa's friend. I claw at my chest, gasping for air as the world spins.

People keep dying because I don't do anything to save them.

Strong fingers lace through my hair and yank me back.

Get over it. Pull yourself together, the little voice in my head whispers. It pulls me back to reality and my greater plan. I need to run and get my family out of Ignis alive. I urge myself to calm down and steady my breathing, biting the inside of my mouth to keep the bile down.

"It would appear the Anzeth only bestowed the gift of actual healing when it is her father that is on death's door," the Priest laughs, looking up at the King. My stomach lurches again as the guilt suffocates me.

"Then she's of no use to me. General Fornous, get rid of this *thing*," he says calmly.

Panic sinks its teeth into me. My eyes go wide at the same time as the Prince's, and he turns to his father with fury rumbling through his eyes that makes me flinch. I turn to scramble away from the approaching general, but Belve's hands wrap around my waist before I can get more than two steps away.

The rattling of chains follows the General's footsteps, a growing smile as he nears.

"I'm going to enjoy this," he whispers before moving his hand to a short sword at his back.

Without hesitation, I bring my arms up the way Evander taught me, and the beast within my core awakens from its slumber, blurring him into a thousand miniscule dots in my vision as the darkness starts to consume my lungs.

"Stop!" Prince Auberon's voice cracks through the room.

The general freezes in his movements, his chin jutting forward in obvious annoyance for the interruption. The darkness snaps back down, swirling in its well uneasily as I blink away the effects of the raw power until my vision clears.

"Unhand her right now," the Prince orders.

The concrete grip around my waist releases slightly.

He turns to his father, and insists, "She can be a Royal Healer."

"We have enough of those, young *prince,*" the Priest says condescendingly.

Auberon's eyes narrow on the Priest, who is unfazed by the glare and shrugs it off. I just want the Priest to stop speaking so I can hear what the Prince has to say.

As if reading my previous thoughts, the Prince says, "War is coming. She will help the Cintis heal faster. We may not need her now, but we will in the future. She could heal those with the plague."

"The plague?" King Cyrus laughs, "It's mainly a mortal problem; why should we care? Let the mortals in the outskirts die. We don't want the other Empires knowing we have someone like her here. We don't want them getting any more ideas. Quintos would know better than to suggest waving an anomaly like *that* in front of those vultures."

The blood drains from the Prince's face at the mention of the name; even the Queen who hasn't spoken a word shifts her weight. I rack my brain at the mention of Quintos, but I can't place it anywhere. It doesn't sound familiar. Maybe he is another General.

I look at the Queen as she resumes being utterly disinterested in the chain of conversation, her face is plastered with powder and kohl. There isn't a single strand of hair out of place in her intricate updo. I study her pulled-back shoulders, and the way her taloned fingers are delicately folded on top of her abdomen. She holds herself like the royalty that she is.

Which gives me an idea.

"I can be useful," I say, "I can be a lady's maid of her highness."

Queen Mellonia perks up at the mention.

"What use would I have of a street rat?" she says with poise, looking down her nose as she always does. She thinks the insult will hurt, but I've heard far worse.

"General Fornous?" I ask, lifting my shackled hands up as if to touch him.

"Get your filthy hands away from me." He moves to strike, but the King stops him.

"Let her," the King says, nodding to me, "Proceed."

I return the gesture and move toward him, cupping his face in my hands, I close my eyes and open my gifts to him. I can see the raging fire of Audor within him. The heat moves towards my gift, and I flinch, expecting to feel its burn, except it feels nothing more than a warm summer's day. The color of his blood is red like mortals, but his is laced with specks of gold and oranges, occasionally a wave of yellow flames crashes against his veins.

I reach out with my gift, feeling for the scarred sliver of skin on his nose, controlling it carefully so as not to let it veer and heal other parts of him. Once I locate the scar, I let the gift do its work, and I open my eyes to watch the scar on his nose fade into smooth skin.

I step back, as the General reaches for the scar, rubbing his finger over the now smooth ridge. As his hands drops, his eyes go wide, angrier than the fire I saw in him.

"Show me," Queen Mellonia urges.

Her eyebrows shoot up and she smiles like a child who just received a new toy. The general turns toward her and she runs her talons down his face.

"Incredible," she gasps.

All eyes are on the General, watching him with newfound wonder. His shoulders are tense and rigid, and I can taste the rage radiating from him. He held that scar like it was his armor, and I just took it away from him.

"Keep her. She might prove to be useful after all. If not, kill her." With that she waves her hand and ascends the curving stairs.

Belve yanks my shoulder back to return me to my cell, but we both halt when the King raises his hand.

King Cyrus tsks, and I can see the wheels in his head turning and concocting a plan as an alarming smile plasters across his face, causing my breathing to accelerate. "Did you think it would be that simple? Do you think I'd let you and your father continue living just because you can heal a scar?"

My thumb finds the skin on my palm, scratching the hard skin as he speaks. I have to bite the inside of my cheek to stop from showing him how his words chill my bones. I can't let him kill Pa. I'll give myself over to the beast before I let that happen.

"I'll give you time to manifest your true powers again, or your parents will die." He waves his hand in the air as if it were a simple request.

My head tilts slightly at his statement, just as dots start to edge around my vision, like each and every dot has a life of its own. I blink quickly, shaking my head in an attempt to clear my vision and focus on his request. "I told you, what happened the other day has never happened before. My healing abilities aren't that strong," I say quickly.

"I'm not talking about your healing powers."

I suck in a sharp breath, and I can't stop my feet from staggering backward. The telekinesis. I shake my head vigorously, opening and closing my mouth to think of an answer that won't instantly get us killed.

"Show me you aren't useless, or your family will pay the price."

CHAPTER 9

"My name is Nobody."
— *Homer, The Odyssey*

The walk back to the cell is eerily quiet.

Even Belve has lost his flair for violence.

I don't look up to watch them leave. I only listen to the lock snapping into place, sealing my impending doom.

My skin beneath the shackles is a bright red. Sprinkles of crimson rise to the surface of the skin, as the battle rages between my healing power and the cold metal digging into my skin fight to see who's stronger.

Like a prick in the corner of my mind, a drive spreads through me. If I can figure out how to use the darkness, then maybe I'll be able to do more than just show him it. I'll use it on him.

I try to tap into the storm of darkness I felt earlier, but it's nowhere to be found. Maybe it's simply a well of power that dried up from my foolish attempts at unleashing myself upon the chains. Had I known there was a limit on my supply of that dark power, I would have conserved it and used it on the King. Especially if it inconveniences him.

However badly I want to unleash the darkness on him, it's a foolish idea. Above having an unknown magical ability to heal, I showed a power of telekinesis at the Hole by flicking the men to the side. That sort of power is only present in the strongest of fae.

I can't help the sinking feeling that they might have done something to Pa. I replay every word that was said, and every single thing I know about how the Priest and the Royals operate. While not certain, it's reasonably clear they don't want me dead just yet. Which begs the question, what would they do if they knew I could heal mortal wounds every time without fail?

I don't know the extent of my own power, and they know even less, being ready to kill me after ascertaining that I cannot heal a mortal wound. If they did, they would have already made their move.

Looking at the Empire's track record, I can only assume that they will keep my parents alive with a knife to their throat to keep me in line, acting as puppeteer. The King will make sure that they stay alive as long as I am, because I will be an unpredictable variable that they can't control without them. Best to have both in case they need to dispose of one if I need punishment.

What good is a puppet without its strings?

Staring at the silver light cascading along the infra stone wall and fighting against shadows deep within the dips of the stone, I slip in and out of sleep. The only sound I've heard since they left has been the rumbling of my stomach. It's not strange for me to go days without food. Days without water, however, is a famine I'm unfamiliar with. Made worse by every drop expended during my hours of sobbing.

Recovering from my delirious shock, I take inventory of my waking nightmare. The cell is as big as Ma and Pa's room back at home. The chain connected to my shackles is spiked directly in the center of the room. Other than a tin bucket and unbreakable chain, there's nothing else in this cell.

A trail of bloody footsteps leads from the door to where Belve deposited me. I must have cut my foot worse than I initially thought, and my gift would have been on overdrive trying to heal everything else.

The chain stops me from making it past the bucket when I try to walk around and bang on the door, or to run my hands along the walls to find loose infra to protect myself with. I try to pull at the chain or break the shackles, yet nothing budges.

Feeling the back of my head, the wound from before is completely healed. The only thing there is clumps of dried blood sticking my hair together. My foot has also healed without a scar in sight, like I didn't lose half my blood on the walk back to my cell. At least the Infra doesn't stop my ability to heal.

The only reason I can think of as to why my head wasn't healed when I first awoke is that I must have had some kind of healing drainage from saving Pa, because the Infra hasn't stopped it from healing since.

The King knows more than he's letting on, but I doubt it's something he will be willing to share with me. Whatever it is, I don't doubt his threat to my Pa's life if I fail to pass this test.

I focus on a pebble in the middle of the cell, with white weblike marks covering the stone. I flex my fingers, feeling my gift thrum through my veins as it completely ignores the darkness. But really, the feeling of hopelessness is what overpowers every other ache or pain within me. I don't know how to start.

How do they fae use their powers? Do they just *think* of what they want to do, and it just happens? Do they command an element with their words? The latter seems like an easier, more doable option.

Taking a deep breath, I narrow my eyes at the pebble. "Move," I order. The faceless stone stares back at me—teasing me.

Show me you aren't useless, or your family will pay the price, King Cyrus' voice echoes through my mind.

"Move," I order again. Still, the stone stays lifeless in the center of the room. The darkness sleeps soundly in the well of my core, unbothered by the turmoil happening. How am I meant to harness the darkness if it isn't even awake?

"Move. Move. Move. Move," I say, over and over again, until a cold sweat runs down my shoulders, coupling with my hot tears of frustration.

Nothing happens.

"Come on," I mutter.

There has to be another way that the fae harnesses their power. This clearly isn't working.

"Move you stupid fucking thing!" I cry, throwing a loose stone at it, watching as it skitters away. "Fuck. Fuck. Fuck," I groan as I hit the back of my palm to my forehead, trying to think of how exactly I can 'manifest my true power'.

What happened in the Hole was fueled by my raw emotions: fear, shock, and rage. I feel all of those things right now, but nowhere near the intensity that I felt that day. We're all doomed if it takes Pa's repeatedly attempted murder just to use my powers.

Hugging my knees, I wrack my head to figure out how to control the darkness and get us all out of here. Golden light starts to cascade into the cell from between the rocks, but I'm still no closer to figuring out how to use whatever power I have. And still, despite my orders and cries of frustration that continue throughout the night, the webbed stone doesn't move.

Even once the sun makes its descent, and my stomach groans from hunger, I can't bring myself to lie on the floor. I can't bring myself to sleep. Every time I close my eyes, I can see the milky hue glazed over Elex's eyes.

That's why he looked familiar when he first came into the cell. That's why he was terrified when he saw Belve tearing at my dress: because he's mortal.

I should have known he wasn't Cintis when I saw that he was a sentinel in unfitted armor without a weapon at his side. I sink to my knees and cave into the ache in my chest, rolling onto my side as my sobs echo through the cell. My tears flow as the night turns into day. I don't stop crying when my throat is raw. I sob even though there are no more tears left to cry.

The cold ground is vicious against my back but leaning against the stone wall that threatens to pierce my skin is worse. I've lain here for what feels like hours, and there has been no sign of Belve.

∾

It's been three days.

Three days where Pa could be going through unimaginable torture or suffering or thirst. Where Ma must have been out of her mind wondering what happened to us. For my own sanity I don't want to entertain the thought that they might have Ma. I need to find a way to get in touch with Ma to let her know that we're alive. I also don't want to entertain the thought that Pa could be dead.

There has to be someone working in the Palace with connections to the general's manor. Ideally, a maid. They're less likely to have some deranged loyalty to that monster. I need someone who can get in touch with her to tell her to forget about us and hide. To leave the city and move to a city far from Ignis. Or even tell her to move in with the baker's boy on the promise that I'll take his hand in marriage once I'm out of here.

As soon as I think about it, I know having a simple life with a kind man will never happen. Now that the King has his hands wrapped around me, the only way I am getting out of here is dead, or at least barely breathing.

If I get myself killed, who's going to take care of Pa? Who's going to rub his back at night and make sure he can breathe without suffocating in his sleep? Who's going to help Ma's elbow when she comes back from work—that is, if she even has work after this whole nightmare.

I can only pray that Evander takes care of my mother like he said he would all those years ago.

I shake my head. Thinking about what I should have done differently won't change the fact that it happened. It's time to face the consequences of my actions.

Staring at the silver light lacing through the walls, I ask myself two questions: Do I regret what I did during the incident? Would I have done anything different? Each time I ask myself those two questions the answer is always the same: No.

I would have brought down the entire forge and every person in it if it meant Pa lived.

I do, however, have one regret: that I didn't kill the Priest when I had the chance.

CHAPTER 10

"The gates of Hell are open night and day; smooth the descent and easy is the way."

— *Publius Vergilius Maro, The Aeneid*

Five days and five nights pass by.

For five nights I've seen silver light decorate the Infra. For four days golden light reflects off the stone into my eyes.

The only face I've seen is Belve's.

On the first day he brought me a blanket. If you can call it that. There are more holes in the rectangular piece of cloth than actual fabric. Patches of yellow stains decorate the blanket, and there's the distinct smell of piss emitting from it.

He does come to feed me every day. Albeit he comes to give me a mouthful of bread and half a bucket of questionable water twice a day.

I can only assume that I have Evander to thank for keeping me fed and not just alive. I doubt the royals would put any effort into making me feel comfortable.

Everyday Belve's footsteps echo through the hallway as the light streaming between the rocks begin to change from yellow to red or purple. Everyday a scowl plants firmly on his face like a tattoo. His hatred towards me burns so deep, I can practically smell the char coming from him.

And every day I'm no closer to moving the pebble. I tried *feeling* the pebble's presence. I tried feeling the presence *around* the pebble, and still nothing.

At some point in the midst of my misery, I wake to keys rattling at the door.

I jerk up, looking at the golden light seeping through the stone. It must be around mid-morning. Before the door swings open, I pull myself onto my feet and right my dress as best I can. The chains rattle at the motion.

Belve walks in without his usual sneer. Faint bruising lines his jaw and circles his eye. I spot a little bit of dried blood in his nostril, and my gift aches to reach out to him at the sight.

"I was hoping they would have killed you by now," he grumbles.

"Day's not done yet," I say, wincing at the gravel in my voice.

He motions for me to lift my hands up and the key goes in. We watch as the chain drops to the floor, and he makes his way back out of the cell.

"What's happening?" I stand frozen in place, unsure where my fate leads.

"I'm taking you to your bedchamber. Now hurry up. I have better shit to do than babysit you," he mutters, trailing out the door, expecting me to follow him like a dog.

With a huff, my feet move along the floor. I want to ask if Pa has been moved to a room, but I'm sure I already know the answer. Plus, I doubt he would even bother to give me a response.

Although exhausted, I somehow feel more prepared than I did when I walked through these hallways five days ago. I study each turn and corridor, building a map in my mind. So far, I know how to get to my cell, the throne room, and nowhere else.

Each time we walk down a new gleaming hallway, my plan to find Pa somewhere down here shatters even more. All the corridors and cell doors look the same. I'd never be able to find him here.

Coming to a stop in front of a black door at the end of a hallway, he flicks his hand motioning me to enter. It feels odd wrapping my hand around an actual door handle. My core tightens at the memory of our broken-down apartment. Everything wore down over time, but we made it work. We made it all our place to call home.

The door shuts behind me as I enter, slamming with a click. I turn the door handle, hoping it will open, but it doesn't budge. I shake the handle and bang on the door yelling for it to be opened.

I know it's useless. I expected nothing less. I wouldn't let my prisoner roam the halls either.

Turning back around, my lips part as I take in the bedchamber. It isn't as big as Evander's room in the Manor, and its color scheme is so at odds with his bedchamber and the rest of the Palace.

Elaborate geometric patterns sprinkle through the room, from the blankets to the two settees, and the plush bed sitting in between two gilded pillars. A writing desk sits to the side of the room, opposite a white door.

I've just moved from one prison to another. Only this time, it's a pretty one.

Walking to the white door, I pull it open, letting my knees sink to the floor from the welcoming sight of a bathtub carved from a giant quartz. The stench emanating from me after days lying in filth and coated in blood, the thought of a bath almost brings me to tears.

A small knock comes from the entrance door, and I fly to the bedside table to pick up an oil lantern, readying to break it into pieces and use one of the glass shards as a weapon.

The door squeaks open, and a girl younger than me steps into the room. She peers up at me through dirty blonde hair, half up in a frizzy mess. I look down to her hands and notice that she's carrying a gold dress and a basket. The sleeve of her dress stops at her elbow, and I can see the 'M' labeled into her wrist. Eyes shoot up in terror as she looks at me and the lantern. I quickly put it back on the table and step away.

"Who are you?" I say softly.

She flinches at the sound of my voice and dips her head to the floor, refusing to make eye contact.

"I will be your servant, madam," she stutters as she drops into a flimsy curtsy.

The basket rattles under her shaking hands, and she swallows between her labored breaths.

"I'm not going to hurt you," I assure her, lifting my palms up towards her, instantly realizing that it's a terrible idea with all the blood coating it. I drop my hands and tuck them into the folds of my skirt, asking, "What is your name?"

She holds her breath and hesitates for a moment before she squeaks, "My name is Maiya, madam."

I flinch at the title. "Please, just call me Althea," I say through a warm smile. I can't imagine she has ever served another mortal in this Palace.

"Yes, ma—Althea," she says quietly, still staring at the floor, "I've come to prepare your bath and ready you for the queen."

My smile falters, "What does the Queen want?"

"I'm not sure. I was only asked to make you presentable for her majesty. Please wait there as I prepare your bath," she says with a little more volume, depositing the dress on the bed before rushing into the bathroom.

Queen Mellonia wants me as her lady's maid after all. I didn't expect to be summoned so soon, let alone to have a room within the Palace walls and to be dressed up.

It does make sense if they plan to keep my gifts hidden from watchful eyes, but they clearly aren't bothered by people seeing my skin. If I'm locked in a Palace, then there would be no way for me to mingle with anyone else.

Maiya slips out of the bathing chamber with her empty basket. "The bath is ready for you, madam. Would you like assistance?"

"Just call me Althea, please. I can wash myself, but thank you for your help, Maiya," I say softly.

She smiles back at me, but it doesn't meet her eyes. Her gaze drops to the shackles, and she grabs a key out of her basket to unlock them. Rubbing my aching wrist, I can feel my gift reach out to heal them the instant they become free.

"My Ma and Pa, have you heard anything about them?" I ask hesitantly.

Maybe she was told to expect such a question and she will report it back to the King. At this point, I no longer care. I haven't heard anything about them in days, and I haven't seen any more of the Palace to build on my map.

"Do they work in the Palace?" she asks so innocently that my chest deflates.

She has no idea what my part to play in all this is.

I shake my head, "Never mind then."

Walking into the bathing chamber, I close the door behind me. The surprisingly clean smell of pine-scented water breaks through the stench of the cell floor clinging to my dress. I make my way to the mirror and blanche at the sight. My dark brown hair looks black as it sits in a tangled heap on my head. Dried blood is splattered from my chest to my forehead, while a river of broken crimson travels down the side of my neck. My cheeks are even more sunken than usual, and a thick layer of blue and purple rests below my eyes from all the sleepless nights.

I shrug off my dress, leaving it by the door. I want nothing more than to burn it and all the memories the fabric holds in its stitching.

My stomach grumbles as I dip my toes into the warm water, lowering myself until only my face is exposed. I stay there for several heartbeats, breathing in the scent of pine, the feel of the water embracing my skin. The heat softens the aching muscles in my back from days of getting well accustomed to the floor. The water turns into a murky brown as the layers of grime soak off me.

By the time I'm done, the water has turned completely black, and I feel guilty leaving Maiya to clean up after my mess.

Letting the water drip in rivulets down my body, I let out a heavy sigh. I feel more refreshed than I have in my entire life. Grabbing the towel, I wrap it around my body over and over again, trying to find a way to hold it to cover as much skin as possible. I shove an arm into the flap of the towel and step out to see Maiya standing next to the chair holding another towel and a brush, motioning me to sit. My breathing hitches as another person sees almost every inch of my skin. Her expression is one of curiosity, as I see her eyes studying me.

Does she think I'm an abomination like everyone else? Is she scared that I might carry some kind of illness?

She pulls the brush through my hair, battling tangles and matted clumps stuck to it, apologizing every few seconds when I wince again. Clasping my hands together to stop them from shaking as her eyes study my marks, I have to fight the urge to dive under the covers of the bed and hide my skin away from her.

Seemingly satisfied with the state of my hair, she sets out putting it in a half-braid, as the rest cascades down my back to hide my skin. Turning she grabs the dress. Opening it and placing it on the floor, gesturing for me to step into the gap she made. I hesitate, not wanting to let go of the towel.

"Please, you must get dressed." There's an urgency to her whisper as she gestures toward the dress once more.

I nod, and with shaking hands, I watch the towel drop to the floor before looking at Maiya. I should be relieved that she's staring at the floor, but I still feel like I've failed Ma for letting another person see my skin.

As she adjusts the dress, the air is forced out of me as she laces me up.

She lifts her hand towards a mirror in the corner of the room, and my blood runs cold. They've ripped me away from my home, and I have no idea if my parents are alive or dead. This dress is just another form of shackles—another reminder that I belong to the Empire.

A mortal would have had to sit for hours stitching each individual bead in this dress just to make coin that's barely enough to feed themselves. I'm sure the material alone would be enough to feed my entire family for a week. And now they've dressed me in a gown that mocks every person in the Remains.

A sheer material covers my collarbones and neck, leaving me exposed for every person to look at as I walk out of the room. I turn to Maiya, hoping she will pull out a scarf to cover the marks, but she continues cleaning the room.

A loud knock on the door causes Maiya to yelp and flinch away from me.

"Hurry up, we need to go. Now," Belve's voice booms.

Maiya scurries around the bedchamber in a flurry, picking up discarded hairpins and cloth, packing it away into her basket before rushing to the door without turning around to say goodbye.

Belve enters as soon as Maiya leaves. He stops in his tracks when he sees me. His lingering gaze makes me feel like I'm in an imposter's body. He drags his gaze from my feet, all the way up my body, stopping at my face. As if in a trance, he shakes his head and the scowl I know all too well returns.

Pivoting, he storms out of the chamber, spitting to the side and grunting as an indication for me to follow.

CHAPTER 11

"If any man cannot feel the power of God when he looks upon the stars, then I doubt whether he is capable of any feeling at all."

— *Horace*

My heels click along the marble as we quickly walk through the various hallways, climbing up stairs and moving in and out of servant accessways. Belve grabs my arm and drags me along with him when he decides I'm not walking fast enough. I look at his waist and notice he has no weapons at his side. Now that my hands are free, there's an all-consuming desire to let Evander's training kick in and drop him to the floor before he has a chance to register. It's an itch that begs to be scratched.

It is an itch that will remain unscratched until I figure out where he's taking me and if there are sentinels ready to punish me for such insolence. Maybe cooperation will get me answers about my parents.

Belve swings open oak doors and shoves me inside, slamming it in my face. My eyes go wide, staring at the dark door and my fingers uncurl as they begin to tremble.

Slowly, I turn around, bracing myself for the unknown.

A loud grumble escapes my stomach as it catches sight of a long table filled with more food than I've seen in my life in the center of the sitting room. It's enough to feed an entire street in the Remains.

Anger replaces hunger as I take in the untouched food. This much food isn't available at the markets in the Square, yet the very people meant to ensure our survival lounge around with more food than they can stomach just for decoration.

Then, my stomach drops when I see Queen Mellonia draped across a red velvet chaise, a golden chalice in her hand. I knew I was going to see her, it was my idea, but I don't feel ready to deal with whatever she throws at me.

This time, there's no skeletal design to be seen on her, only a ruby embossed corset and black satin slip. The same horseshoe arch as in my room is carved directly behind her. The sitting room has the same color palette as the hallways: gold, black, and red.

A servant stands to the side, fanning the Queen with a giant feather as another rubs oils into her feet. A third servant, no older than fourteen, stands to the side, holding a pitcher of wine in one hand and a plate of grapes in the other.

I jump back as an orange ball of fur rubs against my leg. A cat. The Queen of Fire has a cat.

Queen Mellonia takes me in from head to toe the same way Belve did, and she waves her hand to dismiss the servants. They all disappear through a small door hidden at the edge of the room. I want to join them.

I stand rigid, playing with my shaking fingers behind my back.

"You don't look so disgusting anymore. Come closer," she sneers.

She takes a sip of her wine and raises a brow when I don't move from my spot. Fire erupts from her chalice, and she looks at me in warning. I force my feet to move towards my possible death, stopping a few feet away from her.

She rises elegantly, and studies every pore on my face, regarding the hair swooped over my shoulders, and the slight curve in my waist from my dress.

"I suppose you aren't that ugly for a mortal," she huffs and stalks away from me, swaying her hips from side to side as she disappears into a bathing chamber. "Your skin, however, is revolting," her voice is tainted with disgust.

I blink back hot angry tears. *Everyone is going to be talking about your skin. Get used to it,* the voice in my head hisses, irritated. I've spent my entire life hiding my skin, it was mine to keep to myself. Now my skin is no longer my own, it's for the King to parade through the Palace.

You can't let him break you, my own voice growls at the thought, and I nod my head slightly in agreement.

I move to follow but hesitate when I see a butterknife. What would happen if I used it on her? I'm certain Belve is standing outside of the main door, so I'll have to fight him on the way out. I have no idea what's on the other side of the servant's door or if there are more people on the other side.

If I escape, they'll have no reason to keep Pa alive, and his blood would be on my hands. I'll be running through the halls for hours trying to find the dungeons. I need to get more information before I can use the knife on someone.

You don't need to use that on the Queen yet, the little voice chimes, *Take it just in case.*

I don't have much time to consider the ramifications of getting caught with it before the Queen comes back out. Breathing uneasily, I yank the knife from the table and hide it in my sleeve and follow the Queen into the bathing chamber.

Just in case, I tell myself.

A butter knife won't do much damage, but if I can find something to sharpen it then that will help keep me safe. Or at least more able to cause some level of harm.

Queen Mellonia stands in front of a crystal quartz bathtub, double the size of the one in my chambers. This one is carved like a blooming rose, rising into the air and curving over the side. I stare at it for a moment longer, taking in the combination of rough stone, smoothing out at the tips in a pearlescent shine. An idea springs to mind of a rose dagger inspired by the tub.

Balls of fire float in the air like tears dropping into the tub, while black and gold geometric tiles line the floor and climb up the walls.

She clicks her fingers. "Don't just stand there. Hurry up and undress me," she barks.

The sharp whistle of her voice snaps me back to reality and I hesitate for a heartbeat before rushing up to her to begin unlacing the intricate corset. She catches me staring at the tub as my fingers unlace her with unpracticed hands.

"I've always hated that thing," she huffs, "It reminds me of that bitch, Roseus."

She's referring to the Queen before her, who was killed for aging. Apparently, Roseus was once the King's favorite wife. I shouldn't be surprised there's tension between the queens. It's written in their fate to die once the King gets bored of them or finds someone younger.

I wonder if that's why she decided to accept me as her lady's maid, that she believes I can use my power to keep her youthful. I very much doubt that my power can do that even for her to keep me alive.

I stand back once the final lace comes undone, shoving my hands behind my back to readjust the knife so that it doesn't fall. Under the queen's breath, she mutters something about needing to do everything by herself as she steps out of her dress, standing only in her undergarments. Her build is similar to mine, tall and slim. Except there's actually meat on her: one of the perks of hoarding food from her people.

"Let's see how useful you actually are," she quips, sipping her wine again. "I want you to heal me."

My eyebrows knit together at her demand, looking over her skin for any sign of injury or wound. Maybe she's sick? My gift would reach toward her if I could sense something that actually needs healing.

I say nothing, silently urging her to elaborate.

Sighing, she gracefully lowers herself onto a settee tucked against the bathroom wall, chugging the rest of her wine and throwing the empty chalice onto the floor.

"You stupid mortal. I want you to get rid of my stretch marks."

I bite my tongue to hold back a laugh. The King of the Empire of Fire wants the only known being capable of healing others to remove her own natural signs of growth? If Ma heard this, she would be slapping the counter and shaking the whole house with her laughter. This isn't something I thought I'd ever be asked to heal.

As a teenager, she told me that stretch marks are the gods' way of marking their favorites with lighting imprints, and the more a person has, the stronger they are. I didn't believe it, but it did make me feel better. So, I trained my gift to never heal them.

I look at the loose skin at the bottom of her stomach, streaked with laces of white that climb beneath her undergarments. There's more there than I'd expect from a woman with only one child. The Prince must have been a large infant.

"Why—" A whip of fire burns the side of my cheek before I can finish, and I jump back to the wall with a startled scream. A switch inside me flicks, and I feel my anger come alive.

"Don't pretend to know anything, rat. Do as you're told, and *don't* ask questions," she hisses.

A warm sensation trickles down my cheek from where she struck me, and I can already feel my skin fuse back together. A glimmer of amazement flashes through her eyes as she watches. Her lips part as she lifts her hand to my skin to assess the now fully healed wound.

Huffing, she returns to the settee. "Do it. *Now*," she snaps.

My feet jump at her tone, as I drop to my knees before her and place a hand on her stomach.

"I need to keep up with his whores," she whispers.

I bite my tongue, trying to resist the temptation to roll my eyes. I've read books of jealous queens whose kings are always too busy playing with their concubines. But Queen Mellonia is nothing like the soft-hearted women in those fairy tales. She deserves whatever is coming to her.

CHAPTER 12

"Carpe diem, quam minimum credula postero.
Pluck the day for it is ripe, trusting as little as possible in tomorrow."
— Horace, The Odes of Horace

I feel like I'm back in my cell.

The only face I've seen is Belve's and his look of annoyance as he brings me my meals.

I healed them like she asked. I hid the knife in the crook of the pillar behind my bed. Since returning from the Queen's summons, I've paced the bedchamber and check if the door is unlocked after every ten laps. Every time I check, I drop to the floor to see a pair of feet standing on the other side of the door.

Every so often, I check to make sure the knife is still there, and I have to fight the urge to take it out and practice, but I don't. Belve will hear any training that I do.

An idea springs to mind as my pacing brings me to the bathing chambers. The walls are granite, so if I'm careful, I might be able to sharpen the butterknife. Sprinting to the pillar behind the bed, I grab the knife and pause, placing it on the ground.

Taking a deep breath, closing my eyes and holding my hand out to the knife, I try *feeling* the cold metal weapon on the tile floor, picturing it in my head.

"Come," I order, opening an eye to take a peek to see if it has moved. "Fuck it," I grunt, snatching the knife and going to the bathing chamber to assess the walls for the best spot.

It has to be somewhere Maiya won't notice when she cleans. I drop onto my stomach and drag the flat edge of the knife across the granite wall and wince when a high-pitched shriek comes from the motion. I pause, holding my breath, waiting to hear if a sentinel will come barging in.

I stay there for several heartbeats as I break out into a cold sweat before taking a deep breath and resuming in long, smooth strokes. I lie there, sharpening the knife, until my sweat drips onto the floor and metal and granite dust sprinkles all over the tile.

I don't stop until the sun is laid to rest and my neck aches from the way I'm sitting.

Angling the knife to the light to check its sharpness, I touch the edge. It isn't great, but it's enough to penetrate a Cintis.

Scooping the dust with tissue so I don't cut myself, I empty it into the drain, carefully trying to hide any evidence of my disobedience. Jumping to my feet, I go back to pacing and rattling the handle until the light starts to dim.

Various means of escaping flood through my mind, each as unlikely as the one before it, each one blazing into existence like an inferno, devouring the dying spark of the idea that came before it. My thoughts are working so fast I can't distinguish one from the next.

I'll have to figure out a way to get past the sentinel guarding the door of my bedchamber. Before that, I'll need to break the lock on the door. Maybe if I try to slam something heavy over it, the handle will fall off? But that would notify the sentinel that I'm trying to escape. Not to mention that it would be utterly useless.

If I manage to get the door unlocked, then I'll have to knock out a Cintis. They won't be fighting to kill, which is a point in my books. The King still wants to see if I can 'manifest my powers.' But I can barely disarm Evander when he isn't on guard: how do I expect to knock out a Cintis that has already been made aware of my attempted escape?

If only you figured out how to use the darkness, the voice leers.

Breaking the window isn't an option either. It's at least a fifty-foot drop, and while the broken bones will heal, the impact itself will kill me. Like the King said, my death means the death of Ma and Pa. I have no choice but to go through the door.

But what happens when I make it out? I have no idea where my parents are, or if they are even alive.

I try rattling the handle again, and like every other time, it doesn't open. I stand there and trace the pattern of the wood underneath the white paint.

An insatiable feeling of complete helplessness slowly gnaws at my core. I close my eyes, remembering the feeling of Elex's frail ribs beneath my blood-soaked hands. The smell of the boy's blood from the sacrifice. The dagger slicing through Pa's throat and the explosion of red after.

There's too much blood.

The world starts to spin. My hand presses harder against the door, and I let it all out.

My fists and feet meet the hard wood, and I pound. Kicking it like my life depends on it. I let a scream erupt from my throat as I release all the pent-up emotions onto the door. Hitting it over and over again.

Hitting it for what the General did to Pa.

Hitting it for starving the mortals in the Remains.

Hitting it because I've failed Ma.

"Shut up!" the rough voice of a stranger yells. I ignore it, basking in the pain of my fist colliding with the door, feeling the warmth run to my hands as crimson blooms on my knuckles and leaves red smears over the door.

I stumble backwards as the door swings open, and a brown-eyed sentinel wraps his fingers around my throat and pushes me against the wall.

"I said shut the *fuck* up!" he screams, pushing me further back.

As he speaks, his hot breath warms his spit splattered on my face. I struggle against him, trying to move my hands between us to push him away. I reach for the darkness, but the beast cracks an eye and resumes its slumber. My attempts to get him off me only makes him shove me harder into the wall until my ribs threaten to break from the force.

"I have no idea why they have me playing nanny for the King's new whore." His eyes follow the dagger that he trails along my cheek to my neck, slicing the skin on my collarbone. "What I do know is that if you keep this up, I'll take it upon myself to find out exactly why the King wants a *mortal* to whet him. Maybe I'll even break you in."

Does he really think that I'm the King's new whore? Is that the real reason why he allowed the Queen to keep me as her lady's maid rather than just killing me?

A violent shiver goes up my spine as he watches me with excitement. His breath burns my skin as the pounding in my ears becomes deafening. He wants me to misbehave again. He wants to justify his perversions. He keeps his hands around my throat but eases off me as he studies me with hunger. Fuck him. I don't want to let him think I'm afraid. Too many people have seen me weak.

My temper gets the better of me. I inhale sharply before my spit lands just below his eye. He wipes it off with a flick, cocking his head to the side with a depraved grin. I clench my jaw, waiting to see how he will react.

He pushes against the full force of his body and dips his head to my ear. "I do hope you keep this up, mortal."

He releases me and locks the door behind him.

Nothing happens for two days. Belve stopped bringing me food. I should have saved some of the food he brought.

To my shock, there's no dent in the floor from all my pacing, the door handle hasn't fallen off from my rattling, and my mind isn't fried from my useless attempts at using the darkness. Sometimes the beast wakes just to watch my futile attempts, only to curl up and slumber again.

The solitude, boredom and complete helplessness is far worse a punishment than I could have imagined.

I no longer care if a sentinel hears me training. Ripping a strip of cloth from the bed sheets, I use it to tie one of the many pillows to a pillar. Curling my fingers into tight fists, I jab at it, punching it square in the middle, and pivoting as my kick collides with the cushion. It isn't much, but it's something.

Yelling at the beast to move an object has proven completely useless, because the darkness doesn't budge.

Every morning, I fold the blankets and put them at the foot of the bed like I did with the couch at home because it gives me some semblance of familiarity. The most exciting thing I do is change dresses.

Occasionally I stop my training to stare out of the window. It overlooks a garden that never seems to have anyone walking through it except the occasional lone gardener or a sentinel watching over the grounds. Eventually King Cyrus sets the sun over the horizon, and darkness haunts the gardens again.

It's a never-ending cycle of hair-pulling boredom.

When they agreed to let me be the Queen's servant, I thought she would summon me a lot more often.

Thanks to the gap between the floor and the door, I've managed to figure out the sentinel's guard duty schedule. Two hours before sundown, the brown-eyed sentinel from the other night stands watch until an hour after sunup. He stands heavily on his right leg and shuffles the left around. In the shadows, it looks like the left boot is a fraction smaller than the right. The sentinel standing guard during the day coughs periodically. It sounds chesty as if he were a smoker. I can tell he's here because my gift reaches out to try and help him.

Smokers tend to be slower. I'm more likely to outrun him, especially if his lungs won't be able to keep up. If I'm going to run away during the day, I might as well hand myself over now.

The day sentinel won't be back until tomorrow morning, but it'll be a stupid idea if I try to break out of here when he's just started his shift and is still refreshed. No, I'll run away just before morning breaks and the brown-eyed will be tired after a full shift. Hopefully there will be less sentinels on duty in the corridors. *Hopefully.*

Two birds with one stone; I'll get out of here, and I'll kill him.

First, I need to figure out how to open the door. The sentinel has shown his impatience toward me. All I need to do is start taunting him and when he barges in, I'll be ready.

The Palace will still be quiet during that time, so I can get around a lot easier. If I can't figure out how to use the darkness, Pa will die. My only option is to get us out of here. I'm not sure how I'll find him, but I have to keep trying.

Violent coughs drag my attention away from my attempts at using my powers. I can hear the day sentinel on the other side of the door, banging on their chest as they start to choke on their coughs.

My gift pulls me to my feet, running to the door. It scratches against my skin, begging to heal the sentinel.

"Are you okay?" I say, pushing my ear against the door, hearing his coughs settle into a cold wheeze.

"Fine," the sentinel sputters, and I can hear the metal clang as he hits his chest again.

"You don't sound fine."

Jogging to the pitcher of water, I try to locate the one glass I've been entrusted with. Running my eyes through the room until I see the glass on the windowsill, weakly reflecting the sunlight. The sentinel's coughs grow violent once more, which only makes me move faster. Pouring water into the glass, I rush to the door.

"Here, there's a glass of water. It will help with the coughs," I say loudly in case he doesn't hear me.

"I don't need it," he says. At least that's what I think he says.

"Your coughs are going to shake the Palace. A little bit of water will help." My gift hums noisily through me, pushing the sound of his coughs into the shadows.

"I'm—" he starts to say before another cough erupts through him.

"Water," I suggest calmly, but there's more urgency in my tone than I intended.

The sound of keys rattling makes me step back from the door. The sentinel barges through, his olive brown skin turned red with tears running down his cheeks with his dark hair all over his face. Holding the glass out to him, he snatches it from my hand, downing the liquid.

"Don't drink it too quickly, you'll choke." They're words Ma has said a thousand times to Pa.

I can see him watching me from above his glass, like he's waiting for me to turn around and say it was all a trick. Still, he listens, slowing down his pace until his breathing settles, and my gift calms in the process.

He drinks every last drop, wiping his glove across his mouth when he's finished.

"Better?"

He looks me up and down skeptically. "Thanks," he grunts before leaving the room and taking my glass with him.

"That's fine," I whisper, staring at the closed door.

Shaking my head, I grab a pillow and place it in the middle of the bed. Taking two steps away from it, I hold my hand out with my fingers spread wide like it might actually help me control the darkness.

"Come on Anzeth, help me out," I mutter under my breath as I try to move it. Gods, at this point I'll even settle for having the power to light it on fire.

I start to focus on the pillow so hard that my head hurts. Then a knock sounds from the door, not soft like Maiya's, but not so hard like Belve's. Is the sentinel bringing back my cup? The door squeaks open slowly and a mop of red hair pokes from behind.

"I hope I'm not interrupting something," a honeyed voice floats through the air paired with a warm smile dancing across the Prince's lips.

My gift jumps up at the sight of him, wanting to heal him, but I hold myself back. I take in his black suit with golden dragons embroidered into his lapel, but I don't see any sign of injury.

That sentinel said that the King is only keeping me alive to force me to be his whore: the Prince could have the same plan. My eyes dart to the knife hidden on the other side of the room. If I can get to it, then I'll be able to use it. It'll be useless against his powers, but at least I can say that I tried my best.

Straightening my back, I scowl. "I'm locked in here all day and all night. What do you really think I could be doing, Your Highness?"

I stare at him, waiting for him to be like everyone else in this Palace and strike me or yell at me for my tongue. Instead, he fiddles with the handle, red creeping up his neck as if he was guilty of something.

"I know, I'm really sorry about all of this. I managed to get you this room instead of another cell," he says hopefully, but I don't miss the hint of darkness in his voice.

"If you *know*, then why ask such a stupid question?"

Shut up you fool, he can have you killed for that, the voice says.

Snapping my mouth shut, I turn away from him. But the familiar gleam in his eyes and the way my power stirs in his presence gives me a sense of comfort that I can speak freely. Whether that comfort is misplaced, I'll find out.

I continue before he can say anything, "It's just a prettier prison. What I want isn't some pretty room in the Palace. What I want is to be home with my family." I try to soften my voice and coat myself in a layer of innocence. Men love innocence.

It's a little late for innocence, the voice retorts.

"I understand," he sighs, and my nostrils flare as I try to control my rage. "I'm especially sorry about whatever else is going to happen."

My stomach drops. What does he mean?

He finally takes me in, noting my dress and the embroidery climbing up my hands to wrap around my neck, and the cut-outs on my waist with beads radiating outward like the sun. I sway on my feet, resisting the urge not to wrap a blanket around me. Another person is seeing my skin—more than just my hands.

"Did Belve feed you?" he asks suddenly.

"What?" My breath staggers.

He's just pretending to care, the voice says.

"While you were in the dungeons, I ordered him to feed you every day and give you a blanket. Did he do as I asked?" he presses, and I feel like I've been hit in the stomach.

That was his doing? I thought it was Evander using his standing to make sure I'm not completely starved. But it makes more sense that it was the Prince's doing.

"Yes," I nod, not wanting to get into the finer details of what I was actually given or for how long, there are more important things to ask. "Did you ask him to do the same for Pa?"

"I can promise you that your father is fine. We have not brought him any harm." The 'yet' is unspoken. He looks at me for a moment, and sighs defeatedly and moves toward the door.

He places his hand on the handle and stares at it. The motion makes my heart turn in anticipation. I'm unsure whether to breathe a sigh of relief that he will leave or jump for the knife.

He looks up at me in a way that makes my skin prickle. There's a war going on behind his eyes and it feels like he's about to drag me into it.

"Come, I want to show you something." There's a swirl of guilt and need in his voice as he speaks.

He opens the door and walks out, muttering something to the brown-eyed sentinel. My legs refuse to follow him. No, I need to know what he wants to show me. It could help me get out of here. My bare feet pad across the marble as I make my way out the door and pass the brown-eyed sentinel. The air in my lungs disappears when we make eye contact, and he licks his lips. I glare daggers at him then force myself to look away, jogging to catch up to the Prince.

My system is on edge as the Prince takes me down a winding staircase that could lead to the dungeons, but I can't be sure. My fingers roll in and out of a fist, anxiously waiting for an attack, wishing I remembered to take the knife before I left.

"Where are you taking me?" I wince when my question comes out as a stutter rather than a woman who isn't afraid to stand her ground at any cost.

Hold onto that mask, Althea, the voice in my head hisses.

"To your freedom," he states without a moment of hesitation.

My lips part and I have to blink a few times to check I'm really awake. Could he actually mean that? Would he really let me go free?

Everything has a cost, the voice in my head whispers.

Footsteps echo from the other end of the hallway as two sentinels pull open a door for their queen, and Auberon jumps into action, grabbing my hand and pulling me behind a statue big enough to comfortably hide two people. We kneel down, angling ourselves so that we are hidden, but able to see them walking past. Auberon presses his finger to his lips, signaling me to stay silent.

Panic settles beneath my skin. What would happen if Auberon and I were caught here? Would the King take out Auberon's punishment on me?

The footsteps grow louder, and both of us grow stiffer like we could be caught at any moment.

the Queen glides menacingly past, her retinue hurrying to keep up. The two Cintis guards keep pace with practiced ease—marching a step behind her most of the way—only stomping to the fore of the group in order to sweep slow-moving servants out of her path or to wrench open doors before their mistress. An older human woman, her face caught in an eternal pinch of disapproval, huffs a little as she works to match the relentless pace of the Queen—her lips ever moving. I can only assume that she is mumbling obsequious responses to whatever disdainful comments Queen Mellonia might make.

But my eyes are drawn to the heavyset human at the rear of the group—a burly old badger of a man with weathered skin and graying hair that looked out of place in the confines of the Palace. His thick shoulders and sun-roughed face spoke of years of hard work out of doors, and although he wears the same drab uniform as other royal servants the clothes looked shapeless and ill-fitting on him. He looks as strong as an ox, whoever he was, and his role is clearly that of a porter. Bearing the burden of carrying whatever the Queen might decide should come with her. As a porter, he would stoically and silently carry on behind her, whether his responsibility was a chest of clothes, a tray of snacks and drinks, or—as it was today—a gilded statue that the Queen had apparently decided on a whim to relocate.

I felt an immediate surge of sympathy for the old man, his breath wheezing as he stumps after the retinue—bobbing his head and mumbling soft-voiced apologies when the Queen glances back to reprimand him for his apparent slow pace.

As he passes by, I catch a touch of his scent—here in this world of perfumes and incense, the old porter brings the faint smell of sun-warmed leather and fresh green grass.

We watch them go, lowering ourselves behind the statue, trying not to catch the Queen's eye as they pass, until they swept around a corner and were gone.

"Let's go," Auberon mumbles once we can no longer hear their footsteps.

We move from our hiding spot, and he angles his head toward the same direction the group went, and we start walking, picking up our pace to avoid suspecting eyes.

Wherever he's taking me, he clearly doesn't want anyone to know.

Climbing down stairs and turning down more corridors, he comes to a halt in front of an ordinary wooden door, unadorned with gold or dragons, plainer than any other servant entryway I've seen. Looking from him and back to the door, my brows furrow.

"Where are we?" I ask slowly, taking a step away from him as I quickly take in my surroundings to see if there might be anyone else around.

"Behind this door is a secret entrance into the dungeons on your father's floor," he states, and my mind can barely believe what he's saying.

Why would he let me free? Did Evander call in a favor with the Prince to try and help me out? Evander may not have visited me or made sure I was fed, but he could be working on something so much better.

"Should you choose to go through those doors, I will let you know how to find your father and how to get out of the Palace."

Without hesitation I lunge for the door.

"But," he continues, and I freeze as my finger touches the solid wood. *Everything has a cost.* "If you escape, I cannot stop my father or the Priest from hunting you and your family down in every corner of the realm and bringing you back. There are fates far worse than dying on that altar. They will do things to all of you that will make you wish you were dead."

Tears sting my eyes as he speaks. I was planning on getting us out of here. But, I know he's right. My entire life I've been trying to get my family out of Ignis. Somehow, I'll have to get us out of Audor altogether just to give us a fighting chance. If the Cintis don't kill us, then the realm itself will. It's almost impossible to live outside of a city. But what would be even more impossible is making it into another Empire without getting caught because of our bands.

"If you stay, willingly, I assure you that you and your parents' safety will be cared for. Your father will be treated as a guest in my house and your mother will continue to be sent more coin than she knows what to do with. Neither of them will ever have to work again."

Where is all of this kindness is coming from? Could he really mean it?

"I can only protect you and your family within these walls. If you go beyond that, then my power comes to an end." My hand drops from the knob. Even though he's a few steps away from me, I can still feel his hot breath on the back of my neck. "So, you're free to leave, Althea, but if you choose to stay, I can help you," he pauses for a moment before saying, "Please let me help you." There's a sadness in his voice that makes my heart pinch.

I don't know if I can trust the Prince. Beyond wanting to keep me alive, he hasn't proven much else. All I've wanted was for my family to live in better conditions, even if that means being without me. I don't want them to be stuck in the Prince's grip or chained to the consequences of my own actions, but I also don't want them to live on the run because I was too selfish to bear the queen's abuse.

"I want to see him," I say, careful not to let my voice break.

"I know it's hard for you to believe, but you need to trust that I want to make this whole *unfortunate circumstance* a little better for you." His voice is even smoother than before.

"Why should I believe you?" I breathe, suddenly feeling claustrophobic in my own skin.

"You shouldn't. I'm not a good man. I just don't believe anyone should be harmed if they're innocent. And I believe that you and your father are innocent. You were doing what you needed to protect someone you love," he says with a voice that can command an Empire into submission.

"Why?"

"Because I know what it feels like to watch your family get ripped away from you. You don't deserve that."

CHAPTER 13

"The only true wisdom is in knowing you know nothing."
— *Socrates*

I start pulling at the fabric, wishing that I could hide my skin. My lips tighten into a thin line, unsure how to respond to his show of vulnerability.

I want to ask him about Evander, but that would raise too many questions.

"So, will you stay? Will you let me help you?" It almost sounds like he's begging for some reason.

My gift begs to get closer to him. It's the same feeling I get when the need to heal bogs down my mind. But somehow, it's different. Like it's not a wound that the eye can see, but something to do with his soul. I can't explain why, and I can't ask him about it because I don't want him to know any more than he already does about my gift if he doesn't have an answer.

Staring into his eyes, questions storm through my mind. The future is uncertain, but I need to be prepared.

Another Cintis is offering to help me. Another *powerful* Cintis with a powerful family is offering to help me. Why is he acting unlike what I'd expect of the Prince of Fire? He spoke out to save my life and now he's giving me a chance to be free. What's the real cost of staying? What does he want in return?

He could be saying all of this just to manipulate me into trusting him. Maybe the best option for all of us is to let the Prince think that I'm on his side, and I can turn the table around so I'm the one bringing *his* guard down.

I can't forget that he's Evander's best friend. There would need to be some goodness in the Prince if Evander considers him his brother. The Prince helps people in the remains. I may not be able to trust him completely, but maybe what I need is to hope that he's genuine. He wouldn't have offered to let me escape if he wanted to use me. But despite all of that—despite all that he's done—I can't ignore my instincts. I need to tread carefully.

Before I can change my mind, I nod and the tension in his shoulder releases as a small smile crosses his face. He returns the nod and we both walk back to my chambers, where I stand by the edge of the bed and watch him expectantly standing in the middle of the room.

He looks me up and down as a rosy blush climbs up his cheek and he fidgets with his hand. "You didn't answer my question before. Have you been eating? Has everyone been treating you reasonably?" he asks.

I don't answer him as I study the concern in his eyes to search for any sign of malice or fake sympathy. He doesn't falter, taking a step towards me.

"I haven't eaten in two days," I say, not wanting to admit what the sentinel said to me and to forget it ever happened.

As if on cue, my stomach grumbles, and his face contorts with irritation. He shakes his head, turning away from me.

"That's not good enough at all. Stay right here and I'll be back before you know it."

He disappears out of the room without another thought.

I stand there for a few minutes unmoving, barely breathing, until my feet itch to pace. Waiting for a knock to come. After what feels like an hour, my feet stop. I drop onto the settee, thrumming my fingers on the armrest, biting my nails. Impatience and frustration start to boil inside me.

So stupid. Stupid, stupid, stupid, the voice in my head screams at me, repeating it like a mantra, *What did I say about trusting him? Do you actually think he was going to come back?*

Bitter disappointment claws at my chest, and I hit the arm rest, groaning in frustration. Jumping off the settee, I pull out the red nightgown from the drawers and reach around to remove the dress I'm wearing so I can go to bed. The door swings open to reveal a smiling Prince holding a tray with a silver dome and I freeze in place. Our eyes lock before his eyes travel to my bare shoulder. His gaze caresses my collarbones and down my decolletage. He clears his throat and turns his back to me.

"I didn't quite expect *that*," he says over his shoulder. Heat rushes to my cheeks as my fingers fumble to put the dress back on properly with shaking hands. "I didn't mean to take so long to make this. The chef moved some of the ingredients around, and I couldn't find it for the life of me," he laughs.

I freeze part way through doing the laces back up. He cooked for me?

Once fully dressed, I clear my throat. He turns and signals towards the desk, placing the silver tray in front of me once seated.

"Please don't judge it too harshly. I had to make do without some of the ingredients," he says, scratching the back of his neck as the entirety of his face goes completely pink as he moves awkwardly to the settee.

The Prince of Audor is... shy?

He removes the dome to reveal an entire plate filled with vegetables and herbs and an assortment of different meats. My mouth waters as the scent of rosemary hits my nostrils, and my stomach rumbles loudly in response.

The wheels in my head turn as I stare at the Prince. Why did he cook for me? If I weren't so hungry, I would have declined the food for fear of what it might cost me down the line. Instead, I settle for staring straight at the food, completely forgetting about Auberon's existence.

I pick up the fork and spearing a long green vegetable, I pause when it's halfway to my mouth.

"I didn't poison it, I swear," he says like this isn't the first time someone has questioned it.

The little voice from before drowns in gnawing hunger, and I take the first bite. My eyes flutter close as an explosion of flavor comes from the green stalk, and I shove the rest of it in my mouth without hesitating. I make my way through the plate, groaning every time I try a different meat or vegetable. It's a thousand times better than the breakfast Maiya brought me. Between each bite, I'm in utter shock that a prince whose talents I've always assumed were confined to battle is capable of making something so phenomenal. Admittedly, it isn't so hard to beat flavorless soup and stale bread.

A sharp pain goes through my stomach as Pa's face flashes through my mind. Is he getting enough food? Is he being mistreated? He must sense the change in atmosphere, because his expression turns solemn. "I swear on my crown that your father is being fed. I saw to it myself that day in the throne room," he says.

I swallow the bite down with water, suddenly tasting ash. If he saw to it himself, that could mean that Pa could be getting more than just a mouthful of bread.

I can feel the heat of his eyes on me, as he watches me eat from his spot on the settee.

"I can't say I've ever seen someone enjoy my food so much."

I blink at him a few times, looking at the quirk of his brow and the way the small flame from the oil lantern dances in his eyes. I shake my head.

"Thank you, Your Highness. It's truly delicious," I say between mouthfuls, when I realized staring at him isn't a response.

"My friends call me Auberon." His smile is warmer than the one I gave Maiya when I said the same thing.

"I didn't realize the Prince had friends," I say with a hint of humor in my voice to help me forget my own situation.

"Lonely are those who sit on thrones," he sighs, winking at me.

Pushing the plate aside with some food remaining to save for later, I take another sip of water.

"Where did you learn to cook?" I ask automatically before realizing I genuinely want to know.

"As a boy, I would watch the chefs flurry about in the kitchen. I would tell everyone that it's because I was hungry and curious about what things taste like before they reach the plate. It was also my way of making sure the chefs kept their heads. I'm pretty sure everyone saw through the lies. So, I sat there and watched the magic unfold, tasting dishes as the chef seasoned them, watching the way their wrists glided like it were a dance. Cooking isn't exactly princely, so I can only cook when the kitchen has closed for the day," he practically hums, smiling as he reminisces about his days as a child in the kitchen. I smile back, thinking about Ma humming as she experiments with different soups. "What does someone like you do in her spare time?"

I can see why Evander feels threatened by Auberon. The circumstances that brought us here aren't exactly ideal. Yet I feel like if we weren't who we were in this realm, we could have a real friendship.

I can feel the small voice at the back of my head slamming against its walls, warning me to be careful and not to trust him because he's just manipulating me. The truth is, he doesn't need to manipulate me. There's nothing he can't just take. But I feel comfortable in his presence, like I've known him before all of this. Not because his looks rival almost every man in Ignis, but because he fought for me. He stepped in to try and save me from being killed by his father. He told the King of Fire to spare my life. Part of me trusts him enough to know that he isn't going to kill me.

He's just manipulating you for your powers, the voice reminds me.

"I'm an Ironsmith. If I'm not working, I do errands around the house or read. My skin would draw a lot of unwanted attention if I mingled." I shrug.

A sprinkle of the truth is enough to keep someone at bay. He frowns, and nods understandingly, clearly not too pleased with my answer.

"Yes, you're the Cloaked Ironsmith. I've heard of you." His eyes are bright, and it almost looks like admiration.

I expected him to scowl from hearing that a woman is making his weapons.

"I hate that name," I grumble, wanting this conversation to end so I can be left to my own devices

"Yes, I've seen some of your work. I think I even have a dagger that you and your father made." He leans in closer like he's about to tell me a secret. "Don't tell Wayland, but I think you're the best smiths in the forge."

I can't help the heat that covers my cheeks. Years of blood and sweat perfecting my craft to finally be validated by someone from the Palace—the Prince no less. I shouldn't care, yet I do.

"Which one?" I say, trying to hide the pride building in my chest by keeping my eyes on the plate. If Ma found out that the Prince thinks our work is the 'best,' every person in Audor will hear about it with all her gossiping.

"The hilt was carved like a feather. You could see every single strand; it was absolutely beautiful."

Small smile creeps to the corner of my lips. I designed that dagger. I remember feeling the spark of inspiration when I saw a Cintis wearing a feather collar jump back in a fit of rage when a carriage sprayed mud all over. I can still remember how elegantly the feathers moved through the air.

"I'm glad it's to your liking." I give up on trying to hide the smile in my voice as pride gets to my head.

"Yes," he says heavily, and my eyes snap to his. My breath hitches in my chest as his gaze lingers on me with deep rooted intent.

A flicker of gold distracts me away from his stare, and my lips part as he twirls the gilded hilt of a dagger in his hand. "You're wearing the dagger," I say like it's a question. My first instinct is to try to get it off of him. But my second instinct is telling me what a terrible idea that is.

"Of course I am, it's one of my favorites. You should be proud of yourself," he says with a lopsided grin.

Heat covers my skin as an odd feeling flutters in my stomach. *No.* I can't feel like this about my captor. I said that I'd tread with caution, so I need to follow my own advice.

"It was inspired by the wings of the Warriors of Caulus," I say with more vigor than I meant just to get my mind away from his words.

"Fearsome, brave and beautiful."

"Yes, they are." I nod in agreement.

"I was talking about the dagger." Our eyes meet again, and his words from earlier echo through my mind.

What does he get from being kind to me? Why would the Prince of Fire be spending time with his prisoner and *flirting* with her? Whatever the reason, I'm enjoying the attention.

CHAPTER 14

Maiya doesn't arrive when morning breaks.

I could have been out there, roaming the Palace uselessly in search of Pa last night if Auberon didn't show up when he did. He made me realize if I fail in my attempts to free Pa and I die in the process, then I might as well have killed my parents myself.

I also feel like a fool. I shouldn't be feeling pride about my work after my own captor compliments it. Especially when Pa is in his power, and Auberon could easily make Pa's time in the dungeons far worse if I continued being rude. Being 'safe' and treated as his guest is too vague, especially when I have no idea how the Prince of Fire treats *all* of his guests.

The fear of not knowing what might happen to Pa and I kept me up all night. I need to find Evander to give Ma a message from me. She needs to know that I'm okay and that she needs to get out of Ignis.

My back presses firmly against the door as the day sentinel's wheeze distracts me from my thoughts. In truth, it's a welcome distraction. Despite how bored I may get inside the bed chambers; I can't imagine how bored he would be if his entire day consisted of standing outside of the door.

"What's your name?" I question.

Moments pass and he doesn't answer as I suspected he wouldn't.

"My name is Althea," I say, playing with my fingers, hoping that he would at least grunt in response. I sigh when he doesn't, leaning my head back against the door. "My Pa has really bad lungs as well from the smoke." A different type of smoke ruined Pa's lungs, but the coughs all sound the same. "He'd wake the whole neighborhood with his coughs. It would even get so bad that he'd throw up."

I wait again for his response, when he doesn't reply, I continue, "When the weather gets colder, we would always make sure he only drinks hot water, and that his chest is always warm." Sighing, I let my back drag down the door until I sit cross legged on the floor. "Pa lost a lung before I could figure out my powers. Now, every day I worry that he might lose his other," I say so softly that I'm not sure if he heard.

Even though he doesn't respond, it feels nice to talk about my family. It may be a sorrowful story, but it brings me joy thinking about them. Ma and I would take turns going out of the house to make sure there was always enough warm water for Pa.

"Valen," a deep voice says.

A smile creeps onto my face. "It's a pleasure to make your acquaintance, Valen."

Silence paints the room, but now I feel perfectly content with the lack of response. There's a feeling brewing in my chest that feels a little like hope. I'm not sure what exactly I'm hoping for when all Valen has told me is his name, but maybe this means that I have a friend within the Palace. Or at least, a glimmer of hope that friends might be found.

I have always had a gift for making friends. Pa says those are drawn to me, that are drawn to right, whatever that means.

Maiya arrives shortly after with a plate of food. As I watch her clean the room, I start to notice the patches of dried, scaly skin around her eyes and cheeks. Specks of blood vessels rise to the surface on certain parts of the patches. Occasionally she reaches up to scratch it, and I can see her mentally tell herself off for it. My skin jumps to heal her skin, but there's a part of me that thinks she was chosen specifically because of that; to see if I'll flaunt my powers and use it as a way to manipulate her.

Forcing myself out of bed, I move to fold my blankets. She jumps from the ground, placing a hand on the bed. "Just sit down, I can do it."

"Please," I say, "just give me this one thing."

Her frantic eyes soften a fraction. "I'll be placing a new sheet while you bathe. I've prepared the bath for you already."

I close my eyes and nod briefly.

Undressing and stepping into the bath, I let the heat of the water sting my eyes. The water droplets meld with my silent flow of tears. I just want things to go back to how they were. Or at least have some semblance of normalcy.

A knock comes from the bathing chamber door. "Madam, you have a summons. We should get you ready now," Maiya says, and I don't miss the urgency in her voice.

Splashing the warm water on my face, I drag myself to my feet and wrap a towel around my chest. Maiya leads me to sit at the table as she sets about my hair.

"If you, by chance, run into a man named Evander, I believe, could you please let him know I would like to speak to him? He's the general's son. That's only if you run into him," I ask, as desperation claws at me.

She picks at the skin on her neck, notably suspicious about the request asking for someone other than the royal family.

"I would just like to thank him for what he is doing for my family. You see, he demanded that Pa was fed and provided with warmth in that cold cell. There's no need to trouble the King with it: he's a very busy man," I finish off with an innocent smile hoping she doesn't know the truth. I say the last sentence slightly louder to play at her own weaknesses too. Every mortal knows what it's like to be hungry and cold. The King probably already knows that I know Evander's name, and I don't see a safer way to get a message to my mother. I know Ma, she won't just leave her family behind, but I still need to try.

It's a risky lie to tell, especially when I'm telling someone that works in the Palace. Maiya could spread gossip through the Palace, and it could all backfire. But I see no other way to contact Evander.

She nods and gives me a soft smile that kindles hope in my heart. She continues braiding. This time, more hair covers my shoulders, and small golden clips are added into the braid at the top of my head. She hands me a silk black slip dress and a sheer black overlay.

Standing in front of the mirror to admire the work of art on my body, I gasp. A sash of diamonds ties around my waist above the mesh overlay that is decorated with beaded suns all the way up to the base of my throat. The strap of the slip is only two fingers wide, and the patches and lines of my skin show through as if it were a part of the dress. The red line and 'N' can clearly be seen as it stops just before my elbow.

Belve barges into the bedchamber, grabbing my arm and dragging me all the way to the Queen's chambers, shutting the door as soon as I am through the entrance.

Queen Mellonia lies on the chaise with a chalice in hand again, only this time there are no servants around.

"Stupid girl, you're late again. All those years living with rats on the street have certainly not taught you manners," she sneers.

I want to retort that it's Belve's fault for making me late, but I keep my mouth shut. Flexing her index finger, she summons me to her. As I get closer, she stands, lifting her chin up, watching me down her nose.

"On your knees," she barks.

I clench my fist at my sides as my blood begins to boil. I do as she says and lower myself onto a single knee. The marble floor grinds against my bone as I sway slightly, unbalanced.

"Now kiss my feet."

My head snaps up to her. "What?"

A hot rush of heat laces my cheek as the Queen strikes me, and I stare back at her, too stunned to speak.

"What did I say about asking questions?" she snarls.

My hands tremble and my breathing goes ragged as I try to contain the steam coming out of my ears.

I hate her.

I fucking hate this bitch.

Every single one of my instincts screams to stop rebelling against her order. But logic and reason prove that to be an awful idea. Releasing my fingers from my steel fist, I plant them on the ground as I slowly lower my head towards her shoe. When my face is mere inches away from her feet, I inhale deeply, calming my rage before planting my lips on her foot, jumping back the second they touch it.

A high-pitched laugh tears through the air like nails against chalk. "Good. Was that so hard? Now hurry up and undress your queen."

She turns around so that I can undo her laces. My hands ache to wrap around her slender throat, picturing what it would feel like if it were to snap. If the beast wants to help, then this will all be much easier. My fists don't stand a chance against her power, but whatever is in my core might level the playing field. It begs to let the spots take over my vision and make her kiss *my* feet and call me *her* superior.

Rolling my shoulders and glaring at her back, I undo the laces of her dress with trembling fingers, watching the dress fall to the floor in a heap before she steps out and removes her under garments. Sauntering over to the bathing chamber, she steps into the quartz tub and sighs as the water laps against her skin.

"Close that door. Then I want you to heal every scar or blemish that you find," she orders, clicking her fingers at me.

I close the door then walk towards her, putting my hands on both of her shoulders. It would be so easy to push her under and watch her thrash. Her fire is useless against the water. I'd be a fool to think her screams wouldn't draw the attention of the sentinels or servants.

If you shove her head underwater she won't be able to scream, the voice says sinisterly.

I shake the voice off. I wouldn't be able to defeat the horde of Cintis that will come for me if I harm their Queen, and my parents would surely suffer.

Closing my eyes, I let the warmth flow from my veins into her skin. I watch as blazing fire courses through her, circling her heart and her bones in an elegant dance. The flames feed into each other, creating torrents of golds and yellows that pulses through her in time with her heart. I let my power move freely, searching for any organ or bone that needs patching. Going down her diaphragm, my gift catches signs of childbirth.

The amount of scarring is a lot for a single baby. Even Ma doesn't have that much, and she's a mortal. Maybe birthing fae is harder than giving birth to a mortal. Or maybe the real reason that Auberon hung around the kitchen when he was younger was simply because he liked eating, and he was just a big infant.

He probably didn't even make last night's meal after all, the voice sneers.

I force my gift to ignore the trauma to the tissue, and fuse together parts of her reproductive system that are flaking. She should feel the sensation of my gift working, so she won't be able to say I did nothing.

As I move to her arms, my power goes berserk at the band encasing her wrist and the 'C.' I force my gift to ignore it like I tell it to every other time it delves into someone. Before I withdraw completely, I notice something that has my head cocking to the side. The 'C' has a lot more damage to it than I would expect from a Cintis. A mortal's identification mark is nowhere near this mutilated from within. It's as if it had been stamped repeatedly and there was a fight between her fae healing and the imprinting of the mark. I thought that an infant fae's healing speed is as non-existent as a mortal baby. It could be possible that powerful fae are the exception.

Looking closer at the 'C,' I realize that the imprint is far younger than the rest of her. That could only mean that she didn't get stamped as a baby, and had the branding burnt into her skin once her healing developed. They would have needed to stamp her skin hundreds of times just to leave a mark, stamping it again every time it's about to heal, until one day it just stops healing altogether.

I move to the band and notice the same thing. It's like it was tattooed on twice. There's an odd swirl of mystery as I try to figure out the brand's age. Parts of it are as old as her, while other parts are as young as the mark. Opening my eyes, I look at her wrist staring at the mangled 'C.' Even from the surface, Evander's mark looks as clean as every other mortal. My lips part as I notice the band. Its color is unlike any of the other Cintis, whose band is a vibrant vermilion. Whereas hers looks more like the color of red grapes.

I shake my head. The royalty must have a different shade of red, because they wouldn't want to be mistaken for a common Cintis.

"There's nothing more to heal, Your Majesty," I say, releasing her shoulders, keeping my eyes on her wrist.

"So, you're stupid *and* blind? What do you call this?" she says, lifting her hand and her initial requests dawns on me.

She summoned me to fix her broken nail.

I asked to be her ladies' maid. This is what's expected of me. Yet even my gift is offended by the request; to be belittled into healing for the sake of pageantry.

I grip a quartz petal to stop my hands from trembling with the rage surging through me. Steadying my breathing, I reach out to hold her hand. My gift doesn't instantly reach out towards her nail, and I frown. Closing my eyes to concentrate, my warmth seeps into her skin, in my mind's eye I can see the band and her imprint, and the fire in her blood. Nowhere can I see the broken nail. Huffing, I open my eyes and repeat the whole process. I try to convince myself that it's because I'm angry and because of that my gift won't cooperate. Yet my gift reaches out to heal her womb and her branding.

I scour every inch of her fingers, noting that I can't see a single nail.

"I can't fix it, because the nail is already dead, Your Majesty," I whisper, preparing myself for a whip of fire that never came.

"Ironic, isn't it? Your name means healing in the language of the gods, yet you can't do something as simple as fix a broken nail. You know what the 'N' on your arm stands for? Nothing. You are nothing, Althea. You will always be nothing, and when you die, you will continue to be nothing. You truly are pathetic," she laughs in that high-pitch screech.

The darkness snaps in response to my rage, awaking the beast from the Hole.

The black fills my lungs and blurs my vision until I only see faint outlines of colors and millions upon millions of dots. The anger is gone in an instant, and my shoulders ease as the feeling of home swirls through my mind, making me forget about my surroundings. It trickles into my fingertip. Every inch of skin that touches the fabric of my dress buzzes, and it feels like my skin is shifting. Like I'm fully submerged in water, and somehow at the same time water drips off me as I move. Cold prickles tingle across my flesh, swirling around my limbs and tearing at my skin in a sensation that's pleasurable, yet painful.

The colors in my vision begin to shift into vibrant dots as moving figures dance in and out of vision. Everything in the chamber becomes neither here nor there. Just a blur of dots moving in time with imaginary wind, cycling into the earth then back into the sky.

It's like the darkness has lifted my soul into the clouds, wrapping my consciousness with the wind. The darkness tears at my throat, begging to scream with a single goal in mind. To unleash my demons on that wretched bitch.

"King Cyrus, what are you doing here?" the voice sounds so distant, yet so close. I recognize it from somewhere. I can feel her words coil alongside the air, spiraling together to bring the sound to me.

Slowly the glaze over my vision seeps back into my core, taking the darkness with it. At once, air fills my lungs, causing my head to spin. I stumble forward, catching myself on the quartz tub, suddenly aware of my surroundings again.

Snapping my attention to the naked Queen standing in the doorway. I didn't see her move. I try to recall what she said. Did she say someone's here?

My limbs feel frozen like I've peeled off my skin and stepped into something new. I feel rigid as my fingers move up to readjust my dress. The tightness of my skin makes it feel almost painful to move, like I'm still breaking it in.

More noises come from outside the bathing chamber, and I will my feet to move as I stumble over my own steps like I'm learning to walk again.

Nothing about this skin feels right. It doesn't feel like my own.

I follow her out into the sitting room and stop under the doorway of the bathing chamber. Now, my very being feels frozen in place. King Cyrus is splayed out over the chaise, arms up on the headrest, legs splayed open. Women drape themselves over him, across the settee, and on the floor. Three women feed each other, another rubs the King's thigh, and the rest massage him.

These must be the royal whores.

His eyes burn into me. My skin prickles as his eyes take in every inch of skin with hunger. The sheer fabric suddenly makes me feel very exposed and vulnerable. I can't shake the feeling that in this dress I'm like a wrapped present being gifted to the King to play with.

A sickly-sweet smile spreads across his face. He begins patting a concubine on the head, twirling his fingers through her hair and massaging her scalp. He never once breaks eye contact with me.

The naked queen's fingers shake against her taut muscles. She slowly turns and looks at my head, and back to the concubine. Then she turns back to me, her eyes darken, and her taloned fingers are completely splayed.

My heart skips, and goosebumps cascade down my body.

Every single one of his concubines has the exact same shade of brown hair as mine.

"Remember what I told you. You are nothing," she growls, "Now get the fuck out of my chambers."

I lift my skirts up and run to the door, swinging it open with every ounce of strength I have.

"Let's go," I hiss at Belve, walking away before he has the chance to check my tone. My stomach twists and turns as we walk through the Palace. I feel dizzy and I can barely keep my back straight as my breath comes out in short bursts.

I enter the room before Belve turns down the hallway. Sprinting to a bin, I discard the contents of my stomach until nothing else comes out. Everything about the summons makes me feel sick. The floor rushes up to hit my face as I gasp for air, clawing at my chest; the dress rips, and the mask I keep on vanishes.

It's not enough.

My hands move of their own accord as they find my neck. I sink my claws into the material and tear the fabric until a satisfying rip tears through the air.

Crawling to the bathing chamber, my arms scrape against the raw crystal as I pull myself into the tub.

"I hate them!" I scream over and over again, punching the crystal until my knuckles bleed. I ball my fist into my hair, pulling out the clips and the braid.

There's too much on me. Too much material. Too much skin. Too much hair. Hair that's on every single one of the King's concubines.

First the Queen's summons, then the King's concubines. It's too much.

I'm so sick of everything. I just want to go home. I want to go back to my mundane life of working and sneaking out at night to see Evander. I want to go back to being the Cloaked Ironsmith, for all that I used to think I hated having to hide my skin. I want my family to be together again.

I scream into my hands, kicking the tub, tossing and turning. My blood is smeared all over the walls of the tub, spreading over my hands and down my neck. I scream again, seeing the slice in Pa's neck and the hole in Elex.

Rational thought leaves my body, disappearing in waves, and dragging me into a pit of insanity, and I no longer know what's right or wrong.

I've failed them. I've failed everyone. I'm never going to get us out of here. I'm too weak. I'm not strong enough to withstand everything.

We are all going to die here.

The Queen is right. I am nothing. I'm useless and pathetic. I can barely control the dark well of power inside of me. I lost myself and the darkness took over. Not to mention that I spent the first twenty-three years of my life not even knowing I had it. My thoughts churn replaying every second I've spent with Evander, unsure if some of it is just a figment of my imagination. I spent five years with a Cintis who doesn't even care that I've been taken prisoner, because he would have found a way to see me otherwise. He's the General's son. He would have found a way. He would have.

Stupid, stupid, stupid.

My fists collide with the bottom of the tub, sobbing those words like a mantra. When my arms lose energy to continue hitting, I collapse into the tub. My hair sticks to my cheeks from the sweat and tears, and I lie there with my arms curled around my knees.

Deep breaths, Thea. Seven in and eleven out, just like Evander said, my mind echoes. I try to breathe, but the tears only fall harder, making me feel like a failure for not being able to do something as simple as breathing.

No, Evander would have a plan. He wouldn't just leave me in here and wash his hands of me. He cares about me. He said so himself.

Don't fool yourself. No one could ever care about you, the voice sneers, and the pit engulfs me even further into its grip until I no longer know what is real.

My sobs echo through the room, bouncing against the walls until it's almost painful to my ears. The bathing chamber is swallowed by darkness when the sun is put to rest. The tears continue, mixing in with the dried blood.

I don't move when Maiya comes to drop dinner and replace the bin. I don't move when my back begins to ache. I don't move when my mouth becomes sandpaper from my hollow wails.

"Althea?" A warm voice breaks the silence. I tense, and it's like a fist around my heart squeezes. "Althea, where are you?" Concern grips Auberon's voice as it bounces through the bathing chamber.

"Go away," I rasp, pulling my shredded dress tighter.

"Oh gods, are you okay?" His hands are on me before I get the chance to protest, moving over my body in inspection, lifting me to a seated position.

I slap his hands away. He's part of the reason Pa and I are still in here. He could have gotten all of us out of Ignis. If he truly cared he would do everything he could to make sure we're safe even if my family and I were on the run. "I said leave me alone. You're all monsters!"

Hurt flashes through his eyes as he quickly blinks, readjusting his stance without leaving my side. "I'm not going anywhere," he breathes. "Are you hurt? Show me where you're hurt."

He reaches for my arms again, and I jump to my feet to get out of his grasp. I lose my balance, tipping over the tub and my head hits the floor with a thud before the rest of my body makes it down. A sharp pain that pierces over my whole body unleashes a series of whimpers from my lips. Warm hands wrap under my shoulders and legs. I scream, kicking my legs out, hitting his chest and biting his arm.

"Gods, Althea, stop! I'm trying to help you," he yells. I keep kicking, but this time I curl my fist and land a punch square in his nose. He roars and drops the hand holding my legs up.

The door whips open and a sentinel I've never seen runs in, sword drawn. It's always been the brown-eyed sentinel on night duty. Not him. Where is the Cintis that threatened me?

Auberon holds up his hand covered in the blood pouring from his nose. "It's fine. Leave us."

The sentinel looks between Auberon and I, dazed with confusion, before he bows and returns to his post. I shove my gift down to stop from reaching for Auberon. He doesn't deserve my powers. No one in his gods-forsaken family does. None of the Cintis do.

Arms wrap around me once more, tighter this time. "I'm not going to let you go. You can try as hard as you want to push me away, but I'm not going anywhere."

"Stop playing me!" I scream against his chest, trying to shove him away, but he grips my waist so hard it would bruise. "Save me your pity and tell me what you want, so you can leave me alone and be done with these games. We both know you don't actually give two shits about what happens to me."

He stops fighting my kicks and keeps his arms around me instead.

"I hate you!" I scream, "You're just another Cintis giving a mortal attention until you get bored and move onto the next."

"Is that what you think? That I'm only here to play *games* with you? If I wanted to play games, I wouldn't still be here after you broke my nose." His eyes flash with one hundred colors of hurt and betrayal. "Everything I've told you has been the truth, Althea." He pauses like he wants to say more—something that stirs whatever war is going within him. "I've been making sure your father has been taken care of. I came here tonight because—" He closes his mouth in hesitation. "Because I knew you would be bored out of your mind, so I wanted to share my favorite book with you," he says, nodding toward a yellow book on the table, ignoring the blood dripping down his nose, "I've read it ten times over, and I want to share something special to me, with you. Ever since I laid eyes on you at the market, I've been completely entranced by you."

Somewhere in his speech, I must have stopped moving, because he lifts a hand up to tuck my hair behind my ears. His feather-light touch runs down the side of my forehead, and a shudder escapes me. He stares into my eyes with a fierce longing. His words finally sink in, and I push myself away from him.

"What do you mean the market? We met at the Forge."

He sighs, running his hands through his hair he starts to pace. "Shit. I didn't want you to find out like this," he groans with frustration.

"Find what out?" I push, inching back towards the pillar where the knife is hidden. This is what I was worried about. This is why I need to tread carefully. There's more to his visits than what he's letting on.

He stops, looking at his feet before walking to the pitcher and pouring himself a glass of water and chugging it. "Bloody hell, this needs to be wine," he growls as he continues pacing.

I reach into the well of darkness but grasp at straws. Pushing myself against the pillar, I might be able to slide down and grab the knife without him noticing.

"There's no easy way to put this, but we've met before. Well, no. I've seen you before. Many times, actually. You've never seen me, I think." He scratches his jaw and paces quickly up and down the same path I take.

Does this mean he knows about Evander and I? Did Auberon do something to him? Is that why he hasn't visited me?

"I go into the outskirts of Ignis sometimes and give coin to the families of the people who have been sacrificed, or even just to give some to the people on the streets," he says quickly as he paces, like I might miss what he's trying to say if he talks fast enough. "One day, I was visiting a family and you caught my eye."

I hide my hands behind my back so that he doesn't see them tremble. No. This can't be true. None of this can be true. There's no way the Prince of Audor was watching me. There's no way he'd waste his time on some mortal he saw along the street.

His face twitches slightly as before saying, "You were talking to some boy at a bakery, and there was something about that innocent conversation that sparked a cloud of jealousy in me. I wanted nothing more than to be the one you were talking to." He stumbles over his words, talking quickly as though he's opened a dam and it's all pouring out. I followed you home and saw the building you live in, with a rope at the front door. After that, every chance I got, I would walk past your place and hope to see the top of your head bobbing in the top floor window as you move about." At some point during his speech, he stops his pacing, and a blush climbs over his face.

I have no words to say, only the loud beat of my heart feels like an answer. I don't know how to feel. A small part of me feels violated by it. He's been watching me? But there's a bigger part of me—a sicker part of me—that seems to puff its chest at the thought of a prince taking such an interest.

"The only good thing that ever comes from a sacrifice is that I get to see you." A smile seeps into his voice as he speaks. "You always stand at the back with your hood drawn. You're always one of the last people to leave. And you always walk through the forest. If it weren't for my mother, I would have insisted that we drop you back home."

The Prince of Fire looks broken, and his jaw ticks like he just revealed a destructive secret to the world.

Has he been a guardian angel I never knew I had? For once, I want the little voice to yell at me and tell me that he's lying, but it's not there. He knows more about me than I ever realized, yet I know nothing about him.

"Althea, please say something. I beg you." He reaches for my hand and I pull away.

"Why?" I demand.

"I wish I knew how to answer that question."

He drags his hand down his face, shutting his eyes like he's worried he might say the wrong thing. The lump in my throat makes it harder for me to breathe as my mind rages, unsure if I should believe anything he says.

"Try." I need to know what he feels. I need to know if he's telling the truth.

"I honestly don't know how to explain it. It sounds crazy. I was down another street when it felt like your soul was screaming for me to find you. As soon as I laid eyes on you, it was like something snapped into place and that I had to keep looking for you. There's something about your soul that keeps calling me to you. I can't stay away. I don't want to stay away. There's a spark about you that has very quickly become my favorite addiction," he says with unwavering confidence, like he's finally figured out the right thing to say.

A cold sweat breaks across my back. All the times we've made eye contact at the Temple, it wasn't just an accident. He feels it too. He feels the same pull that my gift feels. But I can't let myself give in to the pull. He's the Prince. I'm his prisoner. His kind is brutal towards mortals.

What else does he know? Has he seen me use my powers on Pa? How have I never noticed him before, better yet, why did my gift not react and try to reach for him when he was watching me?

"My Ma, what exactly has happened to her?"

"I know she works for General Fornous. You don't need to worry about her either. On the day you were taken in, I had one of my most trusted men pick her up and move her to another apartment in case they came looking for her. I wasn't lying to you. She has more coin than she knows what to do with, and she knows exactly what is going on."

A breath of relief leaves me, and I rest my head against the wall. "Who was it that picked her up? She wouldn't just trust anyone."

"You may know him because of your Ma. His name is Evander. He's the General's son." A sound somewhere between a laugh and a sob escapes me from his answer. Pa is being treated well, and Ma is safe. And Evander gives a shit. The thought alone could bring me to tears. The tension that has been wrapped around my heart since I arrived dispels. He has no idea about my relationship with Evander.

For the first time since arriving here, real hope blossoms in my core. If I can get him to think that I trust him completely, then maybe he'll believe whatever comes out of my mouth. I don't want to play him after everything he has done, but it may be my only option. Living at the whim of a tyrannical king isn't a life.

I step forward, wrapping my arms around him. "Thank you, Auberon. Thank you for taking care of my family." I smile against his chest.

He stills for a moment. My power stretches its tendrils toward him at the contact, and I pull back to look at the fountain of dried blood from his nose.

"Sorry about your nose," I whisper, lifting my hand up to heal it. I pause to look at him. "May I?"

He nods softly, placing his cheeks against my hand. My heartbeat accelerates at the contact. Without thinking, I open my gift and let it flow through me into him, healing every injury. Yet still, there's an invisible barrier within him that stops my gift from healing him fully. The need to heal him is still there, but for some reason I can't quite scratch that itch.

His lips part as my gift straightens his nose back into place painlessly. "I could get used to having you around," he sighs with contentment.

I shake my head, pulling my gift away. The voice in my head screams to step away and tell him to leave the room. I ignore it, keeping my hand pressed against the warmth of his cheek, gazing at his full lips. The move is intentional, but I can't deny that his words have found their place within me, drawing me closer to him. Especially when my power yearns to heal something that I can't see.

He traces the lines on my shoulder through the rip in the dress, circling his fingers around the patches of different colors. A shiver builds within me from his touch. I'm not sure if my body's reaction is because it's him, or if it's just because I'm being touched.

"It looks like a river," he chuckles before lifting the ripped mesh sleeve back over my shoulder. "You know, I think I like you better in red," he declares, arching a brow consideringly. "I'll arrange for every one of your dresses to be in red. I'll make sure that it covers all of your skin too."

He steps back and walks towards the table where a silver dome sits. He pulls out the chair and motions towards it. "Come, sit. I thought you might like to try another Prince Auberon specialty."

"Actually," I start to say, relaxing all the muscles to make my next sentence sound innocent. "Actually, nevermind. It's silly." I shake my head.

"What is it?" he says, and his eyes shimmer with curiosity. His chest puffs out slightly as I'd expected. A damsel in distress — especially one that acts like a fool — is something a lot of men can't deny.

"Nothing, you wanted to eat dinner. Just pretend I didn't say anything," I say with a placid smile.

"Tell me what's on your mind," he says with the confidence of a prince, capable of fixing any problem.

"It's silly. I've just been cooped up in here for so long. I was going to ask if we could go for a walk. But I completely understand that it's not my place to request such a thing, and it's especially not the right time when you've spent so much time cooking for me," I say softly. The worst thing that could happen is that he says no. The best thing that could happen is that he agrees, and I can start building a map of the Palace.

He thinks about it for a brief second before he pulls his shoulders back and gives me a winning smile like he just saved the day. "Of course we can."

"Really? Are you sure? I would hate for you to get in trouble all because of me." My voice is a pitch higher, and I widen my eyes like a doe. Guilt builds within my core for manipulating Auberon when my end goal is to run away, but I can't push aside the possibility that he might be trying to gain my trust for his own end.

He's a Cintis. He deserves it, the voice says.

He walks to the door without responding, opening it, and swinging his arm across his center like he's bowing. "Lead the way." He winks.

I force myself to blink several times and contort my features into one of utter surprise and gratitude.

It's time I got us out of here.

CHAPTER 15

*"No man on earth may look on forbidden things as you have done
and escape punishment. Especially here, a land so infested with
divinity that one might meet a god more easily than a man."*

— *Petronius Arbiter, The Satyricon*

Thanks to our walk, I have a map in my mind of the way to get from here, to the garden, the throne room and the dungeons. I tuck the precious information away, eager for the Prince to leave so I can go over the map in my mind again and again to make sure I don't forget until I can scribble my mental map onto something more tangible.

But he didn't leave until the early hours of the morning, sitting and talking about everything. We spoke about the books we've read and our mutual hatred for the Priest. He mainly spoke, and I listened. He read passages of the book to me, pausing between pages to tell me how he interpreted the writing.

He told me stories about growing up alongside Evander, but the way he talks about their time together is nothing like how Evander tells it. Auberon speaks of all their bickering with great fondness, and jokes about how Evander used to chase women's tails, and for some reason he stopped in the past few years. Guilt gripped my heart when he said it. I didn't realize I was the only woman Evander brought to his bed. I should have treated him better.

I want to hate the very fact that he breathes. But I don't. I can't bring myself to hate him. Not completely. He's still a Cintis. He still has my life in his hands.

Auberon left me with a book—one that I have no intention of reading. Burning the end of a bone from dinner to use as a stick of charcoal, I start scribbling into the book. Mapping out every inch of the Palace that I can remember. Drawing out the path from the dungeons to the throne room, and from the dungeon to my bedchambers.

I list every single piece of artwork I can recall, to use it as a signpost for the day I get out of here.

The map I have now still isn't good enough. Needing to get to the throne room just to get to the dungeon is an idiotic idea, and I might as well hand myself to a sentinel without even attempting to escape. I need to develop an accurate map, because I'll only get one chance at this.

Hiding the book in plain sight next to the bed, I go back to it every time I remember another piece of this labyrinth. I force myself to sleep for most of the day, because from now on, my nights will be long.

As the sun sets, and the moon is at its peak, I pull the clock from off the wall and lie us both flat on the floor right in front of the door. The sound of the ticking clock threatens to lull me to sleep during the ungodly hours of the night, but I pinch myself to stay awake. Scribbling the time into the book every time the sentinel goes on a break, and how long he stays away for.

The following day, I wait for Auberon again after Maiya brings my dinner, but disappointment covers me like a sheet when Maiya comes in to bring me a book on behalf of him. This one is a political book about the history of Audor. I skim through the pages that repeat exactly what the Acolytes said at the mandatory library sessions.

And like the day before, I practice my fighting, trying to use my power, sleeping in between meals, and the Queen's summons, then staying up all night to watch the sentinel on the other side of the door. His schedule is completely different to the day before, but I don't give up hope. However, my hope that I might be able to control my power is slowly dwindling.

The next night, Maiya returns with another book, and I suppress my disappointment when I don't see the Prince that night either. And then she comes back with another book the next day. Then another the day after. Then yet another book.

A total of a week goes by and Auberon doesn't visit. Instead, the Queen summons me every day to scrub the floor or stand by the wall with a bottle of wine, waiting for her to click her fingers at me to refill her chalice.

I've managed to figure out the sentinel's break cycle. He only has two different break routines that he follows to the very second. Which routine he decides to follow on any given day is still a mystery to me.

Every day I hope and I pray that Auberon comes back, and that I can convince him to take me on another walk so I can figure out a better route to the dungeons.

Stupid fool. Did you really think he would waste his time with you? The voice tells me once Maiya leaves. Part of me doesn't believe the voice because Auberon called me his 'favorite addiction'.

There could never be anything between us, just like there could never be anything real between Evander and I because of how we found each other. Not to mention that he's a Cintis, I'm not. I'm not here willingly, but that doesn't mean he hasn't tried to improve my situation.

Evander never did anything as special as giving me books or cook for me. But as I close my eyes, I can still feel his tenderness. The way his fingers trailed along my back, and the way he never wanted any distance to be between us behind closed doors. He'd hold me, kissing my forehead, and massaging the knots in my back without expecting us to give into passions.

It's been more than a week since I've asked Maiya for him. I can only assume that she either didn't run into him at all, or she didn't really pass on my message. I was hopeful that he'd come see me by now, or that he'd send some kind of message to say that he hasn't forgotten about me. But I realize the risks he'd face just to see me.

The door starts to rattle with the sound of jingling keys. I turn to the window, noting the sun blazing high in the sky. It's too early for dinner, and I've already been summoned today. Could it be another summons? Maybe Auberon has finally come to see me.

I watch the doorknob turn, unsure whether to feel excited by the prospect of a visitor, or dread needing to cater to the Queen. The door opens to reveal Valen. Only this time his hair isn't so disheveled, and his face isn't so red from coughing. I dare say that relief spreads through me instead, but it's quickly tainted by anxiety.

"What's happening?" I say, taking a step toward him.

Belve has been escorting me for my summons, never Valen.

"His Highness, Prince Auberon has ordered that you are to be escorted to the gardens to walk," Valen says mechanically.

"Oh?" I say, turning to face the window.

It's an odd feeling knowing that I can finally visit the area that I've been staring at for days. The odder feeling is knowing that Auberon arranged for it, which only makes me feel guilty about manipulating him to take me for a walk.

"Are you ready?" he says, and this time my gift lurches within me from the sound of the wheeze tickling his voice.

I nod, saying a silent prayer that my silk dress is appropriate enough to bear whatever the weather is like out there.

He moves to the side to let me through, and I pull out the map in my head, ready to start building on it. Maybe there's a secret entrance in the garden that leads to the city?

If it's secret, then how do you expect to find it? The voice remarks, and my shoulders slump in response.

My feet move in time with Valen's as he takes me down unfamiliar hallways with painted ceilings. It's similar to the story in the Temple; King Cyrus' journey with the sun. Only this time Niran is in the painting, soaring through the sky battling nameless dragons. His wings are darker than the night itself, as fire burns between his scales. As he soars through the sky, the flames on his tail drips onto the forest below setting it ablaze.

It is a curious depiction of the story of the Sun, because after the Dragon War only four dragons remain in the council, not the original nine; Shesha, King of Dragons; Leviathan, Queen of the Ocean; Chusi, Mother of the Earth; and Niran, Father of Fire. If Niran is fighting a dragon that isn't any of the other dragons from the council, that implies that King Cyrus was alive before civilization existed.

I have no idea if humans and fae existed alongside the dragons, but I know for a fact that there is no way cities or villages could have survived during that time. The Anzeth ordered their children to kill off the rest of the dragons for a reason; they were destroying the realm.

Either King Cyrus is a fallen god, or he commissioned this painting to keep us questioning the true extent of his powers.

Valen's cough drags my attention away from the painting as my power begs to help him.

"You know that smoking only makes your breathing worse, right?" I say softly in case he takes offence to it.

Part of me wishes that I carried a pitcher of water just to help him out when his coughs become too savage. If this were Belve, I couldn't care less. But something in my core tells me that Valen is different to the other Cintis. It's like the darkness is shining a beacon on him, telling me that he isn't someone to be feared.

"I don't smoke," he says roughly, attempting to clear his throat.

Taking a deep breath, I nod in understanding. "I guess the ash doesn't just affect mortals."

"You could say that."

I have to hold back a laugh at the irony that fae of fire aren't immune from the by-product of their own doing.

As we walk further, there's a pit in my stomach that starts to grow from Valen's response. If what he said was true, there would be more Fae with a cough as bad as his. I'm certain all mortals would be talking about it if that were in fact the case.

I don't get the opportunity to pry further before my breath catches in my chest. There it is. The outdoors. It almost feels like I'll be free once I step through the glass doors. But I know that it's just a misguided dream.

Valen picks up his pace ever so slightly to open the door. He steps back as I near, holding the door open for me. I have to blink a few times in case my eyes are deceiving me. I've grown so accustomed to getting shoved into places that this seems absolutely bewildering.

"Thank you," I mutter as I walk past, stopping as soon as I step over the threshold.

Taking a deep breath, I let the smog pollute my lungs and my gift rumbles to heal the damage. 'Fresh' is not the word that I'd associate with Audor's air, but it tastes far more liberating than anything else I could describe. It reminds me of the walks to and from work that Pa and I would take, or running around the market with a bare coin purse trying to get enough food to last my family a week. It almost feels like a promise that everything will be as it once was, and we can all move on from this nightmare like it never happened.

Valen motions for me to continue, and I move quickly with excitement, unsure where to explore first.

I walk around the garden until I stop in the courtyard by the single tree, glancing up at the struggling plant and its thin leaves outlined against the weak sun—remembering for a moment what it had felt like to creep through the Gardens with Evander before all of this had swept me up in its grasp.

I jump despite myself when a thick, soft voice—as hoarse as the cough of a sleeping hound—abruptly greets me from close by.

"Ay'ap, missy," it grunts gently, the old-fashioned greeting making me think suddenly and painfully of Pa, "See you enjoy t'light as y'should."

I turn my head and realize the old porter from the other day was resting in the shade of the wall nearby, beefy arms folded across his barrel chest, a long-handled woodsman's pipe clenched between his teeth. A rack of clothes was propped up beside him — clearly the Queen was planning several costume changes today.

I am at once intrigued by the old porter — he seems so out of place in this refined Palace — and at the same time I'm put on edge by his presence. If he's here, then her Royal Menace is surely nearby…

Realizing that I am yet to respond to his polite acknowledgement, I mumble a low greeting in return.

His gentle green-brown eyes twinkle for a moment in the wrinkles of his smile.

"Not to fret," he said reassuringly, "She'll not be back for a time. Be eased, lass."

"Thank you," I reply, finding a half-smile on my lips. The old porter seemed so much more 'real' than the others, like he's unbothered by the tyranny of the Empire. So out of place amongst the preening and pretentious courtiers and fawning servants of the Palace. His soft words, world-worn appearance, and laid-back demeanor combined into a certain rough charm that I feel very well-disposed towards.

I study him for a moment as he chews on the stem of his pipe again. It isn't lit—he probably doesn't want to risk the smell of smoke attaching itself to the clothes he is carrying today—but still, it suits him well. It goes with his sun-tanned and wind-wrinkled skin, his bushy whiskers and unkept sideburns, and the bulk and sweep of his muscles. It was clear he has won his considerable strength the old-fashioned way, though years of hard labor and toil, rather than the regimen of exercise and training that kept the Palace sentinels in shape.

I had spent too long looking, and this is not a man to miss the small details in a moment. His lip twitches up into a soft smile, and the twinkle returns to his gentle eyes.

"As out of place as a stag in a henhouse," he chuckles, "Aye. As are you, lass."

"Althea," I said impulsively, extending a hand in the old way—arm held low and palm upward.

As I expected, he responded instinctively, as familiar with the traditions as my own father was. His rough hand wrapped firmly around my own, his calloused palm and strong fingers carrying the sure and certain grip of what Pa always called 'a simple and honest man.'

"Rumner," he returns, then gives a snort as he realizes what I've done, "Ah, there's more to you than a wee slip of a girl, lass. See you know the ways of the field, and there's proper grip in that arm."

"I smithed for my father, before all this," I explain.

"Ah, there's truth there," he nods, "I was a forester and gardener once, myself."

Before we could say any more, Valen glances across at me and taps his spear on the ground. I'm out of time. I nod and hurry away, turning once to wave briefly at Rumner in parting.

Pipe in his right hand, he raises his left in a farewell gesture, and just before I hurried through the door I had enough time to realize the old woodsman's mangled hand was missing the forefinger and thumb entirely.

I wondered to myself what the truth *there* might be.

The sound of crashing draws our attention, and we all turn to see a young man, no older than twelve, jump away from a bush clutching his wrist. A sickle lays discarded on the ground with several droplets of crimson on it.

Without waiting for Valen or Rumner to respond, I run to the boy's side, ignoring Valen's curses.

"What is it?" I say as the gift pulses through me, ready to heal the mortal.

I look down at his hand wrapped around his finger. Blood starts to drip onto the ground and tears well in his eyes.

You're going to get caught, the voice warns.

Not if I do it quickly, I think, glancing back at the approaching men.

"Let me see," I say, opening my gift to him as soon as I touch his skin in an attempt to waste as little time as possible.

Prying his hands from his finger, I can see the wound in my mind's eyes. I force my gift to heal it quickly while I rub my finger over the cut, smearing the blood in the process. The damage is so deep that even the muscle has been torn. I don't let my gift even stop when the men hover next to me, studying the boys cut. As soon as his skin fuses together, I step away with a smile.

"You just had to put some pressure on it, the cut wasn't even that bad," I laugh awkwardly, hoping no one starts asking questions.

"Aye, yer silly lil' lad," Runner chuckles, looking at me from the corner of his eyes.

"I swear it was huge!" the boy protests, holding up his hand and staring at it in complete bewilderment.

"Could'a end up like my old man," Rhumner holds up his hand with the missing fingers, waving it in the air, "missin' yer hand!"

"But, luckily it was just a little cut," I interject knowing well that a 'small' cut would not bleed that much. He could have lost his finger.

"I think it's time we leave," Valen says, and I couldn't be more grateful that he's stepped in.

"Yes, I agree," I say quickly, failing in my attempts to hide how flustered I am.

I start to walk without waiting for Valen to make the first move, trying to ignore all thoughts of what might happen if anyone found out what I did. The King is trying to keep my healing abilities secret, there's no telling the extent he might go through just to keep it that way.

CHAPTER 16

A soft knock echoes through the room. Maiya. She walks in holding a golden tray with a blue leatherbound book sitting to the side of the tray. "I have dinner, madam," she says, placing the tray on the table without a word.

I breathe a sigh of relief when she says nothing about the boy in the gardens. I was stupid. I've put the boy, Rumner and Valen's life at risk for what I did. But truthfully, if given a chance, I would make the same decision.

Grabbing the book, I trace the silver detail embossed onto the cover of the book, and aimlessly flick through the pages to discern what boredom breaker I've been given today.

I scoff. Of course, the blue book they gave me is about Vesi. The waves on the cover should have been my first tell. Flipping back to the front page of the book, my full attention is peaked. The book was written around the time the First Treaty was drafted. This is the first time I've seen anything about what the other empires have done during the signing of the First Treaty.

Turning from page to page, my eyes skim over the words, waiting for something to pop out at me. A lot of the information that is in it is things that I've already heard from the Acolytes; anyone caught trespassing in their waters are taken and used as slaves, whereas slavery is illegal in Audor.

Ma would tell me stories about life before the War and the First Treaty. She said her mother told her, and now it's my duty to tell my own children—which I doubt will ever happen. She said the people in this realm didn't cower in their homes in fear of the Anzeth. The absent gods were nothing more than a myth that granted us life; a hushed prayer that left our lips in gratitude of a fruitful harvest. Everyone says that the War changed us. It changed everything. Now, a whisper of the Anzeth pushes people into an anxious frenzy, for one day, they'll kill us all.

Good, we all deserve to die, the voice adds.

Ignoring the intrusive thoughts, I mentally review everything I know about Vesi to compare notes with the book. The Acolytes spread fear to the humans during the library teachings, and sometimes the Priest mentions the viciousness of the other Empires. They said that when the Feraxians and Vesians started to run low on food, they'd round up mortals and slaughter them for the meat on their bones to feed their fae. But Evander said it's just a lie to stop mortals from trying to run away.

Just like he lied about caring about you, the voice taunts.

Shut up, I hiss back, *He's probably just busy.*

Yes, busy moving on with his life like you were nothing but a bad dream, the voice retorts.

Focusing back on the book, I flick through the pages of things I already know, my fingers stop as a section of the book catches my eye. Sucking in a sharp breath, I re-read the passage;

The Vesians poisoned the shores surrounding Feraxis and Audor to deprive their citizens of seafood and freshwater, and to besiege their warships.

My chest squeezes and my nails dig into the armrest of the settee as I read the passage over and over. The Anzeth have nothing to do with the poisoned water. Those drunken men by the tavern were right. Vesi is the real reason that most of the streams and rivers are now unsafe to drink from.

My fingers tremble as I continue reading through the pages. My eyes take in each and every word on the page as I start to question every single thing I know.

Moving to my feet, I start pacing the room as I continue reading. Before the war, the Vesians intercepted letters between Queen Avani of Feraxis to King Cyrus, changing the letter to say that the Queen is declaring war on Audor. Then, Vesian armies infiltrated Feraxian land and set fire to their crops and villages, and Audor took the fall. They were so fueled by their greed to acquire more land that their selfishness killed millions from every realm.

King Ryven was the first in the Empire to call a truce during the war, saying it's time for 'peace'. Cowards. It doesn't suggest that they were the losing side, only their greed caused enough carnage. Did he have trouble falling asleep at night knowing all the death he caused? Was this book suggesting that the First Treaty was an empty apology for inciting the whole war?

King Ryven is the reason the Anzeth are angry, because they are the ones that destroyed the realm to begin with. Millions of lives have been lost to their rage, all because of their greed.

An image appears in my head to unleash my darkness onto Vesi. Onto King Ryven. But something about the thought makes the darkness stir uneasily.

Why wouldn't the Acolytes preach that the Empire of Water is to blame for all of our suffering? They're the reason our people starve, and perish to plagues, and fall to their death because the earth cracks.

At five years old, I saw my first mortal slaughtered by the Priest on the Altar. I was traumatized at such a young age just because Vesi's greed consumed them and now mortals need to pay the price.

I slam the book shut and throw it across the room as visions of all the blood I've seen spilt in the temple surges through my mind.

I jump into bed and lay there for hours, unblinking, as I stare at the ceiling thinking about what King Ryven did. He single-handedly divided the entirety of Zephryine and caused a one-hundred-fifteen-year-long war.

He makes King Cyrus seem like a saint in comparison.

Maiya knocks on the door louder than usual as soon as sunlight streams through the curtains. She hurries in and begins ushering me out of bed and into the bathing chamber. Leaving my hair brushed and down my chest. True to Auberon's words, she shoves me into a silk maroon dress that covers every inch of my skin.

"What's the matter? Has something happened?" I ask, trying to push down the panic creeping up my spine.

"Queen Mellonia has requested your urgent presence."

What could possibly be so urgent for the Queen? The only possible answer I can think of is that she somehow impaled herself. If she did, I would make a conscious effort to make sure she doesn't heal from it. Unfortunately, if that were the case, I wouldn't be given time to get ready.

Belve and I break into a jog to get to the Queen's chambers. For once, his hand isn't around my arm in a death grip.

We nearly slam into Rumner, the old woodsman, standing silently nearby.

My heart leaps into my throat. It's surprising that he moves so quietly, given his bulk and girth. It was like having a bear sneak up on you in a glade.

"Ay'ap, lass," he grunts in half-apology, "See you there."

"Didn't see you," I grumble, softening my face into a smile as Belve's grip tightens.

He says nothing more, but simply twinkled his eyes in reply, and stands aside to let me and a scowling Belve pass.

We hurry through the hallways, by the time we arrive, a mist of sweat covers my forehead, and patches of the silk turn black from perspiration.

He rushes me inside. The Queen sits on the edge of the chaise, patting a tabby cat on her lap. For the first time, her eyes aren't full of rage. Instead, they're soft and solemn. Almost. Her hair isn't curled and braided in an elaborate updo. She isn't wearing a single item of jewelry, only her nightgown. She looks plain. Like a common Cintis.

"Althea, thank the gods you're here. Please hurry." I stare at her in shock. Did she just use my actual name and say please? She must truly be dying if she's acting with the slightest bit of decency.

Slowly, my feet shuffle toward her, and she pats the space next to her on the chaise to sit. She looks up at me with slightly misty eyes.

"Please, Althea, help him," she pleads, moving the cat onto my lap. He doesn't flinch at the movement. "Help him." My jaw drops. The evil Queen's frozen heart can be melted by a cat. "When I woke up this morning, he was barely moving. He didn't even want his breakfast! Blaze never says no to any kind of food. Tell me that you can do something? You have to do something." Her voice breaks slightly as she pleas.

She's acting so mortal. My heart softens at the tone, and every venomous word she has ever said disappears from my mind.

"I will do everything I can."

Running my hands through Blaze's luscious fur, my gift surfaces, burning hot with the need to heal. Something instinctual makes me pause to leash my gift, afraid to scare the cat away with my power. I close my eyes and slowly let the gift drip through my fingers, rather than plunge into their flesh like I would with a mortal or fae. The cat's blood is nothing like a mortal or Cintis. It's plain and primal. Driven by instinct and hunger. Blaze's blood moves slowly, and my gift urges me to move to the creature's core.

Something sits at its center, blocking the flow. My gift wraps around it, begging for permission to be used. I comply, watching as the clog disappears within my gift. Blaze moves beneath my fingers, jumping out of my hand the instant the stone is gone, sprinting to a bowl at the corner of the room.

Queen Mellonia jumps from her chair and claps her hands like an excited child. "Oh! You're better, Blaze! Come here to Mommy and let me give you a snuggle. You had me so worried, little mushroom," she coos, picking up the cat and nuzzling the feline's neck.

She seems so *normal*. She's like every single person I have ever seen interacting with their familiar.

This can't possibly be the same woman who berates me.

This woman has goodness in her heart and is capable of kindness, yet she intentionally chooses darkness. She wakes up and chooses to be wicked. It makes me wonder where she went wrong, and what could have happened to take away her spark of love.

Dots start to corner my vision like they did in the throne room, and I close my eyes hoping to get rid of the dots. That day at the Hole, the sentinels and acolytes were a blur of white dust. But now each individual dot seems to be filled with color and life. Could they be connected?

No, you're just going insane, the voice says.

Like a switch, she schools her features to look like the wicked queen I know and loathe, looking down her nose at me. "What are you still doing here? You're dismissed," she barks.

Every single thing she has said and done to me comes rushing back. I bow my head and rush out the door before she can abuse me for not curtsying.

Belve and I walk at a leisurely pace back to my chambers for the first time since I've arrived. It gives me the opportunity to take in the paintings and carvings, all holding a feminine touch to them. On this floor, the artwork is a lot less morbid. Here, there are other colors than red, gold and black.

Paintings of women plucking flowers and children dancing in the garden line the walls. Giant jewels, and clusters of gems decorating crowns are encased on podiums all over the corridor, rather than egotistical statues of the King.

I want to ogle the paintings, and study each and every piece of art. But I don't have it in me to. The Queen will never see me as anything more than an on-call healer, rather than an actual person. And I'll never be anything more than Auberon's prisoner. Or a miniscule part of Evander's fae life.

I'm one of the best blacksmiths in Audor, and I may never step foot inside a forge again. I've become nothing more than a glorified beautician.

Rounding a corner, Belve grinds to a halt and bows low at his hips like he's about to pick something up. Confused, I walk towards him and slam into a massive body. I stagger back and drop into the deep bow that mimics Belve's as the beast in my core growls at the man before me.

"Forgive me, Your Majesty, I did not see you," my voice breaks as I address the King.

By Audor's laws, I have assaulted a member of the Royal Family by touching his persons. A crime punishable by public execution.

His deep laugh resonates through the hall. "Man, leave us."

The sentinel bows once more before retreating down the hallway outside of earshot. I can feel his smugness as he leaves. A muscle in my back starts to pinch from bowing for so long.

A smooth finger snakes under my chin, forcing me upright so that my eyes are in the direct line of sight of the King's smirk.

"It is I who should apologize—thank you, even. For it is my pleasure to feel your body against mine," he whispers, and a wave of nausea hits me, making me shudder and try inch away from his touch.

He stalks me backward, and I try to stagger away. He doesn't speak, only stares at me. My heartbeat quickens to an agonizing pace.

Heat radiates from him in pulses that threaten to melt my skin if I'm not careful. A familiar scent drifts into my nostrils that makes my stomach churn. It smells like pine. The same pine that Maiya puts in my baths.

"You're a curious little thing," he purrs, moving his finger down to the neckline of my dress.

He tucks his finger into the tie around my neck, lightly pulling it down to reveal the skin beneath. With his thumb he traces the purple mark that climbs into my skull. I bite my tongue to stop from throwing up as goosebumps storm my skin.

"Truly incredible," he whispers, "More than fae, and so much more than mortal."

I whip my head aside, trying to get away from the stink of his hot breath. He cups my cheek and delicately turns me to face him again. I try to fight against it, but his strength is too much for me, turning his grip from delicate to hostile.

"Your skin is the most beautiful thing in the realm," he mutters darkly as he unties the silk from around my neck, and I push myself as far into the wall as I can.

The world seems to spin as every breath becomes more painful than the last. Bile burns my throat as a cold sweat drenches me, and the need to peel my own skin off my body becomes all consuming. It's as if his words have been tattooed into his flesh, incinerating my very organs.

He drapes my hair off my shoulders. "You should wear your hair up. Do not hide your delicious skin from me," he says in a throaty whisper, running his tongue over his teeth.

Cool air trickles onto my skin as the King slowly steps away and retreats down the hall.

CHAPTER 17

As if with a sixth sense, the brown-eyed sentinel that threatened to ravage me comes as soon as the King leaves.

Please no. Please not now.

There's a look of hungry satisfaction in his eyes as he devours every inch of me before grabbing me by the hair and dragging me through the corridors.

It's as if my mind has gone cold, and my natural flight-or-fight instincts have been stolen by the King. I've become a doe in the forest, waiting for the hunter to make his kill. I'm powerless and drained, too shaken to pull out of his firm grip.

"I liked you better when you resisted," the sentinel says as he yanks open the door to my prison and my body scrapes against the wall, burning my skin.

The scent of pine penetrates my nose, and I have to blink again when my mind fools me into thinking it's the King. The small voice in my head screams at me to move or push back, but I can't. I'm just so tired.

"You're not so feisty now are you, *mortal?*"

His fingers tighten around my throat. I want to kill him. I want to make him suffer. I want the darkness to do its worst on him. But I can't. I'm helplessly paralyzed in my spot. Somewhere in my mind, I can hear the voice yelling at me that I'm not helpless because I *can* fight back. But I'm not sure how much I have left in me.

"Get off me. Please," I choke out as my resolve starts to settle in. If he kills me, then he kills me.

"I think it's finally time that I test you," he purrs, and like a switch, the chill in my mind melts and the beast in my core roars.

No. I can't let him win. I have to keep fighting. I can't let a Cintis think that this mortal body is his own personal toy.

As he starts to drag me to the bed, five years of training in the forest or bedroom with Evander comes out. Howls of pain fill the air as my knee buries itself deep into his groin. His howls of pain. He folds in on himself, and I can't stop my hands from sinking my fist into the space just below his ribs, watching as his form drops to the floor.

"You bitch!" he whimpers, covering his groin with his hands like a makeshift shield, "I'm going to make sure you can't walk because of this." At least that's what I think he says. He's too winded to talk properly.

The darkness flutters, matching my own triumph—a feeling more intoxicating than the adrenaline coursing through my ears. But the beast begs me to do more. It's begging me to kill him. My power surges through me, wanting to heal him from his pain, but I force it back down.

Let him suffer.

A false wave of confidence rushes through me and I drop to the ground with him, digging my knee into his chest to keep him still. His breath cuts short as my fingers thread through his hair, yanking his head back mere inches away from mine to look me in the eyes.

"Try as you might, Cintis, the King will do far worse if you try to tamper with his goods," I hiss, and bile floods my stomach as the words leave me as I am flashed with the memory of his body pushing against me.

Kill him! A choir of voices growl in my mind, making me jump off him.

It's not *my* voice that has been haunting me up until now. No, these voices are far more frightening. Ethereal, yet ungodly. Powerful, but weak. Neither man nor woman. Speaking in perfect harmony in my head.

I snap my gaze back to the sentinel as another groan escapes him, feeling on edge from the multi-tonal whisper.

"You're lucky that's all I'm doing to you. Now get the fuck out of here," I snarl, bringing myself back to reality.

"I'll find a way. No one will be able to save you." He winces as he brings himself slowly upright and shuffles out of the chamber.

I stare at the closed door with my heart wrenching a hole through my chest, until the smell of pine washes over me when I finally take in my surroundings and the eerie silence within the room.

And all at once, a tsunami of emotions hits me and I yank at the laces of my dress with shaking hands. The fabric flutters to the floor and I stumble over it running into the bathing chamber—it stinks of pine.

Of *him*.

Nausea threatens to overwhelm me, the smell overpowers the scent of my lunch on the table.

Snatching a brush off the shelf I scrub. I need to get the imprint of his skin off of me. I have to get his breath off me.

I have to.

I need to.

I scrub my cheeks until they're as red as his hair.

I scrub until my skin burns to the touch. The cold air does nothing to diminish the feel of his heat prickling all over me. I throw a nightgown on, ripping the side in the process.

Tears well in my eyes but refuse to fall. I barely make it to the rubbish tin in time before the contents of my stomach empty.

Hot. It's too hot.

My skin feels like it's boiling, incinerating me from the inside out. It's not just my skin, it's every single part of me: lungs, heart, mind.

Cold. I need cold.

My knees buckle, dragging me to the ground with it. The cool tiles kiss my skin as my tears fall into my hair, dampening the tile beneath my neck. I want to feel the cold in my bones. I need to.

Seven in, eleven out. Cold sweat washes over my body as my mind reels into a tornado of blacks and grays, and my thoughts are nothing but a blur.

Colder. I need the tile to be colder.

The blur from my mind seeps into my vision as the world spins, and the dots that have been haunting me reappears. I squeeze my eyes shut, pushing my cheek against the tile as I roll onto my side. It's still not cold enough.

My hand slaps over my mouth to contain my yelp when I open my eyes. They're still there. The dots are still there. Colors I didn't know existed live within the dots, making up the furniture and the spaces between. Pulsing to a phantom heartbeat. Breathing in harmony

Look at how crazy you are. You're even seeing things, the voice teases.

It's too hot, is all I can manage to think.

No, it isn't. You just have no control over yourself.

The beast wakes, crawling out of its shell, dipping its claws into my gift. My forehead pushes against the floor, trying to consume the chill of the tile. Like the only way I can stop my thoughts from racing is if it's frozen.

Colder. I need it colder.

The darkness threads within my gift, braiding together. My body feels like it's floating, being held by the dots that seem to vibrate even harder. What's happening? Why is it doing that?

I want my mind to stop. I want it to stop reeling as it obsesses about what could be happening to Ma and Pa. I want it to stop replaying the King's words. I want it to stop reminding me about every single thing that has happened in my life. I want to stop hallucinating dots.

I push my forehead harder to the tile. *I need this frozen!*

At once the dots beneath me start to change and the braid of raw power wraps tautly around my chest. Webs of white radiate from all the points where my skin touches the tile, turning it ice cold. Without thinking I scramble away, feeling like the braid of power rips apart, and the webs of white disappear like it never happened.

"What was that?" I manage to say through a choked sob.

First you're an abomination because of your skin, now you're also imagining things.

No. That didn't just happen. I was imagining the ice. I'm just confusing myself with the pattern of the tile.

Telekinesis is one thing, but summoning ice is the power of a Lympha, the water fae. Believing that I might be a powerful water fae living in the Empire of Fire is a crazy enough thought as it is.

Yanking my body from the floor, I jump onto the bed and shove my head into the pillow and scream. I scream and scream until the pillow is completely soaked with my tears. I scream until my body goes limp from exhaustion. I scream until I hear the lock to my chambers click.

Without thinking, I scramble for the knife, and slide it behind my back as a mop of red hair appears in the doorway.

At the sight of my disheveled mess, Auberon snaps his gaze around the room like there might be someone here. "Are you okay? I heard screaming?"

"Fuck off," I say, backing up into the pillar.

He's his father's son. I told you that he just wants to make you his whore, the voice hisses in my mind.

"You'll never make me your whore!"

"What? Althea, no, did something happen? Talk to me." His voice is low and calm, but his body is tense, like someone trying to tame a wild beast.

"Is that why you've been spending time with me, my *Prince*? Get close to the prisoner and force her to do your bidding?" I tighten my grip on my knife, ready to use it if he comes closer.

He lifts his hands up in a hesitant surrender as concern paints his features. "Of course not. All the time I'm spending with you is because I want to get to know you, not because I'm about to force you into anything."

"You expect me to believe that? Your father and the sentinel in one night? Do you really take me for a fool?" I say, darting my eyes around the room as if the sentinel is about to jump out of the shadows.

"What do you mean 'in one night'? Did someone touch you?" His eyes darken.

"I'm a fucking prisoner, of course your kind has been trying to *touch* me since I got here." I laugh like it's the most ludicrous thing I have ever heard.

Who should I tell him about? Belve, the brown-eyed sentinel from the other night, or the King and Queen? I don't want to mention any of them in case this part is a test.

"Where did this mention of forcing and being a whore come from, Althea?" There's a threat in his tone, and I feel like I'm back in the throne room being interrogated.

He takes a step towards me and I go rigid. "Althea," he repeats when I don't answer, "did someone force themself on you?"

My eyes must have given me away because the curtains behind him light on fire.

"Who?" he snarls.

I flinch and his expression softens again, but his eyes promise death.

One by one, everything rushes back into me, like I'm reliving every second all over again; the feeling of the King's skin on mine, the sentinel's threats, the dots, the ice… No. Not again. I can't spiral again. I told myself that I can't let him see me cry, but it's too late. Tears well in my eyes and the need to scrub my skin raw comes flooding back in.

You've become weak. Pathetic. You aren't strong enough to hold onto your mask. Look at you know, crying in front of the Prince *of Fire*, the voice bites.

"A sentinel," I hesitate, struggling to say the words in case the brown-eyed sentinel's threat becomes a reality.

"What did he do?" There's a fire raging within his eyes far more vicious than the flames climbing up the curtains.

"He—he choked me and cut me with his dagger, and he—" I stop as tears well and run down my cheeks. Auberon nods his head slowly, urging me to continue. I look at him, and the care emitting from every fiber of his being like it's wrapping me in a cocoon of safety and taking the pain away. "The sentinel threatened to ravage me." At the words, a sob rips through my throat.

Instantly, the curtains behind him explode into blue flames, and I hurry back with a yelp. Auberon rips his gaze away, waving his hand to extinguish the flames. In a blink of an eye, he's out of the room, slamming the door so hard the room shakes, and a glass falls off the table.

I sit in stunned silence, staring at my empty hands.

What did I think would happen when I told him? Did I expect him to sit through the night and comfort me, or tell me that he'll arrange for another sentinel to stand watch? No, of course not.

He is the Prince of Cintis, and I'm just a mortal.

Stupid.

So stupid.

∼

"Madam, are you ill? Should I call a healer?" a small voice squeaks behind me as I lie on the floor a week later. I've done nothing but spend every second of my day working myself up into a frenzy of emotions that my body has struggled to keep up. Every time I try to harness the darkness, it does nothing but laugh, watching me question whether the ice really did happen.

I've let Pa down. I haven't figured out how to use the darkness. On top of that, I'm under the same roof of a perverted king, and I could be imagining that the darkness created ice.

The only good thing that has happened is that I've stopped seeing the brown-eyed sentinel's shadow on the other side of the door, and the Queen hasn't done anything worthy of note when I'm summoned to play servant.

I can't help but burst into laughter that she would suggest calling a healer for me. After dressing me in sheer *for him*. Dousing me in the smell of him, *for him*. She made me his harlot and I was too blind to notice.

Like the Queen said, I'm pathetic.

My nails dig into my naked thigh, to rein in the rage that wants to lash out at the servant. I need to remind myself that this is exactly what Maiya is—a servant. She's an unwilling victim in the Empire's games. Everything she does, she does because she has to. Because her life depends on it.

She's probably noting the marks on your body to relay to the King, the voice taunts.

I ignore it. Deeply inhaling through my nostrils, then exhaling so vigorously that the world feels like it's spinning.

"No, that isn't necessary. Thank you Maiya. Is it dinner time already?" As the words leave my lips, I frown at the sight of the burgundy light streaming into the room. The sun is getting close to its place of rest.

"No madam, you have another summons." I don't bother correcting her to call me Althea. She isn't here to be my friend.

"Am I scrubbing the floor again?"

"I don't know," she says, bowing her head.

She retrieves a dress from the bathing chamber. The same dress from the night I ran into the King. I fight an urge to retch, although I have nothing left to spill.

She's just doing her job, I have to remind myself. *She's just doing as she's told.*

She holds the dress out and helps me into it before leaving the room without speaking. I close my eyes and take deep steady breaths, trying to ignore the smell of pine, or the way the fabric scratches my skin, or how it did nothing to stop the heat from the King's body emanating into me.

I've been scrubbing my skin raw ever since that night. The red that plastered my skin just hours ago has already faded, leaving me the same unearthly shade of pale.

"Are you ready?" Valen asks, emotionless. I nod, and he moves aside, giving me space to walk past him.

Turning down the familiar corridors to get to the Queen's chambers, Belve clears his throat and angles his head towards the opposite side of the Palace.

My breathing hitches.

He's taking me to the King!

He's going to make me his concubine. He's going to force himself onto me.

No. Don't think like that. He just needs healing.

It isn't a believable truth. A king that sits on a throne and plays with women in his spare time would have no need of my healing powers.

My gaze darts to every single painting on the wall and every mark on the floor, imprinting it into my memory to record in my book later.

"Is my father still in the dungeons? I'd like to see him," I ask, wanting to break the silence to ease the tension running down my spine, and keep my legs from stopping. The question turns the air sour as his lips form into a thin line, suddenly uncomfortable.

"No," he whispers like there's more he wants to say, but doesn't.

"No' he isn't in the dungeons, or no I can't see him?"

"No," he says. It's a single word, but the way he says it tells me a whole story. He isn't saying it in answer to my question, he's saying it in warning from any prying ears.

I nod, understanding his response.

I pause for a moment to collect myself, hearing the incessant and sharp tones of the Queen's attendant haranguing someone nearby. Not wishing to risk a confrontation, I glance at Valen and step back into a doorway. To my surprise, the sentinel hesitates for a moment and then quietly joined me.

"No sense being in the way," he mutters.

The voice grows louder and two people come around the corner to hurry down the hall. I recognize them both from my summons. The Queen's attendant was hovering like a nervous mother bird around Rumner, the old porter, as he carries a hefty load of what looked like expensive glass ornaments—each one nearly as tall as a person.

My heart darkens for a moment as I see his mangled hand struggling to contain the delicate yet heavy burden.

That bitch, I think to myself, *she could have any number of strong and healthy men picking up after her. Why does she always pick on him?*

It doesn't sit well at all with me that the Queen should constantly have the poor old Rumner carrying her things. It was like she chose him deliberately because of his injury, so she could watch him struggle and have an excuse to berate him further.

They passed us in a rush, neither one noticing us off to the side.

And then they were gone, leaving behind nothing but the fading sound of her voice, and the faintest traces of leather and grass in the air.

Valen moves from the wall first, picking up his pace from the delay. There's still another question resting heavily in my mind, and this may be one of the few chances I have to find out.

"What happened to the night sentinel?"

"He's dead," he says darkly.

"Oh. Did the earth take him?" It's one of the most common causes of death for a Cintis: being consumed by the Anzeth when they make the earth crack. Second to war.

"No," he says, "The Prince did."

Reality comes crashing back on who the man is that cooked for me; who read stories to me. He's the Prince of Cintis. He's a Prince of a breed of fae who kill for sport and lie to themselves by saying it's for the gods. My stomach knots when I think of how close his body was to mine a few nights ago. How his fingers grazed my skin as he tucked the hair behind my ear.

He could have killed me. But instead, he killed *for* me.

A large door the color of the Prince's hair swings open, and a bright smile stares back at me.

Speak of the devil.

"You're dismissed for the night," Auberon says without looking at Valen.

The sentinel bows deeply. "Thank you, Your Highness."

An excited gleam twinkles in Auberon's eyes and he gives me a grin to rival that of a child's. I can't return it. Deep within his gaze I swear I can see a war brewing within. It's barely noticeable, but I can tell all the same, because I know now what I'm looking for.

He beckons me inside the room and my feet refuse to move. My heartbeat accelerates as I watch his calloused hands run through his hair nervously.

"What am I doing here?" It comes out on a breath, barely audible. Confusion flickers on his features as he cocks his head to the side.

"I sent a missive to the Queen that I require your services because," he puts his hand on his heart and pretends to stumble, "I have the most grievous wound from training."

He motions for me to come inside again, this time I take a single step. The playfulness leaves his eyes. Not the type of mischievous glimmer like in Evander's eyes, but a genuine innocence.

"You're safe with me, Althea. Please come inside." A hint of sadness taints his sunny disposition. It almost sounds more like an order than a welcome. Walking into the room, my mind reels with all the possibilities behind the purpose of his summons.

I freeze as soon as I see the room. It's unlike anything I've ever seen, and the complete opposite of everything else in this hectic realm.

Everything is plain. Exactly what Audor is not. There's no marble, no patterns, no black, red, or gold. A white stone coats the walls. Circular arches lead into a variety of rooms: a parlor, bedchamber, study, and bathing chamber. Right across from the door, beige and cream pillows decorate the circular bed on a raised dais. A lace net cascades from the center of the ceiling as high as a two-story apartment to encircle the bed.

"Welcome to my chambers. Make yourself at home." His gaze falls heavily on my exposed neck, making me feel naked without having fabric to hide under. "Wait right here," he says as he rummages for something in another room.

Soft candlelight makes for the only decoration, it floods the floors, leading up the stairs of the dais, spilling onto small shelves jutting out of the wall. There are at least a hundred white candles all over the room, casting the place in all the hues of gold and yellow.

"Here," he says. I flinch as he wraps a gold tie around my neck and shields my hair over my shoulders to cover more of the skin. He smiles to himself. "That's better. Didn't I say that you look striking in red?"

I study every inch of him with a delusional expectation to see the sentinel's blood all over his perfectly pressed white tunic. But there isn't even a single piece of string or hair out of place.

You're in Audor. Killers know how to hide in plain sight, the voice says. He may be a killer, but there's no doubt in my mind that he won't try to kill me. He wouldn't do all of this if he were.

"I've been wanting to see you all week," he whispers softly as his gaze penetrates mine with an indescribable hunger. The feel of an imaginary blade against my cheek chokes me when Auberon's heated stare reminds me of the sentinel from that night.

If he's been wanting to see you all week, he would have. Don't fall for it, the voice warns.

I can't help but feel glad that the sentinel no longer walks this earth. Does that make me as terrible as the Prince? How could this man claim to have thought about me when the sentinel's blood soaks his hands?

Actually, I take it back. The thought that the Prince killed the sentinel brings me nothing but joy. But I need to hear it from him. I need to know that it's really true.

Like he's awoken from a trance, he inhales sharply and leads the way into the sitting room. "How did you like my books?" he asks.

Is he such a monster that he can remain so calm after murdering a man? That sentinel deserved to die, but how can he be so detached from it?

"What happened to the night sentinel?" I blurt. Auberon whips around quickly, sparing me a cautious glance.

"What do you mean?" he asks carefully as he walks back to me.

"I know you killed the Cintis that used to stand outside my door at night." My voice drops to a whisper as his eyes darken at the mention of the fae.

"No one lays a hand on you and lives. Death was a kindness he did not deserve." A growl that makes the flames flicker and erupt towards the ceiling sounds from deep in his chest. "I should have ripped his cock off and fed it to him for even *thinking* about doing such a thing to you."

"You killed him. *For* me?" I reiterate, wanting to make sure that I heard it correctly.

"Yes. I will kill any man who tries to get in between us. And I promise you this, Althea, I would kill him all over again if I could," he says in a tone that could cause an earthquake. This can't possibly be the same man who reads to me as I lay in bed, or who tells me that I'm his addiction.

When did he decide that there is an 'us'? My plan didn't involve any sort of 'us.' I just want—no, I *need* something to start making sense.

I turn away and slump on the couch. Blood rushes through my ears and a heavy feeling shakes my stomach. He killed one of his own men, for *me*. Somehow, it isn't the death that bothers me anymore, it's the fact that he went to such extremes in my name.

Auberon drops down on the couch opposite me, and we sit in silence as the candle flames die down to a normal height and the wax pools onto the floor. I can hear his ragged breathing as he tries to calm himself, and I watch as the tightness in his shoulders eases with the fire.

The shadow of the flames dance along the ceiling. I miss home. I miss watching the candlelight from the dining table flicker along the walls as I fall asleep. I miss bickering with Pa and eating Ma's questionable cooking.

"What is happening with my parents," I finally say, trying to get the image of the sentinel out of my head.

He sighs, offering me a reassuring smile. "They're the same as the last time we spoke about it. Your mother has been cooking up a storm in her new place and giving it to some of the people on the streets," he chuckles softly, "Your father is still in the cells, but he is warm and fed." The warmth returns to his cheeks and the sparkle returns to his eyes. Golden strands of hair glow under the light of the candles.

"He has bad lungs. I need to see him. He could die if I don't help settle his lung. He has never gone more than a few days without my gifts," I plead.

My chest contracts as I think about what would become of us if he died all because I couldn't help him.

"Please believe me when I say that I am looking after your father. The Palace healer regularly visits him and has given him medicine to ease his coughs." There's a look of trustworthiness in his eyes that eases my anxieties ever so slightly.

"I'd like to see him either way. I have done everything the Queen has asked. I haven't tried to run away. I haven't caused any trouble. I've been trying to harness my power every day," I beg even though I hear how hollow my plea sounds.

"For you, Althea, I will try to make it happen. But it's not a promise I can make." He hesitates before continuing, "I know exactly what it's like to be away from your family—for them to be taken from you and feel like you're to blame for it because you weren't strong enough." Sorrow bleeds through his voice and my heart breaks at the sound. It's sorrow that can only be felt by someone who has experienced it themselves.

"Did you lose someone?" I ask, leaning forward in my seat.

"Yes. My brother, Quintos."

His shoulders slouch, and my power lurch, wanting to reach for him. I didn't know he even had a brother. I know the King had children to the previous Queens, but they all died along with the Queen at the time. It makes sense now why the Queen's womb had so much damage. It couldn't have possibly been just because Auberon was a large baby.

"How did he pass?" His vulnerability makes me want to hold him and tell him that I understand—that we can work through this together.

Instead, I grip the cushion beneath me. There can never be an 'us.'

Even if I stay their prisoner, I will never be anything more to him than a passing phase.

He shakes his head. "I shouldn't have brought it up. Please forget I mentioned it."

He rises from the couch and flicks back the curtains. The glow of the moon illuminates the silhouette of his profile against the dim candlelight that brightens his eyes.

I stare at my fidgeting hands, unsure what to say. A heavy weight sits on my chest knowing I've upset him with my question. Having the thought of someone you lost resurface in your mind is an anguish I can't even begin to imagine. It's a pain he would have kept hidden away all these years.

"I have to apologize to you for my failures," he sighs, and his form seems to deplete even more. "I've failed to keep you safe, and to keep the world from getting to you. It seems King Ryven has heard whispers of you and has been sending missives enquiring about your abilities." My stomach churns at the mention of the Vesian king. "He only knows that you have the ability to heal another person, but it doesn't appear that he knows the extent of your powers. He also knows about the situation with your *skin*." He chokes on the words as if it hurt him to say.

My breathing grows frantic and the couch groans underneath my steel grip keeping me upright. What could the King of Vesi possibly want with me?

If King Ryven takes me away, I'll never see my parents again. King Cyrus will have no reason to keep them alive.

"What's going to happen to me?" Panic drenches my voice as I speak between shaky breaths. In a heartbeat, he's next to me, tucking my head into the crook of his neck, rubbing my back in slow motions.

"I'm not going to let anything happen to you," he whispers into my hair, "I'll fight for you. I told you that you and your family will be safe as long as I'm around, didn't I?"

I nod in answer. He did say that. And he's proven he's been doing just that. He's taken care of Pa and he's made sure Ma has been kept safe.

"I take care of what's mine," he says barely above a whisper, and a shudder runs down my spine. I become acutely aware of every single part of our bodies touching. From the graze of his knee against the thin fabric of my dress, to the warmth of his hand on my thigh. My legs squeeze together as his thumb draws circles up my inner thigh.

I don't know when I started to be his, but I don't know if the thought upsets me. Part of me knows it's problematic. Still, the other part of me is telling me to ignore it. Even though he killed the sentinel, I feel safe around him.

I let the smell of him consume me, and I relax into his touch. Opening my legs ever so slightly to his roaming thumb. His pauses. His breathing becomes labored. Soft lips lightly brush against my forehead, and the heat of his breath has me suppressing a groan.

He's the Prince *of Cintis. Pull yourself together,* I plead with myself.

I push away from him, telling myself that I will breathe easier once there's distance between us. As soon as his warmth leaves me, an emptiness pierces my heart.

A knock comes from the door, and the smile he wears melts to one of authority, making me forget about our heated moment.

"Enter," Auberon orders, grabbing a glass of wine from beside him and taking a sip from his glass without looking at the sentinel that walks in.

The sentinel holds a wooden chest trimmed with gold, with a golden lock latching it together. His eyes don't roam the room as he walks, his eyes don't even meet mine, he looks at the spot directly before the Prince. He stops, standing at attention when he makes it halfway to the spot he was eying.

"Speak," the Prince commands.

Everything about Auberon is reserved. I can't see any light in his eyes or the honey in his voice.

"I have the crystals for Queen Mellonia's birthday, Your Highness," the sentinel bows as he speaks.

Gods, how old is the Queen turning?

"Show me."

I edge closer to Auberon as the sentinel starts to march to the place that he was eying. Curiosity alights within me as to what Auberon is gifting to his mother. That's a lie, I'm just curious what sort of gifts a Queen will receive from her people's coin.

Bending down on one knee before the Prince, he places the chest on his lap, retrieving the key tied onto a golden chain around his wrist. He starts to unlock it, and I find myself leaning closer without realizing, moving back before anyone notices.

The sentinel bends down, staring directly at the floor as he raises the chest up to the Prince. Auberon flicks the latch open without a single emotion written on his face, and stares at the three crystal flowers laid carefully on three silk cushions.

On the left, hundreds of rubies radiate from the onyx center, like blood dripping from the core. In the middle, clear petals layer and wrap around sapphire, cocooning it like it's being protected by a storm. On the right, a blooming flower, purple petals twirls with white like a tornado. Black thorned vines wrap around it, as though trying to destroy it, but still it remains beautiful.

"Middle one," the Prince says after a heartbeat, like he knew his answer before being asked the question.

"Yes, Your Highness." The sentinel bows his head, raising back to his feet.

"Leave the rest there," Auberon nods to the table under the window.

"Yes, Your Highness."

As I watch the sentinel lowering the chest onto the table and carefully pick up a pillow holding the blue flower, all I can think about is drawing a dagger inspired by the purple flower.

"You're dismissed," Auberon says, leaning back in his seat like the sentinel isn't even here.

The sentinel bows, marching out of the door, carrying the crystal with steady hands. I suppose that a Queen would get nothing less than crystals for her birthday. The only question that crosses my mind now is how much blood was spilt for that crystal?

"I would have picked the purple flower," I whisper, watching as the crystal catches the light from the candles, illuminating the purple within.

Auberon rises from the couch and walks toward the chest. Picking up the purple crystal he holds it in the light, studying it like he's never noticed it before. His steps are slow, calculated, as he makes his way to me with the crystal in hand. The crystal looked ethereal lying delicately on the couch. Now, it looks like an afterthought cradled within the Prince of Fire's hand.

It feels like each step is slower than the last until he stands a whisper away from me, so close that the hand is *almost* touching me.

"Then it's yours," he says so softly, that I could be fooled into believing that this isn't the same man that spoke moments ago.

Taking my hand in his, he gently places the crystal flower in my own. It feels so delicate within my hands, like it may break if I breathe too quickly. But at the same time, it feels like it can be carried through a battle without so much as a chip. It doesn't look right sitting in my hands. It doesn't belong with me.

"Thank you, Auberon, but I can't accept this," I say, shaking my head.

"You can, and you will."

Any hint of softness is replaced with the power that I heard him speak with just before.

Placing a finger under my chin, he gently tilts my head so that I look up at his piercing onyx eyes. His lips are so close that I can practically taste it. All I want to do is close the distance, to feel him against me. To feel safe in his arms.

"The way you look at the flower is the same way I look at you," he whispers, "Keep it."

His hands move to close my fingers around the crystal, and all I can do is nod — too speechless from the gesture. Mortals can only dream of laying their eyes upon such a beauty, let alone to own it.

"Let's get you back to your room," he smiles.

And still, the only response I can give him is a nod. Nothing I could say would surmount to the emotions brewing within me. Awe from its beauty. Gratitude for the gift. Pain from the betrayal I'm causing Evander and every person in the Remains for accepting this gift.

I let him lead the way, following closely behind him. I can't bring myself to tear my eyes away from the crystal. I swear I can see the colors move and swirl, tangling with each other under the light. What would Ma and Pa say if they saw me holding it? Would they be happy for me, or would they tell me how it was made off of the blood and sweat of mortals?

Servants and sentinels bow to Auberon as we walk past. He barely notices them, shooting longing looks my way when he thinks I won't notice. Neither of us utter a word, which I'm grateful for because that means I can study every corridor we pass, and every turn we take.

The familiar sight of my door comes into view.

I pause before walking past Auberon and into the room.

"Thank you, Auberon," I say, hoping he can't hear the conflict within my voice.

"You deserve it," is all he says as I walk in, and the door closes softly behind me before the lock clicks into place.

Sitting the crystal delicately on the windowsill, I stand back, admiring the way the purple deepens into a violet under the moon.

Changing into my nightgown, I try to ignore all thoughts about the crystal to refocus on everything the Prince has told me. I sprawl onto the settee, fidgeting with the book about Vesi. All the books he's given me hold some sort of purpose. He gave me this book because he wants to prepare me for whatever is to come.

I've become a pawn in the politics of the realm.

My stomach twists as I think about all the lives I have seen the Priest take at the altar, all because King Ryven wanted land. It's hard to imagine mortals being treated worse than they are in Audor. I can't even begin to comprehend the sufferings of the mortals in the Empire of Water.

The mortals of Vesi fear the fae not because they kill mortals for sport, but because they feed on them when food runs low.

My mind reels, thinking of all the things King Ryven could do to me if my gifts fall into his hands. Would he use me just to continue the cycle of cannibalism through healing a mortal, just for them to be eaten again? The thought makes me lightheaded.

Not only do I need to figure out how to use the darkness to save my parents, but I need to be able to use it if I'm taken by Vesi.

Moving to the settee to stare out to the garden and the giant tree off to the side, my heart aches remembering how Auberon looked. I can't imagine losing a brother or a sister.

Sudden realization hits me.

Quintos.

The name the King threw at Auberon in the throne room. I see why the thought of his brother makes him so uncomfortable; he's in competition with someone who is no longer alive.

Understanding ripples through me as I realize why Queen Mellonia wanted the stretch marks to disappear. To her, the stretch marks aren't simply a flaw to be erased. Rather, in her mind, healing the outside would somehow heal the inside. She sees it as a scar holding her back from moving on with her life. Because to her, it's a constant reminder of what she lost.

The hinges of the door creak open and close, quiet footsteps enter into the room. I figured Auberon would let Maiya have the rest of the night off as well because he expected to have dinner with me.

"Thea." A deep voice rumbles through the room.

"Evander?"

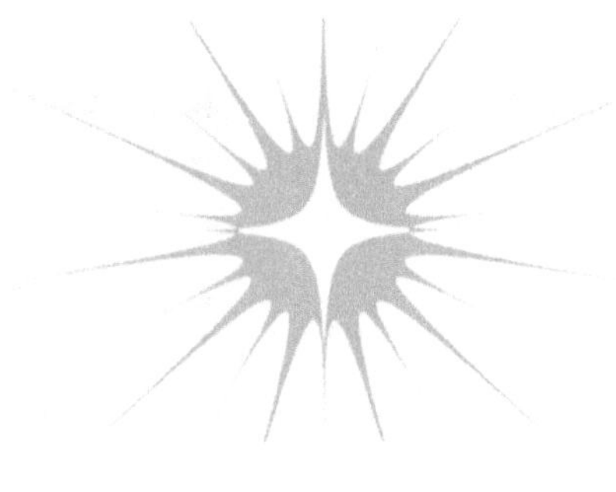

CHAPTER 18

"Basio saepe volam, cui plagam diligo solam.
Many kiss the hand they wish to cut off."
— *George Herbert*

Leaping into his embrace, I laugh as Evander wraps his arms around my waist and twirls me in the air with him. My chest tightens as I breathe in the smell of cedarwood on him. A blissful wave of familiarity and comfort crashes into me.

His arms feel like home. I've missed him. I've missed the feeling of being safe in his embrace. I've missed being able to escape reality with him.

"Gods, I have been so worried," he breathes into my hair, pulling me away from him to assess every inch of me. "Are you okay?"

My core squeezes at the genuine worry lacing through his eyebrows. "If you're not careful, I might think that you missed me," I tease, wishing away this whole nightmare never happened, and that we are back in his room *pretending*. My hand reaches up to his disheveled beard. I've never seen him grow anything more than a light stubble.

"Miss your verbal abuse? Absolutely not, Princess." The mischievous grin I know all too well dances across his lips, and for once I'm ecstatic to see it. Gods, and that wretched nickname even brings a warmth to my stomach I haven't felt in a while. "What do you think of the beard? I figured I might grow it out so you can make a scarf out of it to keep you warm and you can always remember me."

"Oh please, that sad excuse of a beard won't be anything more than a handkerchief." I joke right back, welcoming the light atmosphere making its way into the room—fooling ourselves for a treasured moment into thinking that our argument and my imprisonment never happened.

His hands stay wrapped around me in a gentle grip. Sitting down on the settee, he pulls me onto his lap, tucking my head against his chest, and I tangle my legs between his. His thumb caresses my cheek as he looks into my eyes. It feels like we're back in his bedchamber at Fornous Manor—giggling and gossiping as if everything wasn't crumbling around us. Somehow, he always made me forget where we are and the lives at stake. But that's what he does: he helps me forget about real life.

It's different now. I've just come from the bedchambers of the man Evander has spent the past five years telling me about their rivalry. Gods, even Auberon's gift sits in this room tauntingly. I'm worried about how he might react if I told him that the Prince and I have formed some kind of friendship. Will Evander see our friendship as betrayal, or will he sleep better knowing that I might have a fighting chance with the Prince on my side.

"Have you seen Pa?" I question, hugging him tighter and bracing myself to hear his answer.

He shakes his head, and I tense in his arms. He is quick to add: "However, I've made sure he's the most well cared for prisoner in all of history. I have some sway over the sentinels—I guess being the General's son has its benefits." I push away from him slightly at his response.

"I thought the Prince was taking care of him?" Auberon had said he made sure that Pa had food, blankets and medicine.

"That's beyond me, I haven't seen much of him since you arrived in the Palace," he shakes his head softly. "I will do everything in my power to keep your family safe. I promised you the day you first came into my home, and I am going to hold that promise until the day the Anzeth take me."

I didn't think he remembers saying that to me. I never wanted to admit it to him, in fear that he wouldn't feel the same, but being with him made me feel alive. In fact, it was the only time that I ever felt alive.

The voice in my head usually likes to remind me that he's a Cintis, and that I've spent the past five years uncertain about whether he actually cares about me any more than a mere secret friend. Maybe it's just a side effect of my own self-esteem. But tonight, those voices stay silent, letting all the doubt I've ever had over our relationship wash away. There's no telling what the King might do to Evander if he were caught here. It was selfish of me not to realize that sooner.

"After our argument, I thought you were going to tell your father about my gift." My fingers tremble at the memory of the day at the Hole, and he brings them to his lips and kisses each knuckle.

"Never, Althea," he growls tenderly, moving his face closer to me. "I'd never betray you. What will it take for you to accept that I care about you? In my one hundred years of life, you are the best thing that has ever happened to me. You mean more to me than the sun itself, and I'm afraid I won't survive without you."

"I don't believe you," I whisper under my breath, thinking he won't hear.

Planting a kiss on my forehead, massaging my hand, he carries on saying "Your gift is capable of so much more than you realize, princess. Something about you attracts souls that need healing. Every time I'm around you, every part of me feels lighter, like you've somehow breathed life into my spirit."

I wrap my arms around his neck, letting his words settle in. We sit there, holding each other tight.

"Don't let it go to your head," I whisper, suppressing a wicked smirk, "but I missed you." A devilish smile stretching from ear-to-ear breaks across his face. "Only a little bit though," I say before he gets too cocky. Still, his warm laughter blankets my skin, and his lips crash into mine in a breath-taking embrace and I melt deeper into his arms. My soul feels lighter with the touch of his lips and it's like nothing in this world matters but this kiss.

He lets go of me, and I instantly want his lips back on mine. He stretches his arms into the air and folds them behind his head. "Nope, I didn't miss you at all. Which one are you, again?"

I playfully hit his chest as it shakes with laughter, admiring the way the oil lantern casts a shadow over his smirk.

"It turns out when you're not there, I can actually get a good night's rest without hearing you snore," he challenges, raising an eyebrow, "I always used to think that you tied a herd of oxen up outside my house when you visited. It took me months to realize that wasn't a stampede I heard each night."

"I snore? *I* snore?! You dare!? You make more noise than a team of smiths hammering at their anvils—I never got enough sleep for you to hear me snore!" I taunt right back. He knows exactly how much he snores. I would remind him every week.

Well, at least I used to remind him every week.

Suddenly somber, it strikes me that our night-time rendezvous will never happen again.

I realize that we will each need to be our own escapes from reality from now on.

Sensing my sudden change in mood, he wraps his hands around my shoulders and leans companionably against me.

"I tried to come sooner, but no one would let me near your chambers," he says reassuringly, "They didn't care about me pulling rank either... I'm not sure why, but for the first time tonight when I wandered over I saw that there's no one standing outside."

"Yes, Prince Auberon brought me to his chambers. I think he expected me to stay until at least dinner time." I try to make light of my concerns, but he tenses all the same. The waves of pleasant relief that had washed over us at our reunion suddenly seem to run colder, and I can practically smell his eternal jealousy staining the air between us.

"Why were you in Auberon's private bedchambers?" His eyes turn dark and the muscle in his jaw ticks.

"He sometimes comes to spend time with me here. Auberon just thought that we could go to his chambers for a change of scenery," I say, wanting to show Evander that Auberon is on our side.

"Oh, so you're both on a first name basis now? So, he's thrown all his formalities aside just to try and bed you?" he says through gritted teeth.

"At least someone came to visit me," I say without thinking, making him wince.

I shouldn't have said that. He's been trying to see me—he's risking it all just to be here. Just like he risked exile by spending time with me for the past five years. I shouldn't treat him this way. He doesn't deserve it.

I take a deep breath, squeezing his hand reassuringly. "I'm sorry, I shouldn't have said that. I know you're risking so much by being here. Auberon has been nothing but kind to me. He's made sure I've been fed, he gave me books to read to fill my days, and not to mention he actually stood up for me after a sentinel threatened to ravage me."

It's like he sucked all the air out of the room. "A sentinel did *what*?"

"Auberon killed him for what he threatened to do to me. He made sure that the sentinel will never lay a hand on me again," I say as calmly as possible, wanting to stay in our earlier state of delirium. He untangles me from him and we both jump to our feet.

"Do not fool yourself, princess. He only did it because he doesn't like other people playing with his property," he says darkly.

I am *not* just property. I am neither his, nor Auberon's despite any reference to 'us' or 'mine.' What I don't appreciate is being told who I can spend my time with, my parents did that my entire life, and I'm not going to let someone else dictate that despite being a prisoner.

"He was going to let Pa and me free, but my parents would never be safe if I'm around. There's no need for any jealousy," I say gently, not wanting to escalate things further than I already have.

"I'm not just jealous," he says with eerie calm. "He is not a good man, Althea. There's so much you do not know about Auberon, and more that you don't understand in this realm."

"If there's so much that I don't know, then why don't you tell me? Why don't you warn me about every gory detail of this empire so I can actually be prepared? Better yet, why not tell me how Auberon is somehow an awful person," I say too sharply, that I might as well have slapped him. I sigh, sadness soaking me that the one time I've seen Evander, we end up arguing. "Help me be prepared."

Clenching and unclenching his fist, his eyes burn into mine, but he doesn't say a word.

"Nothing?" I huff disappointedly.

He thinks I've become Auberon's property. He's telling me not to trust the Prince, yet won't tell me exactly why. Evander would get annoyed that the people of the Remains think that he's an awful person just because he's General Fornous' son, yet now Evander stands here accusing the Prince without providing any explanation further than 'he's the King's son'.

Folding my arms across my chest, I shake my head. "Exactly as I thought, you're all talk."

I can tell he is counting to ten in his head. "Trust me, Thea; you need to be careful around him. Don't ever let your guard down when you're near him. Your training won't be enough to take him on, but if you need to, aim for his throat and *run*. Whatever you do, don't let him think that he owns you."

Mine.

Auberon's words echo in my head and I swallow the lump forming in my throat. He already thinks I'm his, doesn't he? I shake my head. No, this is Evander's final attempt at pushing me away from the only person in this Palace who has shown me a shred of kindness, all because of their rivalry. I won't let his childish competition with Auberon change anything, because Auberon and I have our own issues to work out; namely that I'm *his*.

I try to move the conversation in a different and less dangerous direction "Auberon promised to protect my parents as long as I'm here. Whether or not I trust him is irrelevant, because right now I only care about what is best for my family. I need to get Ma and Pa and take them out of here somehow," I beg.

"Are you crazy, Althea? How can you trust that? He's just trying to keep you here so he can use you for his own gain. Tell me, Althea, why would they keep you alive, living like *this*, if they just wanted a beautician for the Queen?"

I shove my hands behind my back, scratching the inside of my wrist. *Crazy*. Does he also think that I'm going crazy? My jaw tightens, unsure whether to feel angry for saying that, or frightened that my concerns are coming true.

Ignoring the comment, I refocus. I'm meant to find him and ask him to get Ma and Pa out of here. "Please Evander, get my parents out of Ignis. They won't be safe if I'm with them. If I stay put and behave properly, then the King might leave them alone." My breath shortens as I feel my desperation choking me. The plan to keep my parents safe hinges on being able to harness my powers.

"No. There's no way I'll leave you here if I'm getting your parents out. I'm not about to leave you with *him*. If I'm getting one of you out of here, I'm getting all of you out of here," he says with utmost certainty.

"This has nothing to do with Auberon. This is about making sure Ma and Pa are safe," I say, trying to get past my frustration.

"This has everything to do with *Auberon*. You're choosing him over your own family," he bites and I drop my hands to my side.

How dare he say that? How dare he think that every single minute of every day that I've spent here hasn't been to keep them alive? If I weren't so worried about them, I would have already tried to escape and not worry about the consequences.

"I am choosing *them* over myself. I am sacrificing *my own freedom* to make sure they're safe. Leave Auberon out of this. *Please,* get my family out of Ignis."

"He's gotten in your head. He's lying to you about keeping you safe, and you're a fool for believing him. You're acting like a stupid child."

I'm not getting through to him. He can't get past this obsession with Auberon.

"I've heard enough, Evander. Thank you for looking after Ma; now please leave."

"I don't want you to get hurt by him. Just promise me you'll be smart around him," he presses and cups my face in his hands. All the anger in his eyes is gone, only raw worry and traces of hurt remains.

I slump into his touch, wanting nothing more than to fast forward to the day that my family and I are out of here. "My parents are my primary concern. The King wants me to display the same power I showed at the Hole, and I don't think I can do that again. He said that he'll kill them."

"I'm sorry for getting angry at you. I promise you that I will never let it get to that. I will never let the King get to your parents. You need to believe in yourself, Althea, your power comes from you. You control it. It doesn't control you. I believe in you, princess." If only it were that simple. I doubt he would be saying the same thing if he knew about the darkness. "I've spoken to your Ma."

"When? What did she say? How is she? Is she okay? How did you manage to get her to trust you?" I ask quickly. I know I've already asked Auberon some of those questions, but I want to hear it from Evander.

"I told her that I'm a friend. I had to assure her by mentioning your love of corn soup and your three favorite mugs just to convince her of that. I told her that I've been making sure you're safe while in the Palace. She wanted me to tell you that once you get out of here, she's going to make her best batch of corn soup." Imagining the three of us sitting at our little table brings a smile on my face. "I've warned her that I'm in the process of finalizing some plans and coin to get all of us out of Ignis."

"And she agrees?" He nods in answer. "What's the plan? I've drawn up a map of the Palace and if you can give me a more comprehensive one to get to Pa then—"

He shakes his head, stopping me from continuing. "You won't be able to step foot inside the dungeons without being caught now that they have more guards on post because of King Ryven. We need to—"

We both stop breathing as footsteps echo down the corridor. With silent feet Evander creeps into the shadows of the bathing chamber.

The cold tile chills my bones as I drop onto my stomach to check for shadows on the other side of the door.

"The coast is clear," I whisper just loud enough for Evander to hear.

Helping me to my feet and pulling me into his arms, his lips meet mine. "I wish I could stay longer, but I need to leave before someone catches us and any hope of escaping will disappear. I'll be back. I promise."

"Thank you for everything, Evander." I nod against his lips. He continues to hold me for a few more seconds before dropping his hands to his sides and disappearing back into the Palace.

CHAPTER 19

"Oderint dum metuant.
Let them hate so long as they fear."

— *Accius*

Sleep didn't take me in the night. The events of the day compounded and suffocated me more cloying than the ash that litters the street.

I always prayed to the Anzeth that things would change, and that my family could get out of the rundown Remains. They listened—but not in the way I wanted. We've been separated and forced to wonder if the Empire is lying when they say we are all alive and well.

I believe Evander when he says that my family is alive, but I still want to see it for myself. As for his claim about Auberon, I don't know what to believe. Since before this whole thing, he was hellbent on shaping Auberon as the bad one in their relationship, but it's all because he can't compare to royal blood. I was the one thing he thought he could keep from the Prince, and his fairytale idea has come to an end.

Light streams through the window as the King wakes the sun from its rest. The sun is red again today. Over the years, a red sun has become more and more common. The Acolytes say the sun bleeds every time the Anzeth wants to remind us of our flaws, and it's a time of repentance and forgiveness. Followers of the Priest will flock to the temple on days like today, kneeling on the floor in prayer until their knees bruise.

Maiya's soft knock breaks the silence before she tiptoes inside and settles down, clearing her throat. Slowly, I turn on my side to face her. Maiya's arms flood with pools of fabric and a giant basket filled with jewels and brushes and cosmetics.

"Good morning, Madam. I will bathe you today."

"There's no need Maiya, I'm fully capable of washing myself. Please rest. You don't need to concern yourself with something so simple," I say, pulling the blankets off and folding it in a neat pile at the foot of the bed. She's learnt to let me do it, she's figured out it gives me some semblance of routine so that I don't go completely mad.

She shakes her head. "The King has requested that I do it," she whispers, tugging at the end of her hair. I hold in a gag as I recall the scent of pine. He's trying to make me his pet; I can't let that happen.

Fighting it means that Maiya will get in trouble. I don't doubt that she will receive severe punishment if she doesn't do what was directly ordered by the King. She's just as much a victim in this as I am.

"Very well," I sigh, picking up the fresh bread and remembering the leftover bread Pa would always be given from the bakery. It never smelt this divine, but the memory makes my stomach ache all the same. I place the bread back on the table while she readies the bath.

"You should eat it," I say once she returns to the room, motioning to the pile of food. She looks at me hesitantly, like I might be tricking her. "I promise I won't tell a soul. The Palace chef is an amazing cook."

She bites the inside of her cheek, eying the food like it has enchanted her. I can see the wheels turning in her head, but all I can focus on is how loosely her clothes fit her, and how frail her wrists are.

"I'd hate for it to go to waste. No one will need to know, I swear it," I urge.

She shakes her head, pulling her gaze away from the plate. "Thank you, Ma'am. I'm not hungry." It sounds as if it physically pained her to say it, making my heart break.

"Even just some bread, it'll help keep your energy up for the rest of the day." I don't stop the desperation seeping into her voice.

"No thank you. Please, the bath is ready," she says like she doesn't want to continue the conversation.

I nod, following her into the bathing chamber. Slipping out of the gown, Maiya looks away as I step into the warm water, holding my breath so as not to smell *him*. My hair floats around me in the water, lapping against my skin as I fidget from having her in the room. I feel so vulnerable.

Get over it, the voice groans.

She starts by scrubbing under my nails and feet, and I choke as she retrieves the pine-scented soap from the shelf and rubs my skin with it, combing it through my hair and pouring oils into the bath to make me smell like pine.

As I step out, she wraps a large fluffy towel around me. She motions me to the table as she always does to do my hair. She moves the mirror in front of me so she can see her work as she goes.

I *really* look at my face for the first time in weeks. My cheeks are fuller than they've ever been. Life has seeped into my hair, and it's like all signs of the life I had as a mortal in the Remains have disappeared.

My blood runs cold as my eyes move down to my neck. *It's moved.* The line that has trailed down the right side of my neck and between my breasts since the day I was born isn't there anymore. Instead, a dark purple line meanders from the side of my chest, around my collar bone and over my shoulder.

I felt like my skin was moving in the Queen's bathing chamber last week. Was it then? We always thought the lines on my body were an indication of an illness affiliated with my gift, but maybe we were wrong. I shudder to think what it might mean.

Maiya does my hair *up,* in a twirl of elaborate braids and knots. A circlet sits in the middle of my forehead, dripping rubies between my brows. The King's demand about my hair echoes in my mind.

Just as she had on that first day, she places the dress on the ground and gestures for me to step inside. Something between a cough and a gasp chokes out of me as she tightens the corset. It's more elaborate and revealing than any dress I've been made to wear.

The skin on my chest pebbles right before it makes way to a swirl of gold, crimson, and onyx fabric. Every single mark on my arms is on full display. The tiny straps crossing my chest does nothing to hide the new lines winding over my skin like thunderbolts. The dress pushes my breasts tightly against my chest, making them spill over the fabric. A belt with the Empire's symbol wraps around my waist above an explosion of satin, embezzled with scales running down half the skirt, merging to a design that looks like butterfly wings.

It's a dress fit for a Queen. Or a concubine.

I feel exposed in every way. The King has decided to take ownership of the secret that has locked me away from a real life. The long sleeves and high necks have been my crutch for so long, that I didn't realize that they were actually my armor.

It feels wrong on me, like I've sold myself to the Empire completely. The pristine fabric is too lavish against my bruised-looking skin. I don't belong here.

Belve clears his throat, drawing me away from my unnatural appearance. And my feet drag against the floor as I follow him out.

My breath hitches as we take the same route as last night towards the Prince's chambers, and Evander's warning rings through my mind. Dressed like this, with the Empire's emblem branded around my waist, there's no denying that my being belongs to Audor.

I spot the dragon-headed golden sentinels guarding the throne room before my heart registers where we are going. I want to stop walking. I want to stop this descent into hell. I don't want to see what games they have in store for me. Not when the sound of Elex gargling for his last breath still lives in my mind. And as they open the great doors, I swear I can still hear him.

My fingers dig into my skin to force my uncooperative feet forward.I almost close my eyes as I enter in fear that his body may still be there. But I know he won't be.

The raging fire feels hotter than last time, but the 'uniform' they've wrapped me up in is what actually burns my skin. Three men loom at the top of the dais. General Fornous still wears a scowl, while the Priest is his usual predatory self; hunched and ready to pounce.But no Auberon.

Heels clicking against the marble, Belve drags me to the foot of the dais, pushing me into a deep bow.

"Look at me," King Cyrus' voice whispers against the roaring fire, making me wince. I roll my hands into fists as my gaze climbs up the stairs to the King. He has the same look on his face that a starved person would have before they take their first bite. "You look truly delicious, Althea. I knew that dress would be ravishing on you."

Every single part of me wants to run back to the room and hide beneath my bed waiting for Evander to come back and erase the King from my mind. If I could scrub my mind from all my memories of the King, I would.

"Don't you feel so much better now that you aren't hiding your skin from me?" he purrs. I don't answer. Nothing I say will please him, and I think I might just vomit all over his pretty dress if I do.

"When your King speaks to you, you answer," the Priest hisses as a whip of flame cuts through the air in front of me.

Clearing my throat, I manage to speak just above a whisper, "Yes, Your Majesty."

He leans back in his throne, stroking the armrest like he did to his concubine. I can feel the heat of his gaze pierce into the plunging neckline of my dress that dips down to my navel.

"You've been such a good little prisoner, Althea, I thought it prudent to reward you for your behavior," the King says in the same way the Priest does before he takes another life.

The throne room door creaks open, and the clanging of chains dragging along the ground punctuated with ragged coughs sends a cold rush through my veins. My gift thunders through my body, ignoring the dread within me and forcing me to turn around.

A woman stumbles in with a collar wrapped around her neck like a dog, and my fingers ache to touch my bare neck. A long pole held by a sentinel attaches to the golden buckle at the back, so she is kept at a distance at all times.

She has the plague.

This is a sick, twisted reward.

The sentinel shoves her deeper into the room, and her feet drag along the floor, stumbling as she attempts to keep up.

"Let her go!" I snarl, moving my feet into the same fighting stance Evander helped me master.

Don't bother acting like a martyr now. You've never stood up for anyone before, the voice says.

He pushes her to the ground a few feet away from me. Her blue lips and the dark blue veins climbing up her neck triggers my gift, sending it into a frenzy as it rattles within me like a caged animal.

"Heal her," the Priest barks.

Edging closer to one of the pillars, I shake my head in denial.

So you're happy to yell at them to free her, but you won't use your gift to save her? the voice says snidely.

Panic settles deep within me. I've already played my part in convincing them that I can't heal anyone facing certain death. If I save her, they'll know that I lied. Everything my family and I endured over the past few weeks will be for nothing if they find out.

"I can't go near her!" I beg, trying to let the frantic beating of my heart seep into my voice. "She'll pass her sickness on to me!"

The comment makes King Cyrus and the Priest howl with laughter. Is this just a game to them? A way to trick me—to force me—into submission. Or do they want me to die?

"Typical mortals. Always so stupid and quick to assume," the Priest shakes out his opulent sleeves and pins me to the spot with a single glance. "I understand the Anzeth didn't gift you rational thought, however, do try to use your brain for once, *girl.* Now tell us, have you ever been sick before?"

Shit. There's no getting out of this one.

He knows that he has me. He knows I can't get out of this one. He knows that every single one of the bruises and cuts his men has inflicted upon me have healed. They need only ask Belve or Maiya. I don't want them to know about the extent of my gift, but I can't keep letting people die when there's something I could do about it. I've always wanted to help people with the plague. This is my chance to make a difference to at least one person's life.

Before I step forward, a daunting thought crosses my mind; will life in a prison outweigh death? I study her brown cloak, her woolen socks, and face clear of soot and dirt as if recently cleaned. I realize then that I recognize her as one of the Queen's maids.

"Perhaps you need more encouragement," the King says, gesturing to the sentinel at the entrance, and a face I know all too well moves from around the corner. *Pa.*

His foot drags along the floor as his arms wrap around two sentinels marching into the room. A strangled gasp leaves him when we lock eyes, "Thea!"

"Pa!" I yell, running towards him. A fiery rope wraps around my waist, whipping me back into strong arms. Elbows flying, and feet kicking, my fingers reach out, in an attempt to dig into my captor's neck. Belve grunts as my broken nails cut into his skin.

"Leave her alone!" Pa coughs.

He's wearing something I've never seen before. Soot doesn't coat his body. They did take care of him, but that doesn't change the slouch in his back or the navy blue under his sunken eyes.

"Silence." King Cyrus' command vibrates down my spine like a spell spilling ice into my blood, making everything freeze in place. "If you don't cure the woman, perhaps you'll be more inclined to use your curious little talents to help your father."

"Leave him out of this." I buck my back, attempting to break loose from Belve's hold.

"Bring him forward," he says, folding his hands behind his back. "Pull that same trick that you used at the forge, and your father dies."

Sentinels dressed in black slither out of the shadows, moving from behind the pillars. Each arrow knocked is aimed at Pa.

I expect to be blinded by red at the edges of my vision. To feel the darkness consume me as I let the dots cloud my vision and flicker every single person in the room out of sight. But nothing comes. Only an empty feeling deep within. A primal pull draws me towards the woman, like something greater than the magic in my veins is calling me to unleash my gift on the woman.

"What will it be?" Nonchalance and intrigue play in the King's eyes.

"Don't do it, girl," Pa's raw voice pulls at my heartstrings. I can't let them kill him. Without the darkness, I have nothing to defend him.

I don't even know if they will just kill my father and the woman as soon as I've done what they want me to do. Or if they'll even let me live. I know it's a vain hope, but if at least two get out alive, it'll be worth it. As long as Pa is one of the people left alive.

"I'm sorry, Pa. I have to," I whisper, feeling like I'm breaking my parents' promise again.

Endless tears stream down the woman's cheek. I wonder if she thinks I'm a monster that only a single tear falls watching her depleting soul. But there's no hatred in her eyes toward me. His tired eyes travel my skin and I see a look I know all too well. Defeat. Hopelessness. Exhaustion.

It's the look of someone that knows that they are nothing more than a pawn to their Empire.

"Promise me," I say, staring at the King, "If I heal her, promise me that you will not bring her or Pa any harm. You will let them both go." He considers for a heartbeat then nods. But not at me. He nods at the sentinel holding Pa.

The noise from the roaring fire drowns out. The feel of my beating heart disappears. All that's left is the sound of cracking. Then, cries of pain. Pa's cries of pain.

I scream, wanting to go to Pa to heal him. Needing to rip the sentinel's hands from him for what he did. But I don't move. Imprinting into my mind the image of the bone in Pa's finger mangle beneath his skin. It's my fault. I disobeyed.

"I'm so sorry. I'm so sorry. I'm so sorry," I mutter.

Tears stream down my face as I look at Pa, cradling his hand to his chest, groaning and hissing between strained breaths.

I did that.

"Don't worry, you can disrespect me nine more times," the King says in a bored tone.

I turn back to the King, look at him through clear eyes. There are no dots in my vision, no beast pushing me closer to the edge. Nothing.

"I'll do it," I say quickly in the delusional hope that I'll get to heal Pa afterwards.

Another snap rings through my mind, and Pa cries louder than he did before. I slap my hand over my mouth before I say another word and hurt Pa even more.

"Eight more times. The correct address is 'Your Majesty'," the King says slowly and calmly, yet all I can seem to hear are Pa's whimpers.

"Yes, Your Majesty," I nod quickly, tasting the salty tears that seeps in between my lips.

I rush to the woman, kneeling and let my fingertips glide over her burning forehead, pushing loose strands of hair off her skin.

"My name is Althea. What's your name?" I whisper low enough that only she can hear.

Blood stains her hands as she coughs, "Mase."

She pauses for a moment, looking over my shoulder at the towering Cintis with their fingers wrapped around the hilt of their sword. "Will it hurt?" she whispers, staring me in the eyes as her tears fall faster.

"Not one bit. Close your eyes and this will all be over soon, Mase." She nods her head shakily, slowly closing her eyes until her breathing softens. My hand finds its way to her sternum, while the other rests gently on her forehead.

My eyes drift shut, and my head dips forward. I breathe in deeply before letting my gift move freely into her, but what it really wants is to help Pa. It plunges into her like a torrent, pushing out of my hands more violently than it has before. She winces at the impact. I try to grasp hold of the gift, but it fights back like it has a mind of its own. My lungs burn as the air rampages back into me.

A broken melody fills the air. A choir singing tunes of sorrow and pain, like an animal stuck in a cage.

My gift moves from her heart, freezing as the darkness takes over. It plunges into the ground, spreading over the room like wildfire, escaping through the front door to cover every inch of Audor—searching for the voice that calls it.

A voice that sounds like home.

The woman starts to buckle beneath me, and I force my muscles to move away from her and I try to snap my eyes open. I don't move. My body doesn't belong to me anymore. It belongs to the gift.

My fingers shake as the darkness nears the voice. My breath comes out more rapidly and my head goes light. I can hear screaming coming from somewhere that feels close, yet so far away.

The beast suddenly drops onto a luminescent floor, like a knight kneeling before his King. I gasp, looking through the eyes of the darkness.

This is the Palace of Air.

CHAPTER 20

"Ite, inflammate omnia."
Go, set the world on fire
— Ignatius of Loyola

Clouds climb around the nine towering thrones that seem to reach beyond the sky. Thick layers of dust dress the thrones. Cobwebs spindle around the legs, crawling up the pale backs covered in gems and chipped paint.

I seem to be floating high above the mountains and within the clouds. The ground below seems to move as we float, overlooking rivers and forest.

Bliss. It feels like bliss. I breathe fresh air into my lungs and it feels so wrong without the combination of ash. Ecstasy trickles into my muscles as my being relaxes and all I can think is that it feels *right* to be here, but so wrong at the same time.

From each cardinal direction, a different colored light pours into the room.

To the east, an explosion of red devours the sky, raging over volcanoes and charred trees. A black shadow is cast over the empire, drowning the lands in ash and poisoning the air with smoke. The Empire of Fire.

To the west, deep purple clouds roam lifeless over barren mountains tinged with yellows and browns. A once fruitful land, reduced to rotten trees. An Empire that smells like decay. The Empire of Earth.

To the south, navy cascades through the sky, dancing with thunderous clouds painted with lightning above a raging ocean. In the midst of the chaos, there is a single speck of silver that seems to call my name, calling me closer like a siren. Every part of my being is weak to that call, and the darkness has no intention of denying it.

The north is the most sorrowful of all the sights. Nothing dwells there, only a cold emptiness. No clouds, no mountains, no color. Lifeless. An empty hole for prayers to come to die. A forgotten glory for the destructive gods.

Help us.

Voices whisper from all around me. They're ageless, toneless neither male nor female. I urge my gift to shift around the room to find the voices, but it refuses, dropping lower to the floor. Is it trying to hide something from me?

"Who's there?" I manage to get the beast to say for me.

Save us, daughter, the voices boom at once.

"Ma? Pa? Is that you?"

I try harder to get the darkness to search the room, to locate the voices, but instead it forces me to look at the floor.

You are the only one that can save us. Hurry.

Their voices come from everywhere in various levels of screeching and wailing. Far away, I can feel Mase convulsing under my hands, yet it's nothing compared to the fear in the voices that fill my head. I can taste their pain—their desire to be liberated, like they're choking.

"Who are you? What do you want from me?" I cough out as ash fills my throat, tearing me away from the fresh, sweet air that has soothed my lungs. My body begins to shake and something solid wraps around my center, trying to yank me back.

Free us, daughter. Only you can save us all.

It feels like an iron fist is wrapped around my stomach. *Why am I here?* I want to scream. I try to open my mouth, to voice my words, but it feels as if my chest is ripping apart and fire has replaced my vocal cords.

Who could possibly have the power to take control of my gift—to drag me to the gods' Palace and bring me to my knees before the throne of the —

The Anzeth.

The Anzeth have summoned me to the Air Palace.

It makes sense. Nine thrones for the nine gods.

Is this throne room meant to be the *great* Empire of Air? The home of the gods that rampage the realm with death for their nonsensical vengeance.

As a child I'd look up at the sky, picturing the gods living in splendor and looking at all of us from their gilded thrones as they decided who to kill next. I thought white light would follow them as they moved, granting an illusion of innocence. The last thing I'd imagine is this hollow shell of *nothing*. Which raises the question, where are the gods?

The darkness slams back into me, tearing over the realm and flinging me through the air until my back collides with cold marble steps and my head smashes into the hard stone. Black spots cover my vision, making my head spin.

The sound of yelling and coughing is white noise at the very back of my mind. I can't figure out what they're saying or even where the sound is coming from.

Just in time, I roll onto my side and my stomach empties out before me. Leaning my head against the cool floor, I let oblivion take me in its comforting, black embrace.

~

A frantic buzz vibrates beneath my skin, uneasy with the need to move, *to search.*

Memories of clouds and sorrow trickle into my mind, stirring me awake from a fitful slumber. I try to pry my eyes open, but a throbbing ache makes me want to stay in this cocoon of rest.

Voices echo in tune against my skull—deep and warm, unlike the wail of despair in the Anzeth's voice. Anger seeps into their hushed whispers, and they breathe my name with a possessive fury.

"She doesn't deserve any of this," a familiar voice argues.

"What happens to her is *none* of your concern," A deep-set growl rumbles from afar. It drags me from the sleep that my being craves. My body protests as I grip the plush blankets around me, unsure whether I want to pull it closer.

Quiet steals through the room. Wherever I am, I'm being watched, and now, my watchers grow silent.

A hand cups the back of my head, cradling me against warmth and the bed dips beneath our weight.

"*Shh*, stay still, Althea, I've got you," Auberon's honeyed voice warms my insides, soothing the fear that poisons my exhausted mind.

"We should leave and let her rest. She exerted too much power trying to help that woman and ended up hurting herself."

Annoyance slips into Evander's voice, and the fear returns. He warned me to stay away from Auberon, yet here I lie in his arms. Will this change his mind about helping me and my family escape?

"If you would like to leave, Lieutenant, there's the door. No one asked you to be here. I'm not going to leave Althea alone after what happened." There's a lethal calm in Auberon's voice, and he seems to take Evander's silence as acceptance.

Evander said I can't let him believe I'm his in any way, but again, Auberon is showing a level of care toward me that I wonder if I deserve. All the secrets and lies that I'm keeping and have told, and he's done nothing but stand up for me in a way that he didn't need to.

My heavy eyelids flutter open to see the familiar sight of my chambers. Evander's stare burning into Auberon, and the guilt of how Evander feels weighs just as heavily on my chest as the thought of what happened to Pa in the throne room.

"Pa, what happened to him?" I rasp. The sound of his fingers snapping rings in my mind and all I can wish for is that I kept my mouth shut.

"He's safe. I've sent the Palace healers to him," Auberon says assuringly.

I shake my head, wincing from the ache. "Let me heal him, please."

Pa is hurting because of me. Pa is being punished *because of me.*

"I promise you that he is being looked after," Evander says, the truth burning in his eyes, but there's a warning to them, telling me not to ask anymore questions.

Sick, injured, alone, and cold. I keep saying to myself that I'll save my family, but all I've done is make things worse.

"I was so worried about you. What happened back there?" Auberon's concern makes me want to tell him everything.

Shut your mouth, don't believe him for a second. If you tell him everything, he'll just think that you've gone crazy. Utterly and completely crazy, the voice says.

For once, I agree with the voice in my head. No one can know that the Anzeth spoke to me. Or at least I think they spoke to me, and I really have gone crazy imagining the room turning into dots.

Assuming that the Anzeth really did speak to me, and that the royals find out... in the worst-case scenario, the Priest takes it as a sign—and not the type of sign I want any part in. With his penchant for killing, I'm certain he will claim that the gods are asking for me to be sacrificed. If I told them what I saw, the Priest may decide that I'm better kept alive, which would be a greater punishment than being sacrificed. There's no telling the amount of security the King will add if the other empires discover that I have a connection to the Anzeth. Any hope of escape will be gone.

"I've never tried anything like healing the plague before," I croak, craving water, gesturing to the pitcher to give myself time to think of a believable excuse.

I want to tell Evander about the Anzeth. He always finds a way to make everything feel better. He'll probably crack a joke about it, we'll laugh, and we'll continue our night like it was nothing more than a bad dream.

What would Auberon do if I told him? Would keep it a secret under lock and key until we figure out what is going on, or will he use it as a way to redeem himself from the shadow of his dead brother.

Evander jumps into motion, quickly making his way to the pitcher like my life depended on it, fumbling with the glass and pouring water with unsteady hands.

The man cradling me in his arms, tenses, and at the same time I do too. Auberon snatches the glass out of Evander's extended arm before I can reach it.

Evander's fists turn white as he watches his Prince tilt my head back, lifting the glass to my lips. I don't have the energy to push it away. I don't have the energy to do anything to stop this petty rivalry.

Maybe one day I can tell them what happened. But that day will not happen until they can both have some semblance of maturity regarding something as trivial as a glass of water.

"I can do it myself," I grumble when Auberon starts to tip the glass.

"Let me take care of you," Auberon says with a voice more delicate than a rose petal. His chest rumbles beneath my shoulder as he pulls me tighter against him, grasping my chin so that I drink.

Neither of us react to the sound of Evander's boots pacing up and down the room with his arms crossed tightly against his chest. He clears his throat loudly, and his jaw ticks as anger more potent than any Feraxian wine emanates from him, which only makes the pain in my chest ache even more.

A warm hand cups my cheek again, gently tilting my head up so that I meet Auberon's eyes. "Forget about him. It's just you and me here. I want us to focus on *you*. I want you to tell me everything that you need."

There's that word again. *Us.*

My gift lurches within me like I'm being called toward the Prince. I look up at him, completely mesmerized under his gaze, like I might find the answers I'm looking for within them. It feels as if an invisible cord has reached from him into me—like a force greater than the both of us combined has threaded together.

The darkness vibrates within me to a hum coming from the cord wrapping us together. Somewhere in the back of my mind, I can picture the floating rings in the temple. It's like we're in one of them—a state of ecstasy as our bodies are feather light, carried into the sky.

"We should let her rest," Evander's voice snaps us out of our trance. I can't help but flinch as the image disappears, and the full weight of my body seems to crash back down on me. And the cord vanishes.

Auberon's finger taps on the bed lightly, at odds with his other hand curled into a fist. He's trying to remain calm, regal even.

"Your presence is unsettling her. It will go easier on everybody concerned if you leave so I can take care of her," Auberon says with a hint of warning in his voice.

Evander, oblivious to the veiled threat, stands at attention with his hands behind his back. "That will not be necessary."

"Maybe I did not make myself clear," the Prince says in a deep whisper that could overpower the sound of a firestorm. "You've been dismissed. Or need I remind you that I am your Prince, *Lieutenant.*" Hostility taints the air, as the two men fight in a silent battle of rivalry and domination. If this is how Auberon treats him, I can see why Evander has little more but disdain for his prince. I don't see two professed great friends right now, but a pair of adolescent boys pretending to play diplomacy and failing in every way. Evander's jealousy is enough to make me want to hurl my empty glass at him for putting everything at risk. I'm grateful for Auberon's attempts to stop Evander from saying anything that might be damaging.

"*Now*, Lieutenant Fornous," Auberon's growl is nearly as earth-shattering as the King's. Evander turns his silent plea at me, but all I can do is turn away.

"Thank you for your help," I whisper. I can't bring myself to watch him back out of the room as a cowed dog, leaving my mouth sour with guilt.

"What happened back there, you flew across the room? Now that we are alone, there's no need to keep secrets." I suppress my grimace because I *need* to keep my secrets.

No matter how much I want to trust him, part of me knows that I risk having anything I tell him find its way to the King. They've already figured out what I'm capable of and where my gifts end.

My hand was forced at the Hole. They know Pa is my weakness. For once, my weakness can help me. They would never believe that I would risk Pa's life by sabotaging myself when attempting to heal that woman. Even the Prince knows how important Pa is to me, so much so that Auberon has been taking care of him.

Auberon. Pa.

Realization dawns on me, and the need to peel myself away from Auberon becomes suffocating. He's the Prince, he would have had some inkling about the King's plan. He would have heard whispers from the sentinels, or heard that something will be happening in the throne room, right?

When I fail to respond, he continues. "They said that you were both shaking. You started coughing blood and became bluer than her. They tried to pull you away from her, but you wouldn't budge." He pauses, as if not quite sure how much to tell me. "I also heard the sentinels say you kept on saying 'save us' and 'help us.'"

My mind reels, thinking of anything else I might have accidentally said that would reveal the truth. The more that they see, the harder it will be to come up with an excuse to make them forget about the whole thing.

An idea ignites in my mind.

I try moving away from him, he resists my attempts for a few moments before reluctantly letting go. I go to sit on the other side of the bed so I can look at his face, and so he can see exactly how exhausted I feel.

"I was telling the truth. I have never laid hands on someone with the plague before. The Priest was right," I pause. "The plague is a disease made by the gods. I am helpless against it."

I let the thoughts sink into his mind, and I watch as a flash of panic crosses his face before he schools his expression back into one of concern. I believe that my lie worked. We've both been brought up believing the same thing; that the plague is the essence of the Anzeth entering us and eating our insides.

"When I put my hands on her and tried to heal her, it was like the plague entered me as well." I let my bottom lip tremble under the weight of all the built-up emotions. "I could feel the Anzeth's power fighting my gift and they wanted to punish me for going against their wishes. I was asking for help because it felt like we were both dying together," I say, thinking about Pa covered in blood at the Hole to get my eyes to water, and my voice to break. It feels like I'm betraying myself by intentionally crying in front of him, but I need to sell my lie.

"That sounds awful," he whispers, reaching his hand out to mine, rubbing his thumb in a circular motion along the outside of my palm. It does nothing to stop the chill that creeps up my spine. There's no concern in his features, only fear.

"I thought I was going to die, Auberon. It felt like the Anzeth wanted to kill me!" I sob, not because of the Anzeth, but because of Pa. "Did she survive?"

In my mind, the blood gushes out of Pa's throat, soaking the dirt beneath him. It wasn't my intention to let him see my tears, but I can't stop them from falling. As they run down my face, all I can picture is how my tears fell into his blood.

He shakes his head slowly, moving closer to me like I'm a fire that needs to be extinguished before it explodes. Any wrong movement and I might break.

I pull my hand away, wrapping my arms around myself as my heavy eyelids refuse to stay open any longer. "It's been a long day, please let me rest." It comes out more like a plea, and I give up trying to keep my eyes open.

He nods, edging closer until his breath caresses my skin, and he pulls the blankets up around my shoulder. A soft finger trails along my jaw, running delicately across my lower lip and causing my breath to catch. The bed dips as warm lips press against my forehead, and I'm not sure whether to focus on the feeling of his finger resting on my lip, or the forbidden kiss.

Stop thinking like that. He could have something to do with what happened, the voice warns as he rises off the bed, closing the door behind him with a soft click.

Even with my eyes closed, all I can think about is the cold nothingness of the Empire of Air. Dusty thrones and a void of darkness, the room hasn't seen life in years, save for save for the spiders who have made a home there. The all-powerful Anzeth who controls every aspect of this realm, who can choose when to destroy every person in it with a single thought, couldn't possibly live somewhere like that.

Unless they don't live there at all.

I always thought the Anzeth would sit on their thrones, laughing as they watch us scurrying through the realm and murdering children in their name. Maybe we were looking at it all wrong. The realm isn't dying because the Anzeth have willed it through *changing* and polluting the way the air acts within the earth and in the water. Maybe the realm is dying because air isn't there at all.

They said they needed my help to be freed. Does that mean they've somehow been imprisoned elsewhere? How could I possibly be the one to save them? Why did they only speak to me when I tried to heal someone with the plague?

Unless it really was a power drain. Perhaps the Plague was too much for my gift, causing my mind to hallucinate the voices and places in the clouds.

I groan, flipping over in the bed. I have more questions than answers, and I feel like I'm going mad with everything that's happened.

Another question rings in my mind as exhaustion begins to seep into my bones.

Why did they call me daughter?

CHAPTER 21

"Perhaps one did not want to be loved so much as to be understood."
— *George Orwell, 1984*

Maiya arrives with lunch by the time I wake up. I'm nauseated enough as it is from the pit in my stomach and the smell of the meal only makes matters worse, and I can't bring myself to eat it.

Grabbing the books Auberon gave me, I skim through them again to find everything there is on the Anzeth. Everyone in the realm agrees: air is the most important of the four elements because it is in all things.

I pull out the book on the history of Audor and the book about Vesi's part in the war, telling myself that I need to reread the books to make sure I haven't missed anything that might explain whatever happened.

Before the War of the Elements, all the Empires lived in harmony with one another. The sun would rise in our Empire and fall in the Empire of the Earth. The Anzeth never interfered in politics. All they did was help the Empires grow crops or keep the land from shaking and skies from ripping open.

Slowly each Empire became more and more greedy, keeping their respective resources to themselves and denying the others any access to it. This went on for years before the war broke out.

213

You know this already. What else? the voice says impatiently.

I trace my fingers over the rough paper, following the veins that live within the material, wondering if the scroll the First Treaty was signed on is anything like this. It was taken from the Palace of Air, so I can't even begin to imagine what it might be made from to harness such immense power.

Whether or not it's true, somehow it made the gods angry enough that when the last royal spilt their essence onto the scroll, the earth divided, creating the Land of the Dead.

A chill rolls through me, prickling my skin. The sun has set. Groaning, I put the book down and take a sip of water, contemplating ripping it apart because it doesn't serve me any more purpose. I breathe slowly as frustration builds within. Nothing in any of the books suggests that the Anzeth need saving.

I can't dismiss the thought that none of it was my imagination, and the Anzeth really did speak to me despite how cryptic their message was. We've always been told the Anzeth are vengeful, but what if they aren't? What if they really are being caged somewhere?

The whole realm could be slowly becoming just like the Land of the Dead; a land of pure black, decayed and ruined, all because the Anzeth took the air away. What if the reason for the realm's destruction isn't because of their anger, but because they're dying, and they're taking the air with them?

The blue book feels heavy in my hands, causing rage to lick my spine. Not only did King Ryven start the war, he's also the one who took the scroll from the Anzeth's home and bound the Empires to it when they signed the First Treaty.

Fermenting in my hatred toward the King of Water won't get me any more answers. Right now, it's the least of my concerns. It has been weeks since the King's threat about my powers, and it's time I start considering that maybe I wasn't imagining the ice.

Whatever the dots are, I need to figure out how to summon them. They appeared at the Hole, when my marks moved, and again when the ice formed. I start changing into a dressing gown to get comfortable before I start the psychological marathon of trying to use my powers.

A knock rattles the door, and I freeze.

A pale hand pokes around the side of the door. "It's just me. I figured I'd check if you're decent this time before coming in." Auberon's voice travels through the air, making me huff.

"What do you want?" I say in frustration. Unlike yesterday, I'm not going to hide my resentment toward him for letting Pa be put in the firing line like that. He promised me that nothing would happen to him if I stayed. Yesterday made it clear that he doesn't have the power to keep my family safe.

"Ah, you're dressed," he jokes, clearly trying to lighten my foul mood.

"I didn't invite you inside. I'll ask again, what do you want? Because frankly, I'm not in the mood to see you. Do try not to slam the door on your way out this time." Folding my arms across my chest, I cock my hip out, putting all my weight on one leg.

Surprise glimmers in his eyes, but that doesn't stop the room from shrinking in his presence.

"I don't need your permission to do what I want," he says as an entertained grin sketches his features. He mimics my posture almost mockingly, and I move to the bedside table, just to add furniture between us.

"No, of course you don't. Instead, you let a dying woman get dragged into the throne room to be part of some experiment while dangling Pa over me," I say sharper than intended.

He blinks for a heartbeat, as if unsure what I might be referring to, which only turns my irritation into rage. His arms unfold quickly, palms facing toward me like he's pleading for mercy. What throws me isn't the way his eyes fill with sorrow, it's the way I can feel his regret. "You have to believe me when I say I had no part in what happened yesterday. I would have warned you had I known they were going to ask you to exert your powers in that way," he says each word with the same sorrow I heard when he spoke about Quintos.

He walks toward me slowly, holding out his hand. The same hand that killed the brown-eyed sentinel. The same hand that tucked me into bed before I fell asleep. The same hand that belongs to the man that Evander has warned me about. I shouldn't want to take his hand, but it's all I can think about doing.

I suck in a sharp breath and shake my head like it might clear my thoughts and remind me why I'm upset. "I don't believe you. Now, answer my question, what do you want?" I ask hoarsely, unable to look him in the eyes for fear that I'll do more than just take his hand.

His chest touches mine before I can step away. Need rushes through me, dispelling my anger as his hand rests around my throat, only then do I realize the bangle on his wrist is identical to the rings in the temple. "I want *you*, Althea." His heated words kiss my skin, and I fire ignites in my core, driving the raw need through me, tempting me to press my body against his.

No. I can't feel like this. I'm not *allowed* to feel this way. Evander and I have a plan to get out of here. I could be leaving any day now, and the last thing I should do is find myself tangled beneath the sheets with the Prince of Fire; my captor.

His hand travels around my waist, settling at the small of my back. It takes everything within me not to let him pull me in tight, because the truth is, I think I want him too.

"I want *you*. Even if the gods kill us today, I'll still want you. I want the way your eyes light up with admiration every time you see a decorative weapon. And most importantly," he pauses, pulling me in tighter. "I want to make you feel like you're worthy of a prince."

My hands find their way to his chest, and I'm not sure if I want to push him away or pull him closer. I know which one I should be doing, but my muscles refuse to cooperate, only placing the slightest bit of pressure. His arms strengthen their hold on me, and I have to focus on keeping myself taunt so as not to fall into his embrace. But it's his eyes that lock me in my position, darkening, pulling me into their onyx void.

"You're mine. There's nothing you can do to escape me. If you try to run, I will follow you into the darkest depths of the earth. No king, fae or mortal will ever take you away from me. I want *you*, and I will not rest until you want me too." His voice is a heavy whisper trailing heat down the side of his neck. The way his honeyed voice runs through is more intoxicating than any addiction.

I can barely breathe from the sharp ache that settles between my legs, and each breath becomes nothing more than a hot pant. My mind is screaming that I'm not his, and no one could ever own me, but my body's reaction to him couldn't disagree more.

The darkness stirs, demanding me to run as far away as I can. I should run. But all I want to do is get closer.

Don't, the voice warns.

Too late, I respond breathlessly, melting into his touch.

His breathing becomes a hot whisper as he presses himself against me, and trails rough kisses from my temple to my neck. "Come to my bedchambers and join me for dinner." A gasp leaves my lips from the rumbling of his chest, sending a wave of desire through me. His hand edges lower down my back, closer and closer to my rear, and his question drowns out to my roaring pulse.

A mischievous chuckle rolls through him like he knows exactly how I'm reacting to his touch. "Now, do I need to carry you? I admit, I'll take great pleasure in feeling your legs on me when I throw you over my shoulder."

My gaze lifts to his, and I almost expect to see stars floating above him from the forbidden ecstasy his presence makes me feel. It feels wrong, but I think 'wrong' is becoming my favorite flavor.

"I asked you a question." He smirks, putting more pressure around my neck, and my back tenses in a battle between wanting to get closer, and keeping myself away.

I nod my head slightly, knowing better than to let myself feel this way around him. Do I want whatever is in his bedchamber? I think I do. I know I should have told him to leave me alone, but I couldn't stop myself from yearning for more.

It's not too late to tell him that, the voice says.

A dark smile spreads across his lips and he moves to a low whisper against my ear. "Good girl."

I bite my lip to stop myself from giving him the satisfaction of hearing me moan. It isn't too late to tell him, but there's no denying that I don't want to.

At once he moves away from me and heads toward the door, leaving me in a hot puddle. The feel of his heat still lingers against my skin, and I want more.He stands by the door, enjoying the power he holds over me.

The walk to his chamber is silent, and I'm grateful to get a moment to regain some ground.

You can't let that happen again, the voice scolds and I know it's right. *He's a distraction, and you need to get rid of your distractions.*

I do need to focus on harnessing the darkness and continue creating a map of the Palace so I can escape. But what until then? Who knows how long it will be until Evander comes back, or until King Ryven decides to take action on his knowledge of me.

As much as I want to get my whole family out of Audor before King Ryven moves, I can't do this without Evander, because he's right, there's no way I'll be able to locate Pa *and* find Ma without getting caught. I don't think my heated moment with Auberon will change Evander's mind about helping me. That doesn't change the fact that I shouldn't be going to his friend's chambers.

Auberon grabs my hand once we reach his chambers and sits me down on a dining room chair, disappearing into another room and returning with a single tray of food. Sitting in the chair next to mine, I squirm under his scrutiny. Or is it the fact that I need to cross my legs tightly as the aftermath of his touch still lingers in my mind?

"Did you think I wouldn't find out?" He grips the armrest of his chair until his knuckles turn white. I go rigid. There's no way he'd know about the Anzeth. Is he talking about Evander? Maybe he saw something in the way I looked at Evander? Did Auberon do something to him?

Bile swarms through my stomach thinking of all the forbidden thoughts I had about him while something could have happened to Evander. Deep down I know that the fear is unfounded in reason.

There could be more about the throne room incident than he's letting on, the voice says, and my hands tangle together, scratching the soft skin on the inside on my wrists.

"I don't know what you're talking about." I try to coat my voice in innocence, and I can only hope I succeeded.

"Maiya told me." My fear compounds with irritation. I knew she would be relaying everything back to the King, but I didn't expect her full allegiance to lie with Auberon. The only thing of note she could tell him is that I was asking about Evander. Unless… *the knife*.

Panic thrums through my blood, and my fingers scratch deeper into my skin, making my gift swarm to heal it. Everything could be ruined if they stop thinking of me as their submissive prisoner that doesn't dare to run. If they know I've stolen a weapon, albeit a pathetic one, my ruse will be done for. There's no telling the hell that would rain down if they've found it. They could stop sending a healer to Pa, or even drag Ma to the dungeons as well.

Maiya must have found it when I was sleeping. I should have hidden it somewhere better. This is all my fault.

Get it together, play innocent and maybe you'll get out of this alive, the voice says.

I school my face into nonchalance, the same practiced expression I hold when I walk through the streets past any Cintis. "As I said, *Your Highness,* I haven't the slightest clue what you are talking about."

"Did you think I wouldn't find out that you've been starving yourself?" Each word comes out like it physically pains him.

"What?" I say as all the fear and annoyance dissipates. Are my ears playing games on me? There can't be any way I heard that correctly.

"You didn't eat at all yesterday, and you didn't even touch the food Maiya brought you today," he strains like he's holding back his true level of anger.

"I appreciate your attentiveness; however, my diet is none of your concern." I try to speak with grace, but the humor that I'm finding in the situation could well result in an undesired outcome if he's so upset over my eating habits. I'd hate for him to discover how little I ate before I was his prisoner.

"Are you trying to weaken yourself?" he says through gritted teeth. He may be trying to appear more restrained than he is, the flame from the candle erupts, reaching toward the ceiling, taking away any humor I once saw in the situation.

"No," I say, confusion washing over me as I stare at him. "I wasn't trying to weaken myself," I start, trying to figure out exactly what I'm trying to say and the reason behind such a dramatic reaction. "For the past few weeks, I have been a prisoner. *Your* prisoner. Pa is rotting in a cell. My mother is all alone without either of us. I'm the queen's *bitch*. Not to mention, the King has been experimenting with my gift. So, forgive me if I'm not in the *mood* to eat, I—" I snap my mouth shut. I've said too much already.

You stupid little girl. You never know when to shut up, do you? Are you trying to break Pa's eight other fingers? the voice snarls.

I want to cower deeper into my seat, or crawl under the table to hide from whatever punishment might ensue from my loose tongue.

The flame behind him sinks lower until it's nothing more than an ordinary candle. Only then can I bring myself to look directly into his eyes, caught in a storm of indecision. His fingers tap against the empty table. With each tap another emotion cascades across his face: Anger, shock, guilt, pity.

The hostility in the air dissipates as his shoulders slump back, defeated almost. Yet his jaw is tight, muscles ticking like he's caught between two worlds. "I *need* you to be strong, Althea." There's no kindness in his voice. It's not an order, but it doesn't feel like a suggestion either.

It's a warning, the voice corrects.

"A war is coming, and if you're weak, you *will* die and there will be nothing that I can do to save you. Tell me you understand." Each word is clear, concise, and there's no mistaking that everything he said is true.

My fingers tremble as they try to resume their assault on my skin, too distraught to even move. King Ryven's interest in me must be far more serious than I thought, which can only mean that there's now a clock ticking for me. And once the time stops, either I become the property of Vesi, or death will ensue.

I nod, unsure what I could say to change my own fate.

"Good," he stands, grabbing a tray from a side table. "Let's eat dinner before it gets cold. This is one of my new recipes." I stare at him, and the warm smile plasters his face of picture-perfect innocence, like he's trying to make up for his reaction. I can't return it, not when the tables of my own situation have shifted to another level filled with deadlier risks.

I stare at my distorted reflection in the gilded dome, wondering how many wrong turns I've taken in life to get here? A lot of people believe that their whole life has been dictated by the Anzeth, and if that's true, what did I do to deserve this?

Auberon removes the dome to reveal a traditional Audorian dish. I inhale deeply to let the smell take over my senses and wipe away my thoughts, even for just a moment. With a reluctant sigh, I reach for the utensils only for my brows to knit together. "There's only one plate?"

"I've eaten already. This is for you," he retrieves the knife and fork before I do, cutting through the meat and bringing the thin slice up to my lips. "Open," he orders.

"I'm not a child!" I protest, pushing his hand back.

Who can blame him when you act like a child? the voice says snidely.

"Open," he says it the same way the King orders silence. Parting my lips, he brings the fork into my mouth to feed me. "Good. That wasn't so hard, was it?" he smirks like he's finally where he's always wanted to be.

I have not a moment to argue with him before he pushes the food into my mouth as soon as I can swallow.

Look at you, being hand fed by the Prince of Fire, cockiness oozes from the voice, and I struggle to feel any humiliation from this. Every part of me enjoys being treated like I'm royalty. It's invigorating seeing a man in power stoop in such a way *for* me. *If only Evander could see you now.*

"I should mention, your father has been released," he says like it's something he just remembered.

"What?" I spray chunks of meat onto his lapel.

"Yes, he was released yesterday and returned to your apartment." he says pointedly.

"Why didn't you tell me this before?" I choke on my food, feeling the room widen like I can finally breathe.

"If memory serves me correctly, we were otherwise distracted." I barely hear him speak, not since he's said something far more important.

He's out.

Pa no longer has to live in a filthy cell. He'll be tossing and turning, wondering what is happening to me, but right now that doesn't matter. I can keep Evander safe and get out of here by myself. My family can finally get out of Ignis. No more sacrifices, no more lying, it'll just be the three of us, and I'll be able to sleep easier knowing that Evander won't be roped into this anymore.

As my mind reels, my relief falters. I still need Evander's help. Even if I get past the sentinel, I don't even know the way out. On the off chance I make it out of the Palace, I'll have to decide between getting Ma or Pa. I won't have enough time to get both, not if I still have to find Ma and Pa. The General wouldn't just leave him unattended without someone watching his every move.

"Why?" I question.

Pa is their leverage over me, it doesn't make sense why they would lose any tool of control. Because none of it makes sense.

"You made a bargain with the King, did you not? Sometimes he has goodness in him, Althea," he says, frowning at the plate as his eyes glaze over, lost in thought. Guilt crosses his features, only to disappear in an instant.

But I didn't make a bargain? In fact, I asked the King to leave Mase and pa unharmed, and he broke Pa's fingers. It feels like a lie even to me to say that the King is a man of his word with matters relating to 'goodness.' Does he think he's made his point by showing me he won't hesitate to harm my family? It serves no purpose for Auberon to lie to me about it, not when the King already has me firmly in his grasp.

Shaking his head he rises to his feet, offering me his hand and says, "Dance with me."

My head jolts toward him at the sudden change of topic. I should go back to my chambers and keep my distance, but all I'll do is stir wondering what might come next.

"What? There's no music, plus, I've never danced before," I say, trying to give him a reason to change his mind, because I don't think I have it in me to deny him.

What I told him is a lie. In the dead of the night, Evander would hold me in his arms as we swayed to whatever tune he hummed. It always felt natural to do, but it felt so wrong at the same time, like I was betraying myself by falling for Evander.

"We don't need music to hold each other," he says with the brightest smile I've ever seen, and I can't help myself from reaching out to let that light embrace me.

He leads me into the center of the chambers, bringing my hands up behind his neck, while his fingers wrap around my waist and pull me close against his body. The peace settling in my chest relaxes my thoughts, and I actually believe that I can leave my worries for later, just like I could with Evander.

"Have I ever told you how much I prefer you with your hair down?" he sighs into my hair, and a small smile crosses my lips.

We sway together, switching our weight from left to right as my head relaxes onto his chest from the circular motion of his hand on my back. We remain locked in each other's embrace for what felt like hours before his hands snake up my front, reaching up to brush his thumb along my parted lips.

Time stills as he stares down at me. The lines around his mouth curves, and I can see each and every mark on his lips. A peaceful bliss stretches between us stronger, and I forget all about how I *can't* want this. The other hand still at my back moves lower, cupping my rear. He stops, patiently waiting to see if I'll pull away. His eyes slowly darken, pushing out the reflection of the flames when I tilt myself toward his hand.

My skin hums at his warmth engulfing me, and his chin dips lower to meet mine. My breath catches with the anticipation of his touch. Heavy eyelids drift close, feeling every inch of his body against mine—from his rough hands pushing me against his hips in an achingly slow rhythm, to the euphoria of heat that his lips leave behind as they glide along my cheek.

This is *the Prince* of Audor, son of King Cyrus. He's seen with his own eyes exactly what I'm capable of, and the death that could follow in my wake. Yet here he is. He saw my skin and didn't run. He saw me at my worst and only pushed harder to be by my side.

He may be a monster, but I've always been interested in dark things.

A hot shiver curls down my spine as his hips push against me. His lips press against mine and I gasp, feeling his smile curve against my mouth. I go completely still, basking in the sparks that dance through my body at his touch. His lips against mine feel like a toxin and a tonic all at the same time.

My breath is stripped from me all at once, leaving a blank space where he once stood. A loud crash sounds from the corner as every single candle in the room erupts towards the ceiling. In the center of it all, a man on fire—not just any man, but the Prince of Fire gripping a sword of flames. Every inch of Auberon is covered in exquisite blue flames of one of the most powerful Cintis.

I'm too in awe that I almost miss someone yelling my name, urging me to run. Then Auberon lunges to the figure yelling for me.

The room turns into an inferno as the figures collide, turning my dress sickly as it sticks to my skin from the flames that nip at me, sweat dripping down my skin.

"Get out of here Althea!" a voice yells. The same voice that's comforted me for the past five years.

Evander.

I'm too stunned to move. The gift within flows through me like a great wave, tightening around my skin as flames lick me. Deep within my core, the darkness vibrates, ready to protect me.

"Stop it!" I scream at the two men, but they don't hear me between the clanging of weapons and their battle cries.

They fight like they're trying to kill.

Evander seems to become one with his blade, flowing with its motion like a stream. His movement is elegant and deadly, like a dancer of death. Each thrust is calculated, strategic, and sharp. He doesn't bother using his magic in his attacks: rather, he uses it as a shield to conserve his strength. I didn't believe him when he said his power lay in his sword, and that it's the only thing that he's better at than Auberon. Now I know.

Auberon is the weapon. He doesn't just wield fire, he becomes it. His power is far superior to Evander's, whose sweat trickles down his face. The heat emitting from the Prince is even too hot for him to handle.

This is a battle between sword and fire.

His fire lashes out, whipping Evander along his sides. Sweat stains Auberon's face as he struggles to keep up with Evander's attacks. But still, it's glaringly apparent that this is not a fight that Evander will win.

A whip of fire burns against Evander's ribs and a strained grunt leaves him. The sight of him in pain carves a hole in my heart.

I fought him at every turn because I wanted to believe that it isn't possible for a Cintis to be good. I became no better than every other person in this realm who couldn't see past someone's blood. I pushed him away because I wanted to believe the lie that I was telling myself— that no person could ever care about me once they see me.

Because you're an abomination, the voice says.

How could anyone ever care for something that defies everything known in existence. Yet, there he was, standing by my side for years, never faltering in his devotion to me, and I treated him like the Empire treats their mortals. Even now, he challenges his Prince and is willing to die to keep him away from me.

Whether or not his rage is from jealousy, the point still stands; he didn't deserve any of the awful things I said to him.

Another pained grunt comes from the fight. Evander's movements are slower, and my gift reaches toward the cuts in his arms.

"Stop!" I yell, stepping forward like it might actually do something. "Stop it!" I scream louder this time, but they're beyond reach, eaten up by bloodlust and devoured by battle.

I was wrong, I thought I would feel the brunt of Evander's disappointment if he found out about whatever is going on between Auberon and myself. Instead, he's taking it out on his own Prince, and it will get him killed.

I have to do something. This isn't a petty rivalry, they're enemies pretending to be civil.

I leave the scene, running around the chambers to find something that I could use to stop them. Frustration takes over as I sprint from room to room, coming up empty handed. Absolute desperation fills me as I start throwing anything I can get my hands on at the pair: a plate, a book, a chair, water. Nothing slows them down.

Five years of training with Evander and I'm useless here. If I intervene, Auberon's flames will probably kill me. But if I do nothing, then Evander will die.

I scream into my hands, as the darkness in my core recedes. It's clear to me that my power considers me the only threat to my safety, not the bloodied, flaming Cintis matching swords blow by blow.

I might as well prove it right.

Agony explodes through me as I throw myself into their carnage. My skin bubbles from Auberon's heat and it blisters my lungs as a knife slices through my rib, ripping through muscle and organs. A blood-curdling scream tears through my chest as I hit the ground, unfazed by the crack of my head hitting the floor as the smell of flesh sears my nostrils.

Deafening silence echoes through the room. My gift scrapes against my skin attempting to heal the blistering flesh. My breath comes short and quick, black spots flicker through my vision, and my blood runs thick and cold through my veins.

Raging red fire enters my mind's eye as my gift plunges into the hand grasping my arm. Evander. Then a blue fire emerges in my mind as another hand cups my cheek. It must be Auberon. My gift spreads through their bodies, healing their burns and cuts, and stealing my breath from me as the overwhelming surge of power floods through our systems.

They gasp as their bodies heal, until my gift is satisfied and only smooth skin is left behind.

I don't have the strength to control the gift, to haul it back into me: to stop it from draining itself into them. It's too busy searching for every single part of them to heal; it's forgotten about me.

"Let go," I cry, as agony strips away my ability to think.

"No, never," one of them whispers. I'm not sure who; the words are too muffled by my own pain. A ringing noise tears through my ears, adding more black dots.

"Heal," I choke, suddenly; the pain evaporates. "I can't—" My chest heaves, struggling to drag air into my lungs, and I no longer feel the piercing burn of my skin—only a cold that chills me to my bones.

So cold.

More hands move around me, their voices are fuzzy. I need to get them away, but their hands are so warm. I don't want to lose that warmth. I need it. If the warmth leaves, I think I might freeze.

Something hot wraps around me, pulling me against a wall of heat. I reach towards the temptress in the darkness, lulling me to let go. To give in.

Save us, daughter. A choir of echoes bounces through my head. *Live.*

My eyes snap open, and I see the outline of a figure looking over me, gripping me. Sleep calls to me, enticing me to shut my eyes and let it all go.

Save us! the voices screeches, and a jolt of energy sends a lightning bolt along the lines on my skin.

I gasp for breath, as a small amount of air trickles back into my lungs, giving me what I need to fight.

"Don't touch me," I manage to choke out, "I can't heal." The pain returns back to my lungs tenfold, and my stomach buckles, throwing me on my side as my gift swarms back into me when two pairs of hands leave my skin. I cry as the gift trickles through me, weaker than it has ever been.

It leaks through my body, cooling burnt skin and soothing charred lungs. The black spots slither out of my vision little by little, as my breathing deepens. I can feel my skin stitch back together, growing back parts that have been burnt off.

In an instant, the room turns back into an inferno. I can't move, I can barely open my eyes.

"You fucking did this," a voice that could shatter glass growls.

"This is your fault as well! I told you to stay away from her. The Empire has done enough to her," Evander bites back.

"You do *not* get to tell me what I'm allowed to do," Auberon hisses.

"She's mortal, leave her alone. We've done enough."

"You hurt her! What the fuck were you doing in my room?" Auberon's voice grows louder, bouncing against the walls in a crescendo.

"What the fuck was she doing *in your room*?" The promise of death rumbles deep within Evander's chest.

"What we do is none of your godsdamn business. All of our plans would have been ruined if she died."

Something smashes. Splinters and shards of glass rain over me, and I am too weak to flinch when something slices through my forehead.

At least no fire is involved this time, the voice remarks.

"You burnt her, and you just hurt her again!"

Another smash. This time, I don't get showered in whatever breaks.

"None of this would have happened if you minded your fucking business. You can get your dick wet elsewhere: leave Althea out of it." Auberon's voice is sharper than any weapon I could make. "Now get out of here or I'll strip you of your title. This is your only warning to stay away from my Althea. Next time, I'll kill you."

"We will see who dies if you hurt her."

"Out!" Auberon roars with royal authority, and my body has the urge to leave the room as well, to heed the command. But I can't move a muscle.

Heavy footsteps grow louder, and then Auberon drops to the ground. With trembling hands, he drags me onto his lap. I want to resist, but my body refuses to listen. My head rolls onto his arm, and I stare bleary-eyed at the ceiling.

Black eyes wide with panic look away from me. He starts to rock me back and forth like it will take all my pain away. His auburn hair tickles my chest as he whispers, "I'm so sorry Althea. I'm so sorry. It was an accident. He came from nowhere. I should have more control over my men. I'm so sorry."

Over and over again he apologizes.

I want to spit in his face. I want to spit in Evander's face as well despite how much I care about him.I was at death's door because of both of their insatiable ego and childish jealousy. None of this would have happened if Evander could just keep it together. None of this would have happened if the Prince weren't trying to claim me.

The love I see Ma and Pa show each other is nothing like this. None of this is love. All of this is a game of pretend.

He's a spoiled Prince that's found himself bored and looking for entertainment. Or am I lying to myself again, like I did with Evander? Am I just convincing myself that I'm not worthy of love? Have I spent so long training myself to hide away, that I've hidden my feelings too?

Is it so bad that I still feel a want towards Auberon—whether that want is lust or love, is it something that I should deny myself?

The torrent of emotions exhausts my already tired body.

In the end, deep, exhausted sleep grabs me and drags me into the empty abyss.

CHAPTER 22

*"We can easily forgive a child who is afraid of the dark;
the real tragedy of life is when men are afraid of the light."*

— Plato

I slept for two days, Maiya said.

I must feel special because the Prince visited me in my sleep, Maiya said.

The cold bath water numbs the ache in my muscles. I've been sitting here for an hour, washing off the accumulated sweat. My gift swirls through me, feigning innocence as if it didn't abandon me when I was dying.

I want to know if Evander is alright, but I have no one to ask.

After two days of rest, the queen felt it prudent that I should be summoned for her 'dire situation.' If it were something to do with Blaze, I wouldn't mind, but I also wouldn't have been given so much time to get ready.

Maiya does my hair up in a braid wrapped up around my head like a crown. She hands me another red dress, dipping low along my chest with a split down the center of the sleeves and down my leg, placing my altered marks on full display.

As usual, Belve scowls as soon as he sees me, grumbling when I don't walk fast enough for him.

A flurry of activity rustles through the queen's chambers. Servants run around making a concoction of different creams and plastering it over Queen Mellonia's bare body, draped over the settee. Something circular and green sits on top of her eyes as her skin is painted in charcoal. Mortals fuss about shaping her claws and toenails, painting them in the deepest of reds.

I'm left standing there for several minutes until she removes the green circles from her eyes. With grace she sits up, and the maids scurry away to give her room to rise.

I want to turn away so she can cover her private areas, but I don't want her to think I'm uncomfortable. And most importantly, I don't want her to feel comfortable.

Her gaze finally rips into mine. Behind her, a fireplace roars to life, creeping up the wall and over the mantle. Violence burns in her when she glares at my skin. She tilts her chin, and behind her threatening gaze, a promise flares to life; a promise that she will be the one to take my last breath.

"Out," her feral voice rings through the chamber.

As each mortal exits the room, the fire in the fireplace grows higher, and the tips of the Queen's hair sets alight. It's almost like she's putting on a show.

When the last mortal exits the chambers, the fire dissipates at once, and a smile crosses the Queen's features as she saunters her way into the rose bathtub. Nothing good can come from her smiling.

"Wipe the mud off," she says, settling deeper into the water and closing her eyes.

Grabbing a cloth from the shelf and pulling up a short stool, I sit behind her. I don't have the energy to deal with another fight, so I do as I am told. My hands are so close to her neck. It wouldn't take much to push her under until she stops moving.

Patches of mud have already dried, and she winces as I scrub to get it off. Every time she flinches or reacts, a sinister smile creeps onto my lip, and a deep satisfaction crawls through me at her pain.

The cloth rips out of my hand. "Useless mortal," she spits, "I have to do *everything* myself."

"Luckily, you have maids to do this," I grumble under my breath, and a fire ignites in her eyes.

"Excuse me?"

I know perfectly well that what she's really intimating is, *Careful what you say next.* If my tongue doesn't kill me, then maybe my attitude will. Because I'm not the bigger person.

"Nothing, Your Majesty," I say sweetly as I rise and give the most exaggerated curtsy I can muster.

The floating balls of fire above the tub grow. The water in the quartz tub starts to bubble and boil, and her hand ignites, glowing as red as her hair. Her muscles tighten as if preparing to lunge

If my death is in her hands, then I won't give her the satisfaction of going down without a fight. Her stupidity in letting me have free range to 'fix her' means that I know all of her strength comes from her legs, and she has a weak left arm.

I summon my gift to the surface, readying it for the impact. A feeling of familiarity settles in, like I'm about to run into the center of a fight between Evander and Auberon all over again. I force the shiver that begs to run up my spine from the memory of the pain to the side, focusing on the Queen *Bitch* in front of me.

Prodding the power, I try to wake it up, I need it—now. But the temperamental thing doesn't seem to think that my life is in any kind of danger. Or maybe I'm simply not angry enough?

An offending trickle of sweat runs down the side of my face, and I swear I see her nails lengthen as she grips the tub.

A knock has both of us look up at the entrance with gritted teeth. An acolyte wearing a black and red robe, with gold stitching, stands far too confidently by the door. I've seen him before: he's one of the Priest's closest confidants.

Shock flickers within me when the queen does nothing to cover her naked body. Does the King not care if others see her bare, or is this her attempt at keeping up with his concubines?

"Now is not the time," Queen Mellonia snaps, and I find myself nodding in agreement with her.

"Come back later," I say with a threatening hint in my voice. The Queen scowls from hearing me speak, nodding her head nonetheless.

"No need. I'll say what I have come to say, then you can resume. However, I would strongly advise against killing the girl, or need I ask the King to remind you what is at stake?" he says; it is obvious he finds his task beneath him.

It's clear the royals aren't planning on killing me *yet*, but that is very different from *keeping* me alive. I look between the two fae expectantly, wanting them to explain what they're talking about. What's at stake?

"Get on with it and get out." She extinguishes the fire covering her hands.

"I have come to tell you that the dragon opened his eyes." A scant whiff of worry edges his voice, and tension fills the air unlike the anger before he arrived. This is far more acidic. Goosebumps prickle my skin as a cold draft whips through the air. "Your attendance is requested at the meeting this afternoon." With that, the acolyte disappears to whatever hell he came from.

No, that can't be all he has to say. How can he say that has opened his eyes and not expand more on that? How many times has Niran awoken that the queen isn't surprised by this information? I thought no one has seen any of the dragons since the Dragon Wars, a lot of mortals think they're a myth. I keep finding more questions than answers.

The Queen throws the cloth back in my hands as she relaxes back into the tub, a silent gesture to resume.

None of the books or lessons I've received would provide any indication on what in gods' name the Acolytes could be talking about. What does it mean if the dragon is stirring? Did they hear the Anzeth's cries as well? I haven't heard any whispers that they might be waking. Most people just believe that they're nothing more than a myth.

If Niran is awake, that might mean Chusi and Leviathan are too, but surely there would be more commotion if they were. If all four dragons are awake, then why would the Anzeth need my help when Shesha would be there to save them, as is his job.

"Are you blind? You've wiped it off already. Now heal it," the Queen's high-pitched voice snaps me back to reality.

Talons shred through my skin before I can register that she's lunged out of the bath, leaving a searing pain in its wake. My gift spasms at the impact, rushing to the open wound and stitching it back together as she strikes me with the back of her hand.

I raise my leg off the floor about to return her assault when I go rigid. I can't fight her back.

"You *bitch.*" Her hands burn my wrists as she yanks my bare skin to her face. "You're seducing him, aren't you? You think I wouldn't find out that you've been trying to steal *my* husband?"

Another sharp pain prickles my cheek as she strikes me again. The darkness in my core boils in response to the red cornering my vision.

"Don't touch me!" I scream.

Twisting my hand from my grip, I stagger towards the exit before I do something I know that will get my parents killed.

"You think that you're so smart, do you? Seducing him with whatever sort of abomination you have in you. The only reason he's interested is because you're his latest curiosity. You are *nothing* but a whore." She lunges for me again. This time, I dodge her assault and run to the sitting room. My body aches to return the fight, but I know it'll just make it even worse.

"I have done nothing with the King!" She stalks toward me like a predator about to pounce.

A high pitch laugh that sounds like it belongs in the bowels of a monster pierces the air. "Do not take me for a fool, *mortal*, I have been alive far longer than you. Cyrus is going to eat you alive. And if he doesn't, then I will."

"I didn't do anything!" I edge my way to the exit.

"I don't believe you, *whore*," she snaps, summoning a ball of fire in her hands. "Why else would he be painting *your marks* on his whores?" she spits.

Ice rips down my spine "What?"

"Get out!" she screeches, summoning a wall of flame that crashes towards me like an avalanche. I spring to the door, which opens before I can get my hands on it. Belve's mouth parts as he stares at the tsunami of fire heading towards us, slamming the door just as I jump through.

CHAPTER 23

"The truth is rarely pure and never simple."
— *Oscar Wilde, The Importance of Being Earnest*

I spent the night pacing the tile floors as my brain wheeled dangerously close to the breaking point. I tried to summon the dots, but nothing happened. Nothing that is happening makes any sense. I want to scream, to throw things—break things. If I succumb to the urge, then they win. I can't let them win. I won't let them. They've tipped my entire life upside down. The last thing I can let them take is what little is left of my sanity.

I force the thoughts aside and try to recall everything I know about the dragons. The books Auberon gave me didn't have anything useful about dragons, but I try rereading it again either way in case I overlooked something.

To Audor, the mighty beast is as powerful a symbol as the sun. They said the reason giant stone dragons sit at the entrance of the castle, and why the King is always seen in armor inspired by a dragon, is to remind us where the powers of Cintis came from, and whose land we are on.

I think that's utter bullshit.

The only reason they don a dragon is to instill fear.

After all the offspring were killed during the Dragon War, the four dragons remaining were forced into separate parts of the realm to stop the breeding of dragons. If Niran is awake, could the Warriors of Caulus be awake too? They could save the Anzeth and leave me completely out of it. They're meant to be slumbering with the dragons, but I've heard countless tavern tales from Cintis who claimed to have seen the warriors on the battlefield during the War of the Elements.

It doesn't matter how long I stare at the pages or file through every single piece of information that I have in my head, I am no closer to finding out what it means if the fire dragon, Niran, is awake. The realm's destruction must have something to do with him waking. The dragons could be the final match that sets this world aflame.

Shoving my head into the pillow, I let the tears fall. I don't whimper, I don't sob, I'm completely silent.

I was never a stranger to tears before all this. Though when I did cry, I made sure it was when no one was watching. Ma and Pa had enough on their plates that they didn't need to also be worrying about my mental state.

I need to pull myself together. Not for Ma or Pa. For me. I have to be strong enough for myself. That's the only way I can make it through all of this.

The next morning, Valen leans against the door like he's waiting for me to figure out why he's here.

"Let me guess, another walk?" I say as excitement bubbles within me.

He nods, stepping back to let me pass. But I don't.

"What are you doing?" he says as I turn my back to him to pour water into a glass.

Spinning on my heels, I offer him the glass while fighting my gift's demands to move closer.

"I can hear your wheeze all the way from here. Drink." I meant to frame it like a question, instead I said it like it was an order.

To my dismay, he doesn't protest, mumbling his thanks as he sips the water slowly. It does nothing to help his breathing.

I bite the inside of my cheek when he stops drinking to cough. What could have caused such an issue if he isn't a smoker and it isn't the polluted air?

Shaking my head, I give into my gift's desires and take a step closer, holding my hand out to him. He eyes my outstretched hand suspiciously, and I shake it, doing my head toward it.

"I'm not holding your hand as we walk," he says in disbelief.

Rolling my eyes, I straighten my arm out even more. "Just take it, let me help you."

There's a possibility that Valen doesn't know about my powers. But that is quickly disproved when he takes my hand hesitantly. There's a fine balance I will have to follow so as not to get either of us in trouble.

I close my eyes and open up my senses up to him, letting my gift rumble through me and into Valen. Immediately, flames roar in my mind's eye, it's almost as potent as Evander's Cintis powers. Between each lethal flame there seems to be a gap that looks like the inside of a mortal, almost as if he isn't pure fae.

Moving into his lungs, my power twists into hysteria. I let my gift take control, jolting to the scar on his chest, the lung right below holds an identical scar like he's been stabbed. Forcing my gift to focus on the lungs, I loosen the reins on my powers, watching as it eases his breathing immediately. I draw it back to me just as his lungs completely heal.

"I wish I could do more," I whisper.

I can do more, but I shouldn't. If he stops coughing or wheezing altogether, the King and every person that knows Valen will know what I did. It could get him in trouble for engaging with the prisoner, and there's no bounds as to what that punishment might be.

He frowns, staring at the floor without letting go of my hands. He takes deep slow breaths with the look of utter confusion sewn across his face. Finally releasing his hold on me, he looks at me with complete bewilderment.

"How did you do that?" he finally gasps.

"It's just a trick I have," I shrug, attempting to wave it off.

"Thank you," he says, searching my face like he's trying to find the words to say.

It feels good to finally be able to help someone after years of keeping my gift to myself. I may not be able to use my powers freely, but the look of gratitude on Valen's face is enough to convince me that I should still try to heal whenever I can.

"Don't worry about it," I smile, "Now, about this walk."

He nods, flashing me a warm smile. "Lead the way."

Neither of us say anything as we walk, yet the sound of his clear and easy breathing is more than enough to fill the silence.

As we step through the door to the garden, the roaring sound of flames snatches our attention. I turn just in time to watch a woman no older than me scramble to bring herself to a stand, and a woman in red in a dress made to look like a skeleton stalks toward her. My gift reacts instantly at the sight of the scar on the woman's face.

"You useless mortal," the Queen's high pitched voice rings in my ears.

I take a step forward to help the woman, only to halt in my steps when Valen places a hand on my shoulders.

"Don't," he whispers, "you'll make it worse."

"You deplorable excuse of a servant, get back to work," she growls.

The woman bows, running back into the room, and the Queen follows suit.

"Let's go," Valen whispers.

Spinning on my heels I head straight toward the barren tree, pacing up and down the yellowed grass furious at the Queen's treatment of her servants.

Valen stands nearby, watching me uncertainly. I know he isn't supposed to concern himself with my distress—unless of course it was to report back to his *masters* —and I definitely don't feel like expressing my frustration to the Prince.

It's almost a relief to see old Rumner ambling placidly out of the doorway behind Valen, placing a heavy hand on the shoulder of the boy I healed earlier, and exchanging glances with the worried sentinel.

Whatever communication passed between them, I neither know nor care, but I am aware of the old porter shambling quietly towards me and lowering himself patiently onto the bench by the tree.

I try to ignore him. I'm not in the mood for conversation.

After a few more moments of tense silence, I hear a low, deep humming. The old man, tapping his pipe on the side of his nose as he leaned back and looked up at the tree, was humming a few bars of some old folk tune to himself.

Despite my rage, I find it… soothing? It's clearly an older song, perhaps even one from the distant days of his youth. To top it off, Rumner had no gift at all for music. His pacing was off, the notes were odd and perhaps out of place, but nevertheless it felt like a glimpse into the distant days of his past.

Finally, I turn to face him.

The humming fades, and his eyes twinkle. I feel a flash of annoyance.

"It's cruel," I say, eventually.

"Many things are, lass," he nods amiably, "Foxes and women and the sea, they all spring to mind. But what cruelty are ye meaning?"

"*Her*," I snarl.

"Oh, aye. She's one of the worst," he grunts, examining his pipe as though he'd never seen it before, "but even a fox cares for its kits, ye ken? Her ladyship is as bad as a broke-tooth boar, and as kind as a hungry buzzard, there's truth there. But she is not without a heart."

"Oh, yeah?" I snap, "Do you know whose it was?"

Valen looks on nervously as Rumner's chortle of amusement rolls around the garden. Despite my fury, there is a purity and wholesomeness to his laugh that threatens to make me smile again.

"The way she treats people is disgusting," I go on, shaking off the moment and focusing on my anger, "She makes you carry the heaviest loads of anyone in the Palace! And you with your…"

I trail off, wondering if he'd be self-conscious about his maiming, and not wanting to embarrass the man.

"Oh, aye, 'me with my'," he grins, lifting his hand without a care and waving it at me, "but 'me with my' is what I mean, lass. Lost it to a tree-felling. No one's fault. Not much call for a one-handed gardener in the Palace grounds, though."

"She picks on you and makes you struggle, every day!" I burst out emphatically.

"Aye, and every day I show everyone that I can still be useful," he nods, his voice quiet, "and thanks to *her*, I still draw pay enough to fill my belly and take home to my own."

"Wait…" I pause, caught off guard, "Are you saying that she… is being kind to you?"

"Well," Rumner sits back, rolling his eyes and making me grin despite myself, "I'm telling ye there's kind and then there's right. I do not think her kind to anyone, there's truth there, but… she does right by me, she does."

"She could just take care of you properly," I growl, unable to help myself.

"I take care of me," Rumner says firmly, with the determination that can only come from those who grew old through hard times, "She but gives me a chance. And she could not risk taking too many under her harpy's wing, or else she would be seen to be soft. She must look to herself, and she is good at that, lass. Aye, she's good at that. But she has a heart, or part of one left. And all those near to her are given a chance to look to themselves."

He rolls to his feet, tucking his pipe away and clapping his leather hat back on his head.

"She's not *kind*," he finished firmly, "Do not think her *nice*. She'll rip yer throat out in a moment, given a chance. Do not let down yer guard. But just know this: there's not a man, woman or Fae in this world that doesn't have a side you haven't seen."

With a final tip of his cap, he ambles off again, leaving only the scent of leather and grass behind him.

And me, pondering his words.

~

Maiya hands me yet another red dress, and to no surprise, my hair is tied off my shoulder in a series of elaborate braids, all braided into one long weft that reaches my mid back.

The King probably ordered her to give me more revealing clothing, not to push me to the limit of my comfort. No, it's so that he can more accurately paint his concubines and get his pleasure from those women that have the same hair color as me.

When Maiya looked away, I managed to hide the butter knife under my dress. Now, walking to meet the queen, there's the ever-present possibility that I didn't tie it tight enough to stop it from falling out if I move too quickly, or sit the wrong way. If I find myself in need of a subpar knife, there is absolutely no way I would be able to pull up the mountain of fabric and reach under the skirt to retrieve the knife in time to dodge an oncoming attack.

I try to think about anything except how frantically my heart is beating, or how my fingers fidget with the skirts of the dress.

The King looks up from her goblet of wine when I walk in. She's reading a book on a settee. I almost forgot what she looks like fully clothed. The dress she wears makes all the dresses I've worn look pathetic. The entire gown is beaded in an array of gems fashioned to look like a phoenix spreading its wings. Even though the Empire has fervently denied the existence of the phoenix, it hasn't stopped royals and noble families from decorating their homes and clothes in the likeness of the creature. Unless that's a lie as well, and the phoenix isn't just a myth.

I hesitate in the doorway. If she isn't going to bring up yesterday's incident, then I won't. I doubt that the queen has miraculously forgiven and forgotten about it though.

Belve shoves me inside and slams the door. Queen Mellonia raises her chin, gesturing to the settee next to her.

The pimple hasn't wavered in its determination to sit in the center of her face. Satisfaction ripples through me knowing how much distress such a little thing is causing her.

I roll my shoulders back and lift my chin like I've seen her do countless times. Strolling over, I lower myself onto the seat with as much grace as possible. I tell myself to pretend to be the night—silent, beautiful, and deadly.

It's nowhere near as elegant as the way she sits.

"I had to miss a meeting because of you," Queen Mellonia says, without looking up from her book. Is the queen so embarrassed by the spot that she would miss a meeting about a dragon waking? It's possible there's more to her stress about a pimple than just her vanity and ego. The King killed his previous wife for getting a wrinkle. Murdering another wife for a pimple doesn't seem too farfetched.

When I don't respond, she sighs and places the book on the table next to her, drinking deeply from the goblet.

"I want you to get rid of the pimple, and," she hesitates, as if unsure whether to say the next part, "I want you to change my hair color." There's a plea in her eyes that eases my defenses.

"Why would you want to change your hair color?"

"You're not changing the hair color, per se, just keeping it the same," she sounds completely unsure of her words.

Her hair is as red as it was when I was a child. The woman before me is a completely different person to the one I met yesterday. This is the Cintis who spoke to her cat like a mortal would. This woman seems human.

"I don't understand," I say.

"This is what I want my hair color to be," she motions to her hair, "it used to be this color, but childbirth changed it to brown." As she speaks, anger trickles through her words, as her shoulders tense.

I sigh, looking down at my hands, "I see."

I don't see. I have absolutely no idea what she means or how her hair color changed.

But there's one thing I do understand--she's as much of a hostage as I am.

We are controlled by the men around us. The day we were born, our lives were sold to men who sit up in high places, who women away so they're seen but not heard. Just like Queen Mellonia, confined to her corner in the throne room.

Despite every awful thing she has said and done to me, I want to help her. I want to do everything I can to make her life a little less awful. She has been forced to believe that her value depends on what she looks like. I may not be able to help myself from feeling self-conscious in my own skin, but I can help her be more comfortable knowing that she won't lose her life from bringing life into the world.

"I'll see what I can do," I say confidently. "Please give me your hand, Your Highness."

Her nails scrape my skin as she places her hand in mine. Inhaling deeply, I close my eyes and send my gift into her, basking in the warmth of her fire. The gift heals the spot, then slowly makes its way to her scalp. Just like her nails, I can't find her hair either. It seems to be dead.

"I have no faith that you'll be able to do this. If you could, you wouldn't let your hair look like pig's shit." My gift returns to me in a flash. "Is that what I need to do? I need to smear my hair in shit to make my husband look at me?" Before I can respond, she spits in my face.

The smell of burnt leather taints the air when the settee behind me catches fire. Flames lick my back as sweat gathers down my spine. Her nails rips into my wrist when I drop her hand—tearing into my skin when I try to pull my hand away from her

"Let go of me," I beg.

I regret ever taking pity on her. How could I imagine she's anything other than a monster? She deserves whatever the King has in store for her.

Short may she reign.

"That's it," she gasps, eyes alight and I can smell the danger coming from her, "It's your hair."

I choke when her claws dig into my skin, preventing me from wrenching myself free. My mind continues to turn in a useless attempt at trying to figure out what my hair has to do with her hair color.

I need to get her off of me, but I couldn't reach for the knife even if I tried. I haven't even felt it move. Maybe I wrapped the damn thing so tightly that I could climb Mount Polis and it wouldn't fall out. Even if I could get it, it would be utterly useless against the Queen of Fire.

She yanks me closer, and my knees slam against the marble floor while my chest hits the side of a settee. Shock thunders up my legs at the impact. My free hand snaps in front of me to stop my head from crashing against the floor. She knocks my hand away, and a loud crack vibrates through my face. My gift springs to life, charging to my nose as blood starts to trickle out of my nostril.

This feels far too similar to the night Belve ripped my clothes in the cell.

I struggle to get her off me. Evander taught me how to use a sword, but he never taught me how to break free from *this*. A rope made out of fire ties my arms together, and my skin heals at the same time it burns, creating a nauseating cycle of exhaustion and pain.

Weak. You'll never win a fight against her, the voice says.

"It's your hair!" Her monstrous screech burns my ear as she pulls my head back by my braid.

"Get off of me, you psychotic bitch!" A side table comes crashing down, splattering glass and liquid all over the floor as I thrash and buckle. I try to wriggle free from her, but the rope only tightens. And burns.

She laughs again, making my stomach coil. "I wonder how much they will like you without your hair!"

Out of the corner of my eye, something silver catches my eye.

A dagger.

The darkness jumps at the sight, arming itself for an attack. Sweat breaks out across my forehead as I try to grasp the darkness and bend it to my will—to use it to get her off me. Every time I reach for that well of power, it's like running my hands through mist; I see it, but I can't touch it.

She yanks my hair harder, and a scream twists through me. Her laughter rings louder in tune with my screams when she lowers the dagger. With a single swipe, the strain in my neck goes loose and I have to brace myself from smashing my head against the floor a second time.

Turning around with all my might, I face the queen and the sinister smile spread across her face, holding a rope that looks oddly like hair in her hand.

Don't flatter yourself. She wouldn't willingly hold anything of yours unless it's hurting you, the voice says.

Her pale knuckles are wrapped in a death grip around the dagger, readying to slice again. Darkness swarms through my lungs and I can feel it shoving me out of my own mind to take control. My heartbeat stops and a cold calm whispers through me as soon as the first white fleck of dust appears in my vision.

My head feels light. Not like I'm about to faint, but like a physical weight has been taken from me.

As soon as her arm moves, the darkness swells through me, swarming into my lungs and changing the air inside it to pure power, hungry for blood.

Queen Mellonia's weight is ripped off me before the darkness can sink its teeth into her. The power tunnels back into my core, leaving me empty and defenseless at her disappearance. The rope around me extinguishes, and my breath returns with such force that a different sort of white dots appear.

"What have you done?" A deep voice booms; rattling every last plate and glass in the room.

I haul myself up and look up to find hungry blue eyes locking with mine. King Cyrus.

"I was teaching her a lesson," the King slips on her mask of boredom.

"Was *this*," the King raises his hand, holding what looks like a brown rope, "part of the lesson?" Darkness seeps into his eyes as he taps his fingers against his sword, and she meets his gaze with a triumphant smile.

"I got what you needed, didn't I?" she mutters.

I swing my attention back to the rope, my hands fumble over my scalp. He's holding my hair.

"You *bitch*," I spit. That hair was like armor that covers my skin. At least it was. What else will they take from me? How much more of me can I afford to lose?

"Leave, Althea," the King commands.

I glare at the Queen one last time before rushing out of the door. I don't wait for Belve to catch up as I sprint to my chambers, holding back the tears that threaten to fall as my heels echo through the hall until I make it to my chamber.

Raging heat creeps over my skin. Grabbing the settee in my room that is not really my own, I throw it as hard as I can across my pretty prison. Wrapping my hand around the pitcher, I toss that too. Next, the useless knife under my dress. Not after fighting the mountain of fabric to get to it.

They've broken me.

They've won.

Evander said that the mask only makes me self-destruct. He was right. Fuck those breathing techniques. It's time to accept this is who I am.

I couldn't care less about what my hair *looks* like. My survival doesn't depend on my vanity. But the queen didn't just cut my hair, she cut away any hope I have of getting through all of this in one piece—without losing myself forever.It was the one thing that has been consistent since I've been here. I was stupid and foolish for believing there might be goodness in her; that we might have some kind of comradeship from our mutual prison.

We are nothing alike. She is a monster.

Maybe it takes a monster to defeat a monster, the voice taunts.

In the midst of my tears, a maniacal laugh rips through my chest. The King made his concubines have my hair color. And the queen honestly thinks shortening my hair gets back at him? She's as stupid as me.

I tear a hole through the gown, shredding it into little ribbons. Feathers explode from the pillows as the butter knife penetrates the fabric.

Crawling my way to the mirror, I grip it with both hands and stare down the woman looking back at me—a tangled mess of uneven hair. Chunks of it go down to my collar bone, while others run sharply along my shoulder.

Pathetic anger rips through me at the sight.

I got what you needed, didn't I? Queen Mellonia's voice resonates in my mind. It's another thing to add on my list of things I don't understand, because I don't know where to begin with explaining why they'd want my hair.

I don't stop destroying the chamber until night creeps in and there's nothing left for me to destroy. So, I sit in the center of the room, in the center of my destruction, and I sob.

CHAPTER 24

"I hate and I love. Why I do this, perhaps you ask.
I know not, but I feel it happening and I am tortured."
— *Catullus*

I sob until my mouth goes dry and my voice weathers.

Just when I think there's nothing left to come out, a sob rattles through my bones.

I don't hear the door opening until warm arms cocoon me, and a honeyed voice whispers sweet nothings into my ear. His kisses plant themselves on my hair like freckles.

It feels strange to cry in the arms of the very person that's partly to blame. It feels like I'm betraying myself for finding solace in a man that I can never fully trust. Not as long as he has the power to take everything—and everyone—that I love away from me.

Despite all the pain and heartache his bloodline has caused me, I still yearn to be closer to him—to have every inch of my skin covered by his.

Evander said I attract souls that need healing. Maybe it isn't what I attract, rather what I'm attracted to.

I've seen the cracks in Auberon's mask, the pain he tries to hide when the topic of his family arises. There's something about him that feels incomplete. Broken. I want to know more about him, to let the sweet melody of his voice find a home in my heart. Yet, he's never felt like a mystery—not like Evander—he feels like an open book, unafraid to let his true desires show. But still, I'm not sure if I'm drawn to Auberon's storm of possessive passion laced with tender care, or the inferno within him.

We are two pieces that have come from completely different puzzles. Though we may fit, it'll never be the right picture unless one of us paints the other in their colors.

His hands run through what's left of my hair. He must think my own vanity is the reason for the destruction of the chamber.Maybe being in this Palace has shifted my view of my own image.

This is something his mother would do. Maybe she and I aren't so different after all.Except, of course, that I laid waste to my room out of despair. Disillusion.

"What happened?" he asks when my sobs no longer shake through me.

"Your mother happened," I grate into his tear-soaked chest.

"Ah," he says, unsurprised in the slightest, "and she did this?" he motions to my hair. Sniffling, I pull away from him, earning a warm chuckle. "You think that I'm going to let you go when you're like this? We're staying right here until I decide that you can be free of me."

No heat runs through me. Nothing tightens. For once, my heart lights up instead. "Far worse has happened these past few weeks than losing something that will grow back. It is nothing."

"I know you'll be fine, and I know you've had the worst thrown your way. But I'm here now, and I'm not going to let what's mine go just because she says she'll get over it." Tilting my chin up, his lips caress mine in an achingly languidness. "I want you, Althea. I'm never going to let my mother anywhere near you again."

It's another one of his promises. If he upholds this promise with as much vigor as he does the other, then maybe I'll be able to heal—mend my broken parts without my gift.

"Thank you." I wrap my arms around him and breathe in his scent of honey.

"It's unfortunate. Your hair was so beautiful," he sighs.

I've never really thought much about my hair. It was nothing more than a means to hide my marks or keep me warm during the winter months. In the Remains, you become reduced to nothing more than your primal instinct to survive against predators and the elements, caring about your appearance is at the bottom of the list of importance.

"Maiya will be pleased to know that she has less work to do now that she doesn't need to fight my tangles," I try to joke to pretend that none of this is a big deal.

"I don't think she will be too pleased about cleaning this place up." I imagine her frail hands picking through the mess, accidentally hurting herself from a hidden shard of glass, and my faint amusement withers. She doesn't deserve to bear the brunt of my breakdown. She's more of a prisoner than I am.

"This is my mess, and it's my responsibility to clean it."

"You don't need to: this is her job. Just leave it for her." He sighs with a hint of annoyance. I pull away from him and this time he lets me go.

"That may be so, but I'm not a child that can't handle the consequences of my own actions." I pause and say to the Prince with more confidence than I should, "Or a man for that matter."

The corners of his lips curve into a grin. "I can't say I often hear women making comments at the expense of men, especially to their Prince. You're much braver than I give you credit for." His amused smirk morphs into his signature warm smile. "You're a good person, don't let anyone take that away from you."

"I'm not a good person," I say, recalling what he said to me by the dungeons. "I'm an idiot."

Another thought flickers through my head; maybe kindness and sympathy aren't personality traits, but a side effect of my gift. My heart howls in anger whenever I see a Cintis, yet as soon as they show any sign of mortality, the howls turn into a pitiful whimper like it did with the queen.

"The War changed everything for everyone, Althea. This is not your pain to feel alone," his shoulders slump, and guilt taints his words.

"Don't pretend life was good for mortals before the War. The Anzeth gave the Cintis a taste of their own medicine," I argue, welcoming the distraction from thoughts of my hair.

Red embarrassment dots his face. "No, but this is a war that all of us should unite in."

"The aftermath of the War of the Elements is far worse than what it was beforehand. The only reason your kind has become so desperate for change is because for once, the fae are suffering." I know that I should stop talking, but I continue regardless, "You have done nothing to make it better for mortals. You are the Prince of Audor—*the Prince,* for gods' sake. If there's anyone who could change life for the mortals living on the outskirts, it's *you.* Visiting a few families is not enough."

I pause, trying to glean his mood. All I find is an unreadable glint in his eyes. So I carry on, "We are starving down there. For weeks on end, we would eat nothing but a bowl of soup. You and I both know there's a lot more food in this Palace alone than there is in the market square—"

"I know, but there's nothing I can do," he interrupts defeatedly, trying to stop my rant.

"You have the power to change *everything,*" I whisper loud enough to be considered yelling, "Only if you actually want to."

"I've been trying, but there's *nothing* I can do," he says with practiced patience.

"Then try harder."

I stand, walking through the feathers coating the floor, ignoring the glass crunches beneath my steps, to gaze out the window.

Sighing, he stands, placing a gentle hand on my arm. "I'm trying. Trust me. This is as much as I can do. Being the prince means very little when King Cyrus is your father," his voice is barely a whisper, yet I can feel his words in my soul. That's all we can do now: try.

Taking my hand in his, he tugs me behind him, leading me out the door. "Come," he says. "Let's go for a walk."

~

He takes me down unfamiliar hallways and spiraling staircases that lead into the unknown. We pass door after door, statue after statue. It's only now that I realize that not a single one of these paintings are of any of the King's children, dead or alive. The only work of art depicting a person that isn't the King was along the walls of the queen's wing.

"Tell me about the dragon," I say, deciding to break the silence.

"I thought you already knew about it. You attended the sessions with the acolytes, right?" he says, bewildered by my question.

"Yes, we had to. Are they real?"

A smile spreads from ear to ear like he's about to tell a child a secret. "Yes."

I stare at him, feeling a faint thread of irritation start to wind in me. "Have you seen any?"

A childish grin tickles his lips. "Maybe I have, or maybe I haven't." He winks.

"They told us that they're all asleep." A statement, not a question. He looks at me warily, unsure where I'm headed with my line of inquiry. "All the dragons and Warriors went to rest before the War of the Elements, correct?"

He readjusts the collar of his tunic, looking around the garden like he's trying to spot wandering eyes. "Yes, that is correct."

"Then why is Niran awake?" He loses his composure for the slightest heartbeat as shock plasters his face, before he attempts to school it back to a fake smile.

"That's ridiculous. You must have started daydreaming too much, locked away in your room." He doesn't look me in the eye, and it becomes too uncomfortable to breathe. Of course, he wouldn't tell me if it were true: why would he?

I could tell him about the acolyte, but it's clear he won't give me the answers that I want. So, I feign resignation. "You're right. Boredom has ways of playing tricks on the mind."

Rounding a corner, he opens a set of thick glass doors. I welcome the chill of the night. It brings me some level of comfort, like I'm back home about to sneak through Ignis with Evander. Had I known we were going outside, I wouldn't have dared the night with a flimsy dress with a shredded skirt that has a newly added split up my leg.

This place makes the City Garden look lackluster and uninteresting. It is far more beautiful on the ground than from my window. Rows upon rows of rose bushes dance across the land, arching over walkways and circling around columns.

As we walk, he tells me more stories about his days as a child, and all his quarrels with Evander; how he would try to steal Auberon's toys, while Auberon stole his snacks. It's hard to believe that they were like brothers.

Our shoes crunch against stone, meandering through flowers and trees, and across a small wooden bridge over a pond illuminated by floating candles. At the sound of our footsteps, the water splashes and movement scurries beneath. We stop atop the bridge, his arm drapes over my shoulder, pulling me against him as the cold makes me shiver.

"I want you, Althea." His whisper trickles down my spine.

The Prince was never meant to be with the peasant. That's the dream of fools; to give them false hope that there's a better future ahead of them. He can want me as much as he'd like, but I don't see a world where we can truly be. We are two opposites that will never make a whole.

"You and I are from two different worlds," I say, looking away from him to the moonlight reflecting against the rippling water.

"Yes, we are," he breathes out, and I look back at his onyx eyes.

"We don't stand a chance, do we?"

"We do, we just aren't letting ourselves take it." I hold his gaze and bask in his warmth before he shakes his head and looks away. "Let's continue. There's somewhere I want to show you."

He takes my hand again and we walk in silence toward a towering tree, with leaves dripping off twigs all the way to the ground. We duck under an overhanging branch, moving towards the middle in complete darkness.

"I can't see anything down here. Let me see your beautiful face." He says desperately. Shadows drown us both, and I can barely make out his silhouette when he snaps his fingers producing a glowing orb of fire. The light catches the leaves above, casting shadows that dance with the wind. The flames lick the wood, but not even a single spark alights under its heat.

"Gods," I breathe, "that's a handy trick."

"You have no idea how much easier it is to sneak out when you can actually see where you're going." His voice carries a whisper of amusement.

"Oh yes, the Prince of Night sneaking out of his Palace to rendezvous with his lovers," I tease.

I can feel him tense by my side. "No, of course not."

"We're both adults here. We can give into the pleasures of our flesh without shame," I say with more indifference than I feel.

My back hits the solid trunk. His fingers wrap around my wrists before I can take another breath, and he forces my hands against the wood above my head, pinning them with one hand. My soul suffers a throbbing ache before it springs to life from the heat that rushes through my tightening core. I shiver, but not from the cool night air

"And did you sneak out in the night to seek *pleasure*?" he mutters darkly against my ear; his lips brushing my cheek. "Did they give you the pleasure that you wanted?"

What we are doing under this tree is not different to the heated nights Evander and I shared. Auberon, too, has taken me under the dead of night sky and tempted my desires. My body trembles as his hips push into me, and his hand finds their way to my breast.

"I asked you a question." His thumb moves in painfully slow movements over the thin material of my dress. The tips harden to painful points under his command. His mouth finds its way to the base of my neck, and a moan escapes me as he feasts on the soft skin, pulling the straps over my shoulders so my breasts are his for the taking.

"I…" I don't have the words to speak. I don't want to think about *that* right now.

His lips don't move from me as his hand snakes into the slit of my dress, hiking it up so that my legs are exposed to the night. His hand skates up my thighs, tracing my skin before he squeezes the bare flesh of my behind. A rush of wet warmth pools between my legs. Cool air teases my thighs and hips, yet my body is on fire from his touch.

"Use your words," his deep voice stirs my core. Long fingers find their way between my thighs, touching me so softly over the throbbing point that I whimper.

More. I want more. Need more.

I can't breathe from our desires tainting the air. But still, I feel intoxicated by it.

We may never truly be together, but if I'm in this prison, should I deny myself such pleasures as they come?

"Are you going to use your words, or will I need to punish you?"

My hips arch towards him and my head flicks back as he places a dangerous amount of pressure on my center. His fingers circle faster and harder, my hips roll on instinct with his movements, hungry for more. My breath comes out hard, only to become ragged when the rumble that comes from his chest sends a wave of heat through me.

"I can already tell how wet you are. I want to feast off you." His voice is a hot whisper against my ear, as his fingers move faster. He drops my arms and pulls the material covering my chest down like it's his greatest nemesis, and his lips find their way to the points. Pleasure blossoms through me, and my chest throbs, wanting more. His tongue swirls around the nipple, dragging his teeth across the tip and sucking. At once, cold air bites my chest and his finger leaves my center, making me whimper. "But girls who don't do as they're told get punished," he sighs.

I can feel him devouring every inch of my naked body. There's nothing hiding my skin from him now.The secrets of my skin are all his.

His fingers lace through my hair, yanking my head back as the other tightens around my throat. My head goes sinfully light as the air to my lungs is cut off. "Now, are you going to be a good girl and answer?" More heat pools between my legs as his fingers tighten. A strangled cough leaves me when I try to speak. "Nod your head if you're ready to obey."

Pressure grows around my neck as I try to nod. The air doesn't feel hostile, it's burning with our hunger.

His fingers loosen around my throat as he grabs one of my hands and puts my hand on his length bulging beneath the seams of his breeches. As if my fingers have a mind of their own, they push against the fabric, cupping his length and feeling it pulse against my palm. An earth-shattering growl vibrates through him as I start to move up and down in slow teasing motions.

He snatches my hand away and grips my hair even tighter. "Did you used to sneak out at night and *fuck*?"

Oh gods. Such a question shouldn't make me so heated, but the rawness in his voice makes my knees buckle. The friction of my nipples against the fabric of his suit exerts another gasp.

"Yes." My mind labors with the idea of feeling him inside of me as he fucks me into oblivion.

"Yes, what?" He pushes me harder against the tree and his hand moves back to my backside and grabs it. Hard.

"Yes, I snuck out." He groans and wraps his fingers back around my throat. He stops when I say, "Yes, I sucked and I fucked until this world didn't feel like it existed. I let him fuck me until I could still feel the marks he left on me for days after."

A lethal snarl rips through the air, and a rage far more dangerous than any power he yields flicks through his eyes.

"You *belong* to me."

I whimper as a primal snarl tears through him; he wraps my legs around him and pushes me against the tree before I can even blink. "And most of all, I own this," he grunts, pushing his finger inside me.

My toes curl at the explosion of sensations, and my head whips back crying in pleasure.

He works two fingers inside me and starts rubbing hungry circles with his thumb. His lips crash into mine, catching my scream as his fingers curve hitting just the right spot. My hips move on their own accord, grinding in time with the rhythm of his fingers.

"That's it, fuck my fingers like only *I* can give you what you want." Piercing pain shoots through me as he pinches my nipple, and my hips plunge deeper onto his fingers as pressure builds in my core, sending me closer to the edge.

"Please," I beg.

"Please, what?" he pushes, rubbing the sensitive skin faster until I'm drowning in the feel of his fingers.

"I need…" I can't find the words to say what I want as the pressure spikes even higher, as my climax nears.

"How many times do I need to tell you? Use. Your. Words." With each word, his fingers push into me, until a third finger goes in, making me scream loud enough for Vesi to hear.

"Fuck me, please!" I scream, seconds away from breaking against his fingers.

My feet drop back onto the ground, and I whimper when his fingers disappear. Frustration builds from the almost climax. Before I realize what is happening, he turns me, pushing my chest against the tree.

The rustling of fabric sounds behind me as he pulls his length out, teasing me with his tip.

The other hand cups my breast, massaging it before my lungs become devoid of air as he slams into me. My cry of both pain and pleasure echoes through the garden. His fingers dig so deeply into my waist that it will bruise. The way he pounds into me makes me stop caring about anyone around. It's been so long that the feel of him stings, and I want to bite into the fabric of my dress.

His pace is relentless. Starved. Burying inside me to the hilt. I lean against his shoulder as pleasure threatens to bury me alive.

"Who do you belong to?" His voice is little more than a burning breath against my skin. Just when I think there's nothing left of him to give, he pushes me down to my hands and knees on the ground, never once removing himself from inside me. The cold soil seeps into my skin, ice against the pyre between my legs.

His moan rumbles through the trees, and I tighten against his length as another wave of pleasure reaches every part of my nerves. "I asked you a question, Althea." Sharp pain rips through my core when he rams into me, even deeper than before. "Who does this *cunt* belong to?"

I can't say it. I can't give him the satisfaction. Because he already has me.

This entire Empire already owns me, and by extension, I'm already at his command. His sweet tongue and rough hands have brought me to my knees for him to take.

With a feral snarl, he slaps my backside and I scream again. The sting is sweet compared to his vicious thrusts that plunge me deeper into the ground with each stroke.

"I'm going to fuck you until you forget about every other person that's been in here. When I'm done with you, you're going to forget how to walk. I'll give you a reason to call me *your* prince." My hand moves to my center, rubbing my desire as the pain begins to fade, replaced by a ravished need to get my pleasure from him.

I push back against his thrust, taking him even deeper. He groans as my muscles tighten around him. He pulls me up so that my back is against his chest, slamming into me faster than humanly possible.

With one final thrust, he releases himself into me, filling me with his essence.

Shock rolls through me on the river of warmth. Since being here, I haven't taken any contraceptive tonic. I pull out of him and turn to face him.

"I'm not taking anything, are you?" I blurt.

He laughs, placing a gentle kiss on my forehead before standing to put his clothes back, swatting off the dirt at his knees. "Don't worry about that, kitten. I've already thought it through."

I sigh as he offers me his hand and pulls me off the ground. The cold air kisses my skin and I shudder. Without his warmth surrounding, the night is icy and unforgiving. I right my dress to find him gone and the orb of fire with him

Ducking under the branches, his heated breath comes out in smoke against the nighttime air. Accepting his outstretched hand, we walk in silence to the glass doors we came through. There, Belve takes one look at our linked hands and his lips tighten into a thin line.

Auberon turns to me with a guilt-ridden grimace. "Belve will take you back to your chambers. I'm sorry about all of this." He bends down, whispering. "Don't forget that you're mine."

In a blink of an eye, he disappears back into the garden, leaving me alone with a man who thinks I'm an abomination.

CHAPTER 25

quod defles, illud amasti.
That which you weep for is what you really loved.
— *Lucan, Lucan; The Civil War Books I-X*

I jolt awake with a start as the door clicks closed. Moonlight still shrouds my chamber, and out the corner of my eyes I can see a figure loom in the shadows.

"Are you awake?" a deep voice whispers.

I sigh in relief, slumping further into the torn pillows, and a smile breaks across my face. *Evander.*

The sound of a sword being drawn grates my ears as I jump into a sitting position.

"What happened? Is someone here? Why is your room like this?" Panic laces his voice. In the shadows, I can just make out his thick dark brows pinched together.

"I did it. No one is here."

Tension creases the air when his gaze travels from my face to my shoulders. "Your hair," he breathes. I can smell the anger roll off him as his mind reels. "If the Prince did that to you, I will gut him in his sleep. Consequences be damned."

"No. No, no. It wasn't the Prince: it was the queen. If you're going to kill her, I ask that you give me the final blow."

He looks unconvinced but puts his sword away all the same. The bed dips against his weight as he crawls closer to me, cupping my cheek in his hands.

No, he shouldn't touch me. I slept with his rival. I slept with Auberon. I betrayed him. Tension burrows deep within my stomach as guilt attacks me. How could I let myself do this? I was so controlled by lust I let his greatest rival take me. Now I am sitting in the same bed as the person that's been by my side for five years, as he pulls me into his tight embrace.What if Evander smells him on me? What if he heard my moans in the garden?

"At least you still look beautiful. I don't think anyone could do anything to you to change how stunning you are." His breath tickles my face as he speaks.

I hold my breath. I don't deserve him. He doesn't deserve what I did.

It feels wrong when his lips meet mine and he kisses me like I'm the last person in the world: like he actually wants me. How could I do this to him?

His tongue slips into my mouth and he explores me like he's never tasted me before. All I taste is *Auberon.*

Despite his passionate kiss, there's no lust in the air, only an emotion I can't quite pinpoint.

"I'm sorry about our fight. I should have been better."

I can still remember the pain of the burns, but I've healed from it already. My betrayal won't be so easy to heal. I was angry at him for risking my escape, but now I'm just angrier at myself for not being able to control myself.

He lets go and when he speaks, seriousness runs deep within every word. This is a side of Evander that I do not know. "I came here because there's something important that I need to tell you, and I don't have long. I bribed the sentinel to give me five minutes alone. But first, how are you coping? None of this can be easy on you, and I want you to know that I will never go anywhere."

All I can do is nod. I have never seen him so worried before, and I think there is fear in his eyes. It makes him look like a stranger.

"I know you'll just put a brave face on and take the mask off once I leave. This won't be easy to hear, but King Ryven of the Water Empire is making demands for you," he whispers.

I knew it was going to happen, it was only a matter of time before he tries to get me. But not so soon. I shake my head. "What could he possibly want with me?"

"I'm not sure. They've found a loophole in the treaty that puts a hold on Audor's trade; they're willing to stop if King Cyrus hands you over to them. You have to pretend that you haven't heard about it. No one else knows I'm here."

Once more, he's risking his life for me.

Pushing off the bed, Evander reaches for me, attempting to get me to come back. He's going to try and comfort me, and I can't let him do that. I stand, dragging my feet along the floor, making an empty path as I pace up and down the room.

"Do they need a healer or something?"

"I have no idea." The bed groans as his feet find the floor and his arms wrap around me like they have a hundred times before. "But I'm going to get you out of here. I promise. They won't take you, Althea. I will do everything in my power to help you escape. I'll get your parents and we can run away to another corner of Audor where it's quieter. I just need two days."

"I need to get out of the Palace. I can't let them take me." I stare at my hands, making a mental list of all that will need to be done before my parents and I to leave Ignis. "How will you get Pa out? He can barely even walk, it's not like I can grow his leg back. We need a wagon and a horse."

His index finger moves to his lips, signaling me to keep my voice down.

"The Empire has stables all over the Ignis. No one will think twice if I go in to get four horses." The whole conversation is making nausea creep up my stomach.

I'm about to agree when I realize the weight of what we're going to do.

"No, one horse for Pa. I don't want someone to leave their livelihood or get sentenced to death for losing so many horses," I say.

They'd get killed for losing just one horse, the voice adds.

"Why are you doing this?" I ask.

It's a question that has been burning on the tip of my tongue. He's taking far more risks than someone that's just meant to be a lover.

"Because I like you, princess, more than you can even begin to comprehend," he says like he has never been so certain of anything else. Running his hand across his face, the deafening silence fills the room.

"What?" I squeak.

I've heard him say he cares so many times before, but I never believed it. Every single word he's said was the truth, now I fear I'm too late. I can't undo what I did.

"It was never about the sex to me, Althea. Never. When I first saw what you did to save your father, I was amazed at what you could do, yes. What really drew me to you was when I confronted you, and you were face to face with certain doom, you weren't scared. In fact, you tried to kill me despite knowing who I was." He looks to be in pain, suffering from buried memories of our first encounter. Pain lances his features as he speaks. He's wrong of course. I was frightened. But also, I was willing to get blood on my hands to keep me and mine alive.

"That doesn't explain anything," I say, resuming my trek up and down the center of the room.

"Please, let me finish," he pleads. At my sharp nod, he continues, "I wasn't planning on letting you get away with it scot-free, I was going to find out more about your gift to use for my own selfish gain. But when you waved Gladius in my face, all of my plans fell apart. Instead, I used you for a different sort of selfishness." I suck in a sharp breath, not wanting to hear that what I've been saying to myself all along was right. "I used you for companionship."

That's not what I thought he was going to say.

He runs his hand through his hair, sighing before he drops into the settee. "That's all it was to begin with. You never said it, but you didn't have to, because you're right. That day, I saw an opportunity, I knew that I could tell you anything I wanted, and you'd be forced to keep my secrets, because what I had over you was so much greater. It makes me sick thinking that I ever thought of you that way."

I walk backwards until I hit a wall, and my legs give out. I slide down to the floor, letting the sharp chill of the tile help steady my roaring mind. "So, you're saying that you don't think like that anymore?"

"Gods no," he groans in frustration, more to himself than to me. "That plan disappeared as soon as I got to know you. You're so strong when you believe in yourself, Althea. You're smart, you're brave, you're caring. You have the most beautiful fire in you that doesn't burn to the touch. Without it my life is cold and empty. Every part of me wanted to share everything with you. That's why I started to bring you food and coin every time we met in the forest, and almost every time after that. I only wish I did more."

My heart aches as he speaks, and I replay every moment we've spent together. All the laughing and the drinking, even the tears. I wouldn't trade those moments for the world.

"Please, I beg of you, don't ever think that you were just someone to warm my sheets. If I wanted to sleep with someone, I wouldn't have gone to the lengths I went to just to be near you." Frustration tips his voice as he drops to his knees and crawls the short distance to me. "At some point through our whole mess, I stopped seeing you as a friend, or an escape, and I started seeing you as something more. You became my whole world."

I didn't notice the silent tears streaming down my cheeks until it soaked into my dress and dampened my knees. He hesitates to touch me, dropping a wary hand around me. He's never proclaimed his innermost thoughts like this.

"I was so scared when you were fighting." I massage my hands like it might be able to get rid of the memory, and he holds me tighter, planting a kiss at the top of my head. Guilt tears a hole in my heart at what I did with Auberon. He didn't even bother walking me to my chambers himself after he did what he came to do. I blurt out, "I thought you were going to die. I kept thinking that I didn't deserve you, and that after all our years together I never told you how grateful I am for you. I spent years forcing down my own feelings, lying to myself that you don't care about me. It was easier to tell myself that I could never have feelings for someone who didn't want me, than to keep my heart away from someone who wanted me completely."

And still, you slept with Auberon, the voice reminds me.

"You don't need to explain yourself," he whispers against my cheek, "I should never have dangled your secret in front of you. I don't blame you for never believing me."

I blame myself for never seeing the truth. I've been so self-absorbed that I didn't see what was right in front of me. I've never seen him exposed like this. He tells me what bothers him, and small secrets about his life, but he's never laid himself bare before. All I can picture is the betrayal he will feel when he finds out about what I did with the Prince. All I can feel is the guilt of knowing that he may never look at me again, and I'll live the rest of my life knowing it would be all my fault.

A fate far worse than any betrayal could result if either of them finds out that I've been with the other. If the other night was any indication, Evander may go straight to Auberon. It will be a fight I won't be able to stop. And I'm frightened because I know who will lose. Evander doesn't stand a chance against Auberon.

Evander can hate me all he wants, but I wouldn't be able to live with myself if he died because of me. I'll tell him once I know it's safe to.

"It's in the past; let's focus on where we are now," I whisper.

"I was so angry when I saw his hands all over you. I wanted to kill him. I wanted to break every single bone in his body." The air thickens with hostility.

I shake my head, rubbing against the rough material of his cloak. "Your jealousy will get you killed. You can't do that, Evander, I would never forgive myself if something happened to you because of me."

"You're worth dying for, princess." My heart skips a beat. "I wish it were as simple as jealousy. He's a bad person, you have to stay away from him."

"You keep saying he's an awful person. What has he done that makes him so awful?" I ask. Part of me is starting to see that Auberon is, but not to the extent Evander describes.

"You need to trust me on this. They don't involve me in discussions, but I know the Prince has conspired with the King to do something bad with or to you. You cannot trust him under any circumstance."

"He's taken care of me while I've been here. He's been the only person to make sure I'm actually fed." Fed forcefully. There's a plea in my words that even I recognize. Am I trying to convince myself or him that Auberon has no ill intent?

He got what he wanted. He bedded you, then left you, the voice sneers.

"He's done more than just keep you fed. You spent five years questioning every single thing I did for you. Why is it that you've known him for all of five minutes and you've stopped asking questions?" He asks without spite, yet the question stings.

He's right. What is it about the Prince that made me ignore all of my reserve? I was skeptical about him at first, but at what point did it all stop? Why did I start trusting Auberon?

Has it been so long that my actions and ignorance stem from a lust-filled mind? How did he manage to bring my guard down so quickly, and make me submit to him even faster?

"What do you even see in him?" he questions.

I stare at him unsure how to answer. What do I see in him? Am I so bored and lonely that I might be walking into the Prince's trap? Where did it all go so wrong that I fell for him and let him do what he did?

A low knock rattles the door that makes me jump. "I have to go, Princess." His lips press on mine and a tear trickles down to salt our kiss. "I promise you that I will do everything I can to get you and your family out of here, and then we can finally be together. In two days. I promise."

There isn't a doubt in my mind that he will bring down the entire city if it means fulfilling his promise. He's never broken a promise before.

The problem isn't that I don't believe him, it's that I know we may never truly succeed. If we get away, the entire Empire of Fire will hunt us down. They won't rest until they find us. Evander will die on the altar for treason. As for me, that future is unknown. Maybe dying would be a greater gift than what the King or Queen might have in store for me.

"You'll get killed if you get anywhere near me. They want me alive. I'll meet you somewhere." Lunging to the side table, I grab the book with my map in it. Flicking through the pages I try to find the best place to meet. "I'll meet you here an hour before the changing of the sentinels," I say, pointing to a spot with a gilded carving of the King a few turns away from Auberon's chambers. I remember seeing a servant's entry nearby, and there's enough room behind the statue to hide.

"Okay, remember what I taught you. When you leave, make sure there is no chance the sentinel will wake up and start making noise so quickly. I'll hide Ma somewhere close, but safe."

"We have to get Pa quickly, before they sound the alarm that I'm gone," I say quickly. It's happening. It's finally happening. We can finally be free. He starts walking to the door. I don't want Evander to leave. I don't want to let him go now that I know his innermost feelings. "Wait, why did you say that you're getting four horses?

He pauses with his hand on the handle. Turning towards me, he whispers, "Because I'm coming with you. I love you, Althea."

As the door closes behind him, I pray that this isn't the last time I see him, and we do make it out alive.

CHAPTER 26

"Homo homini lupis est."
Man is a wolf to man

— Plautus

He loves me.

Evander loves me, and I betrayed him. But we are getting out of here in two days.

As soon as he is gone, I rekindle my acquaintance with the bin, retching from the thought of both their hands on me. What 'plan' could Auberon have that involves me, when he hasn't asked anything of me except to eat? He wouldn't be going through the trouble of debasing himself to act as a servant if his only intention was to bed me. It's hard to imagine an elaborate conspiracy that Auberon and the King would concoct just for me to open my legs.

My mind reels with questions as I set about cleaning up after myself: using my hands to sweep feathers and glass into a corner; piling the torn sheets on the settee; wiping the blood off the floor from the shards of glass that cut my skin.

In the morning, I thought Maiya would be livid when she sees the state of the room. Instead, she looks saddened and tired, which only fuels my guilt. I try to help her again, but she insists I stay seated and out of her way. She cleans the room with practiced ease. Clearly this isn't the first time she's had to clean up the aftermath of a tantrum.

She leaves and returns with baskets filled with new items over and over again.

In the afternoon, she arrives with a comb and shears. She forces me to bathe, insisting I call her when my hair is ready for washing. She massages floral-smelling creams into my hair, rinsing it out only to add another cream.

Worrying about my appearance is still new to me, but now my routine consists of caring what others see. The creams may have made my hair silken, but it still looks like absolute shit.

Maiya places a stool in front of the mirror for me to sit on. Without saying a word, she assesses the damage done to my hair, and the miracle she needs to work to make it the slightest bit presentable.

When she combs my hair, I tense, expecting her to yank at my tangles, but the pull never comes. Each stroke is smooth and unbothered by unruly tangles.

She gets a smaller comb and pulls the hair upwards, snipping at different angles, measuring it from one side to the other. I watch, transfixed, as strands of hair float to the now-clean tile floor. There's a hint of a smile on her lips, and she seems entranced by what she's doing.

Ma's friend would cut my hair once a year, and it would never be anything as intricate as this. She would tie my hair at the top of my head and take the shears to it, then 'fix it' when she untied it.

When Maiya is done, I can barely recognize my own reflection. Strands curve down, shaping my jaw, making my cheeks appear fuller. "You did an amazing job," I say, and she offers a broad smile.

"Thank you," she whispers, before cleaning my hair on the floor and leaving.

Later, as the sun begins to set, keys rattle at the door. A sentinel I've never seen before stands with his hand around the hilt of his sword.

"Come. You've been summoned." He doesn't wait for me to get out of bed before turning away to walk down the halls.

I don't bother rushing to follow him. I take my time getting out, folding the blankets and placing them at the foot of the bed. Leisurely walking to the drawers to put on a robe over the nightgown, and tying slippers to my feet, I gaze into the mirror to adjust the way it sits. If they want me to care about my appearance, then maybe I will do so without the help of Maiya.

Turning away from the mirror, I find the Cintis standing under the doorway, livid. I couldn't care less. I'm tired of being played, but I'm not against playing others. I smile sweetly and say, "Ready? We shouldn't leave them waiting."

His jaw ticks, as his fingers curl around his sword. He must be under someone's command to leave me alone. If only that rule extended to the queen.

His nails dig into his palms from the countless times he sped ahead, only to turn around to find me strolling along, stopping every once in a while to admire the art.

We're walking in the familiar direction to the queen's chambers. Auberon promised I wouldn't receive a summons from her anymore. I had hoped he was a man of his word, but Evander is right, I can't trust him.

He isn't taking me to Auberon's chambers, because that's in the other direction. If memory serves, we already passed the turn that leads to the throne room.

Part of me wants to be summoned by the queen so she can see that cutting my hair meant nothing to me. I want her to know that despite the tears I spilt, she won't keep me broken. I am not the marks on my skin or the cut of my hair. I am so much more.

Paintings of roses and the queens of Audor line the walls as we make our way to the queen's wing. I feel a faint tickle of unease when the sentinel walks past the door to the queen's chambers and waits for me by another set of stairs.

If it's not another summons, or another performance in the throne room, then it's possible I'm being led far worse. The Palace changes from morbid black to blinding gold. The entire hallway is gilded. A mosaic of a dragon and the sun covers the floor as every inch of the place is lit by fire.

Too entranced by the gold, I don't notice that the sound of footsteps no longer accompanies me. Instead, an eerie silence fills my soul.

"Althea," a deep voice rumbles behind me. "I was beginning to think you weren't coming. You're late."

My hands tremble as I hold in my breath. A yelp squeezes out of me as a warm hand touches my waist before I face *him*. The darkness unfurls in my chest, and every fiber of my being screams for me to run.

Before I can move, the King's arms snake around me, pulling me against a mass of solid heat. I bite my tongue not to shriek. I can't let him think he's gotten to me. Not again.

My breath starts to heat through sputtered coughs as my gift goes wild, circling my lungs. I want to roar as fire burns the tissue in my chest. Only a gasp escapes me. Agony rips through me as my throat boils. My gift can't seem to figure out how to fix the damage, because it's like it's still happening.

"I promise you there are fates far worse than death. Come to my chambers, and I will stop hurting you, do you understand?" Tears trickle into my open mouth as I choke. Without even thinking, I nod. As soon as I do, the pain dissipates.

His arms around me leave, and he strolls down the hall. Without his support keeping me upright, my knees buckle, and I stumble against the wall, heaving up dry, ashen air. My gift works quickly, repairing the damage the King did to my organs. I shouldn't be surprised that he has the power to disintegrate a person's insides into cinders, but I am.

The hallway seems to cower as he walks. His presence dominates the high ceiling and gilded pillars.

Sweat coats my body and the silky material of my nightgown sticks to my skin. My lungs squeeze as the claustrophobia settles in. There's too much on me. I need it off *now*. My fingers work at the knot of the robe tied around my waist, frantically attempting to untie it. A scream of frustration leaves me as I rip off the gown that's worth more than what my parents earn in a week.

Maybe he'll get the wrong idea from my lack of outerwear, but I can't bring myself to care in this instance.

A shiver runs through me and goosebumps tickle my flesh as a chill settles on my skin. Pushing myself off the wall, I follow him into another room, not so fast that I seem eager or afraid, but not so slow as to anger the monster.

I freeze in place as soon as I step into his chambers. The room is both exquisite and terrifying.

In the center, a stone fountain ten feet tall spews fire out of a dragon's mouth. The flames flicker out of the beast, spilling over golden mountains and buildings, pooling onto the marble floor without an outer frame to stop it. "Come." His voice calls from an adjacent room. I move towards it, keeping to the edge of the room to avoid the fountain. Gritting my teeth, I force my feet forward, knowing better than to refuse such a command.

Thoughts of the King's skin on me push into my mind, and I try to move them aside, focusing on the possible life or death matter at hand.

If he wants to kill you, he would do it in front of an audience, the voice chimes, bringing me a sense of comfort that I might live yet another day. With it, however, lies the anxiety of what he might do to me instead.

Do his concubines come to his personal chambers or is there a designated room for such proclivities? If the King expects me to be his whore like the queen fears, surely he would house me with them.

The sight of his sitting room brings a wave of nausea.

More gold. My rage isn't founded on the fact that he lives in splendor while the rest of us are left to rot. No. The fury rushing through me is from realizing that this is what mortals have paid for with their blood and tithe.

"Wear that." He points to the dress made of liquid sunlight on the table.

"No, thank you. I'm fine with what I'm wearing." At least that's what I want to say.

Instead, I just stare at it. But I'm not fine with what I'm wearing. The straps are far too thin, the neckline is far too low, and the slit is far too revealing. I might be used to being exposed by now, but I will never be alright feeling this vulnerable.

"Change, or I might find your mother more compliant," he threatens like my disobedience bores him. The temperature of the room rises a couple of degrees, and I know the calmness was a lie.

"Please don't touch her, Your Majesty" I stutter.

Both Evander and Auberon assured me she's safe and far away from the King, but as much as I trust them, I don't doubt the King's capabilities.

"My son may think he's so clever that he can hide her from me, but I know everything that goes on in my Empire." He sips mauve liquid from a crystal glass. "I applaud him for his valiant attempt to keep a secret from me. He saw an opportunity to woo you by caring for your parents, and he took it. From what I hear, it worked, you folded." My rage and embarrassment burn my cheeks. Evander was right, it was all just a plan. "Do not be fooled. Any interest he has in you is distorted and has been quite tactfully executed. Now change."

What does he mean *tactfully executed*? Auberon watched me before I was captured? Was there a twisted plan involving me before I was taken?

I was a fool to think she was safe. None of us will ever be safe as long as we are still in Audor. Neither of my parents are safe. Evander needs to forget about me. He needs to get my parents out first before even thinking about getting me.

I shouldn't be surprised that the King found out about my night in the gardens with Auberon. There were sentinels around, and I didn't keep my treacherous moans to myself. The entire Empire probably knows.

"You're a stupid little girl. You fell for every single one of Auberon's fumbling charms. All we had to do was make sure you feared me, and Auberon would come running to be your knight in shining armor. Why else do you think he would ever put up with your venomous tongue?"

I feel myself grow pale, blood draining away like from a butchered rabbit. It was all a ploy. Everything. From the very beginning, Auberon was lying to me. All the signs were there, and I missed it.

"You've failed. Despite all the time I've allowed, you still haven't harnessed your power. I even tried helping to bring that power out of you, feeling infatuated by my son, hating the queen, and fearing the queen. All that, and you've proven yourself quite useless to me."

Ragged breaths escape my lips, and I steel my spine. No. I can't think about Auberon. Not right now. I need to give him a reason to keep me alive and in Ignis. "I did harness it," I blurt.

He cocks his head, bemused. "Show me," he orders.

Stupid, did you not think before you spoke? Of course, he'd ask for proof—proof you can't give, the voice says.

I still need to try. Attempting to breathe deeply, I yank a gilded ornament from a table, gripping it tightly. Blinking rapidly I stare at the ornament hoping the dots will appear. Nothing happens. The King's fingers drum against the armrest, and I narrow my eyes on the ornament imagining the dots. Again, nothing.

My ability to escape could hinge on these dots that refuse to appear. I need to change my plan. I need to try and get the beast to do it.

Okay, wake up. Summon the dots and turn it into ice, I plead to the beast. *Turn it into ice, my parent's lives and mine depend on it.* It's awake, but only because raw hatred is keeping it awake. *Come on, ice. Turn it into ice,* I command again as the King's drumming becomes more apparent as his irritation rises.

"You've made it clear that you can't use your powers." Disappointment oozes from the King's voice.

"I swear I can, just give me more time," I beg.

With a wave of his wrist, the ornament flies out of my hand, landing exactly where I got it from. "You've wasted enough of my time already. Now change," he repeats, and a pitcher of water starts to boil. "I'll turn around and you can change," he offers without sincerity.

I don't understand what purpose changing serves. It's not the type of gown sacrifices wear, but it is the type of gown a concubine would.

First, his son. And now the King, the voice warns. That will never happen. Not if I can help it.

Still, he stands and makes his way towards the window, leaning against a bookshelf as he stares into the night sky.

Taking a deep breath, my fingers move from muscle memory alone, removing the straps from my shoulders, and shimmying the nightgown over my hips. My eyes never once leave the back of the King's head as I struggle out of my sweat-stained nightgown, my fingers thick and clumsy.

Yanking the golden dress off the table, I pull it over my head, grateful there aren't any laces. The feeling is crushed as soon as I look down; the fabric is so sheer that you can see every single mark on my body. A halter neck plunges down to my navel and leaves my back completely exposed. The sultry nightgown I just yanked off was a better option after all.

Before I say anything, he turns around and I realize he has been watching my reflection in the window the entire time.

My skin prickles under his carnal gaze, undressing me with his eyes. The urge to vomit all over the dress becomes all consuming. I want to scrub my skin raw, burn off any memory of his existence.

The look of hunger changes to one of amazed curiosity, like I'm an exhibition for all to ponder. He walks around me in circles, calculating an equation that he doesn't know the answer to. He ogles every inch of me over and over, until my feet ache from standing for so long.

"How long have you had the marks?" he questions. I don't want to answer him. I want to bask in the delusion that I have some sort of power over the situation, but that's all it is; a delusion. Any rebellion will be useless. There's nothing more I can do but as I'm told.

"Birth." A partial truth. I can only hope he never noted where the marks were before they moved.

"Do you feel them?" An odd question. Maybe if I say that they sting he'll pass it off as a side effect of living in the Remains. And if I'm lucky, it'll ward him away from me like I might transmit my illness to him. I doubt he'll fall for it. My gift will cure an insect bite before it even becomes red. There's no way he'd believe that I'm immune from the plague, but not unclean clothing. I shake my head.

He walks around me again, staring at the branding around my wrist. "I assume the 'N' rather than an 'M' is your doing?" he pries.

"I got bored." I ache for this conversation to be over, as he walks around again.

"I'm well aware. You're far more than that. You're more than the best of fae." Intrigue lances his features, like his statement was a mere afterthought.

"Why did you call me here? I'm not, and will never be, one of your concubines." I suck in my breath as soon as I say the sentence, fearing that voicing my concerns will make them reality.

"You've caused me a great deal of trouble." He takes another swig of his drink. "More people would have starved by your hands."

How in the gods' name is that my fault? I'm not so broken that I'd crumble when my heart strings are pulled in such a way. "You have more than enough food in this Palace to feed the mortals on the outskirts. Don't try to tell me that having to feed one more mouth has jeopardized your people, because I'll be more than happy to return to my old life." My skin is on fire. Not literally, thankfully. My rage has blinded my ability to think straight. He's the one starving us, and he dares try to blame it on me.

My fury leaps when he laughs. "Your life was pathetic. Being here is the most purpose you've ever had." He says each word with careless ease.

"Being the only known healer and playing the queen's pimple remover is hardly a purpose."

"Whatever fate has in store for you now is far worse than what the queen did to you. You'll want to drop to your knees before me and thank me for my kindness."

"I fucking doubt it."

Shut up Althea, before you get yourself killed! the voice yells at me through the pounding in my head.

Breathe. I need to breathe before I say more things that I'll come to regret.

"Ryven is limiting how often and how much grain we can bring from the Kaen to the mainland, starving cities all over Audor. He's agreed to give us free reign to travel between Audor's islands indefinitely in exchange for you. Do you think a man that would starve an entire Empire will be as gracious as I?"he ponders, staring at his empty glass.

The Kings are treating me like a bargaining chip. Vesi started the War of the Elements. I don't need King Cyrus' reminder of what type of person King Ryven is if he's willing to start a war over me.

"Why does he want me? Is he in need of a healer?" Panic has reclaimed me.

"Possibly," he scratches his, "or maybe he wants to see all the exciting ways he can torture you." A smile that's all teeth spreads across his face, and I lose feeling in my feet.

Tomorrow. Evander is getting you out tomorrow. Calm down. You're almost free.

The King lounges on a chaise, tucking a pillow under his head. "Before I consider what to do with you, I want you to feel me."

I take a step back, forcing away the urge to retch. "I said that I'm not going to be one of your whores," my snap comes out like a plea.

You never could figure out when to keep your mouth shut, the voice sniggers as the darkness scrapes its claws against my core.

"I want to know if your powers are worth going to war over. Look inside and heal what you can find," he says impatiently. "I should warn you that I can be very creative with how I punish disobedience. Especially when the person has parents."

A sour taste coats my mouth. I'm powerless to do anything against him. The darkness has no intention of helping me get out of this.

I nod and force myself to move. Each step feels like a boot is digging into my chest. The King's eyes are closed, his hands folded behind his head. He looks completely relaxed. I know that beneath this peaceful exterior dwells a monster.

I hesitate, unwilling to kneel for him. Instead, I bring a chair over, the legs scrape against the floor as I drag it over to where he lays. I can feel him watching me with curiosity as I move about, shuffling things out of the way so I can pull the heavy chair.

Beads of sweat accumulate on my forehead by the time I sit down.

My hand reaches out, stopping just above his stomach. I take a deep breath before letting it drop. The muscles beneath his coat are far more solid than Auberon. I can feel the heat emanating through his clothes, and I'm scared that if I leave my hand on him long enough, I'll burn.

"The clock is ticking, Althea," he muses, and I wince.

Closing my eyes, I relax my mind to let the gift flow into him, but my mind refuses to go willingly. Instead, it yanks me somewhere far, far away.

Blood-curdling screams fill my head and a blinding white light fills my mind before pools of red and black drench through it. The screaming pierces through me and thunders down my spine until my stomach lurches.

The darkness propels me at breakneck speed through the realm; over mountains and hills, plunging into the sea only to be thrown into the sky until my body shatters along the ground.

Through the beast's eyes I look down at the luminescent floor.

I'm once more in the Palace of Air.

The Anzeth has summoned me. Again.

CHAPTER 27

*"As a rule, men worry more about what they
can't see than about what they can."*

— *Julius Caesar*

Agonizing wails fill the air, harmonizing with the screaming. I can't
hear my own thoughts through the noise. The clouds are slate, and in
the distance, lightning tears through the sky, rattling the floor under
my feet.

Stop! the voices beg in unison.

"Stop what?" I screech as their ear-piercing screams rip through my
body, and I drop to the floor.

Help us, daughter! Help us!

"How?" I can't even help my parents, let alone the gods. I can't even
escape without needing someone else's help.

Your powers! Their wails shred my skin. *Find us! Find us!*

My heart thunders louder than their screams, and oblivion looms
in the distance. "Tell me how! Where are you?" I don't even know if
they can hear me through the noise. I don't even know if I managed to
speak aloud.

He will help you. Trust him.

I scream, "Who is *he*? Auberon? King Cyrus?" Not a fiber in my body trusts either of them enough to tell them I've communicated with the Anzeth, let alone to find and save them. Frustration builds within me from their cryptic messages.

Trust him, daughter. Release our children. Release us! Another agonizing scream, and something warm and wet trickles from my ears.

Who? How? Where? My thoughts split apart in cacophony, and nothing makes sense. I know now that I can't trust the royal Cintis. But what about Evander? His face floats before my eyes for a moment, then is torn apart by their wails. Am I to join forces with him? Chase gods? Why can't they just tell me?

They've imprisoned us. We're dying, only you can save us, daughter!

"Who are *they*?" I claw at my ears. "I'm not strong enough. There must be someone else who can help." I couldn't heal someone with the plague. I can't cure Papa's lungs. How can I even dream of helping the Anzeth?

You are power. Find it. Find us! Blinding white light flashes and I jerk my hand away from the King's furnace of a body, and the havoc of the Air Palace.

Sweat trickles down my forehead and the room seems to spin. I can't breathe, I can't stand. The darkness in my core curls in on itself, over and over again like a snake eating its own tail. It's waiting for something, wanting something. It's unhappy with me—its vessel.

The King's eyes are wide open, staring at me like I've just told him a dirty secret he can't believe.

Shit. My thoughts feel like I'm dragging them from a well, the bucket filled with stones, making each thought a labor.

"What happened?" His voice is calm, almost comforting compared to the Anzeth's screams.

My mind goes blank and the ache in my chest goes numb, as if I'm no longer the same person I was seconds ago, and my body is not my own.

"Nothing," I croak.

"Don't lie to me. That wasn't nothing," he says darkly as the temperature rises again.

"I healed nothing," I correct, my mind a muddy pool of confusion.

His lips curl, unconvinced. "The way your body reacted and how you whimpered tells me otherwise." Even in my bewildered state, I don't miss the warning in his voice.

"As soon as I tried, everything went white, and it was so hot that I could feel it in my soul. I couldn't see your body like I expected." Not a lie.

His body moves into a regal pose as he sits up straighter. I've made him feel special—powerful even—that he's so strong that I can't do anything against him. I've made him think that I'm not a threat; far too weak to hit him or look into his body. He might be vain and a man, but he's also a king and politician, he'll see right through this.

People think that a man's weakness is a woman's tears, but they're wrong. It's seeing a woman on her knees and telling them that they're superior.

"If that is in fact the case, then listen very closely to what I am about to tell you next, because your parents' lives will depend on it."

My mask of calm fractures, as my mind is still dazed from the encounter with the gods.

Tomorrow. Evander will get you out tomorrow.

"Don't they always?" I scrape for safe ground.

"Your father's life is in my hands. I can have him killed before you get a chance to blink. I own you, Althea Viteri. I own the air you're breathing, and every single thought you have." I know this to be true, but hearing the King say it brings every one of my nightmares to light. The King stands, towering over my shaking body. Grabbing my wrist, he shoves my red line right before my eyes. "I'm your king. I will always be your king. And when another king takes you, I will still be your king."

I curl my hands into fists to stop my fingers from trembling in his grip. I've had more than enough of these redheaded royals and their games. I'm mute, unable to respond as the fracture in my mind splits deeper to the point of no repair.

"If you go to Vesi, you will do everything in your power to keep your parents alive. You will be his concubine, if he so desires. If he wishes to feast on your flesh, then you will ask him which part he'd like to dine on first. You will get close to him. Should you choose not to, and you find yourself dead, then your parents will find an early grave. You will be my ear to Vesi. When someone comes knocking with questions, you *will* answer."

My blood curdles with each of his words.

"Does this mean that you've agreed to his deal?" I stutter, tasting fear in my voice.

"I haven't decided, but you'll be the last to know. We've already started what we want from you. It would have worked better if we had more time with you," he sighs, leaning back on his chaise.

Realization washes over me. It's more than just my powers. It's always been about my body: the hair, my skin, under the tree. They set out the bait so perfectly, and like a mindless rat, I got trapped in it. I fell for every single one.

Auberon knew the exact moment to show every single time. He knew what to say, and how to act. The meals. The obsession with ownership. His lack of care about harm brought to me unless they've threatened to 'take what's his.'

It was all a lie. All of it.

He showered me in niceties and did the bare minimum, and I *fell for it* like a damn lovesick, naive fool. Evander told me they had a plan, and I ignored him. I'm not sure how their 'plan' involves bedding, but I don't think I want to know.

"You're dismissed." He throws me through the air and across the room with a wave of his hand. The door clicks back shut. With blurry vision I look up to the five sentinels towering above me.

Get up. Stop looking so weak, the voice grinds.

Belve and the sentinel that escorted me are here. Worse yet, sentinels wearing golden armor stare down at me though their helmet.

The only thought flowing through my head is that I have to run away.

I have to leave *now*, before the King decides my fate. I need to get hold of Evander. I need him to take me to Ma and Pa. To get us out of Ignis.

"Get up," a deep voice trails from a silhouette edged with flames. When he steps into the light, I want to scream. But my voice is gone. I'm no longer scared, I'm *furious*. General Fornous, Evander's father. Another enemy on my list. The next time blood splashes on his face, I'm going to make sure it's his own.

Pain sears across my face, and I only just manage to avoid diving head first into the fountain.

"You're lucky I have orders to keep you alive. Those same orders didn't include keeping you unharmed," he says.

The darkness swirls in my stomach, waiting. Ready to kill. It doesn't think I'm about to die, but it doesn't care if I feel pain.

Everything is blurry. No, I can't leave now. I don't know how to get my family out of here without Evander. If I try to run with them around, the General will know that the first place I'll go is to my parents. They know where Ma and Pa are, and I doubt I'll get there before the sentinels with their horses.

I need to get back to my bedchamber and run when there's only one guard at the door. I need to stick to the plan. There's only a few more hours until I'll meet Evander at the spot. They won't ship me off to Vesi before morning. I hope.

"I'm going to my chambers," I say, trying to exude as much confidence as possible, as I turn on my heels and walk between the sentinels who don't move aside when I pass.

Their boots march behind me as they follow me along the hallways. A small sense of victory sits in my chest from being at the front of the group. I don't know if I'm going the right way, but no one seems to correct me.

As I go down a flight of stairs, I start to see floral designs sprinkle over the halls indicating that I'm in the queen's wing. I walk faster through here, not wanting to see the queen because she'll know exactly whose chambers I had just been in.

As I enter my chambers, I try to shut the door but a hand stops it. Shoving the door back, General Fornous marches in, staring down at me. I can see his yellowed teeth through his scowl.

"Until the problem with Vesi is resolved, two sentinels will be posted at the door and two inside," he says, like this is the greatest inconvenience.

"No. I won't let any of you watch me sleep," I say urgently even though I know that he doesn't care.

They can't stay. None of them can stay. I have a fighting chance of taking one sentinel down, but there's no way I can take down four.

"I don't give a rat's ass what you want," he snarls

Impatience seeps from him like he wants me out of his sight as soon as possible. Two golden soldiers step into the room, and the General takes his leave.

No. *No.* They have to leave. I need them to leave.

I can't tell where they're looking because of their masks, and I can feel the events of the night start to creep up my chest.

"Turn around. I'm going to change," I hiss with a false sense of hope that they might actually listen. Neither of them move. The eyes of the great beast stare blankly into the room. I can't escape if there are four of them. I can't even get the stupid knife.

Moving to the bathing chamber to get some semblance of privacy, my heart plummets to my feet from the missing door.

Nothing is going to plan.

CHAPTER 28

"I see no end to my misery but the grave."
— *Johann Wolfgang von Goethe*

I don't sleep, waiting, watching the sentinels in the hopes that they leave. Even for just a moment. But just as I expected, they stand there the whole night stoic within the shadows like a statue. I didn't hear them breathe or shift their weight on their feet.

Instead, I stare at the clock, watching each second tick by until it's time to flee. Every possibility of escape runs through my mind. None of which end up successful so long as I have four sentinels cornering me in this room.

I have to hope that Evander knows what is happening, and he has a backup plan.

We can all leave everything behind and have a *simple* life. Ma could be a cook, Pa can finally retire and maybe there will be a forge wherever it is we go. I don't know what Evander might do

If by some chance I do hold the power to heal the Anzeth, how do I expect to find them? And who is 'him'?

There's no way I would be able to get to them if they were in another Empire because of the red branding around my wrist. Tensions are high after the War: they'd kick me out in a heartbeat. Not to mention, they could be in one of the hundreds of islands all over the realm. The Anzeth should know I'm not in the position to save anyone. Especially if I'm being taken to another Empire.

The real question is what do they need releasing from? Whatever the answer is, I won't be able to get to it from inside this room.

Thinking that I was speaking with the gods has to be my mind playing some cruel joke on me from the stress, or maybe it's just my body going into shock from all of the abuse.

In my exhausted state, I decide that I've imagined speaking to the gods, and when I get out of the Palace, I'm leaving everything about this place and the gods behind.

"I'd like to go for a walk, you've made this room too crowded," I say just as the clock ticks signaling that it's an hour and half before the sentinels change. Which means I only have half an hour to get to the spot. Darkness still covers the sky, and the Remains would all be awake, getting ready for work.

The golden sentinels don't respond, staring at me with their dragon's head.

The door crashes open. "Make it quick," Belve grumbles as Maiya scurries inside with her head down. It's too early for her to be here.

"What's happening?" I say breathlessly before the door can close. But he ignores my question, slamming the door and making Maiya flinch.

She ushers me into the bathing chamber. "What's happening?" I whisper. Her bottom lip quivers in response.

I'm too late. The King has made his decision. This is my *only* chance of escaping. I can't afford to make any mistakes.

I don't pay attention to Maiya as she prepares me until I look down at the black gown that hides all of my skin. Relief and hope washes through me, I can blend in amongst mortals in this dress. They won't stare at my skin or try to peel my dress off me because it's *simple*.

I swallow the lump in my throat, that's why he made me change last night. It was nothing more than a power move against me. To parade me in front of them if he said no. To make them know that I'm Audor's whore.

Belve comes in as the last button is done up. He returns my smile, except there's something dark in it, like he knows something I don't.

"You have another summons, hopefully your last, *mortal*. I hope you die out there," he smirks.

Him. I'll attack him first.

My eyes flick to the clock. I have seven minutes.

Maiya moves out of the room without sparing me a second glance. Belve wraps his fingers around my arm, before I can react, two golden spikes held by the golden sentinels touch the base of my throat.

"If you want one last dance, then just say," Belve spits at my feet.

A glimmer of excitement flashes through his eyes, as if he's hoping I'll take the bait. Something sharp presses against the curve at my waist.

Think, Althea. Everyone has a weakness! The little voice yells at me through my rising panic.

"Is it your intention to keep them waiting? You've let them down enough times, Belve. I wonder how they'd feel to hear that you let them down again." My heart pounds beneath my fake confidence.

His chocolate-brown skin pales at my words. I humiliated him last night in front of his General, and he thinks that hurting me will somehow restore his standing. I'm not sure where they're taking me, but I doubt tardiness is on the agenda.

Victory tugs at me when he backs down. And then his fist collides with my jaw. Pain rips through me as he buries his boot in my stomach, lancing the air from my lungs. His assault threatens to leave a mark— but my gift works faster. The beast swirls urging me to fight back.

Patience, I tell it. *Soon we can have our way with him.*

Pain starts to dissipate as my gift swarms through me. My knees scrape along the ground as hands pull me to my feet, dragging me through the door.

"Let me go!" I scream, stumbling in his grip as I try to bring myself upright. My arms ache trying to fight off his hold and keep from falling.

We're heading in the opposite direction of Auberon's chambers. I need to break free before I lose my opening.

You're weak. Have you learnt nothing? The voice in my head sneers. Part of me wants to succumb, yield to his grip. The other part of me wants to win.

We pass another clock: three minutes.

I wrap my fingers around his thumb, breaking it to get loose as he howls in pain. Stabilizing my knee as quickly as possible, I shove the bottom of my palm into his elbow with all of my strength until I hear a satisfying *crack* .

Even a Cintis can't recover quick enough.

He instantly releases his fingers around me to cover his groin as he drops to his knees, howling in pain. The sentinels behind us just stare at him, one of them is fighting back a laugh.

Kill him, a choir of voices rumble through my mind.

Dots start to edge my vision and the beast roars, coming alive, spreading its tendrils through my lungs as my gift starts to braid together with my gift. But not fast enough.

My fingers wrap around the cool hilt of Belve's sword, yanking it out. My arms raise over my head just as the dots consume my vision, and fire explodes all around me. No burn comes. The smell of smoke never reaches my nostril. White dots swirl all around me like an invisible shield, protecting me from those that wish to kill me.

I feel like a god. Invincible. Indestructible.

I can smell the intoxicating terror dripping from Belve, and I want nothing more than to become his nightmare.

The sword drops before he can react, propelled by the beast. Fire blasts all around as the blade slices through skin, the sound of bone cracking fills the air—and it sounds euphoric. Blood splatters across the floor and his lifeless body drops. And his head rolls to my feet.

"That's for Elex," I spit at his empty eyes.

The thread of power wraps around me as I sprint between the sentinel's, their fires missing their mark. I shove the night sentinel whose hands are before him, attempting to wrap his flames around my shield. I swing the sword, slicing him. I don't know how deep. I don't know where. I can barely see past the flames. I just run.

The second the fire stops, the dots disappear, and the shield leaves with it.

You can't outrun the golden sentinels! The voice warns as my boots bounds across the carpet, sprinting up the stairs taking three steps at a time and passing frightened servants.

I won't be able to outfight them, but I know I can outrun them. I can hear their armor clanging in the distance; four pairs of boots, not two. I have company.

Rounding a wall, my vision starts to go blurry as sweat drips from my back as more boots start to join them. In the distance I can just make out a figure with something sticking out of its mouth.

Rumner.

My feet move faster than they're ever moved, flying across the floor as adrenaline pumps through me, pushing me as the sound of boots becomes deafening.

"Keep runnin, lass," Rumner whispers loudly as I near.

All I can do is nod in thanks as I force my feet to move faster until the golden statue comes into sight. The same statue Auberon and I hid behind to go unnoticed by the Queen.

I can practically smell my freedom already. Evander will be there waiting for me. He'll help us out of here.

My feet don't stop until they buckle behind the safety of the statue. But I don't rest. There's no time. I dart my head around the statue, looking for steel eyes. All I see is a clock staring back at me. It's time. He should be here.

"Where is she?" a voice growls; Valen's voice.

"That way," Rumner yells, but I don't know which way he pointed.

I hold my breath, expecting footsteps to come my way. Instead, they seem to move in the opposite direction.

He should be here already.

He's just late, he'll be here, I say to myself.

I can hear the clock ticking louder than the footsteps of any sentinel that runs past.

Each heartbeat burns as I sit there, cowering behind a golden statue. Five minutes. Each tick of the clock haunts me, weighing heavier on my soul. Ten minutes. He's not coming. 15 minutes.

He lied to you as well, the voice teases.

I refuse to believe it. Evander wouldn't abandon me like this. He loves me. He's probably been caught.

Or he found out about your betrayal.

I can't afford to think about that right now. I can't think of what might be happening to him.

He's probably home lying with another woman, forgetting all about you, the voice says.

I can do this without him. I have to be able to do this without him. I don't know where Ma is, and I don't know the way out. But I'll be damned if I don't try.

Taking a deep breath, I jump to my feet, eying the servant's entrance. Fire wraps around my wrist and fabric burns into my skin. I shirk from the pain, attempting to claw the rope off me, ignoring how it makes them boil. Another rope wraps around my wrist, dragging me out from behind the state. The golden sentinels have found me.

I failed. I couldn't do it. I couldn't free myself. I'll never see my parents again.

I'm too weak to escape by myself that my whole plan rested on Evander, the man who never showed. Did he get caught, or did he change his mind? I don't want to believe it's the latter, but I think the former would hurt more.

I should feel bad about what I did to Belve. I should feel haunted by his lifeless eyes at my feet. I feel no remorse. Regret doesn't weigh on my chest. The only thing I wish is that I made him suffer for longer.

I need to get out of here and I'll figure out the rest later.

They pull me behind them like cattle being led to the slaughter, they walk hurriedly, down stairs and through corridors that I've never been through. I try pulling against them. I try summoning the dots. But nothing. I shriek and I scream and I pull. I can't get near enough to them to attack them, at least I know that I tried.

They pull me upright as we near the throne room, tying my hands together before they stand beside me, making me look feeble between them. I attempt to pull my wrists out of the ropes, but it proves useless. I'm too late.

Scorching heat emanates from inside, and beads of perspiration gather at my collar. Standing at the bottom of the stairs, a black-haired woman looks at me with pure disdain. Her blue dress is a stark splash of color against the flames and darkness of this room.

She's from Vesi. My new owner.

I can feel myself wanting to break, to let the tears rain down my face. But I'm too exhausted to cry. I have to try to be strong, *pretend* to be strong.

Somehow hope still lives within my soul that Evander will come through the doors and save the day. I reach for that hope, holding it tight and letting myself succumb to the delusion that he will still come to save me.

Queen Mellonia stands at the top of the dais, at the bottom of the curving stairs like she was the first time I saw her. She dresses herself in a satisfied smirk as she mouths the word 'nothing' to me.

The Priest and General Fornous stand on either side of the King. My head swings around looking for Auberon, only to be greeted with a shove at my back from the golden soldier.

"Take her to Vesi," King Cyrus declares, there's a hint of annoyance in his tone, like his trade doesn't sit well with him.

My eyes dart around the room, hoping to find Evander within the shadows ready to break me out like he said.

"No," I plead.

This wasn't meant to happen so soon. I need more time. I was meant to escape and leave Ignis with Ma and Pa. We were all meant to be happy together. I was supposed to run and forget about the Anzeth like it was all just a fever dream. I may never get to see my parents again. I'll never be able to look into their eyes and tell them I'm sorry and that I love them.

"You have no say in the matter. You leave today." There's a finality to the King's words. The Priest seems displeased by his King's decision.

No! Evander is giving me my freedom today!

"I'm not going!" I scream, a last useless attempt at trying to get away.

"Remember what I said about your behavior, Althea. I would hate for you to die." His eyes go hungry when he speaks, and I suppress a shudder when the world seems to sway.

"You aren't killing her," the woman in blue snaps at the King, and the flames surrounding the room jump higher. The rise in temperature does nothing to warm my icy core.

He won't kill you, but he might kill your parents for what you did to Belve, the voice says. I don't think he will, he still needs his leverage over me. Killing them won't turn me into his spy.

"You're in my court. Be careful how you speak to me," he warns. "Get this over with. Take her."

Arms close in around me, lifting me into the air. I kick and thrash against their grip.

"Leave my parents out of this! You aren't taking me! I won't go!" I scream the words like a mantra, repeating it over and over. Kicking, biting, shrieking. I try pulling myself away from them. I struggle with all my might. Still, they pull, leading me by the rope unfazed.

Shut up, you idiot. Calm down or you'll get your parents killed before you even get to Vesi, the voice hisses.

Sunlight prickles my skin as they drag me through the Palace doors, scraping my knees along the ground.

This could be my last chance to escape. I have to try. I have to.

I close my eyes and focus on the darkness that hasn't stopped stirring since last night. I try to grab it and bring it to the surface to knock the men away. *Come on. Come Back. Come on!* Every time I reach for it, it sinks deeper into my core until it's unreachable.

"Let her go!"

A torrent of anger and relief floods through me when I see Auberon step through the doors. All I can think about is my own delusion. It doesn't matter how much I hate him, he has the power to stop this madness and tell the Vesian woman to leave without me. He said that I'm his. He wants me for whatever plans he has. He wouldn't just let them take me. He actually cares about me, right? As I think about it, the voice in my head releases a sinister laugh, mocking me. Of course he doesn't. It was all a lie.

The soldiers stop, but they don't let me go. It gives me enough time to get up.

"King Cyrus ordered that she is to be given to Vesi," the other golden soldier speaks without falter.

"He *what?*" The earth seems to shake with his voice.

I want to laugh, or spit in his face. He can stop acting. He can stop pretending that he cares about me. The only thing I know to be true is that he had no idea his father accepted the trade.

Before the golden soldiers can speak, I scream, "He's letting those monsters take me! How can you let them do this?" Thrashing around in their grip, the gold armored gloves start to pierce my skin as they try to hold me down. I wince as they shove me onto my knees. Auberon's rage beneath the surface of his skin starts to boil, and I can almost taste the fire coming from him.

Behind him, the sun reflects off the gold pillars, leaving me blinded to the stark shadows in between. Twirling towers drenched in crimson and gold sundials to remind the mortals that it is the Cintis that yield the flame, and everyone else is beneath them. Spires twist like the talons of a great beasts, spikes protrude from balconies.

His onyx eyes look down at me like bottomless pits; pity, sorrow, guilt.

Coward. He set up bait, and now he's guilty that I fell into his trap.

He is nothing less than the Prince of Audor. I should fear him. But instead, I *loathe* him with every inch of my body. No, loathe isn't a strong enough word.

"I just found out," he states, then looks at the soldiers. "Give us a minute alone."

Where the fuck *is Evander?* I frantically scream in my head.

Adhering to their Prince's command, they drop my arms and I crumble on the pavement.

Auberon pulls me up, and his black eyes stare down at me. Calloused hands cup my cheeks. "You are *mine*," he mutters darkly. Nausea rushes through me and I have to bite my tongue to stop myself from spitting on him, or worse. "Nothing will get in my way of finding you. Nothing. I will come for you."

"Please," I beg, "do something. Help me." There's pain behind his eyes. I'm just like every other mortal to him. He can't help me. Or he won't. I know he dragged me into this *plan*, but still, I beg the Anzeth that it isn't true, and there's a part of him that actually cares about me.

"Auberon, please," I whisper, and his hands drop from my face. Without thinking, I close the distance between us and his body tenses as our chest meets, almost like he wants to turn away. I trace the smooth skin along his jaw to pull his face closer to mine, but beneath my fingertips, his teeth grind and his hand moves to my arm, keeping me at a distance.

I say a silent prayer of thanks that I don't need to debase myself even more by getting closer to him, when he's the one stopping me.

"Take care of my family. I beg you," I whisper, just loud enough for him to hear. He doesn't respond to my request.

"We need to go," the woman in blue says.

He steps away and his eyes drop to the ground, refusing to meet mine.

A soft gloved hand touches my shoulder and I flinch. An indiscernible look flashes over her face, but she doesn't back down. She holds her hand up as sentinels in blue step toward me.

Auberon inches back towards the Palace slowly. "No! Auberon!" I cry out. Two golden staffs lock together in an 'X' when I lunge for him. The sound of the clang makes him wince, and he turns towards the door.

"Wait, Auberon!" I scream again, "Please, Auberon!" He walks faster up the steps, refusing to see my pain as the taste of my salty tears seeps into my mouth.I'm his favorite addition. He wants me. He *wants* me. He's going to stop any second now and tell me that it will be alright. He's going to tell the Vesian woman to go away because I'm *his*.

His foot lands on the very top step, quickly approaching the doors into the Palace. I have to say it. I have to try.

"I love you!" I cry, my voice breaks as I say the words I've never said to a man before. Words I should be saying to Evander. I don't love him. I could never love him. I don't think anyone could ever truly love him. I'm not even convinced his own mother does. But maybe the cursed lie will save me. He whips around to look at me as his face crumbles into splinters of guilt. The doors slam shut.

My lie didn't work.

Evander. I need Evander. Where the fuck is Evander?

"Just another minute, he'll come for me," I beg the Vesian woman. Evander has to come for me. He loves me. He promised me that he'd keep my family safe. He was just late. He hasn't been captured. Why isn't he here?

Minutes go by with my eyes looking for every shadow and every movement, hoping I'll catch his steel eyes. Nothing.

"It's time," the woman declares.

I shake my head. *He's not coming.*

In front of the sea of blue sentinels, I drop to my knees and break. The mask disintegrates to the floor. I'm not strong enough to keep up my own promises. My own voice is right. I am weak. I tried to be strong, for my family and for myself, but I'll never be good enough. I'm weak. I let them down. I let Evander, my parents, and the Anzeth down. And, most of all, I'm *useless*. I have achieved nothing. I have learnt nothing. I have done nothing.

I collapse under the sun, letting the hot angry tears fall onto the ground, heaving and hurling.

The soft gloved hand touches me again and I cringe. Her eyes are soft, pitiful almost; they're the most beautiful concoction of greens. "It's time to go," she breathes, and I scramble up the steps on my hands and knees to get as far away from her as I can.

"Fuck you," I spit, and her expression remains unchanged.

"You can walk yourself to the carriage, or you can be carried. The choice is yours. Whatever you decide, we are leaving here with you," her voice is stern, like the way a mother would talk to a misbehaved child.

Pull yourself together, the voice hisses. *Get up and hold what little dignity you have left. Wear the mask.* The voice sounds a lot like Pa.

"What will it be?" She looks at me, hopeful that I'll pick the right answer.

My bones creak and crack as I lift myself up from the steps with trembling hands.

"Good choice. Now we need to hurry before nightfall," she says. There's a brutal feminine power to her steps as she walks to the carriage. It isn't like the queen's elegance or the King's march, rather a dance that demands attention.

My gaze follows her to the oak carriage dripping in blue silk. There are at least twenty sentinels pulling themselves onto horses when the woman nods at them. She holds the carriage door open, motioning for me to get inside.

Each one of my steps is more hesitant than the other. *Behave or your parents will die. Behave or your parents will die.* The chant repeats itself over and over until I reach the doors.

Turning back around, I take one last look at the place I always thought demons lived, only to find out that I was wrong. The real monsters live in blue.

And now, I'm being taken into the belly of the beast.

I swallow a strangled sigh and get in. She jumps into the carriage and shuts the door behind her. Sticking her head out of the window she yells, "Ride hard for Vesi."

They can drag me to another Empire, but somehow, someway, I'm going to kill King Cyrus. Then, I'll kill everyone else in that Palace.

GLOSSARY OF TERMS

Aecor Lympha

Origin: Empire of Air

A tribe of water fae that can control large bodies of water, such as from a river, pond, or cup.

Anzeth

Origin: Empire of Air

A council of nine gods that controls the air. They live in the Air Palace and are neither man nor woman.

Caulus

Origin: Empire of Air

Status: Asleep

One day, in the dead of the night, an Anzeth snuck out and bred with Shesha, birthing the Warriors of Caulus; a creature not quite fae and not quite dragon, able to harness the wind and soar through the air. The beasts are the greatest race of warriors in history, winning every battle in their path in the name of the Anzeth.

Chusi

Origin: Empire of Earth

Status: Asleep

Chusi, a colorful three-headed winged serpent that can morph and blend into the environments around her. Flowers grow down her spine, as her tails spiral into thorns. Antlers that reach up to the sky crown her head, tipped in gold and silver. Every gem and crystal coats her body, catching the sunlight as she moves along the earth.

She was the great mother, birthing most of the dragons of the first War. The death of all her children hurt her the most. She was the first to slumber. She burrowed herself deep within the earth in her grief. Her tears gave life to the trees, planting seeds for crops to grow.

It's said that the entirety of Feraxis is built atop the wing of Chusi: that's why their lands are so fruitful.

Cintis

Origin: Empire of Fire

The term given to fae that can control fire. The fire move of choice is the whip of flames.

Daskare Lympha

Origin: Empire of Water

A tribe of water fae that turns water into ice. The stronger Daskare Lympha can cover a large village in snow.

Fae

Origin: Unknown

It is unclear whether the mortals or the fae were the first to live in Zephryine. There are three known types of fae; water, earth and fire. The abilities of the fae vary depending on the individual's strength. Heightened speed and senses are reserved for the stronger fae.

The fae are immortal, able to live for thousands of years due to their increased healing speed. However, they can easily be killed through methods such as a sword through the heart, the slitting of their throat, breaking their neck, or a beheading.

Feraxian Wine

Origin: Empire of Earth

Feraxis' number one exported good to Audor. The liquid is a deep crimson with specks of green in it that are naked to the human eye. The secret ingredient that makes the drink so addictive is a closely guarded secret of the Feraxians.

Leviathan

Origin: Empire of Water Status: Asleep

Leviathan, the Queen of the Ocean—a serpentine creature that slithers in the deepest depths of the oceans, harnessing the waters with her very mind. She is the other half of the sun, controlling the moon with her tides. Her mouth is the size of an island, and a tongue darker than the night sky flickers out and devourers all in her path.

Lympha

Origin: Empire of Water

The term given to fae that can control liquid. There are three different classifications of Lympha depending on where the fae was born.

Mador Lympha

Origin: Empire of Water

A tribe of water fae that can only control small bodies of water, including, but not limited to the liquid in mud, rain drops as it falls, the dew on grass, and in some cases the water within a person's body.

Niran

Origin: Empire of Fire

Status: Asleep

The dragon of Audor; a winged beast that breathes fire hotter than the sun itself, and a ball of flame on his tail. He's said to be the most destructive of his siblings, burning everything in his path.

Plague

Origin: Empire of Air

Death Count: The empires have stopped counting.

The plague began when the first crack appeared in the earth following the signing of the First Treaty. As the realm became more polluted, the plague became highly contagious, and those who catch it have approximately 3 days left before they die.

Shesha

Origin: Empire of Air

Status: Asleep

King of Serpents, and the dragon of the Anzeth. He was the strongest out of all his brothers and sisters, laying waste to most of the Anzeth's children during the First War. He has double-armored scales that are impenetrable to even the sharpest of fangs, holding the power to become completely translucent and one with the air, slipping through the world like fog. He can harness air, fire, water, and earth. His strength rivals the Anzeth's power, but his loyalty to them was fiercer than his might in battle.

Terra

Origin: Empire of Earth

The term given to fae that can control the earth. A Terra's powers focuses heavily on the growth of plants and crops. The stronger Terra can move and reshape soil. This has proven convenient with respect to the earthquakes following the signing of the First Treaty.

The Darkness

Origin: Unknown

Also known as 'the beast.' It is an unknown power living within Althea. Not enough information has been acquired about the creature.

Vezen

Origin: Empire of Water

Allegedly a myth. Not enough information has been acquired about the creature.

KEEPER OF THE ELEMENTS

Sign up to the mailing list (https://www.zianschafer.com/contact) to get Chapter 1 of the second book in the War of the Elements series.

Did you enjoy Prisoner of the Elements?
Leave your review on GoodReads.
https://www.goodreads.com/book/show/60297327-prisoner-of-the-elements

ACKNOWLEDGEMENTS

I don't think there are enough pages in the world to express how grateful I am to you, my reader, and every single person that has supported me on this journey. You are all amazing for reading from Althea's point of view, or should I say my own point of view. I did a lot of self-reflection when I was developing her character and deciding what of my own traits I wanted to write on the page. It really was quite therapeutic.

I'd like to especially thank Sophia Behrman, Jade Austin and Samantha Mueller for putting up with my millions of questions, and listening to me rant every week about another turmoil I'm facing or another mental breakdown. Rain, hail or shine, you were all there to get me through the day to either tell me I was being an idiot, or just sit me down and 'show me the way' forward.

Another special thanks to Chris Beattie and Hazel Lockwood for putting up with my pestering. Chris, you are an absolute genius and I really should change your name to 'Google' on my phone, because there isn't a single thing that you don't know the answer to. And Hazel, just wow. The covers you've made makes me absolutely speechless. Even though I had no idea what I actually wanted, you seemed to know.

My amazing beta readers; Taylor, Gina, Mette, Lillian, Cassie and Courtney. Thank you for reading through my manuscript in its most fragile state. You're the real troopers here for interpreting my mess of a manuscript and helping me build it into something astounding.

Now to my friends and family. Thank you for putting up with me. Thank you to my partner for throwing chocolates at me when I was chin deep in editing and thought I wasn't going to make it (if there are any authors reading this, you know the level of anguish I was feeling at this time). I'd also like to apologize to everyone I ghosted during this time as I hermit in my bedroom to try and meet the deadlines that I've set myself.

All in all, thank you everyone!

I love you!

ABOUT THE AUTHOR

Zian Schafer has a love for fantasy romance novels and any novel that isn't recommended for the faint of heart. She lives in New Zealand with her two dogs that thinks they're lap dogs, two rabbits who thinks they're human babies, and her partner. You can visit her at zianschafer.com or on Instagram @zian_schafer or on TikTok @zianschafer.